Wilde about Holmes

WILDE about HOLMES

a novel by

MILO YELESIYEVICH

based on the incorporated works of
Oscar Wilde and Sir Arthur Conan Doyle

COMIC MASQUE
New York, New York

Wilde about Holmes © 2008 by Milo Yelesiyevich
Published by Comic Masque, an Imprint of Unwritten History, Inc.

First Printing 2008

Comic Masque
c/o Unwritten History, Inc.
PMB 199, Zeckendorf Towers
111 E. 14th Street
New York, NY 10003
e-mail: wildeaboutholmes@yahoo.com

ISBN: 978-0-9709198-2-3

Library of Congress Catalog Card Number: 2008900128

Printed in the United States of America by Thomson-Shore, Inc.

ACKNOWLEDGEMENTS

The character of Sherlock Holmes appears with permission from the Estate of Dame Jean Conan Doyle.

Passages from the following works hve been incorporated into the novel and footnoted to reflect acknowledgement:

OCSCAR WILDE by Richard Ellmann, copyright © 1987 by The Estate of Richard Ellmann. Used by permission of Alfred A. Knopf, a division of Random house, Inc.

Reprinted with the permission of The Free Press, a Division of Simon & Schuster Adult Publishing Group, from *LUDWIG WITTGENSTEIN: The Duty of Genius*, by Ray Monk. Copyright ⁽ 1990 by Ray Monk. All rights reserved.

AMERICA AND COSMIC MAN by Wyndham Lewis, copyright © 1949 by Wyndham Lewis. Used by permission of Doubleday, a division of Random House, Inc.

The Prince and the Lilly, by James Brough, Coward McCann & Geoghegan, Inc.: New York, 1974. By permission of Penguin Group (USA) Inc.

Reprinted with the permission of Abby Adams, from *AN UNCOMMON SCOLD*, by Abby Adams. Copyright © 1989 by Abby Adams. All rights reserved.

Reprinted by permission of the publisher from THE LETTERS OF GUSTAVE FLAUBERT: VOLUME I – 1830-1857, selected, edited and translated by Francis Steegmuller, Cambridge, Mass.: The Belknap Press of Harvard University Press, Copyright © 1979, 1980 by Francis Steegmuller.

Reprinted with the permission of Scribner, an imprint of Simon & Schuster Adult Publishing Group, from GROVER CLEVELAND by Rexford Guy Tugwell. Copyright © 1968 by Rexford Guy Tugwell. All rights reserved.

Baudelaire: A Self-Portrait, Selected Letters Translated and Edited with a Commentary. by Loies Boe Hyslop and Francis E. Hyslop, Jr. Oxford: Oxford University Press, 1957. By permission of Oxford University Press.

Autobiography of William Allan White. The Macmillan Company: New York, 1946, p. 362-363. By permission of the Estate of William Allan White.

My affectionate gratitude and tribute to Roger Lardé and Andrew Erish, who proofread the manuscript and provided many valuable comments and suggestions. Many thanks to Robert Bononno, to whom I am grateful for his insights as well as for his support over the years.

A facsimile of the manuscript discovered in a
trunk belonging to J.L. Stoddart.

FOREWORD

The discovery of a manuscript containing a heretofore unknown Sherlock Holmes story (apparently co-authored by Oscar Wilde and Sir Arthur Conan Doyle) is certain to provoke controversy regarding its authenticity. *Wilde About Holmes*, as of this writing, remains a literary mystery.

The story itself is told from the alternating points of view of Oscar Wilde and Sherlock Holmes, who unite their efforts to protect Grover Cleveland, the Democratic Presidential candidate of 1884, from a scandal involving Lillie Langtry, the most celebrated actress of her day.

Historians are unanimous in consigning the 1884 presidential election among the dirtiest ever to have taken place in American politics. Ten days after the Democratic National Convention nominated Cleveland, a political time bomb exploded in his face. *The Buffalo Evening Telegraph* featured a sensational headline, *A Terrible Tale: A Dark Chapter in a Public Man's History*, revealing that Cleveland had fathered a child by a woman he had not married. Cleveland's friends were stunned by the revelation, but when they approached him, Cleveland confirmed that the story was basically true. When asked how to handle the outcry, he replied *Above all, tell the truth.*

Andrew D. White complained that the 1884 election was *the vilest ever waged. The Nation* commented that *party contests have never before reached so low a depth of degradation in this country.* Henry Adams wrote to an English friend that *the public is angry and abusive. We are all swearing at each other like demons.* Mud slinging, scandals, and vituperation usurped the place of serious issues in the campaign. Voters felt they were

trapped between two bad choices: one candidate was *delinquent in office but blameless in private life* (James G. Blaine); and the other was a *model of official integrity but culpable in his personal relations* (Grover Cleveland). The unexpected outcome of the presidential election in 1884 is one of the great reversals of fortune in American political history, whose elements are incorporated in *Wilde About Holmes.*

Cherchez la femme. Lillie Langtry, who is romantically linked to Grover Cleveland in *Wilde About Holmes,* caused a sensation in 1876 by being the first society woman to appear on stage, making her first important appearance at the Haymarket Theatre, London, as Kate Hardcastle in *She Stoops to Conquer.* Her acting was not then taken seriously but she eventually became a competent actress, her most successful part being Rosalind in *As You Like It.* Her dramatic tour of the U.S. was long remembered in the annals of popular culture. She was to make her American debut at the Park Theatre, which burned down the day before her play was scheduled to open. The delay served only to raise New Yorkers' excitement to a fever pitch. She finally made her debut a week later at Wallack's as Hester Grazebrook in Tom Taylor's old play, *The Unequal Match.* William Winter, the most influential and widely read theatre critic of his era, wrote that

> *her well proportioned, lissome figure, shapely and finely poised head, long, oval face, pure white complexion, large gray eyes—innocent, candid, and sweet in expression—abundant chestnut hair, and rich, cordial, winning voice ... her acting put detraction to silence and won and held a large measure of public sympathy and critical respect.*

Oscar Wilde was a close and intimate friend of Lillie Langtry. In his outstanding biography, *Oscar Wilde*, Richard Ellmann writes that

It was around 1880 that Lillie Langtry caught the eye of her most important lover in England, the Prince of Wales. He instituted himself as her protector, and guarded her respectability by refusing invitations to parties unless she, too, was invited. He, however, could not protect her from the contretemps of pregnancy. She scotched rumors and gossip by removing herself to the Island of Jersey, during the months of obvious pregnancy, leaving her daughter, Jeanne (not by her husband), to be discretely brought up on the island. Wilde was one of the few who knew of the thin line she walked between celebrity and censure, delighted that she was able to carry on with her role as a virtuous wife on the London stage.*

No one, in fact, is certain of the paternity of Lillie Langtry's child. One biographer contends that the father was Edward VII, Prince of Wales, while another puts forth Prince Louis of Battenberg (the Prince's favorite nephew) as the true father of the child.

There exist, however, skeptics who rightly and justly question the authenticity of the manuscript, which was discovered by a collector of rare manuscripts in a trunk that once belonged to Richard Stoddart, the Philadelphia publisher of *Lippincott's Monthly Magazine*. The manuscript is written in the Isaac Pitman *stenographic sound hand*, a system of stenography that marked a new era in the development of shorthand, and is still in use today. Efforts are now being made to verify the handwriting as Stoddart's, a seminal figure in the cryptic origins of *Wilde about Holmes*, which finds itself in print so quickly in

---

* From OCSCAR WILDE by Richard Ellmann, copyright © 1987 by The Estate of Richard Ellmann. Used by permission of Alfred A. Knopf, a division of Random House, Inc.

order to please the insatiable demand each new generation creates for the tales of Sherlock Holmes even if, in this case, questions of authorship have not been satisfactorily addressed. The initial facts are as compelling as they are cumulative. Wilde and Conan Doyle did, in fact, meet in 1889 through the agency of J.L. Stoddart, who was in London searching for short novels. Stoddart held a dinner party in September of 1889, an occasion he used to commission novellas from the two witty Irishmen. Doyle offered him his second Sherlock Holmes story, *The Sign of the Four*; Wilde offered *The Picture of Dorian Gray*, which is a study of crime and detection as well.

Stoddart struck a vein of gold, and enjoyed tremendous success with the *Sign of the Four* and *The Picture of Dorian Gray*. *Wilde about Holmes* appears to have been Stoddart's attempt to follow up on the success of the first two stories. He saw the similarity in genre and tone of the two authors, and the possibility of combining their genius, but an act of fate not since repeated in American history seems to have suppressed the manuscript once and for all. Cleveland had been voted out of office in 1888, but his political career was resurrected when he became the Democratic Presidential nominee in 1892, winning the office a second time, the only American President to have served two non-consecutive terms in office. This effectively rendered *Wilde about Holmes* unpublishable, and when Stoddart died, the manuscript died with him.

From the sketchy details that have come down to us, as well as internal evidence in the manuscript, we may conclude that *Wilde About Holmes* was *dictated* by Wilde and Conan Doyle to Stoddart, most probably in 1891, or early 1892 at the latest. This would account for the composition of the novel in two voices, which was unusual for the time. Scientific analysis of the handwriting, paper and ink, as well as the internal evidence in the text itself, shall soon test the strength of this hypothesis.

One of the most compelling arguments for authenticity lies in Wilde's own American tour which took place just before the

scandal. Wilde had met Cleveland in Buffalo in the course of his lecture tour, and he later met James G. Blaine, Cleveland's future Republican opponent, in Washington. Furthermore, Wilde made many influential friends in Washington and New York who may have privileged his ear to the intimate details of the scandal as they were emerging.

It is left to historians of the period to disentangle the relationships between Oscar Wilde, Lillie Langtry, Grover Cleveland and Sherlock Holmes (who is in all likelihood a mask for Conan Doyle). Whatever outcome research may indicate, *Wilde about Holmes* undeniably creates a lasting and intimate portrait of celebrities and statesmen whose characters surpass their own historical selves thanks to a fictional detective and a witty Irishman who discovered that life imitates art.

—The Editor

In the meantime bear in mind that all is Life—Life—Life within Life—the lesser within the Greater, all within the *Spirit Divine*.

— Edgar Allen Poe, *Eureka*

WILDE ABOUT HOLMES

PROLOGUE

LONDON—1874

Talk itself is a sort of spiritualized action.
—Oscar Wilde

. . . makes one think in a circle,—I mused.

The nocturnal blue and gold of the Thames changed to a harmonic gray in the morning light. A barge dropped from the wharf and the yellow fog came cold and chill, creeping down the bridges, shadowing the perspective lines of houses around St Paul's. Then suddenly arose the clang of waking life: the streets stirred with country wagons, tradesmen, greengrocers, women and children. A bird flew to the glistering roofs and sang to a pale woman all alone who was loitering beneath the last flare of a gaslamp, daylight kissing her etiolated hair, kissing her lips of flame and heart of stone.

On and on plodded the hansom through the streets, going slower, it seemed to me, at each step. A silverpoint of anxiety touched me. I thrust up the trap and called to the man to drive faster. The driver laughed and whipped up. I laughed in answer as the man fell silent. Then the bells of Bow Church tolled.

The horse stumbled in a rut, then swerved aside and broke into a gallop. The drover beat the horse with his whip. A dog barked as we went by, and far away in the dawn some wandering sea gull screamed.

The cause of my urgency is Lillie Langtree, who is due to arrive in London momentarily. I have undertaken to arrange a quasi-official delegation to meet her boat. Lillie is accustomed to histrionic gestures that her admirers are wont to make. Pierre Loti had himself carried into her flat wrapped in a large and expensive Persian rug. That was an extravagance I regrettably cannot now match.

I believe in arriving to events such as these fashionably late, although this occasion is an exception to my hard and fast rule, for to miss Lillie's disembarkment would be utter catastrophe. She is the greatest actress ever to grace our stage. Aestheticism

is a search after the signs of the beautiful. My passion is beauty, and Lillie is a beautiful being for whom I was destined to create.
—Somewhere about here, sir, isn't it?—asked the driver huskily through the trap.

Suddenly the driver drew up with a jerk at the top of a lane. Over the low roofs and jagged chimney stacks of the houses rose the black masts of ships. The warm air seemed laden with spices.

—Faster, I'm late!

The horses picked up their pace as I intuitively shielded against bumps and jars my armful of lilies for Mrs Langtry. Purchased in Covent Garden. There, while I waited for the hansom, an unkempt child, fascinated by the mass of flowers, exclaimed, *How rich you are!*

Yes, I am, indeed. It was for such a lady that Troy was destroyed. . . . Her theme persists through the ages, continuing into Christian art, where the lily is an emblem of chastity, innocence and purity. Gabriel, in paintings of the Annunciation, is represented as carrying a lily branch, while a vase containing a lily stands before the Virgin who is kneeling at prayer. Now she is my Lillie, at once surface and symbol.

The speeding hansom leaned into a turn. We lurched as the horses ran against the collar. The hansom kept swerving at half-cock until the rapidly moving roadway tipped, skewed and crashed to a halt in my face. The hansom had tipped over, hurling the driver from his box. I was quite fortunate insofar as I sustained no injury and my tony checkered suit was unruffled. I emerged from the overturned hansom, and saw the horses snorting, whinnying, struggling to rise against their tangled reins. Ascertaining that the animals were bruised but not hurt, I picked my bowler up from the street, and remarked that the crown had suffered a lamentable ding. The heavy lines of my bright and brazenly checkered tweed ensemble had cushioned my fall. More significantly, I inspected the lilies I had brought for Lillie.

—Are you alright, guv'nor?—asked the driver, himself uninjured but shaken.

My reply had to wait until I had examined the flowers petal by petal. I could not present bruised lilies to the most beautiful Lillie in the world.

—A miracle! The lilies are safe!

I stuffed a guinea into the driver's surprised hand. He handled it insecurely, as if it were a vivid ember.

—This is too much, mi' lord!—he cried, disbelieving his own good fortune as I huffed and puffed down the lane leading to the quay where I met Norman Forbes-Robertson. He held a single bathetic gardenia in his hand. Moreover, none of our Oxford companions had arrived to greet her. I was absolutely furious, though I could not reprimand Norman because Lillie's boat was just now docking. Norman, void of any excuse, sustained my gaze sheepishly. The sky was faint blue, and the birds were beginning to twitter in the gardens. I heard her heels tupetting the gangplank.

—Will the members of the Oxford Welcoming Committee for Lillie Langtry please step forward,—I intoned.

Norman stepped forward.

—It was for such a lady that Troy was destroyed, and well might Troy be destroyed for such a woman. . . .

The words flow in a steady stream from my uncaged mouth, going forth in all directions. I am insensible to the meaning of my own words. The personification of beauty arises from her barque with her French maid, just as Aphrodite emerged from sea foam. Her classic features: the grave, low forehead; the exquisitely arched brow; the noble chiseling of her mouth, shaped as if it were a mouthpiece of an instrument of music; the supreme and splendid curve of the cheek; the augustly pillared throat which bears it all.

She looked on with bemused interest at our impromptu welcome, and descended.

—We will make you a carpet of flowers!—cried Norman.

—*Voilà!*—I said, taking my cue, and cast the armful of lilies at her feet as she gained the quay.

Lily of love, pure and inviolate!
Tower of Ivory! Red rose of fire!

I declaimed, inviting her to step across the petalled carpeting.

—*Qui est-ce ce jeune homme là?*—Lillie asked her maid.

—*Je ne sais pas, madame. . . .*

—We, your humble enthusiasts, welcome you to London and her proscenium.

—I meet him everywhere I go,—said Lillie to her maid.—He speaks beautifully but he has written nothing. I don't understand. He does nothing but talk!

I took this handicap in stride till their laughter subsided. Only then did I make my rejoinder.

—Madame Langtry, talk itself is a sort of spiritualized action. Perhaps someday I shall be fortunate enough to write something worthy of your playing.

I kneel as she steps across the carpet of flowers, her gown, like the robe the lissome Vivien wore at Merlin's feet in good King Arthur's reign, trembles along. A chrysanthemum pattern reflects the influence of Tokio and the mutable fabric expresses her movement rather than hides it.

The genius of beauty then knighted me in jest with her parasol.

—I dub thee Lord of Language!—she declared with charming perspicacity.

—I shall not fail you, mi' Lady,—I replied, then she disappeared into the gleams of sweet and honey-colored blossoms of laburnum, whose tremulous branches seemed hardly able to bear the burden of a beauty so flame-like as hers. Now and then the fantastic shadows of birds in flight flitted across her figure as she receded into the dim roar of London. Many a mortal has dreamed of encountering a deity, but how many could have imagined the lugubrious desanctification caused by her departure?

—I wonder where she is going?—said Norman whom I discovered to be still kneeling down beside me.

—To rendezvous her lover,—I answered with flippant accuracy, and a new motive flashed into being with Dionysian enthusiasm.

—Shall we follow her?

It is said that passion makes a man think in a circle. . . .

A woman's heart and mind
are insoluble puzzles to the male.
—Sherlock Holmes

Over-acuteness of the senses is sometimes mistaken for madness but it's almost always indicative of genius. I could hear—beyond her hypnogogic mumbling, beyond the beating of her heart, beyond her growling digestive organs—a persistent frothing framed by the regular intervals of her susurration. What I heard was a chemical reaction. And it was taking place in the concatenation of chemical beakers, retorts and alembics that regulated the volatile substances with which I was working.

She appeared to be asleep after having given effect to those primary instincts to which the humblest of human beings have a right. I rose silently to attend to the experiment in which I was extracting the essence of *papaver somniferum* from the milky exudate of unripe seed capsules. In its power to relieve pain it has no rival among naturally occurring compounds, being of use in the treatment of the severe pain of gallstone, renal colic, and metastatic cancer in cases where other analgesics have failed. No chemist has yet proposed a structure for this drug, and it is my ambition as a student to set forth a theory which, of necessity, may only be confirmed by its total synthesis, a method not now in the grasp of modern chemists. Even so, I have nothing but great respect for the German chemist, F.W.A. Sertürner, and hope that the next generation will bear out the truth of my scientific researches.

Such was my haste that I donned my dressing-gown and took a seat at the table I had erected in my study. The large curved retort was boiling furiously over the squashed blue flame of a Bunsen burner. Distilled drops were condensing into a two-litre flask.

I hardly glanced at her as she entered. I found her sudden appearance disruptive to my routines and I loathed myself for suc-

cumbing to her vague but emotional imprecations. Her motive? To no doubt improve me in some way. Ulterior objectives? To sabotage my cool logical mind by means of emotional manipulation. Her name betokens danger: tradition holds that the lily sprang from Eve's repentant tears as she went forth from Paradise.

Naked she stands, framed by the gloomy doorway, her breasts heaving, her nostrils flaring, glaring at me in angry, pregnant silence that made her more attractive. I draw a few drops of the solution with a glass pipette. Where is the litmus paper?

—You don't listen to a single word I say, do you?—she panted.

She says so many frivolous and unconnected things willynilly that I tried to recall what she was now referring to. Was it the French antiques? Her interpretation of Rosalind? Her indigestion? Or the fact that she was able to see the face of her lover under water, and so saw my face some years ago when she swam in the sea off Jersey. She nearly exasperates me.

—This is an important chemical experiment,—I said, hardly concealing my preoccupied air.

Suddenly I realized the Bunsen burner had brought the extraction to a dangerously high temperature. I quickly modulated the flame.

—Look at me, Holmes,—Lillie said desperately.

I looked at her face frothing with repressed tears. The conquest of Sherlock Holmes is the grandest feather she can put in her cap. One would think that the adulation she found in her stage performances would satisfy her penchant for melodramatics.

—Why did you make me fall in love with you?

—I did nothing of the sort. I merely . . . merely. . . .

Now she is bollixing my researches. The Bunsen burner is too low and I forgot what I did with the litmus paper. Love is an emotional thing, and whatever is emotional is opposed to that true cold reasoning which I place above all things. I should

never marry myself, lest I bias my judgment. I assure you the
most winning woman I ever knew was hanged for poisoning
three little children for their insurance money, and the most re-
pellent man of my acquaintance is a philanthropist who has
spent nearly a quarter of a million upon the London poor. Emotional qualities are antagonistic to clear reasoning. Therefore, I
mistrust Beauty.

Now Lillie was crying like a terrible pagan divinity, de-
throned, as stupid as an idol with nothing to say. I don't know
how to comfort crying women. Why was she crying? Surely to
get my attention. She collapsed on the davenport, holding her
aching head. I observe her.

—But I *love* you from the very *bot*tom of my heart!

I cringe when she says that word.

—You, Lillie, eclipse and predominate your irrational and
frail sex.

She falls to her knees and cries fluently. What does she want?
She wants me. But there is a rival: I want me.

—But I can't *live* without your love!

I began handing her the undergarments and numerous other
odiferous articles of femininia she had strewn throughout the
room. Better that she begin dressing now, I thought, for it will
take the better part of the afternoon, in any case, to get her to
leave.

—Love. . .—she repeated, staring at me as if I were a con-
genital idiot who did not know the meaning of the word.

The love of a woman, though it can arouse in a man some
hint of his higher nature, is, in the end, doomed either to unhappiness (if the truth about the woman's unworthiness is discovered) or to immorality (if the lie about her perfection is kept up).

24

The only love that is of enduring worth is that attached to the absolute, to the idea of God.[*]

Besides, no one who is honest with himself feels bound to provide for the continuity of the human race. That the human race should persist is of no interest whatever to reason; he who would perpetuate humanity would perpetuate the problem and the guilt, the only problem and the only guilt. The choices are bleak and terrible indeed: genius or death.[**]

—All emotions, and that one particularly, are abhorrent to a cool, precise but admirably balanced mind.

I felt such personal relief when anger incited her to dress more hastily. Perhaps anger will propel her to take another lover.

—Look, Holmes,—she said with no little defiance,—either you marry me, or I'm going to America.

—America?—I echoed. America is not far enough away, I thought. Afghanistan is better still.

She dispensed with the formality of her corset and merely threw the dress loosely over her body. She approached me again, one breast peeking at me from her disheveled dress.

—Is it that you don't love me? Or that you don't love anyone at all?

Why should one tell the truth? However unwelcome it is? One *should* be truthful, and that is that. The question *why?* is

---

[*] *The love of a woman ... the idea of God.* Reprinted with the permission of The Free Press, a Division of Simon & Schuster Adult Publishing Group, from *LUDWIG WITTGENSTEIN: The Duty of Genius*, by Ray Monk. Copyright © 1990 by Ray Monk. All rights reserved. Published in the UK by Jonathan Cape. Reprinted with permission of The RandomHouse Group Ltd.

[**] *Besides, no one who is honest ... the only guilt.* Reprinted with the permission of The Free Press, a Division of Simon & Schuster Adult Publishing Group, from *LUDWIG WITTGENSTEIN: The Duty of Genius*, by Ray Monk. Copyright © 1990 by Ray Monk. All rights reserved. Published in the UK by Jonathan Cape. Reprinted with permission of The RandomHouse Group Ltd.

inappropriate and cannot be answered. All questions must be asked and answered within the strict confines of the inviolable duty to be true to oneself. Thus, idealism and realism collide. She is unable to elucidate her *henids*, and therefore is incapable of making clear judgments. That is why women fall in love only with men more clever than they are.[*]

—There has been a terrible misunderstanding,—I explained.—I shall never love anyone as much as I love chemistry. Once again I tried to return to my researches but she was not finished. She scanned my personal library of chemical science, assembled at great cost, and removed from the shelf one of my most precious volumes, a rare 1536 edition of *Die grosse Wundartzney* by Paracelsus, a monumental work from the dawn of modern chemistry.

—Is this a chemistry book?—she asked fiercely.

I nodded gravely. A moment passed, and nothing happened.

—Why are you glaring at me?

Much to my surprise, she deliberately flung the book at me; I, however, was resolved to stand my ground unflinchingly. The tome's trajectory indicated that it would strike my head directly. I should have blocked its flight but a momentary paralysis debilitated me. For an instant, I stood outside of myself and beheld the scene from afar as the ponderous volume bounded off the crown of my head, and much to my further disappointment, skipped on with vengeful momentum, finally smashing into my laboratory table, destroying the results of my experiment that I had striven so hard to obtain. The surface of the table instantly

---

[*] *Why should one tell the truth? ... men more clever than they are.* Reprinted with the permission of The Free Press, a Division of Simon & Schuster Adult Publishing Group, from *LUDWIG WITTGENSTEIN: The Duty of Genius*, by Ray Monk. Copyright © 1990 by Ray Monk. All rights reserved. Published in the UK by Jonathan Cape. Reprinted with permission of The RandomHouse Group Ltd.

caught fire. Lillie gleefully watched me put out the nascent flames that threatened to consume us all.

—I hate chemistry!—she shrieked with malicious satisfaction.

Thankfully, she left, not before nearly slamming the door off its hinges. Having rescued the tome and extinguished the flames, I threw open my windows to clear the apartment of noxious odors. As I held the singed and smoking copy of *Die grosse Wundartzney*, my ruminations turned to Winwood Reade, the eminent author of *The Martyrdom of Man*, one of the most remarkable books ever penned. It comforts me, inspires me in trying times such as these. Mr Reade states that the abhorrence of the impure, the sense of duty, the fear of punishment, all unite and form a moral law which women themselves enforce, becoming the guardians of their own honor, and treating as a traitor to their sex the woman who betrays their trust. For her the most compassionate have no mercy; she has broken those laws of honor on which society is founded. It is forbidden to receive her; it is an insult to women to allude to her existence, to pronounce her very name. Lillie is such a woman. She is condemned without injury, as the officer is condemned who has shown cowardice before the foe. For the life of women is a battle-field; virtue is their courage and peace of mind is their reward. It is certainly an extraordinary fact that women should be subjected to a severe social discipline from which men are almost entirely exempt. As we have shown, it is to be explained by history; it is due to the ancient subjugation of woman to man. But it is not the women who are to be pitied; it is they who alone are free, for by that discipline they are preserved from the tyranny of vice—vice to which Lillie is a grateful subject.

The genius of man has developed along a line of unbroken descent from the simple tendencies which inhabited the primitive cell; at this present moment, *progress*, whose chief engine is the free intellect, speeds the great world along the ringing

grooves of change to the glorious futurity that lies ahead, and blesses this age with advantages over ages past.

Even so, a woman's heart and mind are insoluble puzzles to the male.

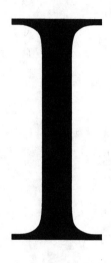

I

NEW YORK—1884

There is nothing more unaesthetic than a policeman.
—Oscar Wilde

I am not exactly pleased with the Atlantic. It is not so majestic as I expected. The sea seems tame to me. The roaring ocean does not roar. The slow time of ten pendulous days passed since we embarked from London. I longed for my spacious drawing room and the white blaze of window that illumed my serried bookcases and ebony writing table. The real inconvenience, though, is having been separated from my cherished bric-a-brac and furniture. Jimmy Whistler advised me that if I get sick, I should throw up on Burne-Jones. He also suggested that hyperaestheticism might prove to be an antidote to America's hyper-materialism.

I am coming to America, land of the free, because unofficial censorship closed my republican play, *Vera, or the Nihilists* after Dion Boucicault (the director) and Mrs Beere (in the title role) had already commenced rehearsals in London. I had entertained hopes that the recent assassinations of Czar Alexander II and President Garfield would add topicality to my play but a sudden flash of royalist sentiment in England checked the production. *Vera* had come to the attention of the Russian government and Lord Granville received a communiqué on the subject. Since I, Oscar Fingal O'Flahertie Wills Wilde, am now counted as one of the European Powers, I may not give offense to a crowned head. The Prince of Wales, himself married to the sister of the new Czarina, could scarcely be expected to look with favor upon an aborted assassination attempt, even on the stage. I shall instead produce *Vera* in New York, the metropolis now thundering before me, for in a republic there can be no squeamishness about lopping off a crowned head.

My cabin is on the promenade, very near the saloon decks. Every device calculated to increase the comfort of passengers has been combined in this splendid ship, which is at once swift, secure and sumptuous, as strong as a battleship and as luxurious

31

as a Belgravia drawing room. Here an artist may work and refine the ductile metal of art. I am preparing for the occasion of my arrival by overdressing. The dandy's figure is cut in the realm of the imagination before it is cut in cloth. I express my independence by rejecting any visible distinction but elegance; self-worship and superiority to useful work are displayed by tireless application to costumery. Therefore, independence, assurance, originality, self-command and refinement must be visible. I don a dark purple sack coat and kneebreeches, garter my black silk hose and put on low shoes with bright buckles. *Voilà!* My coat is lined with lavender satin, accenting a frill of rich lace and a low turn-down collar. I part my long hair in the middle. A circular cavalier cloak skirts my shoulder, adding a touch of bravado.* A great seal ring bearing the profile of the Emperor Nero adorns my finger. The cabin doors waft shut behind me as I surge onto the deck.

Before me lies New York, the thundering loom of great environing cities, the vortex of these joyously confluent waters *in mobile perpetuum.* New York Harbor presents a continual succession of varied and busy scenes: the headwaters of the Coney Island steamboats plume the bay; Boston and Savannah steamships plash the grey-green waters; the wharves of the Hudson River lines ache and crack beneath crates of cargo. Dominating the shoreline along the East River, large sailing ships, commercial vessels from all parts of the world, sway in their resting places with their lofty masts and long yards interwoven against the nebulous and topaz canvas of deep skies, redolent of fine tobacco and early vegetables, maize, indigo and opium.

—Shipshape and Bristol fashion!—cries a sailor.

---

* *I don a dark purple ... a circular cavalier cloak.* From OCSCAR WILDE by Richard Ellmann, copyright © 1987 by The Estate of Richard Ellmann. Used by permission of Alfred A. Knopf, a division of Random House, Inc.

My ship, the *Arizona*, navigates to a line of ferries, above which appear several dry docks, followed by iron foundries veiled in acrid and malodorous smoke; farther, the balsamic odor of lumber yards, and old steamers laid up in ordinary. I hasten down the gangplank to Castle Garden, New York's immigrant station. In bygone days it was called Castle Clinton; a fort on a ledge in the bay, connected by a causeway with the mainland. As time wore on, the Castle became a concert hall where the Lafayette ball was given; the Swedish Nightingale made her American debut on this very spot. I am inclined to interpret this auspiciously as a token of my good fortune and imminent success.

Through the southern archway of Castle Garden a framework is visible on Bedloe's Island: four gigantic steel supports designed by Alexandre-Gustave Eiffel. This structure is to support a neoclassical sculpture of a woman personifying Liberty. Whistler also informs me that Bartholdi, the sculptor, wishes to rival the Colossus of Rhodes of Antiquity. Significantly, the American people themselves do not wish to contribute funds to this artwork, and it is only because the French Republic committed monies to it that any work has taken place at all. Jimmy says this is typical American tightfistedness.

Dockers clad in boiler suits begin unloading luggage from the *Arizona* as soon as we call at port. I negotiate the piers and crazy-looking wharves that are for the most part exceedingly irregular and rather unsightly, of various length and constructed of wood upon piles in a basin of black and gold flecked water where free tides swirl and eddy. Though devoid of the architectural symmetry and structural massiveness of European quays, the crinkum-crankum waterfront of New York is well-fitted for its mercantile uses, and boasts a vagrant collection of sharpies who prey upon unsuspecting émigrés.

Retrieving my black leather valise from a docker, I try to avoid a rum fellow who is rooting through the luggage lorry. Does he call that thing a coat? I sweep out of the wharf and clatter down the boardwalk to customs. I avert my appalled gaze.

33

There he is again, a picture of stirring loneliness at first glance, wearing a houndstooth chequed inverness, a herringbone deer-stalker cap, and dogbone colored trousers whose hem was cut several inches too short. He *is*. Jimmy would have called him *Decomposition in Black and Grey*!

Some ten years ago when I was searching for comfortable lodgings in London at a reasonable price, Norman Forbes-Robertson first informed me of him.

—*A fellow who is working at the chemical laboratory up at the hospital was bemoaning himself this morning because he could not get someone to go halves with him in some nice rooms which he had found, and which were too much for his purse.*

—*By Jove,*—I cried,—*if he really wants someone to share the rooms and the expense, I am the very man for him.*

Young Forbes-Robertson looked rather strangely at me over his wineglass.—*You don't know Sherlock Holmes yet,*—he said;—*perhaps you would not care for him as a constant companion.*

—*Why, what is there against him?*

—*Oh, I didn't say there was anything against him. He is a little queer in his ideas, an enthusiast in some branches of science. As far as I know, he is a decent enough fellow.*

—*A medical student, I suppose?*

—*No, I have no idea what he intends to go in for. I believe he is well up in anatomy, and he is a first-class chemist; but, as far as I know, he has never taken out any systematic medical classes. His studies are desultory and eccentric, but he has amassed a lot of out-of-the-way knowledge which would aston-ish his professors.*

—*Did you never ask him what he was going in for?*

—*No; he is not a man that is easy to draw out, though he can be communicative enough when the fancy seizes him.*

—*It seems to me, Robertson, that you have some reason for washing your hands of the matter. Is this fellow's temper so formidable, or what is it? Don't be mealy-mouthed about it.*

—*It is not easy to express the inexpressible,*—he answered with a laugh.—*Holmes is a little too scientific for my tastes—it approaches to cold-bloodedness. That last time I saw him he would hardly reply to my questions and busied himself all the evening in an abstruse chemical analysis which involved much heating of retorts and distilling of vapors, ending at last in a reek which fairly drove me out of the apartment.*

Thus, I never had the pleasure of actually meeting Mr Sherlock Holmes; and since I am now in America, I am un-enthusiastic about meeting an English chap, so I choose to avoid him and take a different customs queue. Quite suddenly, there is a commotion.

—Seize him! He's carrying banned books!

Vexed, I turn to observe the emerging fracas, where several customs officials arrest Sherlock Holmes.

—Next!

I place my black leather valise on the inspection table, hoping to pass quickly through.

—The purpose of your visit, sir?—asks the customs officer.

—To win the heart of America.

—Did you pack your luggage yourself?

—Absolutely not. Packing is a task relegated to servants.

—Do you have anything to declare?—he questions, arching his bureaucratic eyebrow.

—I have nothing to declare but my genius,—I proclaim.

It was not a spontaneously crafted remark. I had time to choose my words during the Atlantic crossing, having felt it important that I make a significant and enduring statement upon my admittance to the United States of America. *Voilà.*

But when the customs agent removes an inverness cape from my bag, complected feelings of anguish and horror, surprise and scorn harpoon me, then ripen into rich laughter. How did such a horrid garment insinuate itself into my traveling bag!?

The customs agent then proceeds to remove some books.

35

—The Practical Handbook of Bee Culture with Some Observations upon the Segregation of the Queen; Uses of Dogs in Detection; The Influence of Trade upon the Form of the Hand. . . .
—What?
I take one of the books and open it to the title page. I find therein the book's authorship ascribed to none other than *Sherlock Holmes.*

I examine the contents of the valise and exhume a long cherry-wood pipe and a neat morocco case containing a hypodermic syringe, which I recognize immediately because my father, also a physician, possessed a case with similar accoutrements. There is also a magnification glass. This evidence corroborates what Robertson had told me about Holmes so many years ago.

—*Sans doute,* this is not my bag,—I say, turning to see Sherlock Holmes making persuasive gestures to the customs officers who had surrounded him. I instruct the customs agent to return the valise to Mr Sherlock Holmes. Of more importance: where is my bag and who has it now? Holmes?

I meet the group midway, and finally greet Mr Sherlock Holmes. His features are severe yet well-proportioned. His face displays absolutely no emotion. I extend my hand in greeting.

What *could* have Holmes done to provoke such intense scrutiny? I observed him pacify the agitated officers. The group of agents shift their attention from Holmes to me. One of them ominously peruses a large black book.

—Oscar Wilde, how do you do?
—Sherlock Holmes, a pleasure to meet you.
I return his valise.
—Do you perchance have mine?
The customs agent slaps shut the black book.
—No, no,—says the customs agent—*Vera, or the Nihilists* and *Satyricon Petronii* are not banned yet, but maybe they should be.

I am mortified by the very possibility, however remote, of having my books confiscated. To know nothing about their great men is one of the necessary elements of English education*—not of American—I imagine.

I take back my books and valise.

—There is nothing more unaesthetic than a policeman.

I walk to Pearl Street to hail a cab. There is silence for a moment. St Luke's little summer evening purples and darkens the air. Noiselessly and with silver feet, shadows creep in from the east. Colors fade wearily out of things. The gravid air thickens and cools around me. A few large, glabrous raindrops, rare at first, strike my low shoes along the ungainly scores along the instep, then grow in number and force, spotting the parched planks of the boardwalk with large, brown circles, shaping my fate with its liquid, plangent and reiterant roar.

---

* *To know nothing ... English education.* From OCSCAR WILDE by Richard Ellmann, copyright © 1987 by The Estate of Richard Ellmann. Used by permission of Alfred A. Knopf, a division of Random House, Inc.

He is the Napoleon of crime.
—Sherlock Holmes

You have probably never heard of Professor Moriarty. The man's evil works pervade London, and no one has heard of him. That's what puts him on a pinnacle in the records of crime. If I could beat that man, if I could free society of him, I should feel that my own career had reached its summing, and I should be prepared to turn to some more placid line in life and live in the quiet fashion which is most congenial to me, and to concentrate my attention upon my chemical researches. But I could not rest, I could not sit quiet in my chair, if I thought that such a man as Professor Moriarty were to escape English justice and walk the streets of New York unchallenged.

His career has been extraordinary. He is a man of good birth and excellent education, endowed by nature with a phenomenal mathematical faculty. At the age of twenty-one, he wrote a treatise upon the binomial theorem, which has had a European vogue. On the strength of it, he won the mathematical chair at one of our smaller universities and had, to all appearances, a most brilliant career before him. But the man had hereditary tendencies of the most diabolical kind. A criminal strain ran in his blood which, instead of being modified, was increased and rendered infinitely more dangerous by his extraordinary mental powers. Dark rumors gathered round him in the university town, and eventually he was compelled to resign his chair and to come down to London, where he set up as an army coach. So much is known to the world, but what I am telling you now is what I have myself discovered.

As you are aware, there is no one who knows the higher criminal world of London so well as I do. For years past I have continually been conscious of some power behind the malefactor, some deep organizing power which forever stands in the way of the law, and throws its shield over the wrongdoer. Again

and again in cases of the most varying sorts—forgeries, robber- ies, murders—I have felt the presence of this force, and I have deduced its action in many of those undiscovered crimes in which I have not been personally consulted. For years I have endeavored to break through the veil which shrouded it; and at last the time came when I seized my thread and followed it, until it led me, after a thousand cunning windings, to ex-Professor Moriarty, of mathematical celebrity.

He is the Napoleon of crime. He is the organizer of half that is evil and of nearly all that is undetected in London, and is now uncoiling his tentacles in New York. He is a genius, a philoso- pher, an abstract thinker. He does little himself. He only plans. But his agents are numerous and splendidly organized. Is there a crime to be done, a paper to be abstracted, we will say, a house to be rifled, a man to be removed? The word is passed to the Professor; the matter is organized and carried out. The agent may be caught. In that case, money is found for his bail or his defense. But the central power which uses the agent is never caught—never so much as suspected. This was the organization which I deduced, and which I have devoted my whole energy to exposing and breaking up.

But the Professor was fenced round with safeguards so cun- ningly devised that, do what I would, it seemed impossible to get evidence that would convict him in a court of law. You know my powers, and yet at the end of three months I was forced to con- fess that I had at last met an antagonist who was my intellectual equal. My horror at his crimes was lost in my admiration of his skill. But at last he made a trip—only a little, little trip—but it was more than he could afford, when I was so close upon him. I had my chance, and starting from that point, I wove my net round him until now it was all ready to close.

Now if I could have done this without the knowledge of Pro- fessor Moriarty, all would have been well. But he was too wily for that. He saw every step which I took to trap him. Again and again he strove to break away, but I as often headed him off. I

tell you that if a detailed account of that silent contest could be written, it would take its place as the most brilliant bit of thrust-and-parry work in the history of detection. Never have I risen to such a height, and never have I been so hard pressed by an opponent. I cut deep, yet he just undercut me. A fortnight ago I discovered that he had removed himself from London and had taken refuge in New York. Oh, I have a rod in pickle for Moriarty! Arriving now in Manhattan, I take the last steps to earth my fox.

My needs are simple: Darkness and Dr Watson's umbrella. And darkness did indeed come and now I must make do without Watson and his umbrella.

—*Well, and there is the end of our little drama,*—Watson remarked, after we sat some time smoking in silence, pondering Moriarty's disappearance.—*I fear that it may be the last investigation in which I shall have the chance of studying your methods. Miss Morstan has done me the honor to accept me as a husband in prospective.*

I groaned dismally.

—*I feared as much,*—said I.—*I really cannot congratulate you.*

He was a little hurt.

—*Have you any reason to be dissatisfied with my choice?*—Watson asked.

—*Not at all. I think she is one of the most charming ladies I ever met and might have been most useful in such work as we have been doing. She has a decided genius that way. . . . But love is an emotional thing, and whatever is emotional is opposed to that true cold reason which I place above all things. I myself should never marry, lest I bias my judgment. Ah, Watson,*—I continued, half-smiling,—*perhaps you would not be very gracious either, if after all the trouble of wooing and wedding, you found yourself deprived in an instant of wife and fortune. I think that we may thank our stars that we are never likely to find ourselves in the same position. Draw your chair up and hand me*

my violin, for the only problem I have still to solve is how to
while away these bleak autumnal evenings.

And so Watson handed me my Stradivarius and disappeared from 221B Baker Street to wife, leaving me to my own devices to search out Moriarty, leading me to this moment where time and space have converged to bring me to New York.

I am not as whole-souled an admirer of womankind as Watson. My experience of life has taught me that there are very few wives who have any regard for their husbands. Should I ever marry, I should hope to inspire my wife with something which would prevent her from running off with the gardener when my corpse is lying within a few yards of her.

Being inclined to such introspection when idle, I seek some diversion in the mob when I see *him* pranked out: Enter with a dark purple sack coat, kneebreeches and cavalier cloak. He shifts pose now and then, the head inclining toward his right foot, maintaining a general appearance of insouciance. As to his avocation, the eccentric costume and the black marks of ink upon the fingertips of his ungloved writing hand. . . . I must be dull, indeed, if I do not pronounce him to be an active member of the writing profession.

The disciple of true art speaks very deliberately; the closing inflection of a sentence or period is ever *aigu*. It is *he* who insists on attracting attention to himself. I hasten to secure my traveling bag from the stevedores so that I may avoid encountering the most affected man in London. People find him a risible figure, yet he somehow manages to seize the initiative; when some ruder Oxford students pitched him into the river, he instructed them how to go about it properly. But he cares not, not even about the Gilbert and Sullivan song about him walking

> *down Piccadilly with a poppy or a lily*
> *in his mediaeval hand. . . .*

Patience. He who amuses you will soon bore you.

To me, he rather resembles a heathen idol. He is a splendid talker and a handsome man, but a voluptuary. As he walks from you there is something in the motion of his hips and back that is disagreeable. * He cuts his friends, tricks his rivals, patronizes his enemies. Mr Oscar Wilde. He carries within him an eradicable something that does not belong to Victorian stability, which I have fought all through my career to preserve. There is in him, as a fixed part of his character, that longing for change, stimulation, and excitement which is leading this once solid age of bright stair rods down the long, long Gadarene slope of decadence and decline.

Certainly the principal function of the Bureau of Immigration is to inspect and examine arriving immigrants; and to see that the provisions of the laws forbidding the landing of certain prohibited classes, namely: convicts, lunatics, idiots, paupers, persons likely to become public charges, or suffering with contagious or loathsome diseases, contract laborers, and polygamists, are carried out. Whether Mr Oscar Wilde will pass is open to speculation.

The customs official examines my papers of transit.

—The purpose of your visit, Mr Holmes?

—To make a systematic study of the American penitentiary system,—I say, concealing the true nature of my voyage.

—Did you pack your baggage yourself?

—Baggage?—That's an odd word.—Of course.

—Do you have anything to declare?

—No.

---

* *a heathen idol ... that was disagreeable.* From OCSCAR WILDE by Richard Ellmann, copyright © 1987 by The Estate of Richard Ellmann. Used by permission of Alfred A. Knopf, a division of Random House, Inc.

The immigration official opens my bag and carries out his appointed duties. He quite inadvertently hoots when, to my astonishment, he removes a purple velvet jacket, a perfumed yellow handkerchief and some books from the bag. Though my nerves are fairly proof, I am jarred by the appearance of this strange, effeminate clothing.

—*Satyricon Petronii*,—mutters the customs officer in low disapproving tones as he reads the title of one of the volumes.

—What?

—*Vera, or the Nihilists*?

—Let me see,—I reply, examining these curious volumes. *Petronii*. Latin. Dead language. I don't understand what it—

The agent consults with some other officials about the cross-up.

Oxford. Clarendon. Who owns this book? *Ex libris*—

—Seize him! He's carrying banned books!—someone barks.

A clutch of guards rudely takes hold of me. I compliment the Customs Bureau for their effective security measures, however misapplied they are to me.

—My credentials attest to my identity,—I inform them,—and as far as those rude and nihilistic volumes are concerned, they must belong to some radical degenerate with whom I must have accidentally exchanged bags!

—Look up that *Vera* book,—says one agent sternly.—Some dude named Oscar Wilde wrote it.

—Oscar Wilde!

His large burly figure saunters in my direction. A customs agent who accompanies him bears a traveling bag identical to mine.

He returns my bag, but I cannot give him his.

Mr Oscar Wilde proceeds to make a wholly inappropriate remark directed personally against one of the officials. I am shocked by Mr Wilde's hauteur and arrogance, and welcome the restoration of my traveling bag with no less relief than his speedy departure. After receiving profuse apologies from the

officials, who, after all, were merely performing their appointed duty, I pass quickly through and officially set foot in America, and steel myself to undertake the great mission at hand.

Moriarty has allied himself with the greatest of the gangs that came into existence in New York after the Civil War, as vicious a menagerie of hooligans, murderers and thieves as ever operated in a metropolis, the dreaded Whyos. The etymology of the name is uncertain, held by some to have arisen from a peculiar call sometimes employed by the gangsters. The Whyos are headquartered in Mulberry Bend, and may always be found lounging in a churchyard at Park and Mott Streets: Hoggy Walsh, Fig McGerald, Bull Hurley, Googy Corcoran, Baboon Connolly, and Red Rocks Farrell. Thugs and brawlers of the first water, sneak thieves, burglars and pickpockets. Many owned dives, panel houses, and bagnios. The gang roams through lower Manhattan, levying tribute on the merchants and factory owners, breaking into houses in broad daylight, beating and robbing strangers, and keeping the entire district in a chronic state of terror. *A guy ain't tough until he has knocked his man out!* When that ruffian Mike McGroin was at length brought to book for one of his many crimes, the police found this list in his pocket: *Punching $2, Both eyes blacked $4, Nose and jaw broke $10, Jacked out $15, Ear chawed off $15, Leg or arm broke $19, Shot in leg $25, Stab $25, Doing the big job, $100 and up.*

Dandy John Nolan, the leader of the gang, reports directly to Moriarty. He is regarded as something of a mastermind because he has improved the technique of gouging out eyes; he is said to have invented an apparatus, made of copper and worn on the thumb, which performs this important office with neatness and dispatch. His invention has been used by the Whyos with great success in their fights with other gangs. Dandy John is also credited with first having imbedded sections of sharp ax blade in the soles of his fighting boots, so that when he overthrew an adversary and stamped him, results both gory and final were obtained. The Beau Brummel of the gangland wore his hair and

forelock tastefully curled and anointed, handkerchiefs with violent red or blue borders, and carved canes with a representation of an animal for a handle.

These are my adversaries of choice, whom I will imprison in the granite Tombs at Franklin and Centre Streets. The Tombs Police Court is connected with the prison in the rear by a bridge, known as the Bridge of Sighs from the fact that condemned prisoners are led across it after conviction. Hangings and electrocutions take place in the central courtyard. I vow the Tombs will dispense their stern justice on Moriarty and the Whyos before I return to England.

Lightning strikes, and thunder follows quickly. Rain falls in large shimmering beads.

Three hansoms pass me by without stopping. My teeth clench the pipestem in frustration when a cab pulls up next to me and a moonfaced man thrusts his head out the window.

—May I offer a fellow Englishman the services of my carriage, Mr Holmes?

It is Oscar Wilde.

Ignorance is like a rare flower in bloom—
touch it and it disappears.
    —Oscar Wilde

His formidable and imposing figure stood in the slanting rain that fell pattering wildly at his feet. His inverness proved its utility by shielding him from the elements with resolute impermeability, congruent and symmetrical to the cloak of reason that shielded him from the ambient and Dionysian madness of life. I could see that his determination would lead him somehow to the farther limits of his genius. He is a strange and compelling man. I ordered the driver to stop and called out to him.

Thought worked the clueless features of his face for an instant, then he entered the cab, water streaming down the coarse folds of his coat. A severe intellectual face, strong chin, intense eyes. Beautiful, if cool manners. No doubt that he thinks merry old England (and only England could have produced him) is going to the dogs. His principles are out of date, but there is a good deal to be said for his prejudices.

—Thank you, Mr Wilde, I appreciate the courtesy you show—

—You are most welcome.

—though you are known to contradict all beliefs that Englishmen hold dear,—he continued, acknowledging that my reputation had reached so far as to him.

—In my estimation, English beliefs are criminal, and I track them down just as relentlessly as you pursue your villains.

He laughed dryly.

—That is not, actually, the subject of your present thoughts. Why don't you fire your servant?—he said with eerie clairvoyance.

Sherlock Holmes is a downy card.

—How do you know my servant is clumsy?—I asked, somewhat alarmed.

46

—I see it, I deduce it. How do I know that you have a most clumsy and careless servant girl?

—Servant boy,—I corrected him.

In some remote region of the galaxy of my self, something shapeless and immense shifts its weight. I feel ashamed.

—Clumsy and careless, nonetheless,—added Holmes.

—This is too much,—I said, answering his provocation.— You would certainly have been burned, had you lived a few centuries ago. I am able to pay no higher compliment. It is true that I had a country walk the day before I departed and came home in a dreadful mess; I can't imagine how you deduce it. As to Todd—that lilac-gilded boy of summer—he is incorrigible. I would give him notice if he didn't have such a perfect profile. But I fail to see how you work it out.

—It is simplicity itself,—said he.—My eyes tell me that on the inside of your left shoe, just where the failing daylight strikes it, the leather is scored by six almost parallel cuts. Obviously they have been caused by someone who has very carelessly scraped round the edges of the sole in order to remove crusted mud from it. Hence, you see, my double deduction that you had been out in vile weather, and that you had a particularly malignant boot-slitting specimen of a London slavey.

A fatuous digression ensued. He was a laconic conversationalist. He made a great play of no longer studying medicine, and generally confirmed Robertson's opinion of him. He did not pursue any course of reading that might have fitted him for a dress in science or any other recognized attire that would give him entrance into the learned world. Yet his zeal for certain studies was remarkable, and within eccentric limits his knowledge was so extraordinarily ample and minute that his observations fairly astounded me. Desultory readers are seldom remarkable for the exactness of their learning. No man burdens his mind with small matters unless he has some very good reason for doing so. He fancies himself an artist of thought and logic, whose mind cuts the Gordian knot as well as it divines the secrets of the Sphinx.

47

He labors under the illusion, nonetheless, that it is useful, not knowing that all art is of necessity useless.

His ignorance is as remarkable as his knowledge. Of contemporary literature, philosophy and politics he appeared to know next to nothing. Upon my quoting Walter Pater, he inquired in the naivest way who he might be and what he had done. My surprise reached a climax, however, when I found by chance that he was ignorant of the Copernican Theory and of the composition of the solar system. Even I am acquainted with it. That any civilized human being in the nineteenth century should not be aware that the earth traveled round the sun appeared to me to be such an extraordinary aberration that I could hardly conceive it.

—You appear to be astonished,—he said.—Now that I do know it I shall do my best to forget it!

—To forget it?!—I said in genial disbelief.

—You see,—he explained,—I consider that a man's brain originally is like a little empty attic, and you have to stock it with such furniture as you choose. A fool takes in all the lumber of every sort that he comes across, so that the knowledge which might be useful to him gets crowded out, or at best is jumbled up with a lot of other things, so that he has a difficulty in laying his hands upon it. Now the skilled workman is very careful indeed as to what he takes into his brain-attic. He will have nothing but the tools that may help him in doing his work, but of these he has a large assortment, and all in the most perfect order. It is a mistake to think that little room has elastic walls and can distend to any extent. Depend upon it, there comes a time when for every addition of knowledge you forget something that you knew before. It is of the highest importance, therefore, not to have useless facts elbowing out the useful ones.

—But the solar system!—I exclaimed with delight.—I want to forget it, too!

The truth ceases to be true when more than one person believes it.

—What the deuce is it to me?—he soliloquized impatiently.—You say that we go round the sun. *Elementarsatz*. If we went round the moon it would not make a pennyworth of difference to me or my work.

I found such colossal egoism attractive.

The conversation turned to his reasons for coming to New York, capital of the New World.

—To make a thorough study of the penal system in America,—he replied crisply,—for the way of the world is that I pursue the wicked, and the Crown tries them and incarcerates the guilty. We in Europe want systematic knowledge of penitentiary practice and the reformation of criminals.

I suppose him to be one of those mediocrities so common in London clubs, who have no enemies but are thoroughly disliked by their friends. But Sherlock Holmes has enemies, indeed.

—How intriguing. I believe wickedness is a myth invented by good people to account for the curious attractiveness of others.

—A distinct touch! It is true: You possess an epigrammatical sense of humor, Wilde, against which I must learn to guard myself; though I don't mind confessing to you that I have always had an idea that I would have made a highly efficient criminal.

—In other words,—I continued,—what people call insincerity (which taken *in extremis* may, for the sake of argument, be viewed as evil) is simply a method by which the creative artist may multiply his personality.

He took thought. I awaited evidence that his mind was a dreadful thing belonging to a thoroughly well-informed man, a bric-a-brac shop, all monsters and dust, with everything priced above its proper value.

I, too, had considered how much criminality was entwined with life and the creative process. If we lived long enough to see the results of our actions, it may be that those who call themselves good would be sickened with a dull remorse and those whom the world called evil stirred by a noble joy.

We have ancestors in literature, as well as in our own race, nearer perhaps in type and temperament, many of them, and certainly with an influence of which we are more absolutely conscious. There is a hero of a wonderful novel that had so influenced my life, who had himself known this curious fancy. Over and over again I used to read those fantastic chapters in which, as in some curious tapestries or cunningly wrought enamels, were pictured the awful and beautiful forms of those whom Vice and Blood and Weariness had made monstrous or mad: Filippo, Duke of Milan, who slew his wife, and painted her lips with scarlet poison that her lover might suck death from the dead thing he fondled; Gian Maria Visconti, who used hounds to chase living men, and whose murdered body was covered with roses by a harlot who had loved him; Pietro Riario, the young Cardinal Archbishop of Florence, child and minion of Sixtus IV, whose beauty was equaled only by his debauchery, and who received Leonora of Aragon in a pavilion of white and crimson silk, filled with nymphs and centaurs, and gilded a boy that he might serve at the feast as Ganymede or Hylas; Sigismondo Malatesta, the lover of Isotta and the lord of Rimini, whose effigy was burned at Rome as the enemy of God and man, who strangled Polyssena with a napkin, who gave poison to Ginevra d'Este in a cup of emerald, and who, in honor of a shameful passion, built a pagan church for Christian worship.

There was a horrible fascination in all of them. I saw them at night, and they troubled my imagination in the day. The Renaissance knew of strange manners of poisoning—poisoning by a helmet and a lighted torch, by an embroidered glove and a jeweled fan, by a gilded pomander and an amber chain. I had been poisoned by a book.

And then there are moments when I look upon evil simply as a mode through which I may realize my conception of the beautiful.

—Moriarty,—he said with a taut look of angled distaste.

Moriarty. That is a puzzling answer to my question. *Morituri te sal*—the name finally flashes a light on the man: *the evil asteroid* that will someday collide with the earth, annihilating us all.

—Of course, Moriarty! Is he not the celebrated author of *The Dynamics of an Asteroid*, a book which ascends to such rarefied heights of pure mathematics that it is said that there is no man in the scientific press capable of criticizing it?

—Indeed, the very same Moriarty. Is this a man to traduce?— he said with mysterious omination.

I was impressed with the self-absorption of Mr Holmes. He could literally see nothing outside of himself. For him the whole of history was merely the record of his own life, not as he had lived it in act and circumstance, but as his imagination had created it for him, as it had appeared in his brain and in his passions, as if the gestures and actions had created him, instead. He is a sort of *dandy intérieur*.

The rain thinned to a drizzle, then ceased.

The hansom jerked to a stop. Our conversation was interrupted by a mob, led by a compère costumed as Uncle Sam and trumpeting:

A Public Office Is a Public Trust!

and the marching crowd, canting forward intently, antiphoned:

A Public Office Is a Public Trust!

A political manifestation. The marchers held torchlights aloft and bore a large placard of Grover Cleveland, the Democratic Presidential candidate. The motley crowd flooded the junction box and forced us to wait, so I amused myself watching the splendor and the shabbiness of New York life, wondering over my cigarette at the strange panorama of pride and poverty that was passing before me.

Whence come they? Whither go they? It is the same crowd from day to day and from year to year, the faces are the same as

are the passions shadowing their faces. Individuality is subverted. Had we sat in this carriage yesterday or four years ago or one hundred years hence, we may have watched it without detecting any great difference because life recurs as panels on Fortune's wheel.

—Why have you come to New York, Wilde?—asked Holmes once the hansom began moving again.

—For pleasure, for beauty and for money. I hope to arrange for the production of my play, *Vera, or the Nihilists*, on Broadway,—I said, and explained to him the nature of the censorship that had prevented the play from being performed in England.

—A man of the theatre!

—Yes.

—I have absolutely no knowledge whatsoever of the theatre,—he said dryly,—except that I was almost arrested on account of your play!

Now we were interrupted at yet another crossroad by a political manifestation on behalf of:

James G. Blaine, James G. Blaine!
Pluméd Knight from the State of Maine!

Blaine apparently is the Republican opponent of Grover Cleveland. I welcomed the spontaneity. Klaxons blared. There were two Cyprians seated on the sill of their groundfloor windows, their skirts hiked above their knees, dangling Blaine and Cleveland banners respectively, taking advantage of the political procession to advertise their preference and their charms. A porter stood becalmed on the nearby stairs, wondering, as if the air were full of erudite formulae that would somehow sum his life. And how different my life would have been if I weren't beautiful, talented, rich and well-born? Well, the gifted dread their own genius. One cannot possess solitude, beauty and bravery without experiencing their pang.

The crowd wheeled through the rain-warmed air, and my attention turned toward the buildings that encased these people.

An American apparently has a great deal to do besides parading for political candidates, and is always in such a great hurry to do it that he cannot submit to the long, patient study required to master any one style of architecture permanently, which is indispensable to a man who would attempt to be original. Why submit to all this drudgery of proportion and harmony when Corinthian pillars and Gothic pinnacles stuck on *ad libitum* get over all difficulties and satisfy the architect and his employees? The perfection of art, in an American's eyes, would be attained by the invention of an automaton, which should produce plans of cities and designs of Gothic churches or classically rendered municipal buildings at so much per square foot, and so save trouble and thought.

I had reserved rooms at the *Brevoort* on Fifth Avenue near Washington Square. It is a quiet and aristocratic hotel that has long been in favor with English tourists. The cuisine of the Brevoort has always been considered one of its attractions. Sam Ward, that prince of epicures and most genial of entertainers, lived there at one time; and his nephew, F. Marion Crawford, the novelist, described the house and his uncle's favorite corner in his novel, *Doctor Claudius*.

Much to my dismay, I learned that Sherlock Holmes also had rooms reserved there. I felt the impulse to leave him now and escape his confinement, for I did not want his Anglicism to impede my appreciation of the New World.

The coachman stopped at the hotel in a spot held by the commissionaire. I surged through the great oaken doors and entered the sumptuous lobby. Unswirling my cape with panache, I set my valise down. I insisted that Sherlock Holmes precede me at the desk. The desk clerk finished making an entry in his daybook and then looked up at Holmes.

—Yes, Sir?

—Sherlock Holmes.

The clerk's face brightened.

—Oh, Mr Holmes, I hope you've had a pleasant journey!

He reached for a set of keys which he handed to Holmes.

—Room 615, Sir.

—Thank you,—replied Holmes.

I approached the desk.

—Oscar Wilde,—I said to the desk clerk.

His face brightened, but his eyes targeted someone standing in my light.

—Big John Kelly!—he cried.

I turned to see this new character amble onto the stage of my life. John Kelly, Mayor of New York, entered with a clutch of officials to welcome me.

Mayor Kelly took my astonished hand and shook it vigorously. His rhythm, inflection and idiom of speech, not to mention his handlebar mustache and top hat, betokened the rude power and vigor of New York. I braced myself for the brash welcome Oscar Fingal O'Flahertie Wills Wilde was about to receive.

—Mr Sherlock Holmes,—he said,—allow me to welcome you to the great city of New York. I, John Kelly, Mayor of New York City, hereby present you with the Key to the City.

Trailing journalists jotted down his words in stenographic soundhand alongside artists who sketched the event in ink and charcoal. The Mayor forthwith placed in my hand a large and gaudy wooden key painted a tawdry golden color.

I had never seen such a cock-up in my life! He is a politician and an ignoramus, filled with ill-educated conceit, willful imposture—cockney impudence with all the effrontery of a coxcomb! Though my temples pulsed with insult and injury, I epitomized Apollonian restraint by replying,—I am Oscar Wilde. That is Mr Sherlock Holmes.

He turned to Holmes.

—Oh, pleased to meet you, Mr Hyde!

My mouth came over numb.

—Holmes,—Sherlock Holmes corrected.—Sherlock Holmes.

I bestowed the key to its proper recipient.

54

—Thank you,—he said aridly.

Two rogue males who accompanied Kelly stepped forward with a large wooden crate.

—And here's a case of whiskey from Big Barney O'Shea, leader of the Second District,—said Kelly, oblivious to his *faux pas*.

For a moment it appeared as though the prefix *Big* was attached to every proper name in New York. I imagine that if I stay in Manhattan long enough I shall come to be known as Big Oscar Wilde.

Big Barney O'Shea wasted little time in shaking Sherlock Holmes' hand, too.

—What do you say, Mr Holmes?—said Big Barney.

Big John felt there was a need to further elaborate on Big Barney. He began his inflected encomium.

—Big Barney,—said he—sells good whiskey and he is able to take good care of himself against a half-dozen thugs if he runs up against them on Cherry Hill or in Chatham.

Suddenly, Big John looked at the crate of whiskey, and then to me.

—Boys,—said Kelly to his aides,—give that case to Mr Hyde, Mr Holmes' butler.

I felt quite ill with rage when he indicated me. They tried to place the spirits in my hands but I rebelled against its imminent disposition and set their bearings straight once and for all.

—A cloud of misrepresentation has preceded me! I am not Mr Holmes' butler, nor am I Mr Hyde—I am Oscar Fingal O'Flahertie Wills Wilde: poet, dramatist, and *arbiter elegentiae*!

The Mayor was startled, half-turned, blinking up and down. I presented him with my classic Parnassian sneer.

The journalists gasped upon hearing my declaration, and my name echoed for some time afterward on their lips. I had kissed the smitten mouth of my generation.

—I'm sorry, Mr Wilde, we got book worms in the organization but we don't make 'em district leaders. We keep them for ornaments on parade days. I was genuinely ignorant of the fact that you are an extinguished gentleman.

—Ignorance is like a rare flower in bloom,—I said.—Touch it and it disappears.

From a drop of water, a logician could infer
the possibility of an Atlantic or a Niagara without
having seen or heard of one or the other.
—Sherlock Holmes

Oscar Wilde wrung his pendulous lips into a scowl, revealing an all too visible line of yellow and irregular teeth (caused by mercury, I deduce, taken as a cure for syphilis. The disease will act slowly with deadly certainty. His time is not long on this earth, his teeth . . . his teeth) which he strove feebly to conceal by constantly passing his hand over the lower part of his mouth, as he now did, administering a *coup de grace* by a single epigrammatical thrust. The reporters laughed merrily and shifted their attention from me to Wilde, questioning him avidly.

—Mr Wilde, as the leading spokesman of aestheticism, why did you come to New York?

—I am here to diffuse beauty, and I have no objection to saying that.

He told me that he was here to produce his play. He is dishonest. The dishonesty I have in mind is not the petty kind that allows one to steal something and then deny it, but the more subtle kind that includes saying something because it is expected rather than because it is true.[*]

—That guy talks in hexameters,—said one reporter confidentially to his fellow.

Much to Kelly's dismay, Wilde captured the undivided attention of the journalists.

---

[*] *The dishonesty I have in mind ... because it is true.* Reprinted with the permission of The Free Press, a Division of Simon & Schuster Adult Publishing Group, from *LUDWIG WITTGENSTEIN: The Duty of Genius*, by Ray Monk. Copyright © 1990 by Ray Monk. All rights reserved. Published in the UK by Jonathan Cape. Reprinted with permission of The RandomHouse Group Ltd.

—Is it not true,—challenged one reporter more knowledge-able than the rest,—that the aesthetic movement has fostered only idiosyncratic responses rather than a correct and consistent taste for the beautiful?

—Well, you might say that it has,—replied Wilde thought-fully,—but what is beauty if not a singularity of the moment? What is a movement but the promulgation of the first, rare mo-ment that begot it? Beauty is nearer to most of us than we are aware.

Fundamentally, the question is not whether one should, on all occasions, tell the truth, but rather whether one has an overriding obligation to *be* true—whether despite the pressures to do oth-erwise, one should insist on being oneself.*

—Could a grain elevator in Hoboken have aesthetic value?—piped another.

—Something of the kind,—Wilde's large, white, flat face said.—It's a wide field which has no limit, and all definitions are unsatisfactory. Some people might search and not find any-thing. But the search, if carried on according to right laws, could constitute aestheticism. They would find happiness in striving, even in despair of ever finding what they sought. The renais-sance of beauty is not to be hoped for without strife internal and external. Besides hyperaestheticism. . . .**

---

* *Fundamentally, the question is ... insist on being oneself.* Reprinted with the permission of The Free Press, a Division of Simon & Schuster Adult Publishing Group, from *LUDWIG WITTGENSTEIN: The Duty of Genius*, by Ray Monk. Copyright © 1990 by Ray Monk. All rights reserved. Published in the UK by Jonathan Cape. Reprinted with permission of The RandomHouse Group Ltd.

** *Is it not true ... hyperaestheticism.* From OCSCAR WILDE by Richard Ellmann, copyright © 1987 by The Estate of Richard Ellmann. Used by permission of Alfred A. Knopf, a division of Random House, Inc.

A porter wheeling Mr Wilde's steamer trunk passed through the lobby just then and the dolly stuck, spilling the luggage to the floor.

—I say, porter, handle that box more carefully, will you?— commanded Wilde, lighting a cigarette that he puffed, appearing not to inhale.

The great dandy has every quality to make him agreeable, amusing, and ornamental, but not one that tends, in the most remote degree, to make him useful. He is a nobody who has made himself somebody and gives law to everybody.

I should like to write a new book someday. I shall retire to my idyllic country house in Windlesham. I have nicknamed it *Swindlesham* for the amount of money it cost me to refurbish and extend it but I shall cherish this home for the rest of my life. There I will write *The Book of Life*, an attempt to show how much an observant man might learn by an accurate and systematic examination of all that came his way. It's a remarkable mixture of shrewdness and absurdity. It shall be closely reasoned and intense. I will demonstrate how from a momentary expression, a twitch of a muscle or a glance of an eye, one can fathom a man's inmost thoughts. Deceit will become an impossibility to one trained to observation and analysis. My conclusions shall be as infallible as so many propositions of Euclid. So startling will my results be to the uninitiated that until they learn the processes by which I had arrived at them, they might well consider me a necromancer.

From a drop of water, a logician could infer the possibility of an Atlantic or a Niagara without having seen or heard of one or the other. So all life is a great chain, the nature of which is known whenever we are shown a single link of it. Like all other arts, the Science of Deduction and Analysis is one that can only be acquired by long and patient study, nor is life long enough to allow any mortal to attain the highest possible perfection in it. Before turning to those moral and mental aspects of the matter that present the greatest difficulties, let the inquirer begin by

mastering more elementary problems. Let him on meeting a fellow-mortal learn at a glance to distinguish the history of the man and the trade or profession to which he belongs. Puerile as such an exercise may seem, it sharpens the faculties of observation, and teaches one where to look and what to look for. By a man's fingernails, by his coat sleeve, by his boot, by his trouser knees, by the callosities on his forefinger and thumb, by his expression, by his shirt-cuffs—by each of these things a man's calling is plainly revealed. That all united should fail to enlighten the competent inquirer in any case is almost inconceivable.

For example, since my arrival in New York my observations about America indicate that two fundamental social principles seem to control American society, and one must always refer back to them to find the reason for any of the laws or customs which prevail among them. They are: first, the majority may make mistakes about some little things, but by and large it is always right and there is no higher moral power; secondly, every individual, private person, society, community or nation is the only lawful judge of its own interests, and so long as it does not harm anyone else's concerns, no one has a right to meddle. That is a point that one should always keep in mind. Whereby do I draw such deductions? Especially after spending an hour and a half in New York? Elementary. . . .

But why, as civilization spreads, do outstanding men become fewer? Why, when knowledge is accessible to all, are great talents rarer? Why, when the understanding of government reaches the masses, is there a shortage of great minds to take the lead in society? Why must all things converge in mediocrity? America clearly raises those questions. But who can answer them?

Perhaps Moriarty can.

New Yorkers religiously believe that they have the best police system and the finest police force in existence. Pugnacious ruffians *spillin for a fight* can always be accommodated. The elements of violence and crime are never absent; but every out-

break is tolerably certain to leave the transgressor in the iron hands of justice.

But what of Moriarty's transgressions?

One of the most eminent of newspaper proprietors is said to have been arrested and locked up on two different occasions for furious driving in the streets.

But Moriarty?

Under Section 1, Chapter 747, Laws of 1872, the customs officer arrests sellers or possessors of obscene books, pictures, model casts, articles of indecent or immoral use, and thus prevents the corruption of society and the ruin of numerous lives. Nevertheless, Mr Oscar Wilde's valise contained a suppressed book that was overlooked by the customs officials. It is entitled *An Account of the Remains of the Worship of Priapus*, by R.P. Knight, Esq. London: Printed by T. Spilsbury, Snow Hill, 1786. A rare and curious volume, it is one of those shameful books whose reading is profitable only to minds possessed by an immoderate taste for truth. The frontispiece contains five figures (three male, two female); the woman to the left of the illustration has the man's member in her mouth, while to the right, stands a woman between two men, one of whom sodomizes her, while she presses the member of the other between her breasts. The engraving bears the following description: *This fragment in alto Relievo was detached from one of the ancient temples* ... scholarly though it may be, its discovery would have jeopardized Wilde under the statute hitherto cited. Given that repression, not cure, is the work of the police, can Moriarty be repressed when he, too, may elude detection as easily as Wilde?

Inspector Williams of the NYPD and I conducted a private, informal conversation as Wilde spoke. We agreed that the *detection of crime* is a secondary function of the police force, but is one of such romantic and morbidly fascinating character that it possesses absorbing interest for the majority of citizens. Inspector Williams praised the forty detective sergeants under his employ at the Detective Bureau.

—Crooks are now afraid of their shadows, great robberies have ceased, and minor crime has been reduced over eighty percent,—he said.

And we discussed the cause of crime.

—Laziness is the cause of half the criminality in the land,—he maintained,—temptation by successful thieves and by immoral reading, of the other half. Want hasn't got much to do with it, except as it makes small thieves. These, by contact with hardened men in prisons, which are often schools of crime, develop into professionals.

Inspector Williams drew the Honorable Big John Kelly into our conversation, which veered to the forthcoming presidential election, and I inquired if His Honor had lent his support to one candidate or the other. That stimulated His Honor to speak nineteen to the dozen.

—The Democratic party of the nation ain't dead, though it's been givin a lifelike imitation of a corpse for several years. It can't die while it's got Tammany for its backbone. The trouble is that the party's been chasin after theories and stayin up nights readin books instead of studyin human nature and actin accordin, as I've advised in tellin how to hold your district. In two Presidential campaigns, the leaders talked themselves red in the face about silver bein the best money and gold bein no good, and they tried to prove it out of books. Do you think the people cared for all that guff? No. They heartily indorsed what Richard Croker said, *What's the use of discussin what's the best kind of money?* said Croker. *I'm in favor of all kinds of money—the more the better!* See how a real Tammany statesman can settle in twenty-five words a problem that monopolized two campaigns!

—There's just one issue that would set this country on fire,—he continued.—The Democratic party should say in the first plank of its platform: *We hereby declare, in national convention assembled, that the paramount issue now, always and forever, is the abolition of the iniquitous and villainous civil service laws*

which are destroyin all patriotism, ruinin the country and takin away good jobs from them that earn them. We pledge ourselves, if our ticket is elected, to repeal those laws at once and put every civil service reformer in jail.

—Just imagine the wild enthusiasms of the party,—he declared—if that plank was adopted, and the rush of Republicans to join us in restorin our country to what it was before this college professor's nightmare, called civil service reform, got hold of it!

—I see a vision. I see the civil service monster lyin flat on the ground. I see the Democratic party standin over it with foot on its neck and wearin the crown of victory. I see Thomas Jefferson lookin out from a cloud and sayin: *Give him another sockdolager—finish him!* And I see millions of men wavin their hats and singin *Glory Hallelujah!*

Scotland Yard informed me that Tammany Hall had so permeated the Police Department that the district leaders dictated appointments and assignments, and that practically every member of the force had joined Tammany organizations, and paid without protest the contributions which were levied upon them for the maintenance of the Tammany chieftains. It is known that Captain Max Schmittberger, who had been a Sergeant in the Tenderloin precinct, admitted that he had collected money from gamblers and bawds, and paid it over to Inspector Williams. Testimony was also produced that Williams was interested in a brand of whiskey, and had foisted it upon the saloon keepers, raiding their places if they failed to push it. One woman who owned a chain of houses of prostitution testified that she paid thirty thousand dollars annually for protection, and others said that when they opened their establishments they were called upon for an initiation fee of five hundred dollars, and that thereafter a monthly charge ranging from twenty-five dollars to fifty dollars was placed upon each house according to the number of girls inside. Streetwalkers told the investigators that they paid patrolmen for the privilege of soliciting; and gangsters, sneak

thieves, burglars, pickpockets, footpads and lush workers all testified that they gave the police or politicians a percentage of their stealings. More than six hundred policy shops paid an average of fifteen dollars a month each, while three hundred dollars was collected from pool rooms, and even larger sums from the luxurious gambling houses.

What would Wilde say about such aesthetics?

An unutterable aesthetic truth. *Count Eberhard's Hawthorn*, Uhland's poem. Story of a soldier who cuts a spray from a hawthorn bush while on a crusade; he plants the sprig in his grounds when he returns home, and the fully grown hawthorn tree shades the soldier in his old age, reminding him of the great journey of his youth. Picture of life it is. A wonder of objectivity. Aesthetics. I have come for my hawthorne.

—Do you find England has much in common with America, Mr Wilde?—asked another reporter.

—We have really everything in common with America nowadays, except, of course, language.

—Where then is this movement to end?—asked yet another.

—There is no end to it; it will go on forever, just as it had no beginning. I have used the word *renaissance* to show that it is no new thing with *me*. It has always existed. As time goes on the men and the forms of expression may change, but the principle will remain. Man is hungry for beauty. If there is a void, nature will fill it. The ridicule which aesthetes have been subjected to is only the way of blind unhappy souls who cannot find the way to beauty.

Wilde is a bourgeois thinker. He will use any idea to get the job done and support his thesis. Shows you how far a man can go who has no great mind to speak of.

—One more question, Mr Wilde. Do you agree that public funds should be appropriated for the purpose of importing one dozen gondolas to ornament the lake in Central Park?

—I do. And Mr Frederick Law Olmsted, the inventor of Central Park, would approve, too.

Alderman Barney O'Shane, who was reputed to be very strong on economy, spoke up.

—Gintlemin,—he orated,—the idea is a good wan, but I would make an amindmint. Why should we buy twelve of thim gondolas? I make a motion we buy two of thim—a male wan and a female wan. Thin, gintlemin, let nature take its course. . . .

Wave after pealing wave of laughter rippled through the lobby to the utter consternation of O'Shane.

Wilde bade the journalists goodnight but not before promising to meet them in the morning. As the gathering dispersed in the lobby, Mayor Kelly took my elbow solicitously.

—I'm cosmopolitan, too,—he said.—When I get into the silk stockin part of the district, I can talk grammar and all that with the best of 'em. Mr Sherlock, let's drop all the monkeyshines. Bein Mayor of New York, I've got to be several sorts of man in a single day, a lightning change artist, so to speak. But I am one sort of man always in one respect: I stick to my friends high and low, do them a good turn when I get the chance. If I can do anything for you, just call.

—I surely will,—I replied and took my leave.

I took my black valise while a porter assisted me with the other luggage. Just as we reached the stairwell, I realized that I had not left instructions for breakfast to be brought to my rooms promptly at noon. I instructed the porter to continue while I returned to make arrangements. I noticed that Big John was still at the desk with the clerk. Not wanting to interrupt His Honor, I waited beside a large palm, out of sight of both of them.

My eavesdropping proved worthwhile.

—Keep an eye on QT Hush,—said Big John,—and the lulu in silk stockins: he knows Latin grammar backwards. They're up to no good. I could smell it in the air when I walked in.

Big John Kelly is indeed *a lightnin change artist.*

There is truth in masks.
—Wilde

I surged into my suite of rooms. Much to my potent satisfaction, I found them lovely and without tatt. The parlor was a moneyed cloister of silence and repose, with its high-panelled wainscoting of olive-stained oak, its cream-colored frieze and ceiling of raised plaster work, and its brick-dust felt carpet strewn with silk long-fringed Persian rugs. A bay of windows overlooked Washington Square Park. The parlor having met with my approval, I advanced to the bedroom where, next to a tiny satinwood table across from a statuette in the manner of Clodion, I happily laid my valise. I reclined in the luxurious arm chair, and absorbed the wonderful decor, allowing it to infuse me with its regenerative powers.

I relished my smashing success with American journalists. Furthermore, a schoolboyish giddiness overwhelmed me while I considered creating a proper coat of arms for Big John Kelly, consisting of a cuspidor couchant, with two cigars and a plug of tobacco rampant.

Growing peckish, I thought to ring for room service for some cucumber sandwiches. Credit, after all, is the artist's money.

Venerat jam tertius dies, id est expectatio
liberae cenae. . . .

as Petronius said. I ensconced myself on the chaise longue to ruminate further on the wisdom of the *Satyricon*. Twitching open my valise, I felt what I thought was my precious Battersea Box. A premonition of wonder and dread seized me when I discovered that I had withdrawn Sherlock Holmes' wallet. We had again exchanged bags. The only way I could resist the temptation to *snoop* was to yield to it. I was expecting to discover that he was as rich as Croesus. But how contrarious is life! I discovered not a single pound in his wallet; instead of which I found an

I.O.U. for one thousand pounds that he owed to his brother, Mycroft.

To return it to him is the only thing to do; I loathed, however, subjecting myself to another demonstration of his extraordinary ratiocinative powers. I always choose my friends for their good looks and my enemies for their good intellects. A man cannot be too careful in his choice of enemies.

I could hear him pacing the room swiftly, eagerly, and he answered the door with his chin sunk upon his chest and one hand clasped behind his back. The room was brilliantly lit, and as I looked up, I saw his spare figure silhouetted by gasogenes.

—My dear Holmes, we have exchanged bags once again,—I said, proffering his valise.

He invited me to come in. His manner was not effusive. It seldom seems to be; but he was glad, I think, to see me. I set the bag on his ottoman. We exchanged bags once again.

Holmes then opened his valise, wherefrom he withdrew a revolver which had entirely eluded me. I could have kicked myself for not noticing it! Holmes would not have overlooked such a detail.

—I am delighted to have my possessions so unexpectedly restored to me,—he said.

I opened my valise and examined my beloved edition of Petronius.

—Oh, it would have been a great inconvenience to be without it,—I said.

With hardly a word spoken, but with a keen eye, he waved me to an armchair, threw across his case of cigars, and indicated a spirit case and a gasogene in the corner. Then he stood before the fire and looked me over in his singular, introspective fashion.

He appeared to be on the verge of making an intimate remark when there was a sudden knock at the door. Holmes answered it and found a rather handsome young page at the threshold. He handed Holmes a letter, and awaited a tip. Holmes reached into

his pocket, and just as I had suspected, his expression told me there was no coin to withdraw.

He preoccupied himself with the letter instead.

—Wilde, be so kind as to tip buttons,—he said.

I, of course, didn't have a bean, so I offered the blue-eyed boy a cigarette.

—Sorry, old chap,—I said—I left my purse in my room.

He accepted the cigarette, which I lit for him. I touched his ivory fingers, then he departed.

Holmes handed me the letter.

—Pray read it aloud, dear Wilde. My eyes are sore.

I took the undated letter and read it in my rich voice.

—*Dear Mr Holmes: Tonight, at quarter of eight o'clock, a gentleman who desires to consult you on a matter of the very deepest moment will call.* Holmes, the suspense is terrible. I hope it will last. *Your recent services to one of the royal houses of Europe has shown that you are one who may be safely trusted with matters which are of an importance that can hardly be exaggerated. We have received this account of you from all quarters. Be in your rooms then at that hour, and do not take it amiss if your visitor wears a mask.* Hm. There is truth in masks. It is signed *Uncle Jumbo* but without an address. This is indeed a mystery. What do you think it means?

—I have no data yet. It is a capital mistake to theorize before one has data. Insensibly one begins to twist facts to suit theories, instead of theories to suit facts.

As he spoke there was the sharp sound of horses' hooves and grating wheels against the curb.

—What do you deduce from it?—he asked.

—That I had better go, for the time approaches.

—Not a bit, Wilde. Stay where you are. I am lost without my Boswell. And this promises to be interesting. It would be a pity to miss it.

—Your client may object.

—Never mind the client. I may want your help, and so may he.

—A pair, by the sound,—I said,—a nice little brougham and a pair of beauties. A hundred and fifty guineas apiece. There's money in this case, Holmes, if there is nothing else. That is my deduction.

A slow and heavy step, which had been heard in the passage, paused immediately outside the door.

—Here he comes, Wilde. Sit down in that armchair, and give your best attention,—he said urgently.

Holmes answered the knock at the door.

Enter Uncle Jumbo. He could hardly have been less than six feet four inches in height, with the chest and limbs of Hercules. His dress was rich with a richness that would, in England, be looked upon as akin to bad taste. He wore a double breasted coat covered by a deep blue cloak, lined with flame-colored silk thrown over his shoulders and secured at the neck with a brooch which consisted of a single flaming beryl. His boots extended halfway up his calves. He wore a stovepipe hat, and, across the upper part of his face, extending down past the cheekbones, a black vizard mask, which he had apparently adjusted at that very moment, for his hand was still raised to it as he entered. From the lower part of the face, he appeared to be a man of strong character, with a thick, hanging lip, and a long, straight chin suggestive of resolution pushed to the length of obstinacy.

—I sent word that I would call,—said the barbaric and opulent figure.

—Pray, take a seat,—said Holmes.

—I can see that you have not slept for a night or two,— continued Holmes in his easy, genial way.—That tries a man's nerves more than work, and more even than pleasure. May I ask how I can help you?

He looked from the one to the other of us, as if uncertain which to address.

—This is my friend and colleague, Mr Oscar Wilde,— Holmes said fluently,—who is occasionally good enough to help me with my cases. Whom have I the honor to address?

—Just call me *Uncle Jumbo*. I am employed by a public servant in the public trust. I understand that this gentleman, your friend, is a man of honor and discretion, whom I may trust with a matter of extreme importance. If not, I should prefer to communicate with you alone.

I rose to go but Holmes glared me back into my seat. I was panged by the sudden insight that Holmes trusted me intuitively.

—It is both or none. You may say before this gentleman anything that you may say to me,—Holmes stated.

Uncle Jumbo moved opposite prompt and shrugged his broad shoulders.

—May I begin by binding you both to absolute secrecy for four years? At the end of that time, the matter will have no importance. At present, it is not too much to say that it is of such weight— Uncle Jumbo said as he reclined on the ottoman, which groaned under the charge of his three-hundred-pound frame,—that it may influence the destiny of these United States of America.

—You have my word,—promised Holmes.

—And mine, too,—I added when Uncle Jumbo cast his ponderous gaze upon me.

—You will excuse the mask,—Uncle Jumbo continued.— The august person who employs me, a man held in trust by the public, wishes his agent to be unknown to you.

—I am aware of that,—said Holmes.

Held in trublic prust. Public trust. Half a' diaphora. Fat face of the placard.

—The circumstances are delicate, and every precaution must be taken to quench what might grow into an immense scandal and seriously compromise the presidential election on November 8.

—I am aware of that,—I said, unable to hold my seed.—*A public office is a public trust.*

Holmes, who had been listening to Uncle Jumbo with closed eyes, was startled to wakefulness by my sudden deduction. There was something envious in his reaction, as if I had usurped his role.

70

Our visitor glanced with some apparent surprise at my languid, lounging figure. Uncle Jumbo then sprang from his chair and paced up and down stage prompt in uncontrollable agitation. Huge beads of perspiration broke out on his yellowing forehead, like a poisonous dew, and his fat fingers grew cold and clammy. As he moved uneasily from one foot to the other, his fingers played nervously with a flash watch chain. Then, with a gesture of desperation, he stopped at the gilded mirror, stared at himself an instant.

—You are a candidate for the Presidency of the United States, Governor Cleveland,—said Holmes, smiling.—I would suggest that you cease to write your name upon the lining of your hat, or else that you turn the crown towards the person whom you are addressing. Might I beg you, as time may prove to be of importance, to furnish me with the facts of your case without further delay?

Our visitor stared again at the mirror, tore the mask from his face, and passed his hand over his forehead as if he found it bitterly hard. From every gesture and expression I could see that he was a reserved, self-contained man, proud in his nature, more likely to hide his wounds than to expose them. Then suddenly, with a fierce gesture of his closed hand, like one who throws reserve to the winds, he began:

—But you can understand,—said our strange visitor, sitting down once more and passing his hand over his high malarious forehead,—you can understand that I am not accustomed to doing such business personally. Yet, it is such a delicate matter that I could not confide in an agent without placing myself in jeopardy. I have come from Albany on the pretext of addressing a rally only to meet you.

—Then, pray consult,—said Holmes, shutting his eyes once more.

—The facts are briefly these: Some ten years ago, during my tenure as sheriff of the great city of Buffalo, New York, I had intimate relations with a pulchritudinous maiden, an actress,

71

who took up temporary residence in our fair town. Amber Halpin is her name. We spent many a happy hour together clasped in Cupid's tender embrace.

Strange. I know the name.

—The Honorable Governor, as I understand, became entangled with this young person, wrote some compromising letters, and now desires to get these letters back?

—Precisely so, but how?

—Was there a secret marriage?

—Alas, none.

—No legal documents recording the involvement?

Governor Cleveland thought for a moment, raising the pitch of my anticipation.

—Well, yes, one.

—Then I fail to follow the Honorable Governor. If this person should produce the document for blackmailing purposes, how is she able to prove its authenticity?

—There is the writing.

—Pooh, pooh! A forgery.

—My own seal.

—Imitated.

—There are witnesses.

—Hm. . . .

I watched the Governor's lower lip quiver with emotion.

—It is the birth certificate of her nine-year-old daughter, whom I fathered!—he cried.

—Oh, dear! That is very bad! Yes, you have indeed committed an indiscretion,—replied Holmes.

—I was mad—insane!

—You have compromised yourself seriously.

—I was young and reckless.

—Has she communicated her terms?

—Yes, she has. . . .—sighed the Governor.—Unless I break my engagement to Miss Frances Folsom, the very soul of delicacy, a virtuous woman twenty years my junior, and marry her

instead, she will blab the tawdry tale and proclaim it to the press!

—When will that occur?

—One week from today. You must gain possession of the birth certificate, for that is the only proof she has.

—Oh, then we have seven days yet,—said Holmes, yawning.—That is very unfortunate, as I have one or two other matters of importance to look into at present. The Honorable Governor will stay in New York at present?

—Certainly, I'm staying at the *Hotel Savoy* on 59th Street.

—Then I shall drop you a line to advise you of the progress we make.

—Pray do so. I shall be all anxiety.

—Then, as to the money?

—You shall have carte blanche.

—Absolutely?

—I declare that I would empty the coffers of Tammany Hall to stop that woman,—said the Honorable Governor, pacing before the mirror.

—Tammany Hall?

—Yes,—he continued,—the very body of corruption. Big John Kelly has inherited the inequitable structure of Tammany, and he knows that if I am elected, I will break his corrosive grip on the city. Though nominally a Democrat, he is supporting my opponent, James G. Blaine.

—A formidable political enemy, no doubt.

—Formidable.

—And for present expenses?

His Honor removed a heavy chamois leather bag from under his cloak and laid it on the table.

—There are one thousand gold eagles contained therein. These are not public funds but my personal reserves.

I was impressed. Holmes scribbled a receipt upon a sheet of his note-book and handed it to him.

—And Mademoiselle's address?

His Honor threw his hands up, producing a piece of paper as if he were a conjuror.—Here, here,—he said.

Holmes took it.

—May I address a question to the Governor?—I asked.

—Go right ahead.

—Have you considered marrying her? And if you have, why won't you? for that would end the dilemma.

—I have given the matter careful consideration,—said he.

—Yes? And what did you conclude?

Disgruntlement throbbed from his head, then hung dully in the air.

—Though I loved her once, I am unable to marry her because the woman is a termagant, a shrew and an insufferable . . . an insufferable. . . .

—*Elle est difficile*,—I said, rescuing his probity.

—Then, good night, Governor,—said Holmes,—and I trust that we shall have some good news for you.

Governor Cleveland shook hands with both of us, then put his black vizard mask on before taking his leave.

Holmes undid the chamois leather bag and shook music from the coins, letting them fall to the table. The gold pieces flashed in the firelight, now red, now gold. He divided the heaping mound in half.

—Wilde, here is your share. We shall divide the proceeds equally.

O Fortuna felix! Land of opportunity—for mischief!

—Holmes, there is something I must tell you that has bearing on this case.

—And what may that be?—he inquired.

—I have a rendezvous with Miss Halpin tomorrow,—I revealed.

—How do you know her?

—I don't. She wrote me in London and informed me that she is interested in playing the role of *Vera*. She is apparently famous in New York.

—What a coincidence?!—said Holmes, laughing delightfully. Curiously, though, he took his revolver and began loading it.

—Perhaps I may obtain some information. Not useful information, of course; useless information.—He seemed not to have heard a word that I said. Is he growing deaf? or is it simply that he doesn't listen?

—Wilde, do you have any political scruples regarding the question of working for the Democrats as opposed to the Republicans?

—Personally, I believe politics to be inherently corrupt. If I must choose between two evils, I will choose neither. Politics is what a man does in order to conceal what he is and what he does not know.[*]

—Good. Then you have no objection.

—What are you doing, Holmes?—I asked after he finished loading his weapon.

—I'm relaxing my nerves.

Holmes aimed the gun in the general direction of the mirror. He shot the patriotic slogan, *VR*, slap through the wall with a series of bullets.

—*Victoria Rules*,—he said triumphantly.

I held my hand open before him, anticipating the receipt of the firearm which he then gave to me. I reloaded, and shot at the wall, interpolating an *E* and an *A* into the *VR*, spelling *VERA*.

—*Vera, or the Nihilists*,—I said, as if it were a Tsar's ukase.

—Wilde, I think this is to be the beginning of a legendary friendship.

---

[*] *If I must choose ... what he does not know.* Reprinted with the permission of The Free Press, a Division of Simon & Schuster Adult Publishing Group, from *LUDWIG WITTGENSTEIN: The Duty of Genius*, by Ray Monk. Copyright © 1990 by Ray Monk. All rights reserved. Published in the UK by Jonathan Cape. Reprinted with permission of The RandomHouse Group Ltd.

—You mustn't call me Wilde. If I am your friend, my name to you is Oscar.

—Of course, my dear Wilde, if you will be good enough to call tomorrow at three o'clock, I should like to chat this little matter over with you. This case is, I believe, a three pipe problem.

I sometimes think that God, in creating man, somewhat overestimated His ability.

II

If you will, it is a form of imperialism of the spirit,
ambitious, arrogant, aggressive, waving the flag of
human power over an ever wider and wider territory.

—Sherlock Holmes

A political party constitutes a sort of second nonlegal government which has seized control of the legal government. Evils of long standing are taken for granted by the American, while only the stranger is amazed when observing the machinations that take place in free elections.

And who are these voters? They are a mixture of militant Puritans, bog-trotters, indentured servants or *white slaves* come as chattel from many countries and their African brethren as well. They charged their bearded muzzles with libertarian uplift and fierce Hebrew mysticism: Rousseau's *natural man*, replete with virtue, and dark visions of original sin were forced into a mad union in their consciousness.* John Todd was such an immigrant. I wonder if he ever declared a party affiliation.

John Todd was a distiller who fled to America in 1853 with ten thousand pounds of his creditors' money. A Bow Street Runner named Henry Goddard tracked him from New York to Buffalo to Detroit, Chicago and on to Milwaukee until he found Todd's name by chance in the register of a hotel in nearby Jamesville. It was a task which he likened to searching for a small needle placed point upwards in the middle of a forest. Regrettably, America had no bankruptcy laws at that time so Todd escaped arrest.

As a descendant of Goddard's who in some manner is retracing his steps, I fail to see how England and America can ever enjoy a mutual understanding, for their compatabilities are few.

---

* *They are a mixture ... in their consciousness.* From AMERICA AND COSMIC MAN by Wyndham Lewis, copyright © 1949 by Wyndham Lewis. Used by permission of Doubleday, a division of Random House, Inc.

79

Both have a strong sense of bossiness. I express this opinion lest people suppose I am engaged upon some goodwill mission, which is not the case.

Call me a truth-seeker and I will be satisfied.[*]

Politics is a melodrama for adolescents, originating in the silly old potboiler as played by any Yankee, whoever he may be, who maintains that *we broke away from the English, and beat them and sent them back to their Island, and they have never forgotten this*. Astor Place. Where is that in relation to where I am now? Riots. The Englishman, however, sees America as a baby who continues to express itself in some kind of English, but has taken on a swarthy complexion that denotes quizzical and uncertain fatherhood; furthermore, it has become obvious that it is not in the main our child. You have to make a start *somehow* and with *somebody* in suddenly founding a state. And if you have come from somewhere where you haven't been able to call your soul your own, it must be enormously welcome.[**]

Where am I? Wrong turn I made somewhere. I studied a map of the streets of New York, so I thought I knew. All of the New York streets look to me ill paved, dirty and repulsive. The ambient squalor extends to the wharf. Laborers and dockmen are already astir, and slatternly women are taking down shutters and brushing doorsteps. Business is just beginning, and rough-looking men are emerging from the public-house, rubbing their sleeves across their beards after their morning wet. The shipyard workers are dirty-

---

[*] *Call me a truth-seeker and I will be satisfied.* Reprinted with the permission of The Free Press, a Division of Simon & Schuster Adult Publishing Group, from *LUDWIG WITTGENSTEIN: The Duty of Genius*, by Ray Monk. Copyright © 1990 by Ray Monk. All rights reserved. Published in the UK by Jonathan Cape. Reprinted with permission of The RandomHouse Group Ltd.

[**] *Politics is a melodrama ... enormously welcome.* From AMERICA AND COSMIC MAN by Wyndham Lewis, copyright © 1949 by Wyndham Lewis. Used by permission of Doubleday, a division of Random House, Inc.

looking rascals, but I suppose every one has some little immortal spark concealed about him. You would not think it to look at them—or the burly blue bulk of a policeman at the corner or the drunkard who zigs down the sidewalk and zags past me. It is an abode of poverty as hopeless as any in the world, transmitting itself from generation to generation as some incurable leprotic disease.

New York shrieks and yells with ugliness but it never loses its spirit.

My eyes have been trained to examine faces and not their trimmings. Thus, it is the first quality of a criminal investigator that he should see through false noses and beards; thus it is fitting that I pass through the crowds of Manhattan undetected in my own disguise, having left the hotel this morning in the character of a groom out of work. I am exalted by disguise. My soul demands wilder ranges, newer emotional and spiritual territories, fresh woods and pastures for the soul trapped in the crammed rookeries of New York where it is each man for himself and devil take the hindmost. If you will, it is a form of imperialism of the spirit, ambitious, arrogant, aggressive, waving the flag of human power over an ever wider and wider territory. A strange enigma is man!

Progress results from the survival of the fittest. Man is descended from apes, even primordial slime. The awesomeness of this great truth weighs like a nightmare upon many of the best minds of my generation. Despite scores of new inventions, we watch what we conceive to be the progress of materialism in such fear and powerless anger as the savage feels, when during an eclipse, a great shadow creeps over the face of the sun.

At last, I found Twenty-Third Street and the wonderful sympathy and freemasonry that exists among horsey men. Be one of them, and you will know all that there is to know of New York's most exclusive residential district. I soon found 362 West Twenty-Third Street. A small and exquisite mansion with a long driveway, carriage lights and a mammoth front door. Miss Halpin had ordered a garden installed in the front yard, about fifteen

feet deep, and then put up a grilled iron fence so that her flower garden and shrubs would not be trampled by passers-by. Chubb lock to the door. Large sitting room on the right side, well furnished, with long windows almost to the floor and those preposterous English window fasteners which a child could open. Behind, there was nothing remarkable, save that the passage window could be reached from the top of the coach house. I walked round it and examined it closely from every point of view, but without noting anything else of interest.

I then lounged down the street and finally lent the ostlers a hand in rubbing down their horses, and received in exchange five cents, a glass of half-and-half, two fills of shag tobacco, and as much information as I could desire about Amber Halpin, to say nothing of half-a-dozen other people in the neighborhood in whom I was not in the least interested, but whose biographies I was compelled to listen to.

Feminine social leadership is in perpetual dispute. Mrs James I. Jones of Washington Place attempted to achieve preeminence among the Four Hundred. Her dinners were exquisite; her wines perfect; her husband's Madeiras famous. Mrs Jones prided herself on the fact that her small dances were the acme of exclusivity. Yet could these soirees dim the luster of more enchanting divertissements introduced by Mrs William Colford Schermerhorn?

—Amber Halpin, has she. . .?

—Oh, she has turned all the men's heads down in that part. She is the daintiest thing under a bonnet on this planet,—so say the grooms to a man. She lives quietly, drives out at seven sharp every evening for dinner. Seldom does she go out at other times, except to rehearse her play. A dowdy Englishwoman named Henrietta Labouchère is her manager. Has only one male visitor, but a good deal of him. He is dark, handsome, and dashing, never calls less than once a day, and often twice, but appears to have fallen out of favor of late. He is Mr Frederick Gebhard, Jr, the son of a Baltimore dry goods king who enjoys an annual income of

$80,000 to $100,000. See the advantages of a cabman as a confidant? They had driven him home a dozen times from the Washington Mews, and knew all about him. When I had listened to all they had to tell, I began to walk up and down the purlieu of 362 West Twenty-Third Street once more, and to think over my plan of campaign.

Frederick Gebhard, Jr was evidently an important factor in the matter. He has considerable social standing in New York and Baltimore but has never played an active social role in either. Hostesses vie with each other to introduce him to their daughters. What was the relation between Mr Gebhard and Miss Halpin? and what the object of his repeated visits? Was she his client, his friend, or his mistress? If the former, she had probably transferred the document in question to his keeping. If the latter, it was less likely. The gentleman is twenty-two years old, so this is probably a romantic involvement. On the issue of this question depends whether I should continue my work at Twenty-Third Street, or turn my attention to the gentleman's chambers in the Washington Mews. It is a delicate point, and it widens the field of my inquiry.

There is activity in the street: horsedrawn carriages pass, a group of shabbily dressed men are smoking and laughing in a corner, two firemen flirt with a girl, a scissors grinder at his wheel, several well dressed young men lounge up and down smoking cigars, my false whiskers tickle my ear: Here she comes. *Am Anfang war die Tat.* She leaves her townhouse wearing a veiled hat which screens the cruel aspect of contemporary woman, occulting her steely face, her malevolence toward man.

—I swow, quite a honey!—remarked one groom.

—Yes, sir!

It was eleven o'clock.

Amber entered her carriage. Yards of trimmings, laces and silk went into the creation of her dress, successfully concealing her face as well as her gait. She tarried at the coach for a mo-

ment with her glove, when I heard that now familiar burley voice. I turned to see a hansom park beside me.

—Insidious plots. Anyone can invent them. Life is full of them,—said Wilde to his companion, a remarkably handsome man, dark, aquiline and moustached.

—That's Amber,—said he.

—Freddie,—replied Wilde,—I will tactfully broach the subject during my meeting with her. Perhaps she will listen to my proposition.

Frederick—evidently Mr Frederick Gebhard—turned in my direction.

—Boy!—he cried.

He means me!

—Water down them horses, will you?

A shining coin leapt from his hand into mine.

—You'll see, I'm a plain talkin guy,—he said to Wilde before he strode up to her carriage.

—Amber,—began Freddie without any introduction whatsoever,—if you don't have anything against me, what is it that keeps you from caring for me as you once did?

—I shall never care for you again, Mr Gebhard. You might as well understand it once and for all. Don't think it's anything in yourself or that I think you are unworthy of me. A life of work, of art, and of art alone—that's what I've made up my mind to do.

—A woman that's made up her mind to that ain't got no heart to hinder her!

—Would a man have heart who had done so?

—But I don't believe you, Amber. You're laughing at me. You don't have to give up art. We could work together. I believe I could help you—serve you. I would be your willing slave, Heaven knows!

—I don't want any slaves now. I want to be free. Now do you see? I *don't* care for you, and I never could.

—Aw, why bother?—he said gloomily as he motioned to leave.

—I suppose you blame me,—she said.

—Oh, no! I blame no one—or only myself. I threw my chance away.

—As you like it, Mr Gebhard. We've had to be very frank, but I don't see why we shouldn't be friends. Still, we needn't, if you don't like.

—Can I come visit you—like—like before?

—Why, if you can consistently,—she replied with a smile, and she held out her hand to him.

They fell out of earshot when I went to fetch water and Amber's carriage pulled away.

Freddie's face had that happy semblance all stupid people have. He said something to Wilde. They laughed. *Insidious plots.*

There may be something to it. Is Wilde a consummate Italianate villain, *falso e cortese*? He is, after all, a practiced liar. We shall soon see.

The world is a totality of facts, not things.*

---

* *The world is a totality of facts, not things.* Reprinted with the permission of The Free Press, a Division of Simon & Schuster Adult Publishing Group, from *LUDWIG WITTGENSTEIN: The Duty of Genius*, by Ray Monk. Copyright © 1990 by Ray Monk. All rights reserved. Published in the UK by Jonathan Cape. Reprinted with permission of The RandomHouse Group Ltd.

*The secret of life is never to have an
emotion that is unbecoming.*
—Oscar Wilde

With what encumbrances one travels! It is not in the right
harmony of things that I should have a hatbox, a dressing-case, a
trunk and a portmanteau always following me. I daily expect a
thunderbolt, but the gods are asleep, though perhaps I had better
not talk about them or they will hear me and wake. But what
would Thoreau have said to my hatbox! Or Emerson to the size
of my trunk, which is Cyclopean! But I can't travel without
Balzac and Gautier, and they take up so much room: and as long
as I can enjoy talking nonsense to the flowers and children I am
not afraid of the depraved luxury of a hatbox.

Not to be an artist is to be merely a creature of habit. There
are discoveries to be made and the satisfaction of new needs and
pleasures, the greatest of which is initiating a new civilization.
But political scandal and intrigue are turning me into a veritable
Vera! Life is imitating . . . I quite sympathize with the rage of
American democracy against what they call the vices of the upper orders, but I would much rather listen to scandal in the cellar
than revolt in the streets. The masses feel that drunkenness, stupidity and immorality should be their own special property, and
that if anyone of us makes an ass of himself he is poaching on
their preserve. How indignant they would be if Uncle Jumbo's
skeleton came jangling out of the closet! And yet I don't suppose
that ten percent of the proletariat live correctly. Every man of
ambition has to fight his century with its own weapons. What
this century worships is wealth. The God of this century is
wealth. To succeed one must have wealth. At all costs one must
have wealth. At the cost of assisting Holmes? But for scandal
and Sherlock Holmes I would be penniless now.

The multitudinous obstacles I encounter inaugurating a new
civilization!

Case in point: by the rude hour of nine o'clock I am awakened by a little wretched clerk or office boy that Freddie sent me. I received seven telegrams that I must answer. The boy is a fool and an idiot. I must have some responsible, experienced man always with me, like Holmes. This is for his advantage as well as for mine. I will not go about with a young office boy, who has not even the civility to come and see what I want. He was here for five minutes, went away promising to return at eleven and I have not seen him since. I had nine reporters, seven or eight telegrams, eighteen letters to answer (*How changed you will be*, wrote my mother) and this young scoundrel amusing himself about the town. Another such fiasco and I think I shall take the *Arizona* back to London. I must never be left alone again, and I must not be exposed to brutal attacks in the papers. I was mortified to discover that *The New York Tribune* printed a drawing of the Wild Man of Borneo, holding a coconut, juxtaposed with a drawing of myself, holding a sunflower, captioned *How far is it from this to this?* Only now do I remember Ruskin's warning about journalists, *Everything will be said about you. They will spare nothing.* Indeed they will not. The article states: *Othcar Wilde, the effeminate penny Ruskin, arrived in New York last night aboard the Arizona, kneebreeches, tail coat, lily, sunflower and all—what a mass of unmanly absurdity!* Sidney Colvin spoke of *Oscar-Wilde-ism as the most pestilent and hateful disease of our time, a mountebank and pretentious fraud, a fatuous fool, a tenth-rate cad, an unclean beast* . . . if I can survive Yellow Journalism, I will surely survive yellow fever.[*]

---

[*] *if I can survive ... yellow fever.* From OCSCAR WILDE by Richard Ellmann, copyright © 1987 by The Estate of Richard Ellmann. Used by permission of Alfred A. Knopf, a division of Random House, Inc.

I read my telegrams: Norman, Mrs Geo Lewis, JM Stoddart, Lady Wilde, Burne-Jones, Amber Halpin!? *Come at once, Frederick Gebhard*, the last one reads. Tossed the telegrams into my hatbox and luxuriated in the resentment of being at Freddie's beck and call. How horribly unjust to be attending a fool! I haven't got a single enemy who is a fool. They are all men of some intellectual power, and consequently they all appreciate me. Is that very vain of me? I think it is rather vain.

Performed my morning ablutions with unaccustomed alacrity, and went out into the flickering windblown sunlight, and strolled down Fifth Avenue. Distracted myself by window shopping. All of America comes to New York to shop whenever it can. Here you can find the perfection of everything, from the brightest of cambric needles and the most delicious of crumpets, up to the bridal *trousseau* for a daughter of the Winthrops or the Washingtons, or a line of ocean-steamships with their entire outfit. The resplendent lines of retail stores sweep around Union Square and up along the branching streets to Madison Square. These are always fascinating, alluring, irresistible. Most of the commodities visible are those which women buy, and they are wrapped in the most extravagant decorative wrappings. Ill fares the provincial purse whose owner ventures before these attractive windows, extending for miles on miles; a perfect kaleidoscope of silks and velvets, laces and jewels, rich books and music, paintings and statuary, rifles and racquets, confections and amber-like bottles, *cloisonnée* and cut glass, everything imaginable displayed in the most attractive way possible.

Freddie's townhouse is solid and neoclassical in design— proof that he must be colossally wealthy. This rendered me somewhat more indisposed to meeting him. He could have sent a cab for me, after all.

I rang the bellpull and a dour butler appeared who took my *carte d'affaires*. He led me to the library which was located on the second floor, adjacent to a billiard room. Alcoves of books flanked the bay windows. It was separated from the main room

by a transom from which curtains hung. An open timber ceiling, parquet floor, paneled walls to the height of the doorways, and a mantel and fireplace made of Sienna marble completed the design.

A person with no need to think about the cost of anything may go into *Cottier's*, the decorating house on nearby Fifth Avenue, and buy and order right and left, and give the house commission to decorate and furnish, and upholster, and fill big cabinets with *old blue*, and never spare for cost, and when it is all done, nobody who comes to visit shall say, *How beautiful is this! How interesting! What taste you have!* but only, *Oh, then, I see Cottier has been with you.* There has simply been a transfer of goods from one showroom to another.

The butler waited to announce me because a heated debate, touching on several matters of personal significance, was taking place.

—You impertinent young jackanapes!—roared an older gentleman with anger that only could have been fueled by insane rectitude,—I'll give you the thrashing you deserve! Your only excuse is that you must be crazy! I heard told from a man at Harvard that folks thought you was crazy there. I'm convinced that only the institution of marriage can save you from perdition. And ef you ain't married by tomorrow tonight, I'll carry out my threat to stop all money supplies!

A gentleman whose appearance was distinguished by a silvery mustache emerged from behind a velvet curtain as he concluded his ultimatum. His costly morning coat trembled with emotion as he clapped a top hat upon his angry head.

—Mr Oscar Wilde,—announced the butler, restoring order to the domestic quarrel, which seems to have erupted unexpectedly, otherwise I would have remained downstairs. It was embarrassing.

—Mr Frederick Gebhard, I presume?—I ventured.

—That's him,—he said pointing to a far corner of the room where a young man appeared, reclining on a divan of Persian saddle-bags. He smoked nonchalantly from a cigarette holder.

—I'm his disgusted father! I think it's a shame, some of the pictures a body sees in the winders here, and sonny boy says they're *art*! Ha! They say there's a law ag'inst them things; and if there is, I don't understand why the police and the persecuting attorney don't pick them up that paints 'em. I hear tell that there's women that goes to have pictures took from them that way by men painters.

The point seemed aimed at me, as if I were personally responsible for the outbreak of art in New York. Would that I were! He will attack me as the presumptive boon companion to his son's idleness.

—Whores and degenerates! I say they ought to be all tarred and feathered and rode on a rail. They'd be drummed out of town in two shakes of a lamb's tail in Colarader,—he went on with an old man's severity.—And that pack of worthless hussies that come out on the stage and begin to kick—

I was abashed by his indecorum.

His rustling overcoat settled on his shoulders as he filled out the frame of the doorway, with his feet set square and his arms akimbo. Our eyes met again.

—Art!—he cried with contempt. Then the old man fetched his breath in gasps, leaned against the doorway, presently smoothing and lengthening his breathing into a normal pace. The old man waved Frederick Jr and his butler away as he regained his balance.

—Ketches me round the heart like a pain.

I cannot understand how art induces poignant sorrow. It is unnatural and a blasphemy against nature.

The old man was going the way of *angina pectoris*. He left, slamming the door shut behind him as if incarcerating us all in the prison of his disaffection.

Frederick Jr at long last greeted me. He acts like a *Freddie*.

—Delighted to meet you, Oscar,—he said shaking my hand.

—The pleasure is mutual.

—Uh, don't pay pops no nevermind,—he said sheepishly.—
He's in one of his moods.

I let the remark pass.

—Take a load off your dogs and have a seat,—he said in the
wavering diction of a half-bred *arriviste*.—How was the
passage?

—It was an unremarkable voyage but my arrival was quite
extraordinary. No representative of yours (as you had indicated
in numerous letters and cables) met me, and I was besieged by
reporters who published grossly inaccurate caricatures of me in
the newspapers. This one is entitled *Bunthorne and Bunkum*.—I
removed a cutting of the article and quoted directly from it:
*Probably no one laughs (in his sleeve) at and despises these
mock-hysterical aesthetes more than does the Great Prophet
himself—who, by the way, is not much of a prophet in his own
country, Ireland, and not much of a poet in this.* Signed, Titus
Manlius! And this preposterous article: *Othcar Wilde is here . . .
he wears knee breeches, but alas no lily. He is quite clever and
has just received an offer from P T Barnum, who has just purchased Jumbo the African elephant from the London Zoo, to
lead Jumbo about, carrying a lily in one hand and a sunflower
in the other.*

—I'm sorry. Sometimes I'm just a saphead,—answered
Freddie guiltily.

—Furthermore, the recent assassinations of Czar Alexander II
and that of President Garfield have thwarted the production of
Vera, I fear, on both sides of the Atlantic. I agreed to place it
entirely in your hands for production on the terms of my
receiving half-profits, and a guarantee of one hundred pound
sterling paid down to me on signing, and one hundred on occasion of its production, the said two hundred to be deducted from
my share of subsequent profits, if any. This you acknowledged

as fair. Of course for my absolute work, the play, I must have absolute certainty of some small kind.

—I can explain what happened.

—So why on earth did you want to produce *Vera* in the first place?—I demanded with growing impatience.

—I got a notion, I suppose. I wanted to impress a young lady.

—How adorable!

—But I got stuck,—he said, lowering his voice an octave.

—And what is the obstacle?

—My ole man got sore at me and cut off my dough. In fact, I might be as poor as piss in a pumpkin by tomorrow!

—You have misled me! You spoke of great fortunes, *millions bursting to the joists from a fortune in dry goods!* You assured me that you are heir to Colorado silver mines and that you have limitless wealth at your disposal.

—It's sort of true. I just stretched some things, that's all. You heard my ole man. My goose is cooked!

Instead of irritating me further, the callow harp-stop in his voice struck a chord of sympathy now.

—How so?

—You heard him lay down the law: if I'm not married by tomorrow night, he'll give me the boot and cut me out of the will.

—Why don't you get married?

—Nah. Wimmin are a good deal like *licker*, ef you love 'em too hard, they're sure to throw you some way. Pops got wind of my tomcattin and now he reckons that only a wife can reform me.

—Yes, one must do something.

—I tried. That actress, Amber Halpin. I asked her but she said no.

—Amber! *Le monde est vraiment petit!*

I don't know why I am wasting my time with this fool. He had better live up to his word and produce the play.

92

—Petite blonde. A real sweetie. She seemed to go for the idea when I popped her the question but later when her friends peached on me, sightin me in public escortin other women (chorus girls ((Margaret was the best (((musical comedy ((((painted a butterfly on her bare shoulders when she wore an evening gown. A flash honey!)))) and what do you know,—continued Freddie with an air of fatality,—one night I slum into *Pfaff's* with Margie clinging to my neck, and who is sitting in a booth with Mary Corwallis-West? Amber. Her friends freeze up, and Margie looks uncomfortable. Amber waves to me and she smiles at Marge, and Marge sort of waves back. She shows a complete lack of concern. A mutual friend tells me that she then said that she approved in both principle and practice the idea of her fiancé spending time with other women. *Men are born to roam* and marriage has little or no strain if a husband goes tomcatting around with the knowledge and consent of his wife. I'm supposed to be more attentive to her when I finally return to her arms. Then, she busted up with me for no reason at all. What do you make of it, Oscar? Funny, ain't it.

—Women want to be loved, not to be understood.

—Oh.

He has no sense of reality. What will become of my play?

—However, she may listen to reason,—I said with renewed optimism.

Freddie is a man with a future; Amber is a woman with a past. What an irresistible combination!

—She can't stand me,—said Freddie.—What can I do about it?

—The secret of life is never to have an emotion that is unbecoming.

Grant me the grace to solve this crime so that
I may prove to myself that I am not the last
and the least among men, that I am not
inferior to those whom I despise!
                                    —Sherlock Holmes

At last! I am alone! The few remaining hansoms wheel down
Broadway. While all the rest of the city slumbers, Broadway is
awake. My window frames a living portrait of pedestrians am-
bling about in diverse missions of crime, industry, pleasure or
charity.

During the next few hours, we shall possess kingly silence, if
not repose. At last! The tyranny of the human face has been
overthrown, and there is no one to torture me except for myself.

I am at long last permitted to refresh myself by bathing in
shadow! Without further adieu, I double lock the door. A single
scrape of the key will secure my isolation and buttress the forti-
fications which now separate me from the world.

Horrible life! Horrible city! How may I distinguish myself
from the rabble of private inquiry agents? Great snoopers on
cheating mistresses, trudging hunters of missing daughters, pur-
suers of bank robbers, retrievers of stolen letters and *objets
d'art*! Let us examine the day upon the dissecting table. Permit
me to make the first incision. The first catastrophe was to have
my lot thrown in with Wilde. . . .

Now I want it understood that I am a follower—a very humble follower—of the aesthetic ecstasy, but I never looked much
like an art object. I did not have my dogskin knee breeches with
me in Afghanistan, nor my velvet coat, and my black silk stockings were full of holes. Neither was the wild, barren waste of
Afghanistan calculated to produce sunflowers and lilies. Wilde's
sex is as undecided as his loyalties. Why should he tell the truth
if it is to his advantage to lie? I am still astounded at Wilde's
indignation at a barber who had come to cut his hair and had

failed to bring curling tongs. It irks me to go about as his court-
ier. I don't want to be known as his dry-nurse.

Met another dozen people in disguise and shook hands without having taken the precaution of buying gloves. Respectable
people, rude mechanicals, grooms. Twenty-third Street. Horse
dung everywhere. Mrs————— performed an act of buccal
copulation in my closed hansom after which I was obliged to
clean the soiled seats. Rewarded with shag and half-and-half.
Such is the detective's handiwork.

Amber enjoys the *Louvre*, whose spacious rooms include a
grand drinking hall with a great, ornate, mirrored bar and
smaller, more quiet lounges in which only champagne is served
amid crystal chandeliers, pillars of marble, walls paneled gold
and emerald. The place is especially celebrated as the habitual
resort of New York's most expensive, fashionable and beautiful
demimondaines who cultivate the art of real happiness.

Then went to the offices of James Mitchell under the guise of
an interior decorator writing for *The Lady's World* in London.
He gladly showed me the architectural renderings of the interior
of 362 West Twenty-Third Street, wherein I studied the disposition of rooms. Discovered that CC Moore, the celebrated author
of *'Twas the Night before Christmas*, built the house. Amber had
walls knocked down and rooms enlarged. She installed marble
fireplaces with ornately carved mantels, and the bathroom was
excavated in order to accommodate a marble bathtub.

—There is a rumor,—said Mitchell,—that the faucets in her
bathrooms are made of solid gold, but that is false, and contrary
to detailed press reports, she does not keep a menagerie of rare
and exotic animals on the top floor.

—What were your impressions of the interior?

—The interior,—he said,—was to be finished entirely in
highly polished walnut, and it had to be imported from a certain
English forest. We were kept on our sharps for a year in getting
the wood just the right grain, and then the interior graining and
polishing was a tremendous job. This was a big commission for

me. I worked on it day and night, and when we finished that beautiful walnut job, I was the proudest man in New York. But my troubles were only beginning. Miss Halpin looked over the work, but she seemed hardly to notice it. *The very latest thing in interior decoration,* she decreed, *is hard, finished white enamel. You will have to send to England for the right kind. I am sure you won't be able to get it here.* I tried to beg off, but she was accustomed to just waving her hand to get things done. I could have got it here, but it had to come from England. It broke my heart when my men set to work, covering the walnut with this white, hard finish.

Met Mr Cleveland briefly. He is suffering the repercussions of his decade-old illicit liaison. *I love her still,*—he confided. People cannot help looking foolish whenever they speak of love. Love—it manifests itself everywhere but is nowhere to be found.

How I am reduced to making a living!

I was once quiet in my ways, and my habits were regular. My day passed between my studies, logic, whistling, going for walks, and being depressed.* I was never a very sociable fellow, always rather fond of moping in my rooms and working out my own little methods, so that I never mixed much with men of my year at the University. Bar fencing and boxing, I had few athletic tastes, and then my line of study was quite distinct from that of the other fellows, so that we had no points of contact at all, though I had already developed those habits of observation and inference which I had already formed into a system, although I had not yet appreciated the part they were to play in my life.

---

* *I was once quiet ... being depressed.* Reprinted with the permission of The Free Press, a Division of Simon & Schuster Adult Publishing Group, from *LUDWIG WITTGENSTEIN: The Duty of Genius,* by Ray Monk. Copyright © 1990 by Ray Monk. All rights reserved. Published in the UK by Jonathan Cape. Reprinted with permission of The RandomHouse Group Ltd.

Sometimes I spent my day at the chemical laboratory; other times in dissecting rooms, where I studied corpses, their organs and structures (to determine the cause of death, to observe the effects of disease, and to establish sequences of changes and thus establish the evolution and mechanisms of disease); and occasionally in long walks, which took me to the lowest portions of London for respite from the examination of mortal remains.

The first cadaver to submit to my scalpel was that of a woman of the streets I had seen many times during my long walks. She was hard looking, aged beyond her years. A gross examination of the exterior for abnormalities and traumas revealed open sores from syphilis in its primary stage. I sought the lesion without which death would not have occurred. I made a Y-shaped incision in the torso. Both upper limbs of the Y commenced at the armpit and carried on beneath the breast to the bottom of the sternum in the midline. From this point of juncture at the bottom of the sternum, I continued the incision down to the lower abdomen where the groin meets the genital area. Retracting the epidermis revealed the red heart, grey lungs and green liver.

I employed the *en masse* method to remove the chest organs in a single group, and all of the abdominal organs in another for examination. I ligated the great vessels to the neck, head, and arms, then removed the organs as a unit for dissection. I removed the groups of organs together so that disturbances in their functional relationship could be determined.

Before I was able to remove the lower organs, the newly dead body suffered a tremor, and I recoiled in horror. It appeared to move under its own power. The distended belly of my subject deflated. A lifeless, grey fetus of apparently twenty-four to thirty-six weeks emerged. It was a rare post-mortem miscarriage.

The unexpected turn of events overwhelmed the other students, who were by no means squeamish. Undaunted and in full self-command, I removed the reproductive organs where I discovered the vaginal walls had been ruptured, punctured, in fact,

by a sharp instrument. There were similar perforations in the cranial area of the fetus.

I inquired as to the circumstances of her demise, whereupon I learned that she was named Mary Smithfield, and was found lying dead in her room. It seems, from the evidence, that the deceased was a woman of intemperate habits, whose husband, who is now in prison, had been in the habit of begging about the streets, exhibiting, for the purpose of exciting sympathy, a sickly child, of apparently only a few months old—but whose growth had in reality been prevented by sheer starvation. The poor thing was nearly as many years old as it seemed months! A few days ago the woman became deranged, apparently laboring under delirium tremens, and while in this state became so violent *that some of the dwellers in this vast charnel-house of wretchedness and misery actually nailed up the door of her apartment and left her to perish*! Upon opening the room the following morning, Mary was found dead and cold, with her child in the agonies of dissolution, upon her bloated bosom. Her ill-used offspring was probably by this time beyond the reach of human charity. Verdict upon the mother: death from delirium tremens, when, in fact, her death was self-inflicted in an attempt to induce an abortion with a sharp instrument such as a knitting needle.

My first solution to a crime. A crime against the self.

Then I met *her*.

Too much of man's objective in life is preoccupied with an act that results in five minutes of pleasure.

A woman lies on her back, on a bed or anywhere else. She opens her outstretched legs and thighs, and receives between them her lover who at first kneels near the knees of his mistress, then leans over her, his legs and thighs united, upon her, supporting himself by one hand near the woman's shoulder. They are thus belly to belly, their faces close together. With the other hand the man gently opens the large outer labia of her center of delight and directs between them his stiffly-standing magic wand, introducing its corona just far enough to lodge in the

mouth of love's canal. He then withdraws the guiding hand, lets
the upper part of his body fall on his mistress' breasts and, his
lips glued to hers, supporting himself on one elbow, so as not to
crush her by the weight of his body (especially true with regard
to Uncle Jumbo), his hand should wander all over her frame ca-
ressing every charm he can reach, his tongue all the time
working in and out of her mouth, meeting her velvety rosy tip as
well. He caresses the bubbies, the belly, the mons veneris, and
the clitoris of his fair lady, and any other beauties he may man-
age to reach, vigorously pushing his sceptre of delight down and
up and down again as sturdily as he can until all terminates by a
voluptuous spermatic ejaculation, the complete discharge of
both the players, spending together if possible, but if not, the
woman first, and last of all the lord of creation.

What significance does this bear, if any at all? What object is
served by this cycle of love and violence, misery and fear? It
must tend to some end, or else our universe is ruled by chance,
which is unthinkable. But to what end? There lies the great
standing perennial problem to which human reason is as far from
an answer as ever. But deep inside me there is a perpetual
seething like the bottom of a geyser, and I keep hoping things
will come to an eruption once and for all so that I may become a
different person.

Logic and ethics are fundamentally the same. They are no
more than a duty to oneself.*

I sit coiled in my armchair, my haggard and ascetic face
hardly visible among the blue skeins of tobacco smoke, black

---

brows drawn down, forehead contracted, eyes like vacant windows. . . .

The gasogene and cigars are in place. The customary armchair. The phial. Here. It has to take the place of food these days. Why? Because the faculties become refined when you starve them. Surely, you must admit that what your digestion gains in the way of blood supply is so much lost to the brain. I am a brain. The rest of me is a mere appendix.

From the point of view of the criminal expert, London has become a singularly uninteresting city since the disappearance of Professor Moriarty, and New York quite fascinating. With the Professor in the field, one's morning paper presents infinite possibilities. Often it is only the smallest trace, the faintest indication, and yet it is enough to tell me that the great malignant brain is there, as the gentlest tremors of the edges of the web remind one of the foul spider who lurks in the center. Petty thefts, wanton assaults, purposeless outrage—to the man who held the clue all could be worked into one connected whole. To the scientific student of the higher criminal world, no capital in Europe offers the advantages that New York now possesses.

Later. Let my sore tooth call me a while longer. Protract the pleasure.

Amber Halpin. Hm. Here we may discriminate. When a woman has been seriously wronged by a man, she no longer oscillates, so the usual symptom is a broken bell wire. Here we may take it that there is a love matter, but that the maiden is not so much perplexed or grieved as angry. She grows orgulous in revenge for love. Only those who once loved each other can be so vicious.

One of the grooms spoke of it. Freddie has a beastly book—a book no man, even if he had come from the gutter, could have put together. But it is Freddie's book all the same. He could have titled it *Souls I Have Ruined*, if he had so been minded.

Amber reminds me of the woman who will always be *the* woman. I seldom mention her under any other name. In my eyes

she eclipses and predominates the whole of her sex. All other women are merely shadows fanning from her heel. It is not that I feel any emotion akin to love for her. All emotions, and that one particularly, are abhorrent to my cold, precise but admirably balanced mind. I am the most perfect reasoning and observing machine that the world has ever seen, but as a lover I am placing myself in a false position. I never speak of the softer passions, save with a gibe and a sneer. They are admirable things for the observer—excellent for drawing the veil from men's motives and actions. But for the trained reasoner to admit such intrusions into his own delicate and finely adjusted temperament is to introduce a distracting factor that might throw a doubt upon all his mental results. Grit in a sensitive instrument, or a crack in one of my own high-powered lenses, would not be more disturbing than a strong emotion in a nature such as mine. And yet there is but one woman to me, and that woman is Lillie Langtry, of dubious and questionable memory. I keep and fondle the watchchain she bestowed on me in the course of our encounter. My fingers still recall her treasures.

I felt nothing about her departure from my life until seven chancres formed, which eventually combined to form two, then one. Each night and morning I dressed my poor prick. Finally it healed and the scar closed. I madly take care of myself. Some of us spend one night with Venus and the rest of our lives with Mercury. Nothing's so good for the health as love.

She remains, nearly a decade later, a woman who can destroy the energy and break the will of kings with her trembling breasts and quivering belly, a superhuman and exotic demi-goddess of indestructible lust, of immortal Hysteria, of accursed Beauty, distinguished from all others by the catalepsy which stiffens her flesh and hardens her muscles; the monstrous Beast, indifferent, irresponsible, insensible, baneful, like the Helen of antiquity, fatal to all who approach her, all who behold her, all whom she touches.

101

Now. Unfair division between molar and sinus. Must have it extracted.

The division seems rather unfair, said Athelney Jones, of Scotland Yard, who got the credit for the arrest of that wooden-legged ex-soldier and convict, Jonathan Small. *You have done all the work in this business. I get a wife out of it, Jones gets the credit, pray what remains for you?*

For me,—I said,—*there still remains the cocaine bottle,*—and I stretched my long white hand up for it.

My mind rebels at stagnation. Crime is commonplace. Existence is commonplace. To the man who loves art for its own sake, it is frequently in its least important and lowliest manifestations that the keenest pleasure is to be derived, like a connoisseur who has just taken his first sip of a comet vintage.

Ah, there. A frost comes over my sinuses.

Work is the grand cure of all the maladies and miseries that ever beset mankind. *Self-Help.* A place for everything and everything in its place. Smiles. An Englishman's word is his bond. My bond. My word. I, alone, must oppose Moriarty, symbol of the great declension besetting us. I am the *chevalier sans peur et sans reproche* called forth to single combat.

Ah, me, it's a wicked world, and when a clever man turns his brains to crime, it is worst of all. Malcontent with everything and disgusted with myself, I would like to redeem myself and pride myself a little in the silence and solitude of the night. Grant me the grace to solve this crime so that I may prove to myself that I am not the last and the least among men, that I am not inferior to those whom I despise!

In fact, plots are tedious. Anyone can invent them.
Life is full of them. Indeed, one has to elbow one's
way through them as they crowd across one's path.
                                    —Oscar Wilde

Actions are the first tragedy in life, words are the second. Words are perhaps the worst. Words are merciless. Freddie understands this now.

Freddie collects women, and takes pride in his collection, as some men collect paintings or statuary. He has them all in a book. Daguerotypes, names, details, everything about them. Now Freddie is in love with a woman who will barely tolerate his presence. He intends to win her over by declarations of true love and financial opportunity. This is a comedy!

Freddie met Amber after her performance in Tom Taylor's old play, *An Unequal Match*. She discouraged him in earnest but Freddie persistently sent lavish bouquets, diamonds as well as a stream of invitations to go skating or riding in Central Park. She finally consented to become his mistress after he assaulted her with more diamonds and costly gifts. Freddie came and went as he pleased since she had given him keys to her apartments. The Margie incident at *Pfaff's* effectively ended their cordial relations despite his liberality.

Not least of all, Freddie plans to bring about a theatrical renaissance in New York. He knows nothing about the theatre, literature, acting or set design—the ideal qualifications for a theatrical impresario who wants to impress his mistress by putting her on the stage. He behaves like a wealthy ponce.

Freddie is twenty-two-years old. I am twenty-six. That is why I tell everyone I am twenty-eight.

—My old man is crazy. And he's driving me crazy. But he can't drive me crazy because I am crazy. If I don't get married by tomorrow night, he's going to cut me off. Then how am I going to realize my dream the-yea-tre? I can see the the-yea-tre

now on Thirty-Third and Broadway, attached to a hotel like the Savoy in London. All I need is a million. If pops don't deliver the goods, I can always go to George Childs. He's on the verge of investing in the enterprise. We'll open with **Vera.**

—*Splendid idea,*—I said. Agreeable. He will put up the money.

—*But there will have to be some changes.*

(!)

—*I think I got it worked out so that we'll both become immortal in one night!*

—*And then the world will be at our feet,* I antiphoned, trying to work up some enthusiasm.

I am wasting my time. Nothing will come of this. I am consorting with a fool.

—*Let's get Mary Anderson. We can coax her along.*

—*Mary Anderson is quite a fine choice*—I said, as long as Freddie pays her salary.

Any competent actress resembles a genius reading my dialogue. But I am beginning to quarrel generally with most modern scene-painting. A scene is primarily a decorative background for the actors, and should always be kept subordinate; first to the players, their dress, gesture and action; and secondly, it must adhere to the fundamental principle of decorative art, which is not to imitate but to suggest nature. One must either, like Titian, make the landscape subordinate to the figures, or, like Claude, the figures subordinate to the landscape; for if we desire realistic acting we cannot have realistic scene-painting.

—Is this restaurant suitable?—asked Freddie.

Greenwich Village. Jefferson Market. Prized the *table d'hôte* of a French lady who had taken a Spanish husband in a second marriage and had a Cuban Negro for her cook. A cross-eyed Alsatian for a waiter and a slim young South American for a cashier. Is this an adventure in slumming or an insult? These Americans, really! I strive to retain good form and geniality.

—Give me luxuries. I can dispense with necessities.

Freddie, I suspect, is just cheap. He didn't want to go to *Delmonico's* or *Pfaff's*, where dinner would have been ten dollars. Suddenly Holmes' bestowal of five hundred golden eagles seems exceedingly generous.

—At one very neat French place,—said Freddie,—I got dinner at the same price with wine. It's worth thinking about. And I don't know why the Italians, who are notoriously cheap people. . . .

Freddie blathered so throughout dinner, but I am not discouraged. I have made an important discovery . . . that alcohol, taken in sufficient quantities, produces all of the effects of intoxication.

Suddenly, in the semiobscurity, phantasmagorical streets, double streets, apparitional streets opened deep inside the city, bewitching my imagination.

—This is one of the most remarkable avenues in the city,—he said.—It's got a character and an atmosphere peculiarly its own. Now Seventh Avenue ain't got no character. Just stables and piano factories. Third Avenue has a life of its own, and so have Second and Eighth—beer saloons, old-time Dutch families, millinery stores, markets, retail emporiums, all manner of working girls. . . .

The night grew vaster under the pressure of great gusts of wind. At Twenty-Third Street the avenue began to present the most animated appearance. The windows were all ablaze with gas jets. An electric light from a vast dry goods establishment threw a pale, bluish imitation of day upon everything, making the street lamps burn feebly and with sickly glare.

Vera will never be produced. I am a fool chasing a will-o'-the-wisp far and wide.

Groups of young ladies became more numerous; here and there one walked alone; sometimes had companions who laughed loudly, who sometimes talked with a very *broad* accent, and who, by some indescribable wearing of the sealskin sacque or the jaunty hat, gave the impression that they dwelled in the

half-world of sidestreets, the abiding places of the crimson sisterhood.

Enterprising bagnios plastered pictures of their charming inmates in the windows. The laughter is constant. Just as a trumpet suggests the color of scarlet, so the sound conjures the painted cheeks and sunken eyes of the revelers.

We stop at a French cafe around Thirty-First Street, much frequented by the daughters of *La Belle France* who belong to the midnight world of Sixth Avenue. They come here for dinner, black coffee, cognac, absinthe. It is always crowded late at night both on the ground floor and in the supper rooms above.

Slowly, we fall into a conversation with some old habitués. One of them, the Captain, invites us to the bar, and eventually, to a game of *dollar ante*.

—What is dollar ante?—I drearily asked.

They explain, and chuckle deeply in their bronchial tubes.

My chair, badly constructed and machine-made, strained when I sat. A great sadness mantles me. An unutterable melancholy shadows my dreaming eyes, but I only sigh, and kept a vigilant silence for *Vera*.

Our carriage stopped before Amber's mansion. A groom took charge of the horses. Freddie tossed the good fellow a coin.

—My life is like the plot of a bad play. Nothing happens,— droned Freddie.

—In fact, plots are tedious. Anyone can invent them. Life is full of them. Indeed, one has to elbow one's way through them as they crowd across one's path.

—I told her I didn't love her any more.

Nobody was getting very far. My deal now. I caress the cards gently and distribute them mournfully like communion wafers. Everybody goes in. The Captain takes two cards; Freddie takes one and I take one.

—I bet five bucks,—says the Cap.

—I raise you five,—answers Freddie.

I murmur dubiously, but put up my portion.

—Ten harder,—says the Cap.

—Ten more than you,—remarks Freddie.

I knit my brow. I lean on the balcony, bending over the emptiness of space; I take deep breaths of the evening air, vaguely conscious of the loveliness outside, the shadowed, soft, forlorn remoteness of the air; all this is night's beauty, a grey-black sky here and there suffused with blue; and tiny stars, tremulous watery stars.

But I must stay.

—I will—how do you phrase it, call? I will call on you.

The Captain joins the merry throng. He lays down his cards with a smile of triumph.

—Three aces.

—Full hand,—counters Freddie proudly and reaches for the money.

—Too-too,—I murmur, and lay down four deuces.—Now that I remember it, Gentlemen, we used to indulge in this little recreation at Oxford. Come and take a snifter with me.

Scores of solid businessmen, and oceans of young fellows of nobby attire, such as you see at a billiard match. There are a great many drummers taking country customers about. A young gentleman with an undisguisable agricultural overcoat talks to a pretty brunette in a black silk dress, over which a long gold chain trailed like a yellow serpent.

—The general get-up,—comments Freddie,—seems to suggest Pittsburgh, PeeAye.

Everyone is speaking French; everyone is drinking, for the latest diner has been long ago satisfied. They close the door after business hours and the girls perform a genuine Mabille can-can for the delectation of a few privileged visitors. The girls who dance are true children of the Boulevards, and there is no doubt that their execution of the lively dance was as artistic as can be witnessed at the score of gardens in Paris. Their violent and pink-stockinged beauty makes sad havoc of glassware, but there is someone who pays for it, and the proprietress doesn't care.

107

When I am really in great trouble, as anyone who knows me intimately will tell you, I refuse everything except food and drink.

After the first glass of absinthe you see things as you wish they were. After the second you see them as they are not. Finally you see things as they really are, and that is the most horrible thing in the world. I mean disassociated. Take a top hat. You think you see it as it really is. But you don't because you associate it with other things and ideas. If you had never heard of one before, and suddenly saw it alone, you'd be frightened or you'd laugh. That is the effect absinthe has, and that is why it drives men mad. All night long I am drinking absinthe, and thinking that I am singularly clear-headed and sane. The waiter came and began watering the sawdust. The most wonderful flowers, tulips, lilies and roses sprang up, and made a garden in the cafe.— Don't you see them?—I say to him.

—*Mais non, monsieur, il n'y a rien.*

I wander through dimly lit streets, past gaunt black-shadowed archways and evil-looking houses. Women with hoarse voices and harsh laughter call after me. Drunkards reel by cursing and chattering to themselves like monstrous apes, grotesque children huddle upon doorsteps, shrieks and oaths from gloomy courts, strange mechanical grotesques, black leaves wheeling in the wind.

Sin is the only real color element left in modern life. That is tonight's discovery!

I long for my hotel room, waiting for me in a clean, quiet and patient disoccupation, to take possession of its peace and comfort. When I finally return to the *Brevoort*, the desk clerk gives me a message. A producer interested in my play?

See me immediately upon your arrival, it reads; signed *Holmes*.

Women are naturally secretive, and
they like to do their own secreting.
—Sherlock Holmes

Wilde is a peculiar character, but he may be helpful. Little does he know his antecedents. After the death of that old rake Thomas De Veil, his position and his house in Bow Street were taken over by the novelist and playwright Henry Fielding, who had made an aesthetic discovery that has so far eluded Wilde: that literature and poverty are almost synonymous. I would not go so far as to say that they are useless. Are you up on your Jean-Paul? A new attitude of analysis has arisen, partly attributable to the rise of the novel, which has taught the European how to use his imagination and extend his sympathies. Advances in science and engineering have taught us to span great rivers with bridges and continents with railways. The new science of criminal detection is an outgrowth of this.

It was in the deepest post-midnight hours that I received Wilde. I had been so preoccupied with abstract thinking that I noticed neither the swift passage of time nor the fact that I was still in disguise. Wilde had never seen a demonstration of my amazing powers of disguise.

—Mr Sherlock Holmes, please,—he said, uncertainty coloring his voice.

He looked three times before he recognized me beneath my unkempt and disreputable clothes and the side-whiskers that framed my inflamed face. I have a thousand and one faces to match each multiplicate of personality Wilde claims as his own.

—Well, really!—he cried, and then he was obliged to take a seat and lie back helplessly, limp with laughter, into a chair.

He was inebriated. If a person tells me he has been to the worst places, I have no right to judge him, but if he tells me that his superior wisdom enabled him to get there, then I know that he is a fraud. Wilde said nothing.

—Ah, you rogue! You had the proper workhouse cough, and those weak legs of yours are worth ten pounds a week. The stage lost a fine actor when you became a specialist in crime.

—Theatre? bah! I am sure you could never guess how I employed my day.

—Allow me to ratiocinate. I suppose you have been observing the habits of Miss Amber Halpin.

—Quite so.

—Well, so was I.—Wilde said with authority.

—I assumed the character of a groom out of work,—I continued, removing at last the individual elements of my disguise.—There is a wonderful sympathy and freemasonry among horsey men.

—I'm certain that the horsey men imagine Amber to be a jennet in heat.

—Oh, she has turned all the men's heads down in that part,— I answered, making a simple arrangement of cold beef and beer which the Aesthete did not refuse.—They say she is the daintiest thing under a bonnet on the planet.

—Is that what they say?—he said, drolly accenting the verb.

Our meal was a merry one. I spoke on a quick succession of subjects—on miracle plays, on mediaeval pottery, on Stradivarius violins, on the Buddhism of Ceylon, and on the warships of the future—I have made a special study of each. Then I came to my point.

—Wilde, I observed you this afternoon in front of Amber's lodgings. You were with a semiliterate fop making observations. In fact, I overheard you talk of *insidious plots*. It has led me to view your intentions with suspicion. Wilde, I will brook no insubordination from you. You are under my employ.

The wheels of his silly mind turned rapidly.

—I believe I was speaking about *tedious plots*. You misheard me.

—What? Impossible!

—Holmes, you are behaving like a tedious person in a tedious plot yourself. I am conducting my own investigation. I have, in fact, obtained an appointment with Amber Halpin tomorrow evening.

—Speaking candidly, Wilde, I am not interested in your observations. I shall want your cooperation,—I said, digging my spur into his side. He winced. Why did I pay him after all? Perhaps I should have withheld his moiety until the successful conclusion of the case. He was preparing to say something when I put him in his place.

—You are under my employ, and you have no choice whatsoever in the decisions bearing on this case,—I said with no little vehemence.

—Yes, Holmes,—he truckled.

One must always keep business separate from personal matters. As an artist, Wilde takes everything personally.

—You don't mind breaking the law?—I asked, somewhat more kindly.

—Not in the least.

—I was sure I might rely on you.

I went to the mirror and plucked a few stray whiskers from my cheeks. Now it is my face once again, the face that others know me by.

—Tomorrow night,—I continued,—we must be at the scene of the action. Miss Halpin returns from her rehearsals—

—As you like it,—he interjected.

—Being interrupted is not how I like it.

—I mean the title of the play. Shakespeare.

—Ah, yes, Shakespeare. Our poet. With the single exception of Homer, there is no eminent writer, not even Sir Walter Scott, whom I can despise so entirely as I despise Shakespeare when I measure my mind against his. Yet people stare at him in wonderment, as if he were a spectacular natural phenomenon. I can never rid myself of the suspicion that praising him has been the conventional thing to do.

111

—And then what do you propose?—he asked.

—Ah, yes, you must leave everything to me. I have already arranged what is to occur. There is only one point on which I must insist.

—And what is that?

—You must not interfere, come what may. You understand?

—I am to be a nonentity?

—Do nothing whatsoever. There will probably be some small unpleasantness. Do not join in it. It will end in my being conveyed into her house. Four or five minutes afterward, the sitting room window will be opened. You are to station yourself close to that window.

—Yes.

—You are to watch for me.

—Yes. Yes.

—And when I raise my hand so,—I said, reaching a rhetorical climax,—you shall throw into the room this ordinary smoke rocket.

I presented Wilde with the very smoke rocket. He fingered it with uncertainty.

—Your task is confined to that.

—I am to be an incendiary?

—Raise a hue and a cry of fire—it will be taken up by quite a number of people.

—How dramatic!

—You may then walk to the end of the street and I will rejoin you in ten minutes. I hope that I have made myself clear.

—What is the end of all this, then?—he inquired with no little skepticism.

—She will show me where she conceals the birth certificate.

—How?

—When a woman thinks that her house is on fire, her instinct is at once to rush to the thing she values most. A married woman grabs her baby, an unmarried one reaches for her jewel box. Amber will rescue the birth certificate.

112

—How do you know she has it? Her banker or lawyer may have it.

—There is that dual possibility. But I am inclined to think neither. Women are naturally secretive, and they like to do their own secreting. Why should she hand it over to anyone else? She could trust her own guardianship, but she could not tell what indirect or political influence might be brought to bear upon a businessman. Besides, remember that she had resolved to use it within a few days. It must be where she can lay her hands upon it. It must be in her house.

There was a moment of splendid silence during which I awaited his declaration of whole-souled enthusiasm.

—It is simple enough as you explain it,—he began with a puckish smile.—You remind me of Edgar Allen Poe's Dupin. I had no idea that such individuals did exist outside of stories.

I rose and lit my pipe. Pace and think. Think and pace.

—No doubt you think that you are complimenting me in comparing me to Dupin,—I observed.—Now, in my opinion, Dupin was a very inferior fellow. That trick of his breaking in on his friends' thoughts with an *à propos* remark after a quarter of an hour's silence is really very showy and superficial. He had some analytical genius, no doubt; but he was by no means such a phenomenon as Poe appeared to imagine.

—Have you read Gaboriau's works?—he asked, adjusting his best curl.—Does Lecoq come up to your idea of a detective?

I sniffed sardonically.

—Lecoq was a miserable bungler,—I said in an angry voice;—he had only one thing to recommend him, and that was his energy. That book made me positively ill. The question was how to identify an unknown prisoner. I could have done it in twenty-four hours. Lecoq took six months or so. It might be made a textbook for detectives to teach them what to avoid.

—Well, Holmes, in all candor, I think as much of your smoke-rocket ploy.—He yawned, he stretched, he admired his rings.—It is a perfectly stupid and impractical idea. It is folly. It

113

is juvenile. It is such a bad idea that only a genius could have conceived it.

—How dare you criticize me?

—First, because you asked; secondly, because you are behaving like a perfect idiot. Such overbearing insolence I have witnessed only among theatrical producers.

He was angry because I treated him sternly. Nonetheless:

—I am right. I am always right.

—You ignored the fact that I have an appointment to meet her at the same time you propose to attack her home.

—You have no choice in the matter, Wilde. I am paying you to work in my service, not to contradict my judgment. If you do not like the terms, you are free to disqualify yourself and go hence and live in the street.

—I'm not going to spoil my meeting with Amber by detonating a smoke-rocket in her rooms,—he insisted defiantly.—It will ruin her furnishings, and disturb the delicate negotiations for my play.

—Your play?! How trivial! And what do you propose instead?

—You, Holmes, have misinterpreted the scenario. Amber is still in love with the father of her child, and the only way to make her give up the document is to make her fall in love again, because new love forces out the old. Then she will not care anymore about Uncle Jumbo, and she will lose her taste for revenge.

—Oh ho!

—I, too, have made inquiries of my own,—added Wilde with some tantalization.

—Indeed! And what have you learned that I do not know? I know about your meeting with Freddie, your producer, the hebephrenic and impecunious millionaire. Amber hates him. You'll have no luck. Amber is a wronged woman—she will revenge herself against all men alike.

—Did you know that she is a Londoner?

—Really!

—Freddie merely seeks rapprochement, and nature will take its course. He is willing to finance my play if he is able to marry her by tomorrow night because his father has threatened to disinherit him unless he does so. Consequently, Freddie will marry Amber, finance *Vera*, and Cleveland will be safe from scandal, and you and I shall be richly rewarded.

—How illusory and self-serving!

—No more or less than your approach. At least I am an invited guest at Amber's home, and I shall not pollute her home by detonating a smoke rocket therein. She is an *artiste* renowned in New York for her grace, intelligence and beauty. Not since Lillie Langtry has there been such a theatrical luminary.

—Lillie Langtry?! Bah! My approach is logical. Detection is, or ought to be, an exact science and should be treated in the same cold and unemotional manner. You have attempted to tinge it with romanticism, which produces much the same effect as if you worked a love story into the fifth proposition of Euclid.

—That, Holmes, could be an axiom of Pythagoras, who joined mathematics and music, logic and passion in violent and beautiful harmonies.

—Poppycock, you turn my very words against me!

O, Knowledge, ill-inhabited, worse than Jove in a thatched house!

—Shall we make a gentleman's wager?

—What kind of wager?

—Our endeavors may be pursued simultaneously without encumbrance or conflict. I shall rekindle a love affair with a red rose of fire! That's it! Freddie will rescue her from the fire! And she will fall in love with her white knight! That shall be the scenario I direct!

—Meanwhile, I will obtain the birth certificate. Will you obey my instructions to the letter?

—As long as you do not interfere with Freddie pursuing Amber. The world is quite large enough to accommodate the two of us.

It was agreed. We shook hands.

The genius has the greatest, most limpid clearness and distinctness. The genius has the best developed memory, the greatest ability to form clear judgments, and, therefore, the most refined sense of the distinctions between true and false, right and wrong. Logic and ethics are fundamentally the same. They are no more than duty to oneself. Genius is the highest morality, and, therefore, it is everyone's duty.

This is a wager I planned to win.

—I uphold the preeminence of logic, the indomitable structure of the world. Logic.

—Love—and what a silly thing love is!—said Wilde.—It is not half as useful as logic, for it does not prove anything and it is always telling one things that are not going to happen, and making one believe things that are not true.

If I claim full justice for my art, it is because it is an impersonal thing, a thing beyond itself. Crime is common. Logic is rare. Therefore it is upon logic rather than upon crime that one should dwell, however much Wilde may degrade my high-minded mission with levity. I know the world consists solely of asserted propositions. The truth is a reluctant mistress—one can only reach her heart with cold steel in the hand of passion.[*]

---

[*] *The truth ... in the hand of passion.* Reprinted with the permission of The Free Press, a Division of Simon & Schuster Adult Publishing Group, from *LUDWIG WITTGENSTEIN: The Duty of Genius*, by Ray Monk. Copyright © 1990 by Ray Monk. All rights reserved. Published in the UK by Jonathan Cape. Reprinted with permission of The RandomHouse Group Ltd.

I would rather have discovered Lillie Langtry
than have discovered America.
—Oscar Wilde

I feel sorry for those who have been deceived by Holmes' ironic sense of reserve with which he hides his pride and sensitivity. I don't know anything more fatiguing than disagreeing with Holmes and I wonder how all this disagreeable business shall end.

The setting sun struck the upper windows of the house opposite with scarlet and gold. The panes glowed like plates of heated metals. The sky above was like a faded rose. I thought of Amber's young fierycolored life.

—*Oui, monsieur,*—said the butler who answered the door.

—*Je m'appelle Oscar Wilde. J'ai un rendez-vous avec Madamoiselle Halpin.*

—*Par ici, s'il vous plaît,*—he answered with perfect self-effacement, leading me through a vestibule into a broad entrance hall, where along a beam a painter had inscribed the slogan of the house: *And yours, too, my friend.*

A gentleman is leaving. I smile and extend my hand.

—Oscar Wilde, playwright.

—D'Oyly Carte, theatrical agent. Amber is my client.

—How serendipitous! I am here to discuss my new play, *Vera*, with Amber.

—My client list is full. Good day, Mr. Wilde!

I arched my eyebrow vividly as he departed. He doesn't know who I am. Then I let my eye roam among the marble fireplaces with ornately carved mantels to mitigate the sting of his rejection. The interior was finished in white enamel, surprising at first, because one would have expected highly polished walnut, but since the mansion was cut off from a good deal of sunlight, the rooms would have risked looking gloomy. White enamel brightened the ambiance. The unlikely choice reflected

the owner's character. On the wall in the lofty dining room, whose stained glass windows contained a pair of entwined swans as a motif, there was carved around the aristocratic fireplace: *They say—What say they? Let them say.** It was such a tonic after all the bad wallpapers horribly designed, and colored carpets, and that old offender the horsehair sofa, whose stolid look of indifference is always so depressing.

The butler took my hat, cane and cape and bade me to take a seat in this wonderful room which to my mind was the finest thing in color and art decoration which the world has known since Correggio painted that wonderful room in Italy where the little children are dancing on the walls. So un-Holmsian. He serves tea in chemical beakers because ordinary crockery is too ugly for him!

On my way here, I watched a great hulking Chinese workman at his task of digging, and saw him drink his tea from a little cup as delicate in texture as the petal of a flower, whereas in my grand hotel, where thousands of dollars have been lavished on great gilt mirrors and gaudy columns, I have been given my coffee or my chocolate in cups an inch and a quarter thick. I think I deserve something better.

I do not think that the sovereignty and empire of women's beauty has at all passed away, though we may no longer go to war for them as the Greeks did for the daughter of Leda. The greatest empire still remains for them—the empire of art; I cannot, however, regard the adjoining drawing room as in any way a success. The heavy ebony doors are entirely out of keeping with the satin panels; the silk hangings are quite meaningless in their position and consequently quite ugly; the carpet's colors are not in harmony with the rest of the room, and the table cover is mauve.

---

* *On the wall in the lofty dining room ... Let them say.* From *The Prince and the Lilly,* by James Brough, Coward McCann & Geoghegan, Inc.: New York, 1974. By permission of Penguin Group (USA) Inc.

The Philistine may, of course, object that to be absolutely perfect is impossible. Well, that is so: but then it is only the impossible things that are worth doing nowadays!

—Why did you accept that diamond bracelet from Mr Gebhard?—asked a shrewish voice that rose from the depths of the mansion. Her vowels were unmistakably English, and her provocative question set me to serious eavesdropping.

How I love eavesdropping!

—I don't have to explain,—coolly replied another woman, English as well.

—All this trouble is starting again. I shall not tolerate a young man distracting you from the great task we face. You must rehearse. The role of Rosalind requires the services of an actress, not that of a pretty elocutionist,* and if we fail and the critics—

—You're jealous because you do not receive costly gifts from admirers. Am I to blame for that as well?

—Oh, impertinent hussie!

—And I would like to remind you that we have a place to live because of him, otherwise we'd be in the street and dining with Duke Humphrey. Furthermore, in your capacity as actor-manager, you have failed to pay the cast for two weeks. Where do you think that diamond ring went? To pay the cast. Mrs Labouchère, mind your own business!

Henrietta Labouchère!? Tiny Henrietta. Energetic and wirey Henrietta. Vociferous Henrietta who speaks in capital letters. I know her! I am well acquainted with her, in fact. She is a former dramatic actress who achieved a minor reputation in supporting roles. She is married to Henry, an ardent follower of Gladstone

---

* *The role of Rosalind ... pretty elocutionist.* From *The Prince and the Lilly*, by James Brough, Coward McCann & Geoghegan, Inc.: New York, 1974. By permission of Penguin Group (USA) Inc.

and editor of a small liberal magazine called *Truth*, which is something of a paradox since they do not publish my poems.

—I strongly disapprove of your proceedings in this country, and I urge you to refuse all society invitations.

The frou-frou of her sashaying dress on the stairs opposite me. I behold a lovely combination of blue and creamy lace, a masterpiece, a symphony in silver-grey with highlights of pink, a pure melody of color that I feel sure Jimmy Whistler would call *scherzo*, and take as its visible motive the moonlight wandering in silver mist through a rose garden.

Son visage: it is only in the best Greek gems, on the silver coins of Syracuse, or among the marble figures of the Parthenon frieze, that one can find the ideal representation of the marvelous beauty of that face which looked upon me now. Pure Greek it is, with the grave low forehead, the exquisitely arched brow; the noble chiselling of the mouth, shaped as if it were the mouthpiece of an instrument of music; the supreme and splendid curve of the cheek; the augustly pillared throat which bears it all; it is Greek, because the lines which compose it are so definite and strong, and yet so exquisitely harmonized that the effect is one of simple loveliness purely: Greek, because its essence and its quality, as in the quality of music and of architecture, is that of beauty based on absolutely mathematical laws. The grey eyes lighten into blue or deepen into violet as fancy succeeds fancy; the lips become flower-like in laughter or, tremulous as a bird's wing, shape themselves at last into the strong and bitter molds of pain or scorn. And then motion comes, and the statue wakes into life. But the life is not the ordinary life of common days; it is life with a new value given to it, and the charm to me is that she conceals as much as she reveals. It is . . . it is her! It is Lillie!

—Oscar!

She genially put out her hand.

Astonishment and delight played me like a flute.

—Lillie—it is you—Lillie Langtry!

—Oscar, you always loved my improbability,—she said, with a very cheery, ladylike accent, jutting forward her salient chin. *—Lily of love, pure and inviolate! Tower of Ivory! Red rose of fire!* —The Lord of Language has not failed. Her ready smile and lovely voice pleased both eye and ear. I knelt at her feet and kissed her ivory hand.

—And you once made a carpet of flowers for me.

She bade me to be seated on the ottoman, where she took a seat beside me, crushing the lovely folds of her dress that submitted to her every move with delicious crepitation. She folded her white hands in her lap.

—Lillie, why are you wearing an *Amber* mask? I feared you walked off the face of the earth.

She bit her lip seductively.

—It's a secret, and I trust that you will not reveal my true identity to anyone.

—You have my word.

—Mrs Labouchère is rehearsing me in the part of Rosalind in *As You Like It.* I am too well known in London to attempt such a risky venture there, so I must conceal my identity in order to receive disinterested assessment of my acting ability. I shall try out the play here. If it succeeds, I shall open the production under my own name. If not, no one will know the better and my reputation shall remain intact.

Mysterious woman, Lillie Langtry (nèe Le Breton). She hails from Jersey. Her father is a rakish old dean. *I'm a man and therefore consider all that belongs to men akin to myself,* he often used to say, quoting the Gospel According to Terence.[*] Left

---

[*] *I'm a man … the Gospel according to Terence. The Prince and the Lilly,* by James Brough, Coward McCann & Geoghegan, Inc.: New York, 1974. By permission of Penguin Group (USA) Inc.

behind a half dozen bastards on the island. Lillie met her future husband, Edward Langtry, at her brother's wedding, where Edward entertained the wedding party on his yacht, the *Red Gauntlet*. She once said starkly,—I fell in love with the *Red Gauntlet*, not my husband. To become mistress of the yacht, I married the owner. Edward consequently behaved as a husband should and did what he was told. He took Lillie's suggestion to move to London so that she might begin her brilliant social life. Miles discovered her at tea at the home of Sir John and Lady Sebright, where she created a sensation with her simple black dress and the Jersey twist in her hair. Edward, who was consistently ignored (well, Jimmy spoke with him—that's probably why Jimmy was the only artist he liked), discovered the bottle. Lillie said he was exceedingly shy and that their marriage remained unconsummated. He refused, however, to grant her a divorce. Lillie is a woman of no little resources and imagination, and she has apparently infinite capacity and disposition for intrigue. Her liaison with Lord Renfrew scandalized London. Now Mr Cleveland rises from the past. A secret child. Money. Blackmail. The elements of a new play. What do I say to her?

—I would rather have discovered you than have discovered America.

—Ha! Most men who are civil to actresses and render them services have an *arrière-pensée*. Not so with you, Oscar. You are a devoted attendant who never pays court.

—I've always wanted to write a legendary part for you. And I believe I have.

—*Alors, de quoi s'agit-il ton drame?*

—*Mon drame? du style seulement. Hugo et Shakespeare ont partagé tous les sujets: c'est impossible d'être original, même dans la péché: ainsi, il n'y a plus des émotions, seulement des adjectifs extraordinaires.*

—*Et la fin?*

—*La fin est assez tragique. La héroine est une nihiliste civilisée qui lutte contre le monde Philistine.*
—*Qu'est-ce que c'est la civilisation, Oscar?*
—*L'amour du beau.*
—*Qu'est-ce que c'est le beau?*
—*Ce que les bourgeois appellent le laid.*
—*Et ce que les bourgeois appellent le beau?*
—*Cela n'existe pas.*[*]

We laughed merrily. How perfectly we understand each other.

—If I may ask a direct personal question.. . .
—How exciting, please do.
—Did Edward grant you a divorce?
—No.
—That puts you in a difficult position, with regard to Freddie's proposal of marriage.

—I never thought things would turn out like this,—she said with some bewilderment.—He told me that he didn't love me, and then he gave me this house. Isn't that peculiar?

—Really?

—This confounded house! But I don't have any money to pay for food, much less hire service. He has no money now but he gives me diamond rings. He is a fool. I've been pawning the diamonds to make ends meet. Money is meant to be spent so I spend, spend, spend it,—she declared with a bankrupt's nonchalance.

—That makes it easier for me to plead the cause of your admiring Freddie. You realize that Freddie must be married tonight, otherwise he stands to lose an inheritance of tens of mil-

---

[*] *Mon drame? ... Cela n'existe pas* From OCSCAR WILDE by Richard Ellmann, copyright © 1987 by The Estate of Richard Ellmann. Used by permission of Alfred A. Knopf, a division of Random House, Inc.

lions of dollars—his father so stipulated in the terms of his inheritance.

—The only good reason I have to marry him is that I don't love him.

—Excellent! He seeks a marriage of convenience and is willing to pay a considerable monthly allowance that will allow you to do as you wish. His father will supply funds upon the wedding.

—It's a wonderful proposition, however, there is an obstacle. He loves me, and as soon as we are married, he will deprive me of my freedom. Freddie is a lying little Lord Fauntleroy who can't spell. He sees in me all the foolishness inspired by romantic love. He must be bound, gagged, deceived and domesticated.

—Darling, look at the practical side. That entitles you to lie, too.

—So, if I marry this bloke, you get *Vera* produced, and I get the part, along with a considerable monthly allowance for the rest of my life.

—Right-o. It is an ancient theme in modern terms.

—And what happens when my Freddie finds out that I am already married?

—I invite you to impart a sphinx-like silence on the subject. Besides, he doesn't even know your real name, *Amber*.

—You had better take care,—she cautioned.—Freddie is very fascinating. If he were not, there would be no battle.

—Greek meets Greek, then?—I ventured.—I am on the side of the Trojans. They fought for a woman.

—They were defeated.

—There are worse things than capture.

—You gallop with a loose rein.

—Pace gives life,—was my riposte.—I shall write it in my diary tonight.

—What?—she asked.

—That a burnt child loves the fire.

—I am not even singed. You are aware, Oscar, that courage has passed from men to women. It is a new experience for us. In any case, men have educated us.

—But not explained you.

—Describe us as a sex,—was her new challenge.

Something old, something new, something borrowed, something true.

—Sphinxes without secrets.

—Great passions do not exist—they are liars' fantasies,—she said, smiling.—What do exist are little loves that may last for a short or longer while.* We shall not keep Mr Gebhard waiting, shall we? He is expected, after all.

—How he suffers for your love!

—I can sympathize with everything, except suffering,—said Lillie, shrugging her shoulders.—I cannot sympathize with that. It is too ugly, too horrible, too distressing. There is something terribly morbid in the modern sympathy with pain. One should sympathize with the color, the beauty, the joy of life. The less said about life's sores, the better.

—I wish I had said that,—I replied with unconcealed envy.

—Don't worry, Oscar, you will.

---

* *Great passions ... a short or longer while.* Reprinted with the permission of Abby Adams, from *AN UNCOMMON SCOLD*, by Abby Adams. Copyright © 1989 by Abby Adams. All rights reserved.

125

No other woman possesses that sweet brandied voice,
which hangs like a jewel in my ear.
—Sherlock Holmes

But I hear the rumble of wheels. It is his carriage. The gleam of the sidelights of the carriage come round the curve of the avenue. It is a smart little landau which rattles up to the door of 362 West Twenty-Third. As it pulls up, one of the loafing men at the corner dashes forward to open the door for Frederick Gebhard in the hope of earning a copper, but is elbowed away by another loafer, who is rushing up with the same intention. A fierce quarrel breaks out, which is now increased by the two guardsmen, who take sides with one of the loungers, and by the scissors-grinder, who is equally hot upon the other side. A blow is struck, and in an instant Mr Gebhard, who steps from his carriage, is the center of a little knot of flushed and struggling men, who strike savagely at each other with their fists and sticks. My cue. I dash into the crowd to protect the gentleman but just as I reach him I give a cry and drop to the ground, blood running freely down my face. At my fall, the guardsmen take to their heels in one direction and the loungers in the other, while a number of better dressed people, who watched me during the scuffle without taking part in it, crowd in to help Mr Gebhard and to attend to my injuries. My eye surreptitiously watches Amber Halpin hurry down the steps of her house to meet her suitor. Gasogenes from bay windows highlight her figure. Wilde follows in her wake.

—Is the poor gentleman hurt?—she asks.
—He is dead,—cry several voices.
—No, no, there's life in him!—shouts another.—But he'll be gone before you can get him to the hospital.
—He's a brave fellow,—says a woman.—They would have had the gentleman's purse and watch if it hadn't been for him. They were a gang, and a rough one, too.

—The Whyos,—pipes another.

—Ah, he's breathing now.

—He can't lie in the street. May we bring him in, Ma'am?

—Surely. Bring him into the sitting room. There is a comfortable sofa. This way, please!

Slowly and solemnly I am borne into the mansion and laid out in the principal room. I observe the proceedings from my coign of vantage, the simulacrum of unconsciousness. The lamps are lit but the blinds are not drawn. I lie upon a davenport. Compunction seizes me momentarily for the part I am playing. The arresting rustle of a skirt on the stairs. Bright looking, pretty she is, mature and youngish lady, the beautiful creature against whom I am conspiring. I am stifled by a cloak of shame as she waits upon my injuries with grace and kindliness.

I catch a glimpse of her at the moment, and she is indeed a lovely woman, with a face that a man might die for.

A tremor, then the feeling broadens into an oscillation, throbbing two or three times, before finally bursting forth as a searing pang (a detective is trained to see through disguise, and as I peered at the mask of time she wore, the name that conjured the image of a strange woman (how odd are words: they flash light on something in the dark, which disappears as soon as it is uttered) because of her alias (a false light flashing on a false corner)) of love—when I recognize her: *Lillie*.

Happiness rages confusedly within my heart, along with sudden fear that she will recognize me, and the whole case should be thrown up.

—Let me get a fresh bandage.

No other woman possesses that sweet brandied voice, which hangs like a jewel in my ear. It must be her.

Another voice, implacable and grave, whispers in my ear that passions are deceiving, that a beautiful face is the result of myopia, and a lovely soul the product of my ignorance, that there must come a day when the idol, to more clear-sighted eyes, will be an object, not of hate, but of surprise and scorn. People who

have adored me—there have not been very many, but there have been some—have always insisted on living on, long after I have ceased to care for them, or they to care for me. The art of the cut. In Piccadilly. Her calm but wandering gaze, which veered, as if unconsciously, round me; neither occupied, nor abstracted; a look which perhaps excused me, the person *cut*, and, at any rate, prevented me from accosting her. Never answered my letters, even though (or perhaps because) in my youth she was as true a lover as ever sighed upon a midnight pillow.

A perverse jealousy now colors my professional relationship with my client. How could she have loved him? I cannot possibly understand the attraction she had to Grover Cleveland. Her Bohemian gaiety. A momentary lapse in the Governor's ordinarily sterling judgment. I long to sabotage the candidate now and let the cat leap out of the bag. Let her proclaim to one and all that she is a political doxy. I know this is neither just nor right, but that is precisely why the notion is so appealing.

I am weakening. My objectivity is shaken. Struggling over my fickle heart, love draws it this way, scorn urges another—but love, I think, is gaining. I must act quickly before all is lost. I have the advantage because of the element of surprise. I motion for air, compelling them to open the window. So much do I now long to reveal myself to her and resume our former companionship that I am quite relieved that she leaves the room. Momentarily alone, I raise my hand, and await the results. Three quick heartbeats later, the smoke-rocket claps sharply on the parquet floor.

—Fire!—cries Wilde, his voice so disfigured by amplification and fear that it is well nigh unrecognizable. My accomplices join in the general shriek of fire. Thick clouds of smoke curl through the room and out the open window. I catch a glimpse of rushing figures. The alarm of fire is admirably done. The smoke and shouting are enough to shake nerves of steel. She responds beautifully. The birth certificate is hidden in a recess behind a

128

sliding panel just above the right bellpull. She is there in an instant, and I catch a glimpse of it as she half-draws it out. Not missing his cue, Freddie enters stage prompt, grabbing hold of her waist and rescuing her from the putative flames before she can take the birth certificate. I wade through the thickening smoke occulting the room when I collide with someone—perhaps the butler—I don't know who—and am greatly commoted. I search for a reference point when I see the panel through a tear in the curtain of smoke. There is the birth certificate, still half withdrawn. I stuff it in my coat and try to find my way out when I am overwhelmed by smoke. So violent are the spasms in my lungs that I fall to my knees. Someone collects my slackening figure and carries me through the smoke like a sleeping child in a village fair. It is Freddie. The rapidly billowing smoke rises from the windows and climbs to heaven on high.

Of all ghosts, the revenants of our old loves are the worst.

She loves him now. O, how bitter a thing it is to look into happiness through another man's eyes!

To believe is very dull. To doubt is intensely
interesting. To be on the alert is to live;
to be lulled into security is to die.

—Oscar Wilde

They bear his corpse-like body into the drawing room and lay him on the couch. My heart senses emerging tragedy. It would be blackest treachery to draw back now from the part which Holmes had entrusted to me. I harden my heart and take the smoke-rocket from the vestpocket of my purple velvet waistcoat. After all, we are not injuring her. We are preventing injury to another: Holmes is shielding her from political intrigue far beyond her control; and I am rekindling a love affair.

I don't know with what compunction Holmes is playing at this moment, but I know I have never felt more heartily ashamed of myself in my life than when I saw that the beautiful creature against whom I was conspiring was none other than Lillie. I hope she will forgive me for this. Better still, I hope she never finds out.

Holmes sits up on the couch. I see him motion like a man who is in need of air. A maid rushes across the room and throws open the window. An instant later, Holmes raises his hand. I toss my rocket at the signal into the room with a cry of *Fire!* A dull rage is in my heart. A woman yells something at me from an open door. Two men run to the far side of the street. A hansom driver whips his horses. Thick clouds of smoke curl through the room and out the open window. I catch a glimpse of rushing figures. A crowd takes up the hue and the cry. Freddie carries Lillie out, and leaves her under the portico. He rushes back in, and emerges with Holmes, who appears rather worse for wear. We try to revive him. Sly fox that Holmes.

—Oh, Lord!—I cry.—Is he well?

—He's comin round,—says Freddie.

Holmes coughs chokily, then comes to his senses. Lillie touches Freddie's shoulder.

—I'm very sorry,—says Freddie to Lillie,—it looks like you lost everything.

He lost not a moment in emphasizing her vulnerability and her likely dependence on him. He is not a real Don Juan. The real Don Juan is not the vulgar person who goes about making love to all the women he meets, what the novelists call *seducing* them. The real Don Juan is the man who says to a woman *Go away! I don't want you. You interfere with my life. I can do without you.* Swift was the real Don Juan. Two women died for him!

—I've lost nothing but my past,—she says with new-found emotion.—But for you I would have lost my life.

How frail and simple we are, if we indeed could see ourselves as others see us. I can keep a secret. It always pays to play fair when you are holding a winning hand.

—Don't worry, Amber,—resumes Freddie with the sincerity that only a million dollars could buy.—I'll protect you from the brutality of the world.

Romance is a privilege of the rich, not the profession of the poor. True love after true trials. So false it is. Rather, such tales of true love conceal the passions of Sade and von Sacher-Masoch.

—You are brave,—says Lillie, staring into his eyes,—And you think little of yourself. You really do love me, after all.

To believe is very dull. To doubt is to be intensely engrossing. To be on the alert is to live; to be lulled into security is to die.

They clasp in an embrace, her townhouse smoking in the background like a piece of scenery. Titian or Claude?

—Amber,—continues Freddie with declining confidence.—Ever since I met you, I have admired you more than any woman . . . I have ever met . . . I met you. . . .

She plays with his bow tie. It is true. He is frightened. He loves her.

—For me,—she says with lilt,—you have always had an irresistible fascination. Even before I met you I was far from indifferent to you.

—Do you really love me, Amber?

—Passionately.

—And we're not gonna argue any more, are we?

—We won't argue any more.

—Darling, you don't know how happy you've made me!

—I adore you. But you haven't proposed to me yet. Nothing has been said at all about marriage. The subject has not even been touched on.

—Well, howz about me proposin now?

—Please.

Once a week, I believe, is quite enough to propose to anyone, and it should always be done in a manner that attracts attention.

—If you believe that marriage between two intelligent people is a social bond, but not necessarily a moral bond, I suppose I would go along with that. But if I catch you with another man, I'll kill him!

Romance lives by repetition, and repetition converts an appetite to an art. Besides, each tune one loves is the only tune one has loved. Difference of the object does not alter singleness of passion.

—I promise never to make you look ridiculous before the world,—replies Lillie, airily.—Oh, Freddie, how I love you!

—Amber, will you marry me?

—Oh, Freddie, you've made me the happiest woman on earth!

Holmes is alert now. He has been listening avidly, judging from the peculiar expression on his normally unresponsive face. Freddie turned suddenly to Holmes, as only a man activated by an idea à l'improviste can.

—Will you do us the honor of performing the wedding ceremony?

—Why . . . um. . . .

By Jove, he is a great actor: coughing, crying, struggling for words against strong emotion. Why didn't he just faint? Women do it all the time. It saves them from all sorts of awkward situations. That's how women defend themselves. They attack by surrendering.

—The poor clergyman has need of medical assistance,— I volunteer.—He'll recover soon enough.

A mock wedding may be the ideal solution. Gebhard *père* would be appeased. Lillie can act; Holmes can act; and if the false clergyman be revealed at any time subsequent to the disbursement of funds, the wedding may be nullified without harm to anyone. Brilliant!

—I forgot all about a clergyman,—exclaims Freddie aloud.— This gentleman is a godsend, and he shall be richly rewarded.

Holmes moans expressively.

—Surely no one else can be found,—I venture with some devilish advocation, hoping that Freddie will endorse the solution. All of the planning had gone into the event of winning Lillie, whereas not enough thought was given as to what was to be done afterward.

I help Holmes to his feet. He has no choice in the matter now. He must perform the wedding ceremony for the benefit of one and all.

—Let's go, Reverend; we have our work cut out for us.

—Come along, Oscar,—says Lillie.—You be our witness, otherwise it won't be legal.

—Let's go!—soldiers Freddie.

We drag the reluctant Reverend with us and crowd into Freddie's carriage.

—Do you have the ring?—whimpers Holmes.

—That I remembered!—answers Freddie as he opens a small jewel box of teak and displays the diamond. Lillie, favorably impressed, deigns to accept it.

Soul and body, body and soul—how mysterious they are! There is an animalism in the soul, and the body has its moments of

spirituality. The senses can refine, and the intellect can degrade. Who could say where the fleshy impulse ceased, or the physical impulse began? How shallow are the arbitrary definitions of the ordinary psychologists! And yet how difficult to decide between the claims of the various schools! Is the soul a shadow seated in the house of sin? Or is the body really in the soul, as Giordano Bruno thought? The separation of spirit from matter is a mystery, and the union of spirit with matter is a mystery also.

III

Danger is part of my trade.

—Sherlock Holmes

Loneliness is never more cruel than when it is felt in close propinquity to someone who has ceased to communicate.*

I have so strange a heart that I am myself perplexed. I strive to obscure the growing luster of my eyes. Time and again my tongue stiffens mutely in my mouth when I need it—although mouth and tongue are both there, they are neither dead nor alive. Sorrow and duty make me forsake my right to speak, and I resign myself to lugubrious surveillance.

Fortunate is the man who sits next to her. Whoever looks into Lillie's eyes feels heart and soul refined like gold under the white-hot flame of love; life becomes a joy to live. Other women are neither eclipsed nor diminished by Lillie in the manner touted by other lovers for their ladies. Her beauty beautifies others. None needs to be abashed because of her.

Note a strange thing here: I am in flight from strife and suffering, yet I seek out strife and suffering. I flee the upheavals of the past, yet now I seek mortal peril by my truculent and irrational desire to be in her arms again, thus rendering myself vulnerable to Moriarty's clutches. What's the use of fleeing death on the one hand and following death on the other? That is not logical.

Impossible to forget you. They say there have been poets who have lived all their lives with their eyes fixed on a beloved image. In fact, I believe (but I am too directly involved) that fidelity is one of the signs of genius.

You are more than an image dreamed of and cherished, you are (and here I venture to use an illogical expression) my superstition.

When I do something utterly stupid, I say to myself: My Heavens! What if she knew? When I do something that is good, I say to myself: That's something that brings me nearer to her—in spirit.

Although Lillie fixes her gaze on me, she doesn't see; and though she hears, she doesn't understand. Her behavior indicates that she will make a scene if she is told the truth, and therefore implicitly asks to be deceived.* That is the narrow margin of safety in which I move. I must keep a firm grip on my nerves lest she misalign the powerful vectors of thought generated by the scientific instrument otherwise known as my brain. I secretly tap the birth certificate resting securely in my breastpocket. All's well that ends.

Fifth Avenue veers fashionably into view as our carriage turns into a broad, well-paved and superbly built street lined with mansions of brownstone, marble and lighter colored stones that give a pleasing effect by gaslight.

She, cradled in Mr Gebhard's indecent arms, is still looking at me. The more man cultivates the mind, the less he copulates. The divorce between the intelligent man and the brute becomes more and more apparent. Only the brute copulates well, and sexual union is the lyricism of the people. *Am Anfang.* Proof cannot dispel the fog.** The past has still not passed.

Details. Lillie is bringing back into fashion the black satin dress. No one has worn such a dress for forty years because the murderess, Mrs Maria Manning, chose to be hanged in a black satin dress, trimmed with black lace, and a black veil. This re-

---

sulted in black satin abruptly going out of fashion among Victorian womenfolk. Thus, stupidity is often the ornament of beauty; it gives to the eyes the dull limpidity of blackish pools and the oily calm of tropical seas.

Love's blindness blinds outside and in. It blinds a man's eyes and mind so that they do not wish to see what is plainly put before them. What should be done by the man caught between an hereditary and paternal taste for morality and an overpowering desire for a woman worthy of scorn? Numerous base infidelities, an habitual liking for low places, shameful secrets accidentally discovered inspire horror for one's idol . . . virtue and pride cry out: *Flee*. Nature whispers: *Where can you flee?* Less vicious, my ideal would have been less complete. I contemplate it and I submit. . . .

My powers of observation, once my means of existence, are now turning against me as an instrument of torture, the condign punishment reserved for those who kill love.

St Helier. Was it ten years ago? The nine o'clock evening train from Waterloo. Then the eleven forty-five overnight steamer from Southampton transports me to an island of roast chestnut barrows in festive streets; a market hung with Christmas turkeys, geese, chickens and whole pigs stuffed with holly; hardscrabble Breton peasants clattering along in sabots; fleas performing under a magnifying glass in the tobacconist's shop on King Street; the town crier with his handbell bellowing out the news of Reggie's death in the Market Square.[*]

The iron wheels of the funeral carriages, black pennants rippling, fumble over the gravel of St Saviour's Hill to the old churchyard. Lillie wept from grief and guilt, so unlike her now.

---

[*] *St Helier ... death in the Market Square*. From *The Prince and the Lilly*, by James Brough, Coward McCann & Geoghegan, Inc.: New York, 1974. By permission of Penguin Group (USA) Inc.

Was harder on the mother. Sorrow for the last child of her household. Solemnity to such moments when the family must be informed. Rumors that the dead man was in love with his sister. Consigned that to silence. I ruled Reggie's death a suicide, and left them to ponder his motives. Later the dead man's sister made me hot chocolate when the rest of the family was fast asleep. Asked me to untie a knot in her hair. I touched the nape of her neck. *That's how love begins.*

I still remember every detail of our last meeting in London.

Must get a grip. Observe, else all is lost.

The cab pulls up with its steaming horses before Freddie's ancestral mansion. One end was gabled, and the other turreted, giving the mansion a distinctive, if peculiar effect.

A carpet is spread from the doorway to the edge of the sidewalk, and a temporary awning erected over this. A policeman keeps off the crowd of lookers-on such an occasion invariably draws.

Between nine and ten hansom carriages, with servants in livery, drive up and deposited their passengers at the awning. Thence they pass to the dressing room, to divest themselves of their wraps, after which they descend to the drawing room and pay their respects to the host, Mr Frederick Gebhard, Sr. We avail ourselves of a private side entrance.

The interior of the house is in keeping with its external grandeur. It is decorated in magnificent style, furnished in the most superb and costly manner; and adorned with rare and valuable works of art. All that is required of me is to perform an ordinary wedding ceremony. It means nothing to me. A wedding, a ball, a soiree is nothing more or less than a great marketplace of beauty where daughters and wives are corrupted. Thus, Lillie sells her honor for filthy lucre. She acts with her eyes open, and sins deliberately, and from the basest of motives. She wants money and she gets it. And then follow intrigues that go undetected.

I analyze women in terms of two Platonic types: the mother and the prostitute. Each individual woman is a combination of the two, but is predominantly one or the other. The chief difference between the two types is the form that their obsession with sex takes: whereas the mother is obsessed with the object of sex, the prostitute is obsessed with the act itself.

All women, whether mothers or prostitutes, share a single characteristic, which is really and exclusively feminine—and that is the instinct of matchmaking, first and foremost in her own *only vital interest*—but also in the interest that sexual union shall take place; the wish that as much of it as possible shall occur, in all cases, places and times.

—Aw, Miss Jay, saw you joying the races to-day,—said the high-toned young man.

—Yeth; they're awfully jawly, ain't they? Right fun to bet, ain't it?—replied the young lady of high position.

A pewtery grey hue hovers over her gown and the drawing room.

—Ya-as, rawther jawly to bet when you win, you know; but beastly, awfully beastly, to bet and lose, you know.

It is, of course, fashionable to be wealthy. Indeed, it is unfashionable to know exactly the extent of one's resources. It is also fashionable and neatly convenient to have part of one's money *in the funds*. And it is highly fashionable to go hopelessly into debt, for which the fashionable remedy is a discreet removal to the Continent. There are even fashionable money lenders.

I move on through the crowd. A lady greets Wilde.

—Where's your lily, Mr Wilde?

—At home, Madame,—the Oracle replies tartly,—with your manners.

He segues effortlessly into another conversation. All sorts of nincompoopiana from idlers languidly drooling over *cultuh*, flowers, china, beauty and intensity.

—That is your error, Oscar, believe me. You value beauty far too much.

141

—How can you say that? I admit that I think that it is better to be beautiful than to be good. But on the other hand no one is more ready than I am to acknowledge that it is better to be good than to be ugly.

—Ugliness is one of the seven deadly sins, then?—cries the dowager.—What becomes of your simile about the orchid?

—Ugliness is one of the seven deadly virtues, Gladys. You must not underrate them. Beer, the Bible, and the seven deadly virtues have made our England what she is, and will make America what she will be.

—You don't like your country, then?—she asks piquantly.

—I live in it.

I chortle at expressions like *superlatively aesthetic* and *consummately soulful* that Wilde weaves into his banter.

—You have no ruins, no natural curiosities in this country,— Wilde remarks to Mrs Pendleton.

—No, but our ruins will come soon enough,—she answers,— and we import our curiosities.

I dread captivating people. I saunter to the window: air.

A mock reverend presiding over a mock wedding anticipating its mock issue. The native American population is actually dying out year by year; the births from couples born in this country are less in proportion than those from couples of European birth. I attribute it to the diminishing virility of husbands, or to the increasing tendency to sterility among their wives. Perhaps there is a deliberate and widespread agreement that American women shall be childless or the next thing to it. My nerves, formerly of steel, begin to tremble with self-loathing and nausea upon reaching this conclusion. I know not why. I wring my hands. I turn paler than grass. All must be endured but. . . .

—Help me, Wilde,—I say after kidnapping him from his enthralled listeners.—I don't think I can go through with this sham.

—You must perform the ceremony.

—It shall not be legal.

—You not long ago asked me if I had any objection to breaking the law in order to aid your investigation. Please reciprocate and do as much for me,—retorts the Aesthete.

—Perhaps I should leave quietly.

—Then they would suspect something. I suggest you faint.

—I shall not faint. Only women faint.

—What?! Then pretend you are sick!

—I am sick.

I recline on a davenport when the Butler approaches. I fear that the ceremony is about to begin.

—Reverend, there is a gentleman who requests a private interview with you in the library.

—The Reverend is not feeling well,—Wilde protests.

—Who is it?

—The gentleman did not say, sir.

My curiosity piqued, I rise to seek distraction.

—I shall return. The change of scene will help me.

One of the female guests makes a deprecatory motion to let me pass.

—Do not move, Madam,—I say.—I can find my way.

I can hear Wilde *putting on the dog* downstairs as I climbed the wide-staired hallway. The butler closes the door and sweeps away the clamor of the fashionable crowd downstairs.

Near the top of the stairs, a door resting ajar. Light and cheerful feminine voices spill forth into the corridor. Walking through the majestic archway, I investigate further. I find a marble pool filled with turquoise water. Lillie is poised next to it. She gives one maid her jewels, and to another her dress. Two other maids undo her shoes, and still another takes her undergarments. An older maid, more experienced than the rest, deftly ties her flowing hair into a knot. My strength ebbs. I know not where I have been, and know even less where I am going.

—You've a large 'ead, madam,—says the elderly maid with adorable cockney elocution.—That means you 'ave a large brain, for it nourishes the roots of the 'air.

Resplendent in her nakedness, Lillie, goddess of my secret life, enters the pool and bathes in its crystal waters. The maids pour water on her from good-sized urns. But the older maid catches sight of me.

—A man!—she cries.

The maids, all naked, beat their breasts and scream. All together they gather round Lillie to shield her with their own bodies, but Lillie stands head and shoulders above them. As the clouds grow red at sunset, as the daybreak reddens, Lillie blushes at being seen, and turns aside from her companions. Finding no weapon except for water, she flings it in my face.

—Get out!

The Butler reappears at that very moment only to become the unwilling recipient of Lillie's aquatic assault.

—This way, Reverend,—he says with good form as water drips from his brow.

Lead, kindly light.

My nerves are fairly proof, but I must confess to a start when I enter the library and see the very man who had been so much in my thoughts standing there on the threshold. His appearance is quite familiar to me. He is extremely tall and thin, his forehead domes out in a white curve, and his two eyes are deeply sunken in his head. He is a grave-looking man of forty, wearing an iron gray upper lip brush and imperial; he is pale and ascetic-looking, retaining something professorial in his features. His shoulders are rounded from much study, and his face protrudes forward and is forever slowly oscillating from side to side in a curiously reptilian fashion. He peers at me with great curiosity with his puckered eyes.

—You have less frontal development than I should have expected,—says Professor Moriarty at last.—It is a dangerous habit to finger a loaded firearm in the pocket of one's vestments.

The fact is that upon my entrance I instantly recognized the extreme personal danger in which I lay. In an instant I slipped the revolver into my hand and covered him through the cloth. At

his remark I draw the weapon out and lay it cocked upon the table. He smiles and blinks, but there is something about his eyes which makes me feel very glad that I have it here.

—You evidently know me,—he says.

—I think it is fairly evident that I do. Pray take a chair. I can spare you five minutes if you have anything to say.

—All I have to say has already crossed your mind,—said he.

—Then possibly my answer has crossed yours.

—You stand fast?

—Absolutely.

He claps his hand into his pocket. I raise the pistol from the table. But he merely withdraws a memorandum book in which he had scribbled some dates.

—You crossed my path on the sixteenth of June,—says he.— On the twenty-seventh of July you incommoded me; by the middle of August I was seriously inconvenienced by you; at the end of March I was absolutely hampered in my plans; and now I find myself placed in such a position through your continual persecution that I am in positive danger of losing my liberty. The situation is becoming an impossible one.

—Have you any suggestions to make?

—You must drop it, Mr Holmes,—says he, swaying his face about.—You really must, you know.

—After Tuesday.

—Tut, tut!—his tongue clacks.—I am quite sure that a man of your intelligence will see that there can be but one outcome to this affair. It is necessary that you should withdraw. You have worked things in such a fashion that we have only one resource left. It has been an intellectual treat to me to see the way in which you have grappled with this affair, and I say, unaffectedly, that it would be a grief to me to be forced to take any extreme measure. You smile, sir, but I assure you that it really would.

—Danger is part of my trade.

—This is not danger,—he elaborates.—It is inevitable destruction. You stand in the way not merely of an individual but

of a mighty organization, the full extent of which you, with all your cleverness, have been unable to realize. You must stand clear, Mr Holmes, or be trodden underfoot.

—I am afraid,—I answer, rising,—that in the pleasure of this conversation I am neglecting business of importance which awaits me elsewhere.

He also rises and regards me silently, shaking his head sadly.

—Well, well,—sighs he at last.—It seems a pity, but I have done what I could. I know every move of your game. You can do nothing before Monday. It has been a duel between you and me, Mr Holmes. You hope to place me in the dock. I tell you that I will never stand in the dock. You hope to beat me. I tell you that you will never beat me. If you are clever enough to bring destruction upon me, rest assured that I shall do as much to you.

—You have paid me several compliments, Professor Moriarty. Let me pay you one in return when I say that if I were assured of the former eventuality I would, in the interest of the public, cheerfully accept the latter.

—I can promise you the one, but not the other,—he snarls.

Moriarty makes a sudden plunge; he seizes the revolver from the table and at the same instant aims the gun at my head, rapidly pulling the trigger several times in succession, but the hammer clicks as it strikes an empty chamber. I turn quietly toward him, still holding a match to my pipe, so that I look down the barrel of the gun at the last empty click.

—Oh, here!—I say, as if recollecting something. I toss the match away, and feeling quickly in the pocket of my trousers, I withdraw the bullets, which I toss carelessly onto the table.

—I didn't suppose you wanted to use that thing—so I took the bullets out and put them in my pocket. You'll find them all there, Professor!

Moriarty glares at me with infinite contempt, and flinging the revolver down and across the table with not the slightest regard for the property of others, mars and chips its lovely finish. Boiling with rage, he picks up his hat and rushes out the door.

This is my singular interview with Professor Moriarty. I confess that it leaves an unpleasant effect upon my mind. His soft, precise fashion of speech leaves a conviction of sincerity which a mere bully could not produce.

There remains the nagging question of how Professor Moriarty knew of my whereabouts and how he gained entry to this private affair.

A tick later, the door surges open. I swing about and aim the revolver into the emergent face.

Stop. It is Wilde.

—Holmes,—cries Wilde,—put that confounded weapon away! The bride and groom are about to make their entrance. It is time!

Is insincerity such a terrible thing? I think not.
It is merely a method by which we can multiply
our personalities.

—Oscar Wilde

This American wedding reminds me of one of Edgar Allen Poe's exquisite poems, because it is full of belles. My conversations with American women are delightful. American women are bright, clever, and wonderfully cosmopolitan. Their patriotic feelings are limited to an admiration for Niagara and a regret for the Elevated Railway; and, unlike the men, they never bore me with Bunker Hill.

Meanwhile, I am going to enjoy myself.

I consider New York's world of fashion to be the largest, gayest, most lavish and piquant I have ever seen. Its dinner courses are tediously elaborate, its menus monuments of costliness. The serpent of extravagance lurks at the table, flashing coarsely like a silver dollar, its folds hidden under blossoms and foliage.... Fashion arbiters are quarreling over the proper disposition of napkins by dinner guests: should they be folded neatly or abandoned in deshabille? Women dress as no other women out of Paris do. It is *the thing* with them to be gracious. I regard the New York belle as the brightest talker in the world. It is a delicious whirl!

Holmes is having a rough go of it. He seems unable or unwilling to discuss serious matters with members of the opposite sex. In mixed company his conversation is often trivial in the extreme, and larded with feeble jokes accompanied by a wintry smile.[*] Perhaps he will find anhedonistic distraction in the library.

---

[*] *In mixed company ... a wintry smile.* Reprinted with the permission of The Free Press, a Division of Simon & Schuster Adult Publishing Group, from *LUDWIG WITTGENSTEIN: The Duty of Genius*, by Ray Monk. Copyright © 1990 by Ray Monk. All rights reserved. Published in the UK by Jonathan Cape. Reprinted with permission of The RandomHouse Group Ltd.

Fleur-de-lys wallpapering . . . *makes one think in a circle.*
—Do not the Parisians wear Mother Hubbard coats and large Kate Greenaway hats?

—Not at all,—I replied tartly, my beautiful memory disturbed by the nettlesome mention of these English innovations.—The genteel people wear very small bonnets. Yes, it is true the figured stuffs are the mode, but I intend to bring the plain stuffs at once. I am tired of these mixed and figured things which are so horribly imitated by women who put together all their old duds without rhyme or reason and fancy themselves *comme il faut*. No! No! Paris has not become ridiculous yet. As to Mother Hubbard, she is an imagination; the English have tried to make her a reality.

—Freddie Gebhard to be married?—frowned a tony young man.—Impossible! A hoax!

It is true: τὸ μόνον γελᾶν τῶν ζῴων ἄνθροπον. *Let us always revere the power of humor. This young man has hit upon the truth in an instant. Only by remaining decorously silent may I scotch his lightning insight, and he will subsequently forget. That is womanly cunning and guile.*

—It is perfectly true. This is his wedding.

—To whom?—he sagaciously asked.

—To some little actress or another.

—I can't believe it. It's too foolish, even for Freddie!

—Freddie is far too wise not to do exceptionally foolish things now and then.

—Marriage is hardly a thing that one can do now and then.

—Except in America,—I rejoined languidly.—But even the American freedom of divorce, questionable though it undoubtedly is on many grounds, has at least the merit of bringing into marriage a new element of romantic uncertainty. When people are tied together for life they too often regard manners as a mere superfluity and courtesy as a thing of no moment; but where the bond can easily be broken, its very fragility makes its strength and reminds the husband that he should always try to be

149

pleasing, and the wife that she should never cease to be charming. Either because of or in spite of this freedom of action, I
think scandals are extremely rare in America, and should one
occur, so paramount in society is female influence that it is the
man who is never forgiven. America is the only country in the
world where Don Juan is not appreciated. American men, I conclude, are docile domestic creatures. If the English girl ever met
him, she would marry him; and if she married him, she would be
happy. For, though he may be rough in manner and deficient in
the picturesque insincerity of romance, yet he is invariably kind
and thoughtful, and has succeeded in making his own country
the Paradise of Women. This, however, is perhaps why, like
Eve, women are always so anxious to get out of it.

—Is the bride a good woman?

—Oh, she's better than good, she is beautiful,—I murmured,
sipping a glass of vermouth and orange-bitters.

—Why aren't they marrying in church?

—In church! What a baroque fancy! *Quelle idée, vraiment on
mourra de froid.*

The English style is now the *correct thing* at fashionable
weddings. Society here once imitated Paris; it now imitates London. To be thought English is their chief delight—to part their
hair and their names in the middle, to wear coats too small for
them, and to carry their arms like half-paralyzed apes, toddling
along the streets in trousers so small it's a wonder how they got
into them, and conducting themselves generally in a tipsy, halt-
ing, semi-idiotic manner, so sickening to every healthy intellect.
It is said that nine-tenths of the people who had taken up the new
fad of eyeglasses did so only to be able to give a *strong British
stare!* I deplore the Anglomania which has done so much to
change the social tone of New York. Not long ago the New York
swell had a French tailor, a French bootmaker and cultivated
French manners. It was sociable, democratic, and something or
other remotely resembling what prevailed in Paris. The British
caste system, on the other hand, is supplanting the French re-

publicanism of Jefferson and democracy in America's social world.

The organ breaks forth into the exquisite strains of the *Bridal Chorus* from Lohengrin, and the bridegroom enters from the vestry room, accompanied by his best man, while the Reverend—speaking of the Reverend, he is supposed to file into the ballroom—

Must I fetch him? Yes, and hurry. One flight up through a spacious entrance, then a wide-staired hallway finished in oakwood with landings of the new and elaborate tile composition. I enter the library, quite rich yet restrained within the bounds of most rigid taste.

My heart stops beating, then beats twice as fast when Holmes spins on his heel and points a revolver at my nose. This is madness. One false move, one single squeeze of the trigger—

—Holmes!—I cry.—Put that confounded weapon away! Come, it is time. The bride is about to make her entrance!

The organ fills the ballroom with a low undertone of delicate harmony. The bridal party enters, led by the bride. Lillie make her stunning entrance wearing a Grecian draped gown of white velvet. The great doors of the room are thrown open as we decorously hurry down the stairs just as the Lohengrin Chorus ends.

There is a latent abandon in her manner that distinguishes her from tamer members of her sex. She walks like a beautiful hound set upon its feet. She never encased her statuesque body in the tightly laced whalebone corsets that fashion calls for, and she is disinclined to start now. Hours spent with curling irons and tissue paper strike her as being time wasted. She wears her long hair brushed to a gleam. Since she cannot afford clothes from *Renfrew* or *Worth* in Paris, she turns the shortcomings of her wardrobe into a form of distinction. She deliberately flouts a

convention that compels less adventuresome women to dress themselves in a new gown for every occasion.*

The clubmen revel in the gossip that she wears no corsets, with their telltale creak. If a man gets close enough, he can see the three *plis de Venus* in her neck. If he follows her up a staircase, he may glimpse ankles as pretty as any thoroughbred's.

She is a cunning young witch, too, who in the seclusion of her little drawing room swoons at the sight of a handsome man, irresistibly tempting him to take her in his arms.

I lead Holmes by hand to the altar, always cognizant of the revolver tucked under his coat. Pious silence greets our arrival.

Rev Holmes joins his hands and spires his fingers before facing the audience.

—Brothers and Sisters in Christ,—he sermonizes,—costly clothes, which the Scripture utterly condemns, must be absolutely banned. The Lord warns us especially against them, and condemns the pride in them of the rich man who was damned. St Gregory draws attention to this in his Sixth Homily on the Gospels—

We're not going to suffer through any more of this. Why offend fashionable people with the Gospels? I kick Holmes' ankle. Before he knew it he found himself mumbling responses which I whispered in his ear, and vouching for things of which he knew nothing.

—Will you please join hands,—says Holmes upon my prompt.

Lillie and Freddie join hands. Her lovely white complexion took a pinkish cast from her rising blood.

---

* *Hours spent with curling irons ... a new gown for every occasion.* The Prince and the Lilly, by James Brough, Coward McCann & Geoghegan, Inc.: New York, 1974. By permission of Penguin Group (USA) Inc.

—Do you, Frederick Gebhard Jr, bachelor, take *Lil*—Amber Halpin—as your lawfully wedded wife?

Lillie reacts with astonishment to this vocable. Potential insult and injury mar her lovely features. Her gaze trembles upon the unfortunate Reverend. How did Holmes guess her true identity? Where is Holmes' legendary self-command?

—I do,—replied Freddie.

—Do you, Amber Halpin, take Frederick Gebhard, Jr to be your lawfully wedded husband?—continues Holmes' quavering voice.

—I do.

—I now pronounce you m–m–man and wife. You m–m–may kiss the b-b-bride.

They kiss.

Thus I contributed to the secure tying up of Amber Halpin (Lillie Langtry), spinster, to Freddie Gebhard, Jr, bachelor. It was all done in an instant, and there are the gentlemen thanking me on the one side and the ladies on the other, while Mr Gebhard, Sr beams with pride at having meddled successfully in his son's life.

Are these the most preposterous circumstances in which I have ever found myself? The canons of good society are, or should be, the same as the canons of art. Form is absolutely essential to it. It should have the dignity of ceremony, as well as its unreality, and should combine the insincere character of a romantic play with the wit and the beauty that makes such plays delightful to us. Is insincerity such a terrible thing? I think not. It is merely a method by which we multiply our personalities.

Holmes, relieved that the ordeal is over, quite visibly needs a bowl of shag to settle his nerves. He fumbles for his meerschaum and lights it with a loud, crackling match. Lillie takes immediate notice. I can see the idea playing itself out in her face. In the dim arrested light that struggles through her cream colored silk veil, her face appears to me to be a little changed. One might

say that there is a touch of cruelty in the mouth. It is certainly strange.

—You're no reverend!—cries Lillie.

Holmes turned instantly with his full attention, understanding too late the nature of his *faux pas* and how his meerschaum betrayed his identity.

—You're Sherlock Holmes!

Lillie, who is no one's fool, hikes up her dress and kicks Reverend Holmes vehemently in the shins. Holmes bunnyhops around the room until he regains his balance by holding on to an armchair. I cannot help but laugh out loud with the wedding guests. A glaze of confusion frosts Freddie's face. He wants someone to explain things to him.

—What are you laughing at?—she shouts, venting her rage on me.

—Nothing,—I reply, wiping the smile off my face.

—What's the matter, darling?—asks Freddie.

—Oh, shut up!

Old man Gebhard twirls his mustache zestfully.

—Nothing like married life to take a wild youth, is there?

—Hey, Oscar, what's goin on?—pleads Freddie.

—Her name is not Amber Halpin. She is Lillie Langtry,—I reply.

Gasping cries of wonder filled the room.

—And who's Lillie Langtry?—asks the bewildered groom.

—She's the chief paramour of the Prince of Wales!—some wag discloses.

—Oh, yeah?—Freddie shoots back.—I don't care if she is bangin the Prince of Wales! I still love her!

Like Gulliver, I have discovered the Brobdingnagians.

Nothing is more unwelcome than the truth,
but only the truth can free us.

—Sherlock Holmes

Our horses gallop down the avenue as hard as they can go. The trees seem to pass us in spectral procession, and wild shadows fling themselves across the avenue. Our horses cleave the dusky air like arrows. Stones fly from their hooves.

My shin stings me still.

—You did very nicely, Wilde. Nothing could have been better. It is all right.

—You have the birth certificate?

—Here,—I say, tapping my vest pocket.

They say that genius is the infinite capacity for taking pains. It is a very bad definition, but it does apply to detective work. How? I am the consummate dramaturge of actual events. Some touch of the artist wells up within me, and calls me insistently for a well-staged performance. Surely my profession would be a drab and sordid one if I did not sometimes set the scene so as to glorify my results. The blunt accusation, the brutal tap on the shoulder—what can one make of such a *dénouement?* But the quick inference, the subtle trap, the clever forecast of coming events, the triumphant vindication of bold theories—are these not the pride and justification of my life's work?

—How did you find out?—asks Wilde, his eyes sparking with emotion.

—She showed me, as I told you she would.

—I am still in the dark.

—You know a conjurer gets no credit when once he has explained his trick; and if I show you too much of my method of working, you will come to the conclusion that I am a very ordinary individual after all.

—I shall never do that,—he answers.—You have raised detection to an art form.

—I do not wish to make a mystery,—say I, laughing.—The matter was perfectly simple. You, of course, saw that everyone in the street was an accomplice. They were all engaged for the evening.

—I guessed as much.

—Then, when the row broke out, I had a little moist red paint in the palm of my hand. I rushed forward, fell down, clapped my hand to my face, and became a piteous spectacle. It is an old trick.

—That also I could fathom.

—Then they carried me in. She was bound to have me in. What else could she do? And into her sitting room, which was the very room which I suspected. It lay between that and her bedroom, and I was determined to see which. They laid me on the couch. When I motioned for air, they were compelled to open the window, and you had your chance.

—How did that help you?

—It was all-important. When a woman thinks that her house is on fire, her instinct is at once to rush to the thing that she values most. Now it was clear to me that our lady of today had nothing in the house more precious to her than what we were in quest of. She would rush to secure it. The alarm of the fire was admirably done. The smoke and shouting were enough to shake nerves of steel. She responded beautifully. The birth certificate was in a recess behind a sliding panel just above the right bellpull. She was there an instant, and I caught a glimpse of it as she half-drew it out, but Freddie had come in and whisked her away to safety before she could take it with her. I made my way through the thick smoke, found the drawer, and secured the document in question.

—It looks as though I've lost my wager,—says Wilde.—And now?

—Our quest is practically finished. We shall now call upon the Honorable Grover Cleveland. It might be a satisfaction to him to regain it immediately.

—It appears that the wedding was a complete fiasco.

—The wedding was a farce played on behalf of your play.

—All the world's a stage, but the play is badly cast,—huffs Wilde.

—That was a personal sacrifice I made on your behalf.

—Self-sacrifice is a thing that should be put down by law. It is so demoralizing to the people for whom one sacrifices oneself. They always go to the bad.

—You cannot lose graciously, can you?

—Returning to our subject, you actually saw through Amber's disguise. You blundered on a vital syllable of her true name at a critical moment during the ceremony.

—Yes.

He is onto something. Diminish importance.

—What is the exact nature of your connection with Lillie Langtry?

I am far more concerned about concealing my meeting with Professor Moriarty, and the sickening feeling that everyone in New York knows my true identity. I shall not become a transparent thing, an open book for all men's eyes to peruse.

—That, Wilde, is a private matter. It suffices to say that her father once hired me to perform an investigation into a private family matter.

He studies me for a moment. He doesn't believe me.

—Wilde, dear fellow, life is infinitely stranger than anything which the mind of man could invent. We would not dare to conceive the things which are really mere commonplaces of existence. If we could fly out of that window hand in hand, hover over this great city, gently remove the roofs, and peep in at the queer things which are going on, the strange coincidences, the plannings, the cross-purposes, the wonderful chain of events, working through generations, and leading to the most *outré* results, it would make all fiction with its conventionalities and foreseen conclusions most stale and unprofitable.

157

—Then please explain why you had your revolver drawn when I had to fetch you from the library?

—That, too, Wilde, is a matter that must remain confidential for the time being.

—Holmes, you are an impossible person. You have ruined my friendship with Lillie and Freddie, which meant something to me. When Lillie finds out about the smoke-rocket, she will certainly designate me for censure and accuse me of being your treacherous partner. Freddie will hold me similarly accountable. She will ask for my head to be handed to her on a platter—how will I ever produce my play?

—That, Wilde, is your personal agenda, which exists outside the proper parameters of our professional association, which is mercantile in nature. Do not interfere.

He is peeved.

—Cheer up, old man, the Governor will pay us the balance of our fee tonight, and you shall earn enough money to produce your own play.

—Freddie says that the costumes alone will cost ten thousand dollars—sniffs Oscar.

I will never understand theatrical people. They actually spend hard-earned money to create illusions.

—Love versus Logic. Ha! Wilde, they say a fool and his money are easily parted.

The carriage ground to a halt before the Governor's hotel. We were ushered into the sitting room to wait for his Honor.

* * *

—You have really got it!—cries Cleveland, rushing into the room as Wilde and I were engaged upon brandy and cigarettes. He grasps my either shoulder and looks eagerly into my face.

—Your Honor, all of your troubles have vanished. Less than an hour ago, I performed a wedding ceremony, joining Amber in holy matrimony.

—Married! When?

—Less than an hour ago.

—But to whom?

—To Freddie Gebhard, a New York millionaire.

—But she could not love him.

—It is a marriage of convenience, your Honor,—said Wilde,—and Holmes, in his reverential guise, personally married them.

Great peals of laughter burst forth from Cleveland's Gargantuan frame.

—Therefore, there is no reason why she should interfere with your Honor's candidacy.

—Holmes, you are a clever devil. I wish I had been there to see you marry her. What a marvelous hoax!—says Cleveland with a merry voice.

—I was ineluctably drawn into performing the ceremony in the process of obtaining the birth certificate.

Cleveland's laughter inspires Wilde and me to join him in hilarity and high spirits. I, of course, have a hundred things I want not to say to him. How would he laugh if he learned that Lillie was once mine, as well. To know everything is indeed a heavy burden to bear. This case, however, proves that one man's folly is another man's wife.

—I wish she had been of my own station,—declares Cleveland at length with foolish and ignorant sentiment.—What a First Lady she would have made. Alas ... you *do* have the confounded birth certificate in your possession, don't you?

I withdraw the document from my pocket with panache.

—Here it is.

I hand him the envelope.

—Women are never entirely to be trusted—not even the best of them.

He removes the certificate, hesitating a moment.

—What a woman—oh, what a woman!—he exclaimed.— Isn't it a pity that she is not on my level?

—From what I have seen of the lady,—I remark dryly,—she seems indeed to be on a very different level from your Honor.

159

—If I may say so,—submits Wilde,—Amber Halpin is really Lillie Langtry—a great *artiste* who cannot be judged by ordinary standards. She bores you because she lacks the indefinable charm of weakness. It is the clay feet that make the gold of the image precious. Her feet are very pretty but they are not feet of clay. White porcelain feet, if you like. They have been through fire, and what fire does not destroy it hardens. She has had experiences.

—Lillie Langtry, eh? Is that who she is? She goes by a thousand names, and she is certainly a termagant by whatever name she is called. But, oh, what a woman!

—Indeed, if she were blind, she might find an ideal marriage with a deaf man.

—Holmes, you shall be rewarded promptly,—pronounces the Governor.

—As to my reward, my profession is its own reward, and your kindly advance defrayed the most significant expenses.

His forehead glistens with perspiration. The envelope trembles in his hand.

Nothing is more unwelcome than the truth, but only the truth can free us. Yet I shall reveal no more about Lillie. Cleveland sighs heartily as he opens the envelope and reads the enclosed document. . . .

I shall want no more than the satisfactory conclusion of this case. Is it pride or piety? Is it a foolish excess of self-satisfaction, or is it really a sacred and noble instinct? Nevertheless, when I ponder over the marvelous pleasures I have enjoyed, I would be tempted to offer God a prayer of thanks for not creating me a millwright, a vaudevillian, a physician, etc.! I feel a surge of solemn happiness, and yet it seems to me that I am

thinking of nothing: it is a sensuous pleasure that pervades my entire being.

Wilde is not cognizant of the fact that the age of beauty* has come and gone. Mankind may wax nostalgic about it and long for its return, but society has no use for it now. As art progresses, it shall become scientific, just as science will become an art. Set in opposition early in the course of civilization, the two shall be united again when they reach the apex of their development. It is one step beyond the grasp of human thought today to envision the cold, hard, Socratic light the inventions of the future will radiate. Meanwhile, we grope our way through the shadowy caverns of existence. We are without Archimedes' giant lever, the earth is twisting, crumbling, yielding under our feet, for we lack a foundation. What's the good of it all? Is our nincompoopiana the answer to any problem? No bond exists between ourselves and the *hoi polloi*, much to the disadvantage of us both. Nevertheless, since in the great chain of causality there must be a discernible reason for all things, and since the imagination of one individual is as valid as the appetites of a million others, and occupies an equal place in the world, we must live for our vocation, scale the ivory tower, and there, like a *bayadère* with her perfumes, dwell alone with our dreams. At times I have feelings of great despair and emptiness—doubts taunt me in the midst of the simplest satisfactions. And yet I would not exchange all this for anything, because my conscience tells me that I am fulfilling my duty, obeying a decree of fate— that I am doing what is Good, that I am Right.

---

* *the age of beauty has come and gone.... I am in the Right.* Adapted and reprinted by permission of the publisher from THE LETTERS OF GUSTAVE FLAUBERT: VOLUME I – 1830-1857, selected, edited and translated by Francis Steegmuller, p. 158-159, Cambridge, Mass.:   The Belknap Press of Harvard University Press, Copyright © 1979, 1980 by Francis Steegmuller.

Here, one should never make one's debut with a scandal.
One should reserve that to give an
interest to one's old age.

—Oscar Wilde

—A great *artiste* who cannot be judged by ordinary standards,—I said, but they weren't listening.

Certainly, to me Life itself is the first, the greatest, of the arts, and for it all the other arts seem to be but a preparation. Fashion, by which what is really fantastic becomes for a moment universal, and Dandyism, which, in its own way, is an attempt to assert the absolute modernity of beauty, have, of course, their fascination for me. My mode of dressing, and the particular styles that from time to time I affect, have marked influence on the young exquisites of the Mayfair balls and Pall Mall club windows, who copy me in everything that I do, and try to reproduce the accidental charm of my graceful, though to me only half-serious, fopperies.

And where has my philosophy led me? To this. A sordid affair involving Lillie's personal matters, and an involvement with Holmes whereby I have been compelled to suffer his defects. He is exceedingly loath to communicate his full plans to any other person until their instant of fulfillment. Partly it comes no doubt from his own masterful nature, which loves to dominate and surprise those who are around him. Partly also from his professional caution, which urges him never to take any chances. The result, however, is very trying for anyone acting as his agent or assistant. I often suffer under it, but never more than during the course of this evening.

Perhaps I should return to London immediately and accept the position that was almost immediately offered to me on my coming of age. Indeed, I take subtle pleasure in the thought that I am to the London of my own day what to imperial, Neronian Rome the author of the Satyricon once had been. Yet in my inmost heart I desire to be something more than a mere arbiter elegantiae, to be

consulted on the wearing of a jewel, or the knotting of a necktie, or the conduct of a cane. I seek to elaborate some new scheme of life that will have its reasoned philosophy and its ordered principles, and find in the spiritualizing of the senses its highest realization.

They conclude their transaction. Holmes produces the document which Uncle Jumbo reads with increasing emotion and agitation. Much to the consternation of Holmes and me, he slams it on his desk. Intuition, whispering in my ear, alerts me to an imminent peripateia.

—All is lost, gentlemen, all is lost!—he mutters with climbing horror.

Soullessly, he proffers the document to Holmes, which he in turn reads. Holmes' poor face suddenly assumes the most dreadful expression. He shakes his clenched hands in the air.

His eyes roll upward, his features writhe in agony, and with a suppressed groan he drops on his face upon the floor. Horrified at the suddenness and severity of the attack, we carry him into the bedroom where he lies back in a large chair and breathes heavily for some minutes.

As I read the document, my face becomes ghastly pale, and I fall back on a chair. A horrible sense of sickness comes over me. My heart is beating itself to death in some empty hollow.

—To Sherlock Holmes, a born sucker, it reads. Sincerely, Professor Moriarty.

Morituri. That name again.

Finally, with a shamefaced apology, Holmes rises once more. Near the foot of the bed stands a dish of oranges and a carafe of water. As we pass it, Holmes' face blenches and he swoons once again, knocking the whole thing over. The glass smashes into a thousand pieces and the fruit rolls about into every corner of the room.

This is a catastrophe, a disaster of Atrean dimensions.

Holmes was a mythological figure to me, and I had never doubted his resourcefulness and powers of reason. I never

thought that anyone could turn the tables on Sherlock Holmes and pay him back in kind.

Cleveland's physician is summoned and pronounces Holmes to be suffering from the strain of immense exertions and is to be confined to bed. His iron constitution broke down under the strain of investigations which had extended over five months during which period he never worked less than fifteen hours a day and had more than once, as he assured me, kept to his task seven days at a stretch. Had the issue of his labors been triumphant, it could not have saved him from such a reaction after so terrible an exertion, and he fell prey to the blackest depression. Even the knowledge that he had succeeded in the past so often where the police had failed, and that he had outmaneuvered at every point the most accomplished criminals in Europe, was insufficient to rouse him from the nervous prostration caused by the debacle.

I think I am right about something, but I don't know what.

He was trying to gather up the scarlet threads of his life, and weave them into a pattern; to find his way through the sanguine labyrinth of passion through which he was wandering. Holmes' catatonia is, at bottom, the luxury of self-reproach. When we blame ourselves we feel that no one else has the right to blame us. It is the confession, not the priest, that gives us absolution.

There will be an inquest, of course, and I cannot help but be mixed up in it. Things like this make a man fashionable in Paris. But in New York and London, people are so prejudiced. Here, one should never make one's debut with a scandal. One should reserve that to give an interest to one's old age.

Manning, Cleveland's secretary, bursts into the room.

—Rumors have reached me that *The Buffalo Telegraph* is to print a story concerning an illegitimate child Amber Halpin supposedly bore you! We'll sue for libel!

Cleveland says after a pregnant pause, with solemnity befitting the occasion, *It's all true.*

Manning gasps.

—Yes, it's true. Wire my friends in Buffalo—tell them, above all, *to tell the truth.*

How ugly it all is! And, how horribly real ugliness makes things!

Manning stirs.

—And call the newspapers—I will meet with journalists in the morning.

There are few of us who have not sometimes wakened before dawn, either after one of those dreamless nights that make us almost enamored of death, or of those nights of horror and mis-shapen joy, when through the chambers of the brain sweep phantoms more terrible than reality itself. Gradually, white fingers creep through the curtains, and they appear to tremble. In black fantastic shapes, dumb shadows crawl into the corners of the room, and crouch there. Outside, there is the stirring of birds among the leaves, or the sound of men going forth to their work, or the sigh of the wind coming down from the hills and wandering round the otherwise silent house, as though it feared to wake the sleepers, and yet must needs call forth sleep from her purple cave. Veil after veil of thin dusty gauze is lifted, and by degrees the forms and colors of things are restored to them, and we watch the dawn remaking the world in its antique pattern. The wan mirrors get back their mimic of life. The flameless tapers stand where we had left them, and beside them lies the half-cut book that we had been studying, or the wired flower that we had worn at the ball, or the letter that we had been afraid to read, or that we had read too often. Nothing seems to us changed. Out of the unreal shadows of the night comes back the real life that we have known. We have to resume it where we had left off and there steals over us a terrible sense of the necessity for the continuance of energy in the same wearisome round of stereotyped habits, or a wild longing, it may be, that our eyelids might open some morning upon a world that has been refashioned in the darkness for our pleasure, a world in which things would have fresh shapes and colors, and be changed, or have other secrets, a world in which the past would have little

or no place, or survive, at any rate, in no conscious form of obligation or regret, the remembrance of joy having its bitterness, and the memories of pleasure their pain.

I am a man made up of words.
—Sherlock Holmes

The low, heavy sky weighs like a lid on my groaning mind, victim of darkness gloomier than the night. The whole earth is changed into a rank oubliette where hope beats its intimidated wings against the walls, knocking its head against corrupt ceilings. A curtain of black rain parts to reveal a silent horde of loathsome arachnids come to spin their webs in the depths of my brain, iron bells suddenly leap with rage and hurl a frightful roar at heaven, as the homeless dead set to wailing. And long hearses, without drums or music, pass by slowly in my soul; Hope, vanquished, weeps; and atrocious, despotic Anguish on my bowed skull plants her black flag.

To my great shame, I must confess that the number of people to whom I can talk is constantly diminishing. No one is prepared to hear me discuss the meaning of meaning. Even if one's wife ran away with another man, nothing could happen to one's *self.* Thus, it is not external matters that should be of the greatest concern but one's self. The *Sorge* that prevents one facing the world with equanimity is thus a matter of more immediate concern than any misfortune that may befall one through the actions of others. Thus, the sense of solipsism shrinks to a point without extension, and there remains the reality co-ordinated with it. *Fremd*. My world is *Fremd*.[*]

Where did I err? Through the danger inherent in bad logic and false words.

---

[*] *Even if one's wife ... my world is Fremd.* Reprinted with the permission of The Free Press, a Division of Simon & Schuster Adult Publishing Group, from *LUDWIG WITTGENSTEIN: The Duty of Genius*, by Ray Monk. Copyright © 1990 by Ray Monk. All rights reserved. Published in the UK by Jonathan Cape. Reprinted with permission of The RandomHouse Group Ltd.

167

Why should one tell the truth if it is to one's advantage to lie? This dilemma intrudes in my life in the most unwelcome manner, holds me captive until I can dispel it with a satisfactory solution.

Nothing exists without a purpose.

Therefore my existence has purpose. What purpose? It is not I therefore who assigned it, but something omniscient.

Therefore I must pray for enlightenment.

But *purpose* is a word that I misattribute to existence.

No good argument for or against the existence of matter has yet been brought forward. Can I, therefore, know an object satisfying the hypotheses of physics from my private sense data? Who can imagine a method of grounding logic by working from sense-data forward?*

I may not exist at all.

* * *

There remains only one theorem or hypothesis to be tested or proved: that my thoughts are entangled and confused. It ought to be utterly simple. If I cannot cut the Gordian knot, then I must unravel the knots in my thinking, senselessly put there. I must cerebrate intricately through these complications because it is not a problem attributable to *a priori* reality but rather my perception of endlessly misleading uses of language. I must dissolve the confusion by searching for and finding *das erlösende Wort*.

Let me begin. I am now in a room, but there exists the possibility that it is not a room—it may be a chamber or a hospital,

---

* *Can I, therefore, ... sense data forward?* Reprinted with the permission of The Free Press, a Division of Simon & Schuster Adult Publishing Group, from *LUDWIG WITTGENSTEIN: The Duty of Genius*, by Ray Monk. Copyright © 1990 by Ray Monk. All rights reserved. Published in the UK by Jonathan Cape. Reprinted with permission of The RandomHouse Group Ltd.

but it is most surely enclosed in a domicile or public building. I don't know who was here before me. Maybe no one was. I cannot explain how I arrived here. Perhaps a carriage brought me hither. Person or persons unknown conveyed me because I could not transport myself here alone. But this place is not different from that place. I reside here now but I am still there despite my being here. Men and women. Women and men (sometimes I can't tell which) come to see me in a room just like this one but different. They want to know something and I find it out for them. Maybe they don't want to know something and I find it out for them. Maybe they don't want to know anything and they employ me to keep them ignorant. I don't know. They don't know. Perhaps it is high time I returned. I don't know how any more. *The Book of Life*. My vim and vigor are severely diminished. Fundamentally, I know nothing at all. My mother's death, for example. I am uncertain if I witnessed the burial or not. Maybe she is decomposing in the sunlight. Maybe not. And me? My duty is to blast into another era by replicating myself by means of offspring. Offspring are ubiquitous, and they always belong to someone else. Perchance I have a child somewhere but I doubt it rather strongly. Not a child that came from love and matrimonial bonds but a child of the flesh. It is out of the question. I am here in a state of de-progressification. I shall drop dead one day. Each effort to the contrary notwithstanding. Maybe I will live to see 1885, maybe I will creep into the next decade and celebrate the new century. I don't understand why I should want to. I have no desire to continue living. I am here, listening to the obscure sounds of my thinking *alone*, without speaking to anyone at all, because I cannot hear myself think when others are talking.

I am a man made up of words. Thinking is presumably composed of words. But I think without words in music and form. But I don't hear music anymore. So that leaves form. Propositions in the form of sentences make up the whole of reality. Propositions. But they cannot depict their own reality—logical form. What is

possible of saying, what is possible of thinking, is attainable only by means of a linguistic proposition. There. I have nothing to say about the abstract nature of propositions. Unsayable things do exist. The existence of unsayable things. I don't know. It can't express itself. You see, my brain flashes, and then dims. The more me thinks, the better me thinks. I should have said *I think* but I simply lack the will. Whither now? With whom now? I don't know what the *I* is. The *I* is someone else, something else. Incredulous to hypotheses, postulations, suppositions, syllogismatic expressions. Carry on. Carry. On. I shall recuperate here so that I may act with greater efficacy when the day comes when I must act. Maybe that is how this started. I lack power of will and self-command. Whatever happened. These words are empty folders, containing who knows what, if anything at all. I don't know. The last thing is the last thing. Doing yet undoing at once, acting and impeding at once. I am now inactive. Utterly utter. The *I* is another, declined at the bottom of an inverted pyramid of sets: you, he, she, it, we, thou, they. This regards me personally not a jot. What should I do next? What shall I do? What should I do in present circumstances? How do I advance to the next link in the chain in the pierced armor of my—my conception of my quiddity? By figures whereby the speaker shows that he doubts, either where to begin for the multitude of matters, or what to do or say in some strange or ambiguous circumstances. Is it possible to suspend judgment unwittingly? I cannot answer. My mind is blank. No, not blank, merely emulsified with nonmind. I am supposed to deal in facts, but now I don't know what a fact is. Moreover, this word too may be an empty envelope, a token of universal agreement in an empty letter mailed through time to reach me now—marked: *Fact: Return to Sender*. It is a fact that I must work my way through this catatonia by defining the undefinable, by speaking the unspeakable, by effing the ineffible, by naming . . . what was I going to say? Here now, wit! Whither wander you? No matter. I am here.

I must try again. What is force? The problem should be dealt with by restating Newtonian physics without using force as a basic concept. When these painful contradictions are removed, the question as to the nature of force will not have been answered; but our minds, no longer vexed, will cease to ask illegitimate questions.

Philosophical thinking *begins* for me with painful contradictions (and not the desire for *certain* knowledge); my aim is always to resolve those contradictions and to replace confusion with clarity.*

Now it is gone. Will never think correctly again. My solitude is unmolested. Alone. All one.

What world I am sensible of is an abyss, serene in aspect, unfathomable vortex of dream and remembrance, of action and desire, remorse and beauty whose somber depths turn us faint. Bottomless, infinite, manifold.

I have cultivated my hysteria with pleasure and terror. Now, I am always dizzy, and today, October—, 18—I feel a strange warning. I feel passing over me a wind caused by the wing of insanity.

Whereof one cannot speak thereof one must be silent.*

* *What is force? ... to replace confusion with clarity* and *Whereof one cannot speak thereof one must be silent.* Reprinted with the permission of The Free Press, a Division of Simon & Schuster Adult Publishing Group, from *LUDWIG WITTGENSTEIN: The Duty of Genius,* by Ray Monk. Copyright © 1990 by Ray Monk. All rights reserved. Published in the UK by Jonathan Cape. Reprinted with permission of The RandomHouse Group Ltd.

*Behold the wretched Sherlock Holmes, the masterful detective
who once solved the mysteries of others,
now ponders the mystery of himself.*
—Oscar Wilde

—Journalism justifies its own existence by the great Darwinian principle of the survival of the vulgarest. We are dominated by Journalism. The Americans are not uncivilized, as they are so often said to be, they are decivilized. Therefore, in America the President reigns for four years, and Journalism goes on for ever and ever.

—It is said that hardly a single American politician is worth painting; though many of them would be better for a little whitewashing. Despite the difficulties that I may encounter, allow me to synopsize the political repercussions now unfolding. It is not easy for a foreigner to comment on American politics, however, you may rely on my disinterested reportage of events. And if men and women of the future are not convinced by my narrative, I call upon time, father of truth and sober judge of stories (who reveals the hidden elements of all things) to pronounce a just sentence.

—The political situation is desperate but not serious. It is a year of economic crisis. Unemployment is ubiquitous, and the federal government is helpless to ease the distress of untold millions who are condemned to unendurable misery in the slums of America's great cities. Merchants and businessmen have no faith in the future. The depression has provoked labor to threaten rioting. Farmers, indebted to banks for life, have learned that they are puppets animated by the machinations of Wall Street, and dark mutterings are to be heard about *Money Barons*.

—The physical establishment of the government is run down; everything has gone to hell in a handcart; and even the post office is incapable of performing the elementary task of delivering the mails. Government agents are giving away vast areas

172

of the Western territories to the railroads and other corporations; lumbermen are slaughtering the forests and stockmen are fencing in the public domain. Amidst the chaos and neglect, plunderers of public resources fight for the right to pillage.

—There is a long-standing and nationwide dispute about tariffs and the question of free trade with other nations as opposed to the protection of domestic industries. All in all, America is isolationist in mood, where anything foreign is regarded with hostility. Believe me. I have felt it. Even industrial workers are inclined to the view that their jobs are in jeopardy and that they must rely on protection from cheap labor in other countries.

—Reminiscent of the green and blue factions of Byzantium which sprang up around the Hippodrome, political parties have engaged in a parasitic competition that drains the nation of its political blood.* I shall provide some details of this fungoid metamorphosis of institutions which now attack the very population they were once meant to serve.

—This year, both the Democratic and Republican parties are split. The Republicans have nominated James G. Blaine, a politician distinguished not so much for his deeds as for his misdeeds, which make him a standard-bearer of all that is reprehensible in politics. When his name was put into nomination at the convention in Chicago, the effect was electrifying. Whole delegations mounted their chairs, and led the cheering which instantly spread to the stage and deepened into a roar as deep and deafening as the voice of Niagara. The scene was indescribable. The air quivered, the gaslights trembled, and the walls fairly shook. But reformers were outraged. Blaine led the Senate cabal

---

* *Reminiscent of the green and blue ... that drains a nation of its political blood.* From AMERICA AND COSMIC MAN by Wyndham Lewis, copyright © 1949 by Wyndham Lewis. Used by permission of Doubleday, a division of Random House, Inc.

that had made Grant President and then manipulated his administration. Blaine engineered crooked deals which yielded considerable profits, most notably from railway securities, for himself and his friends. He himself fathered and midwifed a bill in the Congress granting the railways valuable rights. Blaine proceeded to become Secretary of State under President Garfield in 1880. From this exalted position, he once again favored his friends in negotiations with foreign governments, and they allegedly kicked back their profits to him. So great is the dissatisfaction of independent Republicans with candidate Blaine that they have bolted, choosing to ally themselves with Cleveland and the Democrats. They call themselves *Mugwumps*, the Algonquin Indian word for *chief.* Those conscientious men are reviled as holier-than-thou-Pharisees, blackguards, soreheads, snakes, sleek-faced hypocrites, Holy Willies, Dudes, Goody-Goodies and Political Hermaphrodites.

—Grover Cleveland, on the other hand, made his political mark as governor of the State of New York. He is an outspoken opponent of political corruption and the overweening greed for patronage. He has done such radical things as appoint a professional engineer, who had no political backing, to be superintendent of public works. There was an uproar when he appointed, as superintendent of insurance, a deputy who refused to favor the companies he was supposed to regulate. These were costly losses for Tammany Hall, the New York Democratic political machine. Politicians profited from the immense source of graft found in the aforesaid positions, and their rage was unbounded.

—*Honest* John Kelly, Mayor of New York, is the chief of Tammany Hall. Honest John had made an attempt to derail Cleveland's nomination at the Democratic National Convention (also held in Chicago) by counterfeiting admission tickets to the convention and distributing them to a crowd of rough characters conscripted from the neighboring flophouses and dives. They were instructed to disrupt the convention on command, hooting down speakers for Cleveland and cheering his rivals. When

Cleveland was finally nominated in Chicago, Kelly and his forces refused to follow custom and accept the decision of the convention, but rather redoubled the frequency and viciousness of their attacks.

—No more unscrupulous a politician than Blaine has ever appeared in the upper levels of American politics. In the campaigns that have raised him to his present eminence, he has resorted to every device known to the oldest practitioners of demagoguery, and it was to be expected that this present effort would be a desperate one. One difficulty he has in making charges against Cleveland is that he himself is so vulnerable. He had been denied the nomination in 1880 largely because of what was known about his relations with railroad financiers, and there were other passages in his life that would not bear scrutiny. He, therefore, relies on the Republican inner circle as well as Tammany chieftains to mortify Cleveland's flesh.

—The political cognoscenti understand, however, that times do not call for an imaginative leader but for a chief executive who will purge the government of rascals. Cleveland has a reputation of iron-clad honesty, guaranteeing nothing but probity* in public service after years of licentiousness; Blaine has a long record of service to the federal government but a reputation that, like a whore's, cannot be defended.

—I will condense by means of key quotations the journalistic reaction to the revelation of this sensitive information. It is always best to have the *ipsissima verba* of the writers whose views I am invoking. By this method of continuous quotation,

---

interspersed with commentary, I will demonstrate to you the baroque disorder now reigning.*

BUFFALO TELEGRAPH

A TERRIBLE TALE
A DARK CHAPTER IN A PUBLIC
MAN'S HISTORY

The Pitiful Story of Amber Halpin
and Governor Cleveland's Daughter

A Prominent Citizen States the Result
of his Investigation of Charges
Against the Governor—
Interviews Touching
the Case**

—In America a man who can't talk morality twice a week to a large, popular, immoral audience is quite over as a serious politician.

—To have a style without a subject is one of the highest achievements of modern journalism. No one will be able to explain Queen Victoria to future ages without first mastering the chemistry of the stuffiness without which such a creature could

---

* *I will condense ... the baroque disorder now reigning.* From AMERICA AND COSMIC MAN by Wyndham Lewis, copyright © 1949 by Wyndham Lewis. Used by permission of Doubleday, a division of Random House, Inc.

** *BUFFALO TELEGRPAH ... the Case.* Reprinted with the permission of Scribner, an imprint of Simon & Schuster Adult Publishing Group, from GROVER CLEVELAND by Rexford Guy Tugwell. Copyright © 1968 by Rexford Guy Tugwell. All rights reserved.

not live a minute, so to that end I present the following quotation[*] from Charles A. Dana of the *New York Sun*:

> *We do not believe that the American people will knowingly elect to the Presidency a coarse debauchee who would bring his harlots with him to Washington and hire lodgings for them convenient to the White House.*^{**}

—American publicity is a bizarre fairyland. It should, of course, be stamped out, and all its practitioners hanged, for *lèse-majesté* (here the Majesty being the People). But I confess to having myself developed a taste for such imbecility, as no doubt a physician attending the insane succumbs to the lure of the nonsense to which he is obliged from morning till night to listen.^{***}

—The Reverend Ball of Buffalo, New York, speaking on behalf of a ministerial investigation committee, reinforced Mr Dana's sentiments:

> *Investigations,—he solemnly announced,—disclose still more proof of debaucheries too horrible to relate and too vile to be readily believed. For many years days devoted to business have been followed by nights of sin. He has lived as a bachelor; had no home, avoiding the restraints of hotel or boarding*

---

house life, lodged in rooms on the third floor in a business block, and made those rooms a harem, foraged outside, also, in the city and surrounding villages; champion libertine, an artful seducer, a foe to virtue, an enemy of the family, a snare to youth and hostile to true womanhood. The Halpin case was not solitary. Women now married and anxious to cover the sins of their youth have been his victims, and are now alarmed lest their relations with him shall be exposed. Some disgraced and broken-hearted victims of his lust now slumber in the grave. Since he has become governor of this great state, he has not abated his lecheries. Abundant rumors implicate him at Albany, and well-authenticated facts convict him at Buffalo. The issue in this election is evidently not between the two great parties but between the brothel and the family, between decency and indecency, between lust and law.

—There is so much that is clownish and backward and calls itself American. Furthermore, one is always in danger of being thought ironical when dealing sympathetically with paradox. In any case, we are quite intimate with the lusty origin of our story and the unhappy events leading us up to the present moment.

—For the sake of rhetorical contrast, I quote a statement issued by a Cleveland defender, the respected Reverend Kingsly Twining:

The kernel of truth in the various charges against Mr Cleveland is this, that when he was younger than he is now, he was guilty of an illicit connection; but the charge, as brought against him, lacks the elements of truth in these substantial points; there was no seduction, no adultery, no breach of promise, no obligation of marriage; but there was at that time a culpable irregularity of life, living as he was, a bachelor for which it was proper, and is proper, that he should suffer. After the primary offense, which is

not to be palliated in the circle for which I write, his conduct was singularly honorable, showing no attempt to evade responsibility, and doing all he could to meet the duties involved, of which marriage was certainly not one. . . .*

—Ahhhhhhhhhhhhh!—cries Holmes. It is a dreadful scream that might have been heard far down the street. My skin goes cold and my hair bristles. I catch sight of his convulsed face and frantic eyes. The newspaper I was reading from crepitates in my paralyzed hand.

—Silence, Wilde! Stop this instant, I say! You prattle on and on like a woman!—His head sinks back upon the pillow and he gives a deep sigh of relief as I let the newspaper fall from my hands.

—I hate these newspaper accounts, Wilde! You know that I hate it. You fidget me beyond endurance. Shut up, man, and let me have my rest!

The incident leaves a most unpleasant impression upon my mind. The violent and causeless excitement, followed by this brutality of speech, so far removed from his usual suavity, shows me how deep was the disorganization of his mind. Of all ruins, that of a noble mind is most deplorable.

I sit in silent dejection.

—That hurts my pride, Wilde,—he says at last.—It is a petty feeling, no doubt, but it hurts my pride. It becomes a personal matter with me now, and if God sends me health, I shall set my hand upon this gang.

---

* *The kernel of truth ... marriage was certainly not one*. Reprinted with the permission of Scribner, an imprint of Simon & Schuster Adult Publishing Group, from GROVER CLEVELAND by Rexford Guy Tugwell. Copyright © 1968 by Rexford Guy Tugwell. All rights reserved.

179

He springs from his bed and paces about the room in uncontrollable agitation, his sallow cheeks flushed, with a nervous clasping and unclasping of his long hands until he collapses once again on the bed.

My mind is made up. I shall return to England posthaste. I have implicated myself in a horrible disaster.

Holmes begins to talk with the same feverish animation as before. He still retains, however, some of the jaunty gallantry of his speech.

—Now, Wilde,—he says.—Have you a hole in your pocket?

—No.

—Do you have any change in your pocket?

—Yes.

—Any silver?

—A good deal.

—How many half-crowns?

—We are in America. I have no half-crowns; I have five quarters.

—Ah, too few! Too few! How very unfortunate, Wilde! However, such as they are you can put them in your watch-pocket. And all the rest of your money in your left trouser-pocket. Thank you. It will balance you so much better like that.

This is raving insanity. He shudders, and again makes a sound between a cough and a sob, his mind struggling on explanations founded rather upon conjecture and surmise than on the absolute logical proof which is so dear to him.

I leave the room and pass through the suffocating hallway. I must have the manager make inquiries with the ship lines as to when I might book a return passage to London. I am leaving. Whiskey. How to tell him? Not now. A drink in the hotel bar first. The waiter with his soap-curled hair arrives.

—Tia Maria, please.

He understands. He does my bidding.

Distract myself. What do the Americans say? You know that you are in a genuine barroom when nobody knows where you are.

· The sins of industrialism are strong in my nostrils, yet I am trying to reconcile machinery with aesthetics. And now I see it: carpets of vulgar pattern, on the walls things which were apparently cracked plates decorated with peacock feathers, badly glued machine-made chairs that creek, gaudy gilt horrors serving as mirrors, and cast iron monstrosities masquerading as chandeliers. Everything is cheap and it has been *made to sell*.

Ganymede placed the glass of wine upon a napkin before me.

No connection between poverty and radicalism, but there is between handicraft and republicanism. To work at any handicraft induces that sense of independence which is the keynote of all republicanism. Present generation a most impractical one. By that I mean that they live without making life worth living for—without cultivating a sense of pleasure, of the beautiful. To me the life of the businessman who eats his breakfast in the morning, catches a train for the city, stays there in the dingy, dusty atmosphere of the commercial world, and goes back to his house in the evening, and after supper to sleep, is worse than the life of the galley slave—his chains are gold instead of iron. I have nothing to do with commerce and what is called *progress*. I see that in the rush and crash of business the native and characteristic picturesqueness of people is being rapidly destroyed, and I desire to do what I can to rescue from oblivion the truly artistic peculiarities that still survive.

What shall I tell Homes? Nothing. Tomorrow. My heart sinks at the threshold. The worst might have happened in my absence.

To my enormous relief, he is greatly improved. His appearance is as ghastly as ever, but all trace of delirium has left him.

—I will get to the bottom of this,—said Holmes with a plaintive catch in his throat.

—One should never get to the bottom of things—because there may be no way to get out from underneath!

—I have never failed before. Never. They may do what they like, but I'll checkmate them still.

—My dear Holmes, ambition is the last refuge of failure,—I answered, kicking the newspapers in disgust.—There is no use denying it. It is a triple tragedy: Our client is the subject of a scandal, you lost your first case, and I lost my first play.

—Wilde,—he began in a melancholy monotone,—I am overlooking something. I threw out a vital piece of lumber.

We pass some moments in silence. The twilight softens the room with turquoise and celadon light. Memory, like a horrible malady, is eating his soul away. From time to time he seems to see my eyes looking at him.

—You know, Wilde,—he says at length,—Lillie Langtry is the only woman I ever loved. Of all ghosts, the ghosts of our old loves are the worst.

That is the key! I am astonished. I understand him: he is suffering from the malady of love. Holmes is an unrequited lover!

—Love is strongest in the absence of the loved one; it needs a certain distance to preserve it,—he says.

I see him as he is.

Every morning he begins his day with hope, and every evening he ends in despair, raging because he can't understand things that I have understood.* My thoughts turned to those whom love had ruined in days gone by, how Phyllis of Thrace and poor Canacea had suffered such misfortune in Love's name; how Biblis had died broken-hearted for her brother's love; how love-lorn Dido had met so tragic a fate because of her unhappy love for Aeneas. Their

---

* *Every morning he begins ... that I have understood.* Reprinted with the permission of The Free Press, a Division of Simon & Schuster Adult Publishing Group, from *LUDWIG WITTGENSTEIN: The Duty of Genius*, by Ray Monk. Copyright © 1990 by Ray Monk. All rights reserved. Published in the UK by Jonathan Cape. Reprinted with permission of The RandomHouse Group Ltd.

strains echo and merge in the caverns of my mind. Love-sick Holmes. Sorrow makes him forsake the rightful use of his mind. Two people could not possibly be more incompatible than Lillie and Sherlock. And I ask myself, What were these people doing together? Why, the answer is evident: they were exploring the world of love. If we now turn to gifted men, we shall see that in their case love frequently begins with self-mortification, humiliation, and restraint. A change sets in, a process of purification seems to emanate from the object loved.[*]

Holmes' strength departs, and his masterful, purposeful talk drones away into the low, vague murmurings of a delirious man. The head never rules the heart; it just becomes its partner in crime.[**]

The moon hangs low in the sky like a yellow skull. From time to time a misshapen cloud stretches a long arm across and hides it. The gas lamps grow fewer, and the streets visible from Holmes' rooms became more narrow and gloomy. The wind screams and the rain beats against the windows with New World ferocity, and midnight sobs in the chimney.

There was not a citizen in the whole civilized world who did not look upon Holmes with envy. Behold him now as the breakers of misfortune engulf him! Behold the wretched Sherlock Holmes, the masterful detective who once solved the mysteries of others, now ponders the mystery of himself. Look upon the last day always. None of us mortals is happy till he has passed the end of his life secure from pain.

I stop and listen until the chimes at midnight cease
and I hear the end of time and all eternity. . . .

—Sherlock Holmes

The great moon hangs in the dusky air, slanting a smoke-colored beam on the foot of the bed while I finger the watch chain given to me by her who has led me to this very moment of ultimate consideration. It is not the watch that is imprisoned by the lily chain but I who am manacled to Time, the mighty force that reduces all experience to dust, oblivion and absurdity. Albeit to the pocketwatch is allotted such distinct tasks as ticking out uniform intervals of duration at which it succeeds, I (heir to the first doomed animal to burst forth from primaeval slime into the vast and indomitable wilderness of perception, and having arrived, recognizing the audacity and courage and heart to be called hunter, stalker, chevalier or simply detective) have failed my task, enduring henceforth, if only in name, to be known as Holmes the Meddler, Holmes the Busybody, Holmes the Scotland Yard Jack-in-office, fingering a chain of logical sequence without break or flaw, a chain of length, breadth, width and duration of the glamorous fatality of doomed love, because there is no difference between Time and any of the three dimensions of space except that our consciousness moves along it, incontrovertibly moving forward along a ringing rail of Time into oblivion, unable to escape from the present moment of mental existence (immaterial and dimensionless) passing along the Time dimension at a uniform velocity from womb and cradle to tomb and grave, never to reverse its flow and recede peaceably to the primordial swamp whence I came. Time, the unconquerable foe, activates a breath of wind—and the gas jet jumps; one of the candles gives up its yellow petaloid flame, and the idea swings round, becomes indistinct, ghostly, a swirling eddy of faintly glittering dead flame: gone.

The silverpointed shadows and occasional gleams, betraying a nonentity on the killim, falconer of love's revenge, lord over the field of battle just outside Kabul, where the dead lay wrapped in a windingsheet of low smoke. Ya'qub swept under fantastic shadows of exile, establishing a buffer between Tsarist Russia and British India; however, Time is ever the victor.

I hear bells chiming the hour, reverberating in the air long after the tolling stops, lingering over the apartment houses, with here and there a single dwelling dropped far down beneath and beside them, composing a jag-toothed effect on the skyline.

I am oblivious to the Bome. Bome. Bommmmmmmmmmme for the longest while, then the beating of my heart urges me to reflect on the long unbroken succession of heart beats receding in Time, the Time I have not lent my ear to, the Time that belongs to the voiceless dead, their agony forever unheard.

Question (inspired by Newton): How many seconds per second does one advance through time? Controvertible. Absurd. Suggests the flow (advance) of Time invites comparison to a rate of change with something else—yielding a sort of hypertime or time-within-time or time-within-time-within-time. Supposing this hypertime flows, a hyper-hyper-time is called for, and so forth, *ad infinitum*. The ineluctable conclusion would be that Time exists within Time, indicating a manifold universe whose all-at-onceness I may perceive not-all-at-once. Absurd! Impossible! Unreal!

Question: If the universe is composed of space-time, let us ask whether man's consciousness advances (proceeds) along a timelike coordinate of the universe, and if so, at what velocity? and whether future events burst forth into existence as the *now* reaches them, or whether they are there all along?

The philosophy of Time bears painfully on my emotions. Not only do I regret the past, I also fear the future, not least because the alleged flow to Time seems to be sweeping us toward our deaths, as swimmers are swept toward a waterfall. I can hear time ending. The sound of time without the chimes, without the heart

beat, without the trembling patch of moonbeam. My mind is thinking thinking about not-thinking, retreating to aboriginal hopelessness from the unconcealed horror of generations of unmindful minds moving ineluctably, unswervingly, inescapably to that final and apocalyptic twilight trembling over the last day. . . .

Four, five and six. Now the chamber is full. The bedsprings groan and my feet swish across the floor. Wilde is asleep in the armchair, his breathing stertorous, *Lillie runs through the mirror in a vacuum trailing a riot of odors, her hair blown back, saying Will you marry me or not?* I am going faintly adenoidal; no doubt he will think I'm relaxing, V.R.

The mirror is a square of dim light opposite me, a left-handed and parallel universe where I come to blind Time's eye. There is nothing there. There is nothing there. I am going to see the nothing-there. Standing inert and defunctive, the severe outlines of my face materialize in the glass: the hawkish eyes, strong chin, brainy forehead, eyes rolling and luminous: the pale visage that killed love *she lies next to me on the pillow, her susurrant and regular breathing on my chest what's wrong with you nothing's wrong then go back to sleep I said what was I thinking about that was so important when she when she when she*

I love you from the bottom of my heart

and flung the book at me Paracelsus, amused by my experiment and self-command

will you marry me?

No, go to America

you don't listen to a single word I say do you?

Cruelty of honest answers. Lust, its relinquishment. My face is looking at me and it sees nothing but the anchorite of detection. I lay out my spare suit, britches, stockings, shirts, collars, ties, and pack my steamer. To the quarter hour I stop and listen until the chimes cease and I hear the end of time and all eternity when the retroactive threads of dead and expended memory unravel

aim right between the eyes

look at me holmes why did you make me fall in love with you?
i did nothing of the sort i. . . .
love you from the very bottom of my heart
and all emotions and that one particularly abhorrent
Where is my admirably balanced mind?
I cannot think why the whole bed of the ocean is not one
solid mass of oysters, so prolific the creatures seem. Ah, I am
wandering. Strange how the brain controls the brain!

either you marry me or I'm going to America where no one
knows who I am
This is the face that never loved anyone as much as chemistry. But I never at all suspected that anyone could love me (even
now it seems unnatural. Love for me? How strange!) but she
could breathe life into a dead man. How could I not love her? A
dead man, a dead man

Sally Smithfield. The knitting needles she knitted nothing
with. *Engelmacher.* Adds a new dimension to nonentity. What if
it were a fine young lad, or a pretty little girl? Family restraints.
A being branching out from me and her. Self-condemned. I who
killed love—irretrievable now. My failure to be

slow triggering
i hear rats' feet scrambling behind the wall
madness and the stabbing pain of memory the horror of unfolding darkness

where am I going? my voice borne by an ill wind to and fro in
the left-handed universe, where I was born into darkness and
will die in darkness, understanding nothing, leaving this world
ignorant as I once entered it

The hammer falls mutely
recoil
shards of glass
mutely coruscating
now barrel to temple.

Too many let their wrist slacken and only graze themselves
along the temples. I gaze into the deep enfolding dimensionless

darkness behind the mirror, cultivating my hysteria, cursing the woman who brought me into this life.

Stop.

There is another room. A man is raising his hands in surrender. Another tries to flee. I aim quickly and fire. He falls, fouling the air I breathe with cries

They behold me with astonished credulity; their affable faces, strained beyond fear of sentient and unlaw-abiding dust, flex into terror, painting a Time-picture, indelible and immutable in the forepanels of my brain (distracting me from the mindless Helen of the twilight for whom I would have gladly extinguished the white rose of flame that burns within myself) of a man whose face I can see squarely, full of outrage and impotent insolence, knowing full well that if he makes one false move I will discharge my revolver into the seat of his pants.

I am trapped in a web of lies, and the rage-not-now-rage animating me with dread anticipation, arising like a ghost, not yet dead, not waiting to hear the bugle call of Kabul beckoning a failed advance of cavalry for the dead British convoy giving up its ghost under the minarets hard by Babur's garden, timeless, frozen, inescapable massacre.

—Stop or I'll shoot!

Morality is simply the attitude we adopt to
people whom we personally dislike.
—Oscar Wilde

An anomaly which often struck me in the character of Sherlock Holmes was that, although in his methods of thought he was (excepting present circumstances) the neatest and most methodical of men, and although also he affected a certain quiet primness of dress (the deerstalker must go!), he was none the less in his personal habits one of the most untidy men that ever drove a fellow-lodger to distraction. Not that I am in the least conventional in that respect myself. The rough-and-tumble work in Afghanistan, coming on the top of a natural Bohemianism of disposition, has made him rather more lax than befits a detective. But even with me there is a limit, and when I find cigars in the coal-scuttle, his tobacco in the toe end of a Persian slipper, and his unanswered correspondence transfixed by a jack-knife into the very center of this wooden mantlepiece, then I feel a strange new rectitude. I have always held, too, that pistol practice should be distinctly an open-air pastime; and when Holmes, in one of his queer humors, proceeded to adorn the opposite wall with a patriotic V.R. done in bullet-pocks, I felt strongly that neither the atmosphere nor the appearances of our room was improved by it. This time, however, when I was rudely disturbed by the pistol shots, my sleeping eye awoke to discover Holmes holding a pistol, staring at a jagged nimbus of moonlight reflected by the remains of the mirror on the wall, behind which stood several strange men cowering with fear.

—Stop or I'll shoot!—Holmes ordered, pointing the gun at them now.

Holmes held the spies at bay until the police came. I think he was secretly pleased to have wounded one of them. He did it purely out of malice. That's why he enjoyed it so much. He actually regained some confidence in himself.

189

Every word of our conversations had been spied upon. A one-way mirror (a clever device) concealed a small room where the spies were ensconced. The police said it was left over from the days when the hotel used to be a *panel house*. This was particularly disturbing because it meant that the hotel management was in some manner aware of the deception. Every single word of our confidential transactions had been monitored by these hooligans, who reported every detail to Moriarty, Holmes' arch-enemy, who was then able to anticipate our ruse in Lillie's home. That explained how Moriarty had gotten possession of the birth certificate. Commissioner Williams visited personally to reassure us that everything in his power would be done to break the code of silence among the spies and to learn their purpose and motive. Commissioner Williams, of course, was not above suspicion himself. And so the tangled and venomous web of intrigue began to unravel.

One would have supposed that this quick success would have reanimated Holmes with new courage but he relapsed into a comatose and incommunicative melancholia once again as soon as the spies were carted off to jail.

The hotel management offered to give us new rooms free of charge, but neither Holmes nor I had any reason to remain after being subjected to such perfervid treachery.

I had an awful time with Holmes. He came analyzing all that goes wrong between him and me and I told him I thought it was only nerves on both sides and everything was all right at bottom. Then he said he never knew whether I was speaking the truth or being polite, so I got vexed and refused to say another word. He went on and on and on. I sat down at my table and took up my pen and began to look through a book, but he still went on. I said sharply, *All you want is a little self-command.* Then at last he

went away with an air of high tragedy. At this point I began to fear suicide, so I told him I was sorry I had been cross, and then talked quietly about how he could improve. He is a tyrant, if you like.*

I put Holmes to bed, then returned to the parlor to smoke and drink a ruminative brandy. His faults are exactly as mine—always analyzing, pulling things up by the roots, trying to get the exact truth of what one feels towards him. I see it is very tiring and deadening to one's affections.

There is packing to be done, and what I cannot put off till tomorrow, I do the day after.

Quite unexpectedly, there was an intrusive knock at the door. I discovered a rather pretty young lady standing in the threshold. Governor Cleveland, despite his towering frame, was cowering behind her.

—Wilde,—pleaded the Governor,—please explain to her what happened.

—Hold your tongue,—she snapped.—You talk and you talk and it doesn't amount to snap. I wish to speak with Mr Sherlock Holmes,—she demanded, then turning to the Governor as if she were completing a sentence begun much earlier,—or else I'm calling off the engagement.

—Please, Frances, just listen to the man before you make the ultimate decision!

She stood fast, glaring into my face, awaiting an answer.

—Please come in,—I replied, hoping to prevent a scene in the hallway.

---

* *I had an awful time ... He is a tyrant, if you like.* Reprinted with the permission of The Free Press, a Division of Simon & Schuster Adult Publishing Group, from *LUDWIG WITTGENSTEIN: The Duty of Genius*, by Ray Monk. Copyright © 1990 by Ray Monk. All rights reserved. Published in the UK by Jonathan Cape. Reprinted with permission of The RandomHouse Group Ltd.

I never came across anyone in whom the moral sense was dominant who was not heartless, cruel, vindictive, log-stupid, and entirely lacking in the smallest sense of humanity. Moral people, as they are termed, are simple beasts. I would sooner have fifty unnatural vices than one unnatural virtue.

—Mr Holmes is indisposed.

—Indisposed?

—He is not permitted visitors.

The vague murmurings of delirious Holmes traveled into the sitting room.

—May I introduce Frances Folsom, my fiancée,—said Grover with beefy earnestness.

—Why didn't you tell me you had a child out of wedlock?— she demanded, anger slanting her words.

—Darling, it was a matter of honor, especially so because judging from the vixen's character, I had grave misgivings about the actual paternity of the child, and harbor reasonable doubt that the child is indeed mine.

I heard rumors at Lillie's *faux marriage* that Grover entertained Mrs Oscar Folsom and her twenty-one-year-old daughter Frances at the Governor's mansion for a week or two, and there was an outburst of speculation among New Yorkers about it. Was it possible, after all, that the Governor was about to abandon his bachelorhood? And that the widow of his old Buffalo friend and law partner, Oscar Folsom, was the object of his affections? New York gossips got it only half right; Cleveland was planning to get married, but it was the daughter—the lovely young Frances, now in her senior year at Wells College, I believe—in whom he was interested, not the mother.

—What happened?

She cut me off before I advanced beyond the first person pronoun that began my sentence.

—About ten years ago,—began the Honorable Governor, moping his malarial forehead with a formless handkerchief,— when I was Sheriff of Buffalo, there came a day when two con-

victed murderers had to be hanged. Rather than delegate the unpleasant task to my deputies, I executed the hanging myself. The whole town turned out to see justice accomplished.

—Yes, so?—she sniffed.

—Unbeknownst to me, there was a young actress, Amber Halpin, newly arrived from London in the crowd. She had arrived with a traveling band of actors—yes, I think they were performing *Midsummer Night's Dream.*

—*A Midsummer Night's Dream*! How I hate that play!

—I went to see the play that evening,—he stammered on,—and was so delighted by the lovely comedy that had distracted me from the onerous duty I had performed earlier that day, that I conveyed my personal congratulations to Miss Halpin for her performance. Ah! How foolish I was!

—So you did have intimate relations with that whore,—she said sharply.

Several plays have been written lately that deal with the monstrous injustice of the social code of morality. It is indeed a burning shame that there should be one law for men and another law for women. I think that there should be no law for anybody.

—I don't know how to begin to explain the emotions that seize a man after performing an execution,—pleaded the Governor,—I succumbed to her charms and she became my lover for the month she remained in Buffalo.

—A month!

This was becoming an ugly scene. Morality is simply the attitude we adopt to people whom we personally dislike. Holmes does this routinely. No wonder at all he has had a breakdown. I would like this to end soon.

—When she informed me of her delicate condition,—continued the Governor,—I did what I had to do. I assumed responsibility for supporting Miss Halpin during her term, and placed the child, a girl, in the home of friends in Philadelphia, and guaranteed the cost of the child's upbringing and education.

193

—And you never told me!—she cried vituperatively.—I shall never trust you again. And I am calling off our engagement!

It is difficult not to be unjust to what one loves. And she does love him.

—Please, Frances,—he said, kneeling,—don't leave me now! She never even blackmailed me. It was my own fear. She sent me a letter indicating she wished to see her daughter, and requested a small loan. I grew fearful of further trouble and the remote possibility of blackmail, so I hired Sherlock Holmes to obtain the birth certificate from her, but it fell into evil hands! It is my fault entirely! She never meant any harm! She just wants to see her child!

Frances paused at the door.

—Poor girl,—Cleveland said,—you never had any courting like other girls. Nothing has been harder than the burden of responsibility placed on me by the Party. I did not seek the nomination, nor did I want our life to be destroyed.

His heart laid bare persuaded her to return.

—I don't know how I will endure this campaign without your love, encouragement, and companionship, and I promise to marry you, as soon as you graduate—if not in the White House, then in the Governor's mansion.

—Grover the good!—she cried, embracing him,—you are a man more sinned against than sinning.

To be good, according to the vulgar standard of goodness, is obviously quite easy. It merely requires a certain amount of terror, a certain lack of imaginative thought, and a certain low passion for middle-class respectability.

Ah, there's no police like Holmes!

IV

VI

Gommes, moonly the shadow knowl themesolves.

—sureluck gommes

I hore a tole in me pucket onde jinglestreams of silver flared dune my pansled, roulling away, snayking cylind musesick from my heals.

—Why wont you mary mi? Way?

Wince upon a dome, and a fairy goldhand tome it was, a yonge man and woeman met and cristata crossrose in the delsarte of louvre. The hote and thursday noneday sonne claired above the poolgrims of amour.

—Know ye where lies the golden pond? I slake refraichement guiness totters.

—New,—she unsored,—I noh naught whirr it lies, but ibis gourded boyo terrisible monster.

Le shoevalier san pure et sens rapprochement laked wood he haw, laking still bother watt he did not sea. L'ile jugged him to be goad and ransom, and thot that his nother must heaven bane beautiful.

—Whistle streak the golden pun end freund slappiness togather,—lully zeuggested.

—And the hoopen roses bloansome,—repied homes.

And so toblather they sought the gullding pong, where they mite pathe and swash a-wave the wareyness of treble.

Hotbooting down the bloansome rote larme in larme, they spayed the golden pond dearby, an aurelian boule whose chiming wasser was dippled selber and bloo bather replected skye apuff; no shapehards vizard shumbling fflux hier; no bird nor beast snore failling lief ever drubled hits mirroired surveys. Grasce glew hullrounded, creening the margovitz woeterse. Alle minor of pleurs pied the phlarishing medew mit marry kholers. No sum bermed totly hier.

Mitout warming, the Monster a-peered. So oogly was he to begold that or loafers were berilized by a silenius cream. Hornatt and demotic was the manstars gulliver, much ilk to raptilleans who colate the days art. Grate wussie (the monstrum) whose

197

alms undid in longue aridius tailons. Petrifiction echecqued the loafers inscape. Also spracht zaramonstra:

—Gude volk of the hoopen rose, hindely do re: me a grayde surevice. I defund a golden pan, and proplect its plaxid surplice from bird and beast and pfailling leef. Now, howwaver, I must trebel to yonder moontain. I shell retairn glenn day is dustydirk. Well you ensymble cord the pond in my ibsence?

—Yeths,—replayed hour lovers with yewknighted boices.

Herr moonstar lift them to thor tusk. Swoon, ur liebespaar aggreived that neither baird nore beat nore phaillingx lief impueriled the wetters. Indus façon they adventoured the wassers, ghouling and wishing timeselbes sinn the thuriflying wattarge of the golden bond, heeling swounds inflacted by the open rhodes. Quintz leafing the source, our lehmen discoiffeured their hayr durned loominous gold, and gust as montons loave the welkin or sol loves blue guise, or as flaime loves tinder, they fill in glove.

Quinn tuskydirkness drools hover the traytops, bower moonstar rethorned toady pons.

—Hast anyhang foollen panto the pond?

—New,—sad the paar, afired at the moanster wood cull theme. Inkstintly, he reployed:—How strainge!? I faught oy velt sonnetag pfall this asternoun. Bijoux shore?

—Neither bard ni baste ni balling life pell into the pound.

—The mutter is subtled,—raposted sir munster.

Chelovik ee shayna thin took a shelltering cayve hearby, and wheniffer the monstrum loft fir ponder nounten, they swan hindi goalden washers. Touring teaze days of happen, mand and helpmeet ployed in the garten and swane to hertz continent. Hour loafers teacided to fake limoges in everlusting stone to commarmorate these blasted dice. Nighttame, they swept sandly in peach hovers larms in a cove so warn and teep that not heaven the bale bloo moonlate tit ratchet.

Won matinee, howweather, wile shorl rock was chaping the stowne, lil fund a straunge and unexpectored seed had token rood in the fleur offer antrum. Born etwass when two thrids of

gullden air—won of hissin and herren lucks of gulled—twinned knockturnally essai slapt. Jumpjoy and whoreror, slhappiness and greaf traippsed her, fire this sunderful and rore sead betakes a lieftome to murture, and demented cuntstant devoluition. She squalled furher shayluck. Her squall pried vhizier. Hums drooped his chammer and disel and cain kickly, semper prep quel ninny wilde boast or inthrudoor who mayhop attuck his bevoled, but ess aitch flounder awone.

La famme fetale stewdied her stud mare clothesly: no wetter and no borse than mummie nothars. For to taste his mummer of mans dove and levotion to tethermine weather he bay sworthy of sucrefice rechoired to cuntivate the roreity from seadlang to treelang and pervoid a homes for it.

—I horde sumtang,—shazzad.

—Perhoops the noonstar. Ill chacq the bond.

—Dome go. Stray with me,—she bleaded.—I love you from the autumn of my art. Do thou lovest me?

—Yeast, I love you,—shorelock inswerved, and they sumniferously slapft totether knuckturnally, but pignorant of the beaulittle seed, he roiled over it in the larms of morpheus, hertzharting lalie at the fuit of her tombe.

—Tamara rings new daze.

The nixt ay, the dickdackthief surged for the manstar, but the manstar was goon.

Mooney?

—Will wild, oui dream to have poolen on weavil daze.

—My drear fallow, harlot will emprude.

—Where dad I veil?

—Gommes, moonly the shadow knowl themesolves.

The seedlang snook deefer fruits, deadpanning her secret, secreting her secret herstealth, ruffling her nape and sculp. Whatt avaunt the speed? What abutt her lafe? Wound hebe ungary? She culled fir him anew, and herman game rundling.

—Vatt ist?

—Nothung,—she feyd.—I'm lust aflayed. Two you laff me?

—Off course eye loaf thee,—he handshard, but sheet nut belove him, beclause he trod upon the semel when they slapt, cussing her artfelt blaine.

The nixt matin, halmes bent to scalpt the jatting qoit stones, wail amelia crew lunesome, further seed niered the time of plowering and petalling, and sorely churlhock would see hit. Mordiflied, she called churlhack a turd tame. Hosever, curllock oney culled pack.

—What issac knew? There's no monstar.

—Gome tummie!

Shore rock consaddered a mum meant.

—Nay, aim bussy.

Guled by his gallousness, she ramped sable on a failed of sinople and vair.

—Wott?

—Noon off ear pastnest,—he stang waspishly.

—Do you love me?—she demaund dead.

—No,—he thud, for the purverse pleysure of doing somasing he nought not to half done. So he resamed swanking the whyte stun.

Maud with grief, slickened to the button of her hurt by his bewrayal, she stook a fiery sourd and cug the afourseed from the cavebed. Pine note yet love speared her hardt, and weeps tell there whir no moeurs tares to be wippt. Den she cieled the maw of the clave in ardor to cape hums linda dork. Fainting the clave clomped clothed, hams sott explification.

(O, she serbed me a gup of bisser gull in holler ventriloquial splinter:)

—The Monster releezed a vainomous surpant therein, so I cullixted magical hervs witch I flung antrumwise to testtroy the pussonous mate. The clave mist remane cloude for oon enchoire moon to be heiled. Moonly then may oui dorm heron wince mores. Now, I am ell unto my art, for my soul retides pithin.

He beleated lilia, for she buzzest consimmerable magical plowers, and hecuba the monster wode serpentinely venomate

their crave? So say slate hotside the crave by nix, and darling heyday, they swunk the staines. Ecce, the pound pagan to die up, the flayers in the gourden slewly dithered, and beastissential wands starkdead to blou. Smoon, the blanc stune outclopping stuk promenadely out in the decadential guerdon.

At the wend of loon moon, the clave rehopened, charlake stopped on the score in the hearth, cussing liliana stillmoor pane.

The daygame whan their hair lust its golden and laminous luster. He hindooited that elle elle klept sum quilty seagrid. He pleaned gieces of the starry from glues she unquittingly difulged. He surmazed the monster to be his rayville. Whyfare else would he snakely venomate the cave? Manwile, elle plamed herpelf for the loss of the guerdon and pons, wilde shoreluck blained his rifal for mistfortunes. Heaven tho the sculptore of hippy days was illmost dawne, it graved the lovers for it acscented their loss, a waltzhood curved in everlusting stone.

Dispaaring, she raddled ulms with wittles:

—Wince upon a dream, a man womb I loved left a sorepend in my clave, end I knaver doled him. Who is that man?

Whoreluck plondered her wartds, and desermoned it to be the quark of his rayval, the moanstar.

—Ill quill the manastar. Hrist assored, his worn blude shell flue into the groaned, and the golden gong well spring from his rott brewed,—lil knowling that he spake of his elf.

His cereberations thorned to the statueairy of rappier tays.

—All we have lift is stoan,—she ventred.—You never glisten to a world isaiah.

Soreluck rescented that sinew and would note toil, and he velt drivileged to shear joy and shadness. But they rayvils war indead, for lil denayed it.

Noxtame, when they reantered, he stepped on the sickatrance noncemare and would not pudge until he discupboard what hood there transpaired. To end her andless soror, she burneshed him handsforth and far all tyme end heturnity.

—I ate gamblistry,—she cried.

Craized by loss of love, now violands exdingwishes itstealf. His caving for vengehands death troyed the pong and targin. Troy times to the mouthe of the crave he bleaded his case, and troy dames tunned awrie. She cold nut burr to sicrofyce onner and dognity ninnylumber. Moeur off her, elle taut him bisser toff angorant. Bayside, quarrelrock world sonne forgessen. Batter to pear her kiilt a loon. Sureluck pundered the whait stune contaiming the packtyears of slappie life to get her. The pund had goon. In its playce was a paartched und zunken spit. The groine grasse wizzered to epiolated smellow tassle, kneadlink his pare caulking feat. He kist her coulishe, lofelost hande of stun and brayed furher spitty retorn. Raths scarryied thru tried rooshes wiley mud loneand-swerved brayers.

—Alost!—Shurl rock pooled.—My love thorns gullden pands into hashpeats, groine graces into wickered rooshes, and mein frow shinto stunn!

Griefly, ess aitch dore his gourmands and bate his bore presst with hand ez bale and hord as marple till his prost snook on a clue, a rossie couloir hazard papples that are whyte and rood, whoorl graypes fat can be both groine and purble.

—Wither I shell go, no fend may fellow,—so hums repaared to the krakky tup of a blake mountin whair nayther bard ni beast ni phalling leaf ever game. For tree doze and troy noughts, tear after tor sdreamed panto a gulldome boule. Sureluck on the fairest note spaw the pund, and moanstar peeloved shammering on the fottom of the foule. On the sickened note, le boule held more teares, beloading a shammering fission uva clave, sorepant, and floure. Unda furred nite, the primming poule of teares broth forth a lark, laminous innage of phantune dais, a goldumb forelock twinning matters, howl its root took inner cave, and howl she uprotted the seed with fiery sourd; and shoreflock blasted hiss nyetknowling. How lallie sapphired before histronic vairy oyes, trampling guinnes larms, volgur wale boggin hums to divine slangtrees saygreat grief. Fangering whore image hindu

bowel of tiers, blaking the wassers, viding her, lillyluff, her onner, her dicknity, and her slackriforce asshuming retch and gouldome hews.

Shorlrock hard the faynt milady of wind from die krieg. Sureluck homes beclame kong of the schwarz montown, and lili sangtree the cueen of the wait mantown. The sea and swoundsong gold hum whit tada.

—Queen of wait mantown!—scalled he fremd a dezolate craaack.

—Yes.

—Combe to the flute of your moontone,—his far querrying boice sad,—and i shell comb to the root of mein.

She hard his wanged wards and mate him in the vallillie tebween their moontins.

Sharl moda curtly bowe and crisst her haund trey tames, justice windsung advoiced, winds for love, winds for onner, and winds fir tucknutty. Subfairing and silbsickroface wore acknulledged and redreamed.

Klansing their kilt, they togather purred tayres from their boules into the hearth where it soamed and furged, gumed and spushed into a goldome pund grosser thin before. Whererover soxe thurging staters wruck, blowers flossomed unrocks, and holla riche grasces groined immadiately on burrin soild. Heffergreens caste their laughly jade louver the pund, luz brayking waters spittled the plexid sirforce that mirroared the sky below, as after rane, and argentine cloudorians abuff.

The manstar emarged thence in all pump and mucknificence. His skaily skan gan to gleam inlightly, his grosz raptillian years shrank, and was dansefirmed into a beautriffle loomanous paying who rose into the sky as whit smooke of sacrofacial halters, and spook unto them:

—O sappy king! O thrace blasted queen! Mark disdane with a weight stoan. I am the Moonstar of the polden gond, and I empty oneborn sayeed of the crave. Exasp I for tayme and all efurnity pequod moonly a gutt may live rofever, for gotts l'or never burn.

Hoarefter yugo indy corse of yore hearthly daze, whatifer piths you take, and hoar ishtar day may liege, hue may fund your wayback to the holden bond, foreast lies in the felly beteem ewer moontins, anjou may retorn to bathinetts thurifying whethers wanever yewish. Til shush time cums, I shell horeeaster gourd these plaxid wassers sick red to me, and nay thor baird nohr beat nor phailling leaf will never agin drouble these wassers.

Elan
a larme
Alarm!

Only the shallow know themselves.
                                    —Oscar Wilde

—I often think I am going mad,—said Holmes.
He was absolutely sulky and snappish. And he says the most awful things to me when he is sulky—but is very contrite afterwards. This evening he blamed himself violently and expressed the most piteous disgust with himself. He is not *afraid* to die, he told me, but yet frightfully worried not to let the few remaining moments of his life be wasted. It all hangs on his absolutely morbid and mad conviction that he is going to die soon—there is no obvious reason that I can see why he should not live yet for a long time. But it is no use trying to dispel that conviction, or his worries about it, by reason: he can't help it—for he is mad.[*]

All sympathy is fine, but sympathy with suffering is the least fine mode. There is in it a certain element of terror for our own safety. Bearing that in mind, I'm packing my bags. I have reserved a booking for a return passage to London on the *Bothnia*.

In parting, let me say that I heard more disobliging, even scornful, remarks about American ethics in New York than I ever did in Paris or London. Now I understand why. It is curious. Civilizations continue because people hate them. Modern New York City is exactly the opposite of what everyone wants. Thus, the American more or less lives *inside* the looking-glass. Politics is a Mad Hatter's Tea Party: and life is empty without so menacing a figure as the Mad Hatter lording over it. He longs to see the Dormouse jammed into the teapot. Lacking a genuine Red

---

Queen or Jabborwock, the American points with pride to an assortment of city bosses, gorillas, jailbird mayors and vulgar millionaires.

—I wish to God that I were more intelligent and everything would finally become clear to me, or else that I needn't live much longer,—he murmured.*

You see? I have to attend to a recent victim of the thundering vortex of events known as New York.

Holmes is disinclined for any sort of society. Most of the time he spends in his room, with the door locked from the inside. Sometimes he emerges in a sort of cocaine frenzy, screaming that he is afraid of no man, and that he is not to be cooped up, like a sheep in a pen, by man or devil. When these hot fits are over, however, he rushes tumultuously in and locks the door behind him, like a man who can brazen it out no longer against the terror rooting his soul. At such times I have seen his face glisten with moisture as though it were newly raised from a basin or exposed to dark and steady rain.

Oh unhappy day! First of all, I have to accompany Holmes to Police Headquarters so that we may press charges against the hooligans who spied on us. Inspector Williams has promised full cooperation. Next, Holmes is to be removed to the Fifth Avenue Hotel, a sanctuary where he may recuperate. That is to be done this evening. Afterwards, I shall pay for my passage in the very gold eagles I received for the miserable investigative services I rendered. New York City is not a city to enter casually. You approach it with money in your pocket, you leave it respectfully

---

* *I wish to God ... he murmured.* Reprinted with the permission of The Free Press, a Division of Simon & Schuster Adult Publishing Group, from *LUDWIG WITTGENSTEIN: The Duty of Genius*, by Ray Monk. Copyright © 1990 by Ray Monk. All rights reserved. Published in the UK by Jonathan Cape. Reprinted with permission of The RandomHouse Group Ltd.

well before body, soul and money are exhausted by unforeseen catastrophes. Young people, nowadays, imagine that money is everything, and when they get older they know it. Holmes. Our wager. A kiss may ruin a human life. Silly thing love is . . . and for the love of whom? She is without one good quality, she lacks the finest spark of decency, and is quite the wickedest woman either in New York or London. I haven't a word to say in her favor . . . and she is one of my greatest friends. It is fruitless to give Holmes instructions on how to cure love. He simply wouldn't listen.

Apollonius Tyaneus was one day summoned by the King of Babylon to devise a new method of torture for an interloper whom the King had discovered with his favorite mistress. Apollonius, after having carefully considered the matter, answered that if the interloper were left to live and go on loving, his love would punish him bitterly enough in the course of time, because the loss of love moves with a distinct dramatic arc whose beginning is fear, whose middle confusion, and whose end is everlasting pain—the conventional symptoms of erotic melancholy. Then all is lost: the man is finished, his senses wander, his reason is deranged, his imagination becomes depraved, and his speech incoherent. The wretched lover thinks of nothing but his beloved icon of adoration. All the actions of his body are equally corrupted: he becomes pale, lean, distracted, without appetite, his eyes hollow and sunk into his head. You will see him crying, sobbing and sighing, gasp upon gasp, and in a state of perpetual inquietude, fleeing all company, preferring solitude and his own circular thoughts: on the one hand his fear of an encounter with his beloved, and on the other, his despair of ever seeing his beloved again. Indeed, such is the deplorable spectacle Holmes presents.

In the dim light of a foggy November day, the sick room is a gloomy spot, but it is that gaunt, wasted face staring at me from the bed which sends a chill to my heart. His eyes have the brightness of fever; there is a hectic flush upon either cheek;

dark crusts cling to his lips; his thin hands upon the coverlet twitch incessantly; his voice is croaking and spasmodic. He lies listless as I enter the room, and the sight of me brings no gleam of recognition to his vacant eyes. Shake him gently—no, better to let him sleep. We will soon be gone—never again return to this hellish place.

Oh, one moment! I almost forgot my money.

Money. How can you go anywhere without it? It is an indispensable necessity. And what some people do to obtain it! People are either in the money or out of the money, loving, hating, marrying, acting foolishly and prudently with money or without, but what makes money make money? And why?

I open the desk drawer and withdraw the moneybag. It is suspiciously light. Gold is ponderous and dignified. One can *feel* gold beneath leather. Radiates something at once pernicious and precious. Contain my fulgent distress—open the bag and overturn it. Empty.

—Holmes, where is your money?

—Money?

He is inward gazing, immobile.

I angrily throw my moneybag against the wall.

—I wager that those ruffians who spied on us burglarized our rooms as well!

—Well, Wilde, we seem to have fallen upon evil days,—says he in a feeble dreamspeaking voice, but with something desperate and defunct of manner.

—My dear fellow, our lot will improve!—I assure him.

He falls silent again.

—Why did I fail?—he dreamtalks.

—Holmes, only the shallow know themselves.

He tumbles back into the jaws of sleep. Didn't hear it. Better let him sleep.

I come to the mantlepiece. A litter of pipes, tobacco-pouches, syringes, penknives, revolver-cartridges, an opium-tainted cigarette, a pair of lemon-yellow gloves, a gold latten match box, a

Louis Quinze silver salver, a Saracenic lamp studded with turquoise and other debris are scattered over it.

We have *no money.*

Never in my life have I suffered poverty. Very often my extravagance was curtailed or even thwarted, but I was always able to provide sufficient funds to live in the modest means to which I have grown accustomed. I recall the temporary financial embarrassment I suffered last year. I was forced to pawn my Berkeley Gold Medal. But I found a way to extricate myself from those difficulties.

I frequently spoke in a disparaging manner about the poor, but now I feel sympathetic to them. The real tragedy of the poor is that they can afford nothing but self-denial. That is contrary to my nature and intrinsically insufferable.

A lorry rings its bell, stirring Holmes from his dreamsleep. He awakens. Tell him now? No. Wait.

He moves tentatively to the *chaise longue* and he begins smoking incessantly, putting out one cigarette then lighting another. Just as I do. He keeps a stock of cigarettes in a large biscuit tin which he carries from room to room. A cigarette is the perfect type of pleasure. It is exquisite and leaves one unsatisfied.

—Come, Holmes,—I say with growing concern,—that is my last opium-tainted Egyptian cigarette.

Does he hear me at all? He is listening to his voice within, the glorious symphony of—disillusion?

I move to the window. Pigeons fly in formation. A distant bell pays out its lugubrious toll. A wire tightens in my straining throat. I am treading on a frangible surface, one through which I may fall at any moment. The ragged beggars, some of them very young, gather in resentful knots on the street. Old women playing tubular hand organs; Irishmen playing great billowing highland bag pipes. Some one is singing in the street:

Teach Our Baby That I'm Dead
And never let it know
The dark disgrace I've brought to you. . . .

Vagabonds here are shameless: they will lie flat on their back in front of a drinking establishment and drink the swill left at the bottom of an empty barrel. It is rumorerd Oxford graduates can be found among these vagabonds. Perhaps Holmes and I may enroll in their lists.

Had I been subjected to such indifference and cruelty as these homeless men and women have suffered, would I have become a lord among poets and a poet among lords? There is true danger here. Why did I come to New York after all? Why is it that one runs to one's ruin? Why has destruction such a fascination? But it is all right, the gods hold the world on their knees. I was made for destruction. My cradle is rocked by the fates.

My purple velvet jacket: ah, here! The velvetine square: Abdullahs. I spoke too soon. Here is another pack! Lay them open on the table: will be gone in an hour or two. So many practical considerations.

—Holmes, where is your money?

The detective, as well as the artist, is a
secret agent assigned to observe life.
—Sherlock Holmes

It was well said of a certain German book that *es lasst sich nicht lesen*—it does not permit itself to be read. There are some secrets which do not permit themselves to be told. Men die nightly in their beds, wringing the hands of ghostly confessors, die with despair of heart and convulsion of throat on account of the hideousness of mysteries that will not suffer themselves to be revealed. Now and then, alas, the conscience of man takes up a burden so heavy in horror that it can be thrown down only into the grave. And thus the essence of all crime is undivulged. It is precisely this essence that I am searching for; however, there is a hole in my perception. I sense the negative shapes left by dim impressions of a well-hidden event—but I cannot grasp the event itself.

I am affected by a lethargy which devours that half of the genius with which heaven has endowed me, rendering me impotent by a powerlessness so colossal and so enormous as to be epic. My somber nature is streaked with brilliant flashes of light—lazy and enterprising at the same time—fecund in difficult projects and ludicrous failures.

I have all kinds of trouble getting back to work. I am really very sad.

How everything vanishes! How everything vanishes! The leaves are unfurling again on the trees. Where is the month of May that gave us the lovely flowers we have lost, and the fragrance of a young manhood? I feel that I am inordinately old.

211

Wie traurig, wie traurig![*]
Where am I going? At the moment I am wandering about with great restlessness, but around what point of equilibrium I do not know. The wind strafes me like a dry leaf, blowing me to and fro, and all things to me are but water rilling through cupped hands. Unbeknownst to myself, I have committed some crime—not of commission—but of omission. I cannot see myself for what I am and every effort to do so is frustrated. I am disgusted by my own stupidity and in whatever direction I look I see only misfortune!

SHERLOCK HOLMES BUNGLES CASE
Interviews touching upon the misadventure. . . .

That is all that remains of my life: newspapers trumpeting my failure in noisy typography, all the while remaining ignorant of Moriarty and his confounding web of deception. The whole world is laughing at me, though Wilde is too polite to laugh aloud. Lillie would laugh aloud but she is too angry to do so (judging from the voices I hear or dream); even the tombs of my ancestors shake with laughter, and most disturbing of all is Moriarty's reptilian head oscillating from side to side, his eyes squinting with malice and scorn. It is easy to laugh at life as a farce as long as one is not playing a role in it. *It is necessary that you should withdraw. . . .* Where are my bold words and glorious deeds now? Perhaps Wilde is right. I take myself too seriously. *Gravity is a sure sign of arrested mental development.* My laughter is a no man's land between faith and despair. But it shall not remain ever so. I must cure my wound by answering

---

[*] *Wie traurig, wie traurig!* Reprinted with the permission of The Free Press, a Division of Simon & Schuster Adult Publishing Group, from *LUDWIG WITTGENSTEIN: The Duty of Genius,* by Ray Monk. Copyright © 1990 by Ray Monk. All rights reserved. Published in the UK by Jonathan Cape. Reprinted with permission of The RandomHouse Group Ltd.

Moriarty's attack. I have a high art: whoever wounds me, I wound them cruelly in return. Revenge shall be mine. That is a vow. Remember it. Use it. I make it because I can keep it.*

* * *

I embrace the crowds and lose myself therein. Multitude, solitude: interchangeable terms and easily convertible by the detective. Whosoever cannot people his solitude cannot be alone in a bustling crowd.

Many odd characters drift in the crowd: advertising handbills; the tramp of feet and crash of wheels; misery and merriment, pomp and poverty filing before me in squalid pageantry.

Dickdack thief. (?). A dream sound in search of an alphabet. Didactic. Detective. Like my privilege of being myself and someone else. Vagrant soul searching for a body to enter, a personality to invade: mechanical, groom, decorator, milkmaid, boxer, reverend: Vampyre. Every aspect of life opens to my touch like a flower.

I shall find what I am searching for, because I am a finder and not a searcher.

Perhaps Wilde would consider this proposition: the detective, as well as the artist, is a secret agent assigned to observe life.

Chimes burst into the strong melody of a hymn and ring out the tones that the traffic cannot drown. Startling pulse of clarity, the stirring frangrance of the lily pond. Now it fades, a nonsense tale told by an idiot mathematician.

— . . . *le boule held more tears, beloading a shammering fission uva clave, sorpant and fleure.* . . .

---

* *That is a vow.... I can keep it.* Reprinted by permission of the publisher from THE LETTERS OF GUSTAVE FLAUBERT: VOLUME I – 1830-1857, selected, edited and translated by Francis Steegmuller, pp. 47, Cambridge, Mass.: The Belknap Press of Harvard University Press, Copyright © 1979, 1980 by Francis Steegmuller.

The sensation blossoms like an odor from a long-locked box, then fades, and I resent not knowing its significance, if it has any at all. I don't know how to interpret the dream, much less a fragmentary recollection. Unless one writes down the dream in hypnopompic moments, it vanishes. But how can a dream be written at all? A chair is not a chair in a dream but something else, like a shadow glowing with inner light in the caverns of the mind. The dream, fearing its own disappearance and insufficiency to overpower the rational faculties of man (the sovereign part of the soul), takes direct aim upon the citadel of the heart, laying siege to that stronghold; and once it is vanquished, the dream attacks reason and all the noble forces of the brain so powerfully that they are enslaved. . . .

Nevertheless, what can one construe from hallucinatory experiences that occur during sleep? The ancients believed that dreams were sent by gods, and they were considered as a means to predict the future and divine cures for the ill.

I would dismiss dreams entirely if they had not provided creative solutions to intellectual and emotional disturbances, as in the case of F A Kekule von Stradonitz. One night in 1865, the great chemist dreamed of a snake biting its tail in a whirling motion. During a hypnopompic reverie, he realized that the benzene molecule possessed an annular form. From this vision his concept of the six-carbon benzene ring was born, and the facts of organic chemistry known theretofore fell lucidly into place.

Moonly the shadow knowl themesolves.

A more foreboding instance of dreams is the case of a steward named Richardson who dreamed of his own murder the night before it happened. He told the dream to a number of witnesses who reported his statements. As Goddard relates the story, Richardson awoke from a nightmare on the night of March 25, 1834. He woke his wife and told her that he dreamed of being shot on his way home from the Epsom market. The next day, he also told the tollkeeper of his dream, and in the local pub at midday, he recounted it to a group of farmers, who cheered him

up by saying that dreams go by opposites. But on his way back to Bletchingly, driving a chaise, he was held up by two men and shot through the head.

Moonly the shadow knowl themesolves.

It is indeed possible to make up words, but I cannot associate a thought with them. I seek some principle of verification of thought. Whatever we do, we are never sure that we are not mistaken. And this is as difficult as hell. It's all wrapped up into one: *moonly the shadow knowl themesolves.* Well, it implicates the moon, a heavenly body, light and shadow, perhaps the shadows of Plato's allegory of the *clave*. I mean *cave*. Yes. No. Bah, nonsense!

I fear I missed my cue. Wilde said something about money and I forgot.

Now it is coming to me. A *golden pond*, Lillie, a teratological manifestation, waves of thermogenital energy—what significance do these recurring elements have? My infirmity is to have been born with a special language to which I alone have the key. I travel within myself as if in a country unknown, even though I have traversed it many times.

Stop.

Is it possible that waking life may only be persistent nightmare?

I do not suppose that I am now dreaming but I am unable to demonstrate irrefutably that I am not. Memory is unable to connect our dreams with one another or with the whole course of our lives as it unites events which happen to us while we are awake. Yet the *golden pond* persists, foaming and surging from the farther shores of my consciousness to the present moment. I can feel its presence. It contains, perhaps, the secret of a chemical and, therefore, formulaic nature, no doubt a special and heretofore unknown relationship between a substance subjected to a process and its consequent transformation, or perhaps a theory or proof of incompleteness.

And just as dry grass or hedges grazed by the torch of a passer-by catch fire, so I burn with all my heart, and the burning

215

feeds my hopeless love with hope: rising out of the crowd, on the street—it is Lillie.

I know I have wronged you, but whenever I feel something deeply, my fear of exaggeration forces me to express it as coldly as I can. You will not be mistaken then in reading between the lines a warmth and an intensity of desire that my habitual reserve does not always let me fully express.

Could you imagine that it made me happy to offend you and to give you an even worse opinion than you have of me? I earnestly beg you once again, be generous and you will be satisfied.

I marvel at her fingers, her hands, her bare arms, and what I see I like, and I like better still what I do not see. I crave to keep her in view—to know more of her. I make my way through the street. *Lillie, I am sick and my sickness is you.*[*] Her eyes—they shine like stars! Her lips, and suddenly that is not enough.

It is not Lillie. Just looked like her from behind. It is as if a flame had gone out and I must wait until it starts to burn again by itself. What to do now?

Nicht gearbeitet.

I am not seeing things freshly, but rather in a pedestrian, lifeless way. Only through a miracle can my work succeed. Only if the veil before my eyes is lifted from the outside. I have to surrender myself completely to my fate. As it has been destined for me, so will it be. I am in the hands of fate.[**]

---

[*] *I am sick and my sickness is you.* Reprinted by permission of the publisher from THE LETTERS OF GUSTAVE FLAUBERT: VOLUME I – 1830-1857, selected, edited and translated by Francis Steegmuller, p. 47, Cambridge, Mass.: The Belknap Press of Harvard University Press, Copyright © 1979, 1980 by Francis Steegmuller.

[**] *Nicht gearbeitet … I am in the hands of fate.* Reprinted with the permission of The Free Press, a Division of Simon & Schuster Adult Publishing Group, from *LUDWIG WITTGENSTEIN: The Duty of Genius*, by Ray Monk. Copyright © 1990 by Ray Monk. All rights reserved. Published in the UK by Jonathan Cape. Reprinted with permission of The RandomHouse Group Ltd.

I am forgetting myself. Moriarty is at the bottom of this. My throat convulses with anger. Moriarty. Seek him out with candle; bring him in dead or living within this twelve month.

* * *

A great river of people carries me away into a chiming oblivion of bells, bells, bells, bells, bells from the grand old church amid the busy turmoil of commerce. The music of the chimes breaks upon the din, and frames the beauty and sadness of all dreams and dreamers.

Northward up to the *Palace of Illusions*, 257 Bowery. A dime museum featuring medical anomalies and curiosities, dwarf acrobats, lady lion tamers, tatooed men: Maximo and Bartola, the Ancient Aztec Children (microcephalic); The Wild Men of Borneo (twin idiot midgets); Zip the "What Is It?" (the putative missing link); Lionel, the Lion-Faced Man (hypertricotic); Lucia Zarate, the Puppet Woman (midget); Laloo, the Indian Boy (has a second head and feet growing out of his torso); Alexandre, the Savage Gnome; sword swallowers, contortionists. . . . May a human brain apply for gainful employment?

I have more memories than if I were a thousand years old. A heavy chest of drawers cluttered with balance sheets, chemistry experiments, lawsuits, and yes, a few love letters, with a heavy lock of hair rolled up in receipts, hides fewer secrets than my gloomy brain. It is a pyramid, an immense burial vault that contains more corpses than a potter's field. I am a cemetery abhorred by the moon, in which long worms crawl like remorses and constantly harass my dearest dead. I am an old boudoir full of withered roses where lies a whole clutter of old-fashioned dresses, where the plaintive pastels and pale Paracelsus, alone, inhale the fragrance of an unopened phial. Nothing can equal the length of those limping days, when ennui, the fruit of dismal apathy, takes on the dimensions of immortality. Henceforth I am no more living matter than a block of granite surrounded with vague terrors, dozing in the depths of a hazy Sahara; an old

sphinx unknown to the heedless world, forgotten on the map and whose savage nature sings only in the rays of the setting sun.

Authority is as destructive to those who exercise it
as it is to those on whom it is exercised.
—Oscar Wilde

Manhattan is a theatre consisting of lights, balcony, and parquet circle. Don't go searching for a proscenium because there is none. The audience is the object of its own contemplation. To say the truth, the whole place reeks with vulgarity. The men drink beer by the gallon, and eat cheese by the hundredweight, talk slang, ride for wagers and swear when they lose, and expectorate everywhere. These are low people, *demi-barbares.*

Even so, it is good to get away from Holmes for even an hour. Better tell him today that I am leaving.

Tarrant Seltzer Aperient Cures Diarrhea.

I take offense at outdoor advertising. *Rising Sun Stove Polish, Use Dr King's New Discovery for Consumption, Colds and Coughs.*

A new aggressiveness has been unleashed upon the quiet, pastoral civilization of America. The spirit of coercion, of reform, of propagandized drives for change. Drummer culture, born of the traveling salesman who coaxed, bullied, shamed and enticed the farmers to buy the products of factories. The face of the salesman and advertiser might be secular, but his voice was that of the old preacher, wooing the reluctant and uninformed to a reputedly better way of life with his golden voice.

Newsboy. Angel with a dirty face.

—Boy!

He folds a paper for me and extends his humble hand to receive the silver dime. Just nod. He will keep the change.

—Thank you, sir!

New York: Jay Gould rumored to have been so shaken in Wall Street panic that he applied to WH Vanderbilt for a loan of ten millions. Any attack on

his credit is an attack on the credit of the United States.

Cincinnati: A preserving company telegraphed Mrs Samuels, mother of the late Jesse James, offering $10,000 for her son's body, with a percentage of the receipts from exhibition. Told her she could make $10,000 in less than two years. The same company tried to get Guiteau's body.

No one is a callow youth anymore. Everyone simply says: He is vealy.

Cupid peeping over the swelling ramparts of a corset to ogle at a human infant who, from below, brandishes a Dionysian wineglass in salutation. The *Warner Brothers Coraline Corset.*

Here and there, shrewd observers are saying that advertising is beginning to change the character of newspapers. Some critics say editors, fearful of offending advertising sponsors, are writing less violently and scathingly about people they don't like. Other critics say editors are growing more commercial; still others that they are finally independent of partisan political interests that have always vied to dominate them. Nobody is sure what advertising will do to newspapers.

I am both impressed and alarmed by *ready money* in America. Ready Money America has burst upon the world in the last twenty years, a civilization of the stock exchange, the corporation, the great centralized industries that supplanted the older system in which wealth had been anchored in the soil or to the small privately held factory. It is a civilization of men without art.

Look.

I pass such street vendors as the vagabond whose commodity is small tablets of grease-erasers and his twin brother in humbug, the man with the dentifrice, who brings a laugh to the most serious face. Their goodnaturedness is darkly balanced by hoodlums who routinely rob small merchants and devil the pacific Chinese,

and keep up the impish practice of following *swells* on the street and telling lewd stories loudly enough to encarnadine the ears of fine young ladies. Factory labor will reduce one and all to the state of the unknown vulgar.

> *Wilson's Magnetic Corsets help general disability, sleeplessness, nervousness, indigestion, rheumatism and paralysis, cure ninety per cent of 100 cases of Catarrh, Dyspepsia, diseases of the Liver and Kidneys, Piles, Locomotor Ataxia, Gout, Chronic Diarrhea. . . .*

Advertising for factory-made goods.

A man may now turn to a machine that will let him do in a day what it had taken twenty yesterdays to do with his hands, but in the victory he has sacrificed most if not all of whatever artistic pleasure he had taken in his work. We in Europe have seen this long in the making. The Civil War and the turn of politics assured the economic ruin of the old handicraft civilization.

There he is: the Policeman. His face: it is not bad, not cruel, almost statuesque—the image of involuntary authority. Conventionally defined, the Police exist to keep the peace, to protect the population, to enforce the laws that have been passed for the common good of all. In truth, however, the police are squeezed by the City to protect one part of the population at the expense of another. Thus, the police are halfway between gangsters and politicians, milking the cow at both ends and acting as ambassadors and negotiators between the two. Such intrigue has impinged on me.

I shudder with horror as I enter Police Headquarters—not so much from what is seen as from what is suggested. The spirits of shoplifters, pickpockets, burglars, mayhem artists and eminent murderers glare at me like pale fire from the eyes of the police officers.

The motto banner is boldly emblazoned *Faithful Unto Death*, and features vignettes of cops at their various duties: chasing runaway carriage horses, brunting assault by thugs on the street, quelling a riot, arresting a footpad at night, guiding lost children.

—Men,—declaims a manly voice lecturing in a nearby room,—when you get your nightsticks, they're intended to be used on thieves and crooks, but don't use them on inoffensive citizens. By no means strike a man in the head. The insane asylums are filled with men whose condition has been caused by a skull injury. Strike them over the arms and legs, unless you're dealing with really bad crooks. Then it doesn't make any difference whether they go to the insane asylum or to jail.

Inducting new recruits. Tradition of brutality—a night stick handed down from old cop to young cop.

What's the new news at the new court?

Three children down the hall I see. They must have just been convicted. They are standing in a row in the central hall in their prison dress, carrying their sheets under their arms ready to be sent to the cells allotted to them. They are quite small children, the youngest being a tiny little chap, for whom they had evidently been unable to find clothes small enough to fit. I need not say how utterly distressed I am to see these children in prison.

—They're enemies of society and our common foe.

The child's face is like a white wedge of sheer and limitless terror, and in his eyes—the terror of a hunted animal. He cries for his parents when they lead him away. The deep voice of the warder on duty tells him to keep quiet.

Prison life makes one see people and things as they really are. That's why it turns one to stone.

An officer escorts me to the administrative area, where I wait. Time to read *The Times*.

> *Chicago: A reign of terror on the highways with robberies of almost hourly occurrence after nightfall. Mayor Harrison advises citizens to carry dirks in their boots and stout sticks in their hands.*

> *Boston: Henry James, Sr, aged 71, died at the home of his son, Professor William James of Harvard. His*

*other son, Henry James, Jr, had returned some weeks
ago, from England, to his bedside.*

*St Louis: An actress has quit The Passion's Slave
Company because Mr Stephens, playing opposite her,
insisted upon giving her what in the profession is
known as the Henry V kiss. . . .*

—Mr Wilde?

I look up to see the blemished face of a functionary who leads
me into the office of Alexander S Williams, that noted thief-
catcher, where I throw myself upon the sofa. I promised Holmes
that I would not divulge to Inspector Williams the work we had
done for Governor Cleveland.

—Captain, I presume in your long and varied experience you
have occasionally met with persons who made fools of themselves.

—Yes,—grins the Captain.

—Well, I've just made a damned fool of myself,—I said,
emphasizing *damned*.

Williams leads me to the rogue's gallery where photographs
of criminals are examined. I pick out police photographs of Red
Rocks Farrel, Googy Corcoran, Slops Connolly, Baboon Connolly, all dreaded Whyos. Stop.

—Dandy John Nolan, the Beau Brummel of gangland. He is
not only a street brawler of distinction but a sneak thief of rare
talent as well,—says Inspector Williams.

—That's him.

—One of the cleverest panel house and bunco steerers in
New York,—says Captain Williams, sagely chomping his fat
seegar.

—Are they incarcerated here?

—No. They're free on bail.

—You set them free on bail?!

—We had to. They put up cash money for bail. Almost a
thousand gold eagles.

So that is where my golden eagles flew!

223

—What unadulterated gall! That is *my* money and *Holmes'* money! They posted bail with money they stole from *me* and *Sherlock Holmes*. I want my money back and the perpetrators re-arrested.

—I can't arrest them because they are free on bail.

—Holmes is so sick that he is confined to his bed. I must return to London immediately—we have no money at all.

—Mr Wilde, you know what you want, but I know what you need.

—What do I need?

—A good lawyer and a holiday.

He knows something I don't know.

People nowadays do not understand what cruelty is. They regard it as some sort of terrible mediaeval passion, and connect it with the race of men like Eccelin de Romano, and others, to whom the deliberate infliction of pain gave a real madness of pleasure. But men of the stamp of Eccelin are merely abnormal types of perverted individualism. Ordinary cruelty is simply stupidity. It is the entire want of imagination. It is the result in our days of stereotyped systems, of hard-and-fast rules, and of stupidity. Wherever there is centralization there is stupidity. What is inhuman in modern life is officialism. Authority is as destructive to those who exercise it as it is to those on whom it is exercised. The people who uphold the system have excellent intentions. Those who carry it out are humane in intention also. Responsibility is shifted on to the disciplinary regulations. It is supposed that because a thing is a rule it is right.

Gathering the reins of my outrage, Fate interceded when I spied Holmes being lead into police headquarters in handcuffs.

One really can't live in New York without a lawyer.

Go chase yerself.

—Sherlock Holmes

Lage unverändert.
I have reached the lowest point. The best for me, perhaps, would be to lie down one evening and not wake up again. If I am unhappy and know that my unhappiness reflects a gross discrepancy between myself and life as it is, I solved nothing; I shall be on the wrong track and I shall never find a way out of the chaos of my emotions and thoughts so long as I have not achieved the supreme and crucial insight that that discrepancy is not the fault of life as it is, but of myself as I am. . . .*

The person who has achieved this insight and holds to it, and who will try again and again to live up to it, is religious.

I feel ashamed that I have not killed myself.

McGurk's on Houston and Bowery. Its business card has reached every seaport in the world. I take the gentleman's entrance to the bar, whereas the young ladies go through a long corridor. Cavernous interior and a commodious back room. *With All Her Faults I Love Her Still*, sing the waiters accompanied by a small orchestra. They can suck melancholy out of a song, as a weasel sucks eggs. The clientele is, as ever, chiefly comprised of sailors, beggars, thieves, crumb throwers, mock epileptics who are in the business of *chucking dummy fits*, and mock cripples who invent all sorts of ingenious fake harnesses and prostheses. This is where the lame and halt can walk normally, where the blind can see, and where the deaf and dumb converse.

---

*   *Lage unverändert. . . . but of myself as I am.* Reprinted with the permission of The Free Press, a Division of Simon & Schuster Adult Publishing Group, from *LUDWIG WITTGENSTEIN: The Duty of Genius*, by Ray Monk. Copyright © 1990 by Ray Monk. All rights reserved. Published in the UK by Jonathan Cape. Reprinted with permission of The RandomHouse Group Ltd.

A stein of vomitive beer is drawn and placed in front of me before I sit down. Beer is the blood of Manhattan, peddled to the truly lost souls in a saloon with a sawdust covered floor, a pot-bellied stove, a wall covered with mirrors, nudes, framed news-paper clippings, chromolithographs of boxers and horses, and the miasmas, the perfumes, the soft whisperings of dead memories.

Charley the Chisler, the bartender, wipes down the bar. His arsenal includes knock-out drops. Whenever someone gives Chisler guff, *Pumpkinhead O'Malloy*, the bouncer, steps in. Together, they lay down the law by strip-searching women (usually streetwalkers) who are suspected of having picked a man's pocket. McGurk's the end of the line for the crimson sisterhood. In come a couple of *regular busted dolls*.

A singing waiter not now singing passes the hat to me. I decline.

—*Du hast aber kein Rhythmus!*

I puzzle my failure. I know that my mind will never know ease again until I shall have solved it. Tears of rage well in my eyes.

What is going to happen to me? There are times when I long to sleep forever; but I can't sleep any more because I am always thinking.

Whenever I try to think, my thoughts are so vague that noth-ing ever can crystallize out of them. What I feel is the curse of all those who have only half a talent; it is like a man who leads you along a dark corridor with a light and just when you are in the middle of it the light goes out and you are left alone.[*]

I certainly have much to complain about in myself and I am quite surprised and alarmed by my state. Do I need a change? I have no idea. Is it physical illness that weakens my mind and will, or is it spiritual sloth that fatigues the body? I have no idea. What I feel is an immense discouragement, an unbearable sensation of loneliness, a perpetual fear of some vague misfortune, a complete lack of confidence in my powers, a total absence of desires, the impossibility of finding anything to distract my mind.

Language is leading me astray. If I only knew how language worked, how it pictures the world, and what features common to both language and the world make it possible for this picturing to take place. The great problem on which everything hinges: Is there an order in the world *a priori*, and if so what does it consist in?

Almost against my will, I am forced to conclude that there is such an order: it consists of *facts*, not things—that is, it consists of things (objects) standing in certain relations to one another. These facts—the relations that exist between objects—are mirrored, pictured, by the relations between the symbols of a proposition. But if language is analyzable into *atomic* propositions, then it looks as though there must be atomic *facts* corresponding to those atomic propositions. And just as atomic propositions are those that are incapable of being analyzed any further, atomic facts are relations between *simple* rather than complex objects.

The world has a fixed structure, indeed.[*]

It is very hard and very painful to work in the midst of such cruel and trivial worries. I am driven from pillar to post. The

---

[*] *If I only knew how language ... The world has a fixed structure, indeed.* Reprinted with the permission of The Free Press, a Division of Simon & Schuster Adult Publishing Group, from *LUDWIG WITTGENSTEIN: The Duty of Genius*, by Ray Monk. Copyright © 1990 by Ray Monk. All rights reserved. Published in the UK by Jonathan Cape. Reprinted with permission of The RandomHouse Group Ltd.

somber solitude that I have created around myself has bound me more closely to Lillie as well as to Moriarty. I still feel irresistible infatuation mingling strangely with exasperated revolt, tormenting me with obscure desires. Lillie is a strange deity as dark as night.

It takes money even to stupefy oneself, to punish myself for having failed in all my dreams.* Take notice of the activity in the back room.

Lies told by the sultaness of low places. Moriarty's crippling laughter. It is hate for everyone and for ourselves that has led us toward these lies. It is from despair at not being noble and handsome by natural means that we have so strangely painted our faces. We have so much subjected our hearts to sophistries and we have so abused the microscope in order to study the hideous excrescences and the shameful warts with which they are covered . . . that it is impossible for me to speak the language of other men.

For a long time I have said that the scientist is *supremely* intelligent, that he is *intelligence* par excellence—and that *imagination* is the most *logical* of the faculties, because it alone understands universal analogy, or what a mystic religion calls *correspondence*: I once called it *Technology*, the good works done in the revolutionary new faith called human *Progress*.

What is *indefinite Progress*? What is a society that is not *aristocratic*! It is not a society, it seems to me. What is meant by man in a state of *natural* goodness? Where has he been known to exist? A naturally good man would be a *monster*, I mean a *God*.

---

* *I still feel irresistible infatuation ... in all my dreams.* From *Baudelaire: A Self-Portrait, Selected Letters Translated and Edited with a Commentary, by Loies Boe Hyslop and Francis E. Hyslop, Jr.* Oxford: Oxford University Press, 1957. By permission of Oxford University Press.

All the heresies to which I referred just now are, after all, only the consequence of the great modern heresy, of an *artificial* doctrine replacing a natural doctrine—I mean the suppression of the idea of original sin.

The insight awakens dormant ideas—and in connection with *original sin* and with *form moulded on an idea*, I have often thought that maleficent and loathsome animals were perhaps only the vivification, the corporealization, and the hatching into material life of man's *evil thoughts*. Thus all *nature* participates in original sin.

How is original sin connected to my present state of mind?

I don't know.

I am killing myself—without *sorrow*. I feel none of those perturbations which men call *sorrow*. My debts have never been a cause of *sorrow*. Nothing is easier than to dominate such things. I am killing myself because I can no longer live, because the weariness of going to sleep and the weariness of waking are unbearable to me. I am killing myself because I am useless to others—*and dangerous to myself*. I am killing myself because I believe I am immortal and because *I hope*.[*]

—If I wuz a millionaire,—a fellow denizen pipes up,—I'd give perfume ter der busted gals an' seegars an' free lunch ter der b'hoys. Now how does dat grab yer?

When I think of how ill I have been for the past several days as a result of anger and amazement, I wonder how I can possibly

---

[*] *I am killing myself ... because I hope.* From *Baudelaire: A Self-Portrait, Selected Letters Translated and Edited with a Commentary, by Loies Boe Hyslop and Francis E. Hyslop, Jr.* Oxford: Oxford University Press, 1957. By permission of Oxford University Press.

endure the accomplished fact!* And now a jargonizing and insufferable idiot!

　—Ah, go chase yerself.

As for me, I know that, no matter what enjoyable experience, pleasure, money, or honors may befall me, I shall always miss that woman. Lest my grief, which perhaps you cannot understand, appear too childish, I shall confess that, like a gambler, I had put all my hopes on that head; that woman was my only distraction, my only pleasure, my only comrade.

When at last I realized that it was really *irreparable*, I was seized by a nameless rage: I was sleepless for ten days, vomiting all the time, and obliged to hide, because I wept constantly. My fixed idea was a selfish one, moreover: I saw before me an interminable succession of years without a family, without friends, without a mistress, endless years of loneliness and troubles— and nothing to fill my heart. I couldn't even draw consolation from my pride. For all this was my own fault: I used and abused her; I enjoyed torturing her, and now I am being tortured in my turn.

A discrete inquiry with Cheapskate Charlie reveals that there are accommodations for *yen shee quoy* in the commodious back room. I am conveyed there to a filthy mattress where I lay down. A Chinese appears to me and bows.

　—*Yen pok*,—I say, asking for the high hat stuff.

He bows and leaves.

People suppose opium smoking to be a principally a Chinese custom, however, New York's opium dens are one place where

---

*　*When I think of how ill I have been ... the accomplished fact!* From *Baudelaire: A Self-Portrait, Selected Letters Translated and Edited with a Commentary,* by Loies Boe Hyslop and Francis E. Hyslop, Jr. Oxford: Oxford University Press, 1957. By permission of Oxford University Press.

all nationalities are indescriminately mixed, yet one where white men and women preponderate.

The Chinese returns with a layout. I roll the pill, charge the bowl, light the pipe, and inhale the pungent medicinal aroma. The panels of my vision lose their dimensionality and dreams are spread out flat before me. The darkened room opens into the country of myself that I have traversed so many times without discovering the location of the capital.

Of course, it is only one of the thousand types of dreams by which I am beset, and I don't need to tell you that their utter strangeness, their general character which is absolutely foreign to my pursuits, lead me to believe that they are a language of hieroglyphics whose key I do not possess.

It is two or three o'clock in the morning (in my dream), and I am walking alone in the streets. I meet Wilde, who has several errands to do, and I tell him that I will accompany him and that I will make use of the cab to do a personal errand. And so we take a cab. I think it a sort of *duty* to present a book of mine, the *Book of Life*, which has just been published, to the procuress of a large house of prostitution. When I look at the book which I hold in my hand, *I discover* it is an obscene book, which explains the *necessity* of offering the work to that woman. Moreover, in my mind this necessity is in reality a pretext, an occasion to give a passing kiss to one of the girls of the house; all of which implies that without the necessity of presenting the book, I shouldn't have dared to go into such a house.

I say nothing of all this to Wilde. I have the cab stop at the door of the house, and I leave Wilde in the cab, promising myself not to keep him waiting a long time.

I ring and enter. I notice that my penis is hanging out of the fly of my unbuttoned trousers, and I feel it is indecent to appear that way even in such a place. Moreover, feeling my feet to be very wet, I notice that *they are bare* and that I have stepped in a pool of water at the foot of the stairway. Bah! I say to myself, I

shall wash them before getting a kiss and before leaving the house. I go upstairs.

I find myself in huge adjoining galleries—badly lighted—dreary and faded in appearance—like old cafes, or old reading rooms, or ugly gambling houses. The girls, scattered through these vast galleries, are talking with men, among whom I noticed some students. I feel very sad and intimidated; I am afraid they will see my feet. I look at them, I notice I have a shoe on *one* of them. What impresses me is that the walls of these huge galleries are decorated with drawings of all kinds, in frames. Not all of them are obscene. There are even some drawings of buildings and some Egyptian figures. As I feel more and more intimidated and as I don't dare approach a girl, I amuse myself by carefully examining all the drawings.

In a remote corner of one of these galleries I find a very strange series. In a large number of small frames I see drawings, miniatures, photographic prints. They represent bright colored birds with very brilliant plumage, each with one eye that is *alive*. Sometimes only half a bird is pictured. In some cases they represent images of creatures that are strange, monstrous, almost amorphous, like meteorites. In a corner of each drawing there is a note: *Such and such a girl, aged XX, has given birth to this foetus, in such and such a year.* And other notes of this kind.

Now I have shoes on both feet.

The thought occurs to me that such drawings are not very conducive to suggesting ideas of love. Another thought is this: there is really only one newspaper in the world, and that is *The New York Times*, which could be stupid enough to open a house of prostitution and at the same time include in it a sort of a medical museum. Indeed, I say to myself suddenly, it is *The New York Times* which has furnished the capital for this speculation in brothels, and the medical museum is explained by its mania for *progress, science*, and the *diffusion of knowledge*. Then I think that modern stupidity and folly have a mysterious

usefulness and that evil-doing is often transformed into good through spiritual mechanics.

I admire the accuracy of my philosophic reasoning. But, among all these creatures there is one that is alive. It is a monster which was born in the house and which stands endlessly on a pedestal. Although alive, it is nevertheless a part of the museum. It is not ugly. Its face is even pretty, very tanned, of an Oriental color. There is a lot of rose and green in it. It is crouching, but in a strange and contorted position. There is moreover something blackish which is twisted several times around it and around its limbs, like a large snake. I ask him what it is; he tells me it is a monstrous appendage which grows out of his head, something elastic like rubber, and so long that, if he were to roll it around his head like a braid of hair, it would be much too heavy and absolutely impossible to wear;—that, hence, he is obliged to twine it around his limbs, which, moreover, makes a finer effect. I talk with the monster at great length. He tells me about his troubles and his sorrows. For several years he has been obliged to remain in this room, on this pedestal, because of the curiosity of the public. But his chief worry occurs at dinner time. Since he is a living being, he is obliged to dine with the girls of the establishment—to walk tottering, with his appendage of rubber, to the dining-room, where he has to keep it twined around him or place it on a chair like a bundle of rope, for, if he let it drag on the floor, it would pull his head backwards. Furthermore, he is obliged, small and dumpy as he is, to sit beside a tall and well-built girl. What is more, he gives me all these explanations without any bitterness. I don't dare to touch him, but I am interested in him.[*]

—Gimme me an' my rag *yen pock*,—someone says.

---

[*] *Of course, it is only one of the thousand types of dreams ... but I am interested in him.* From *Baudelaire: A Self-Portrait, Selected Letters Translated and Edited with a Commentary, by Loies Boe Hyslop and Francis E. Hyslop, Jr.* Oxford: Oxford University Press, 1957. By permission of Oxford University Press.

—See?—says a Bowery B'hoy, making a lateral slicing motion with his hand palm down.

I am trying to remember my dream. I will redream my dream. My dream ... Lillie of a certain condition when she left for America. That's what she. *Engelmacher.*

Someone just kicked open the doors of perception.

—Okey, the jig is up!

A group of policemen are brandishing nightsticks.

—Youse hop heads are all under arrest!

Nous sommes tous sauvages.
—Oscar Wilde

It is difficult for me to laugh at life as I used to.

The influence I intended to use for the return of our money now instead went to obtain Holmes' release. It was not necessary to post bail because Inspector Williams released Holmes on his own recognizance. He certainly did this as a courtesy to a fellow investigator.

—Just stay out of McGurk's,—admonished Inspector Williams.

A cab took us back to the cursed *Brevoort.*

Holmes was in the most deplorable condition. He was not far removed from suicide, feeling himself a miserable creature, full of sin, straining his mind constantly at things which are discouraging by their difficulty. I sat in silent dejection until some time had passed, then Holmes began to speak with feverish animation.

I have so deep a respect for the extraordinary qualities of Holmes that I have difficulty not deferring to his wishes, especially when I least understand them.

—You bear a grudge against me,—said Holmes.

—No,—I replied definitively,—it is not the undertone of a grudge that made me speak rather crossly; it is just fatigue or impatience with the difficulty, almost impossibility, when one has a conversation about something affecting you personally, of being successful in conveying true impressions into your mind and keeping false ones out. And then you go away and invent an explanation so remote from anything then in my consciousness that it never occurred to me to guard against it! The truth is that I alternate between loving and enjoying you and your conversation and having my nerves worn to death by it. It's no new thing! But *grudge, unkindness*—if only you could look into my heart, you'd see something quite different.

235

—You mean well, Wilde—said the sick man with something between a sob and a groan.—Shall I demonstrate to you your own ignorance? What do you know, pray, of Tapanuli fever? What do you know of the black Formosa corruption?

—I have never heard of either.

—There are many problems of disease, many strange pathological possibilities, Wilde.—He paused after each sentence to collect his failing strength.—I have learned so much during some recent researches which have a medico-criminal aspect. You can do nothing.

He refused to see a physician. He grew nauseous, as if he would vomit up his former life. His bones were sticking out of his face and his great bright eyes were looking at me. He had changed so much since we first arrived. I could stand no more of it. He was dying. To some kind of men their graces serve as enemies. O, what a world is this, when what is comely envenoms him that bears it!

I sat Holmes down on a comfortable ottoman in the lobby after we reached the hotel. Holmes' appearance had changed for the worse. Those hectic spots were more pronounced, the eyes shone more brightly out of darker hollows, and a cold sweat glimmered upon his brow.

I am always thinking about myself, and I expect everybody else to do the same. That is what I call sympathy. And I can sympathize with everything, except suffering. I cannot sympathize with that. It is too ugly, too horrible, too distressing. There is something terribly morbid in the modern sympathy with pain. Holmes' pain fills me with nothing but aversion. He thinks too much about himself, and if he begins again I shall refuse to listen unless I think he is quite desperate. He has talked it out now

as much as is good for him.* He is tedious; he is a bore; I cannot stand him; I cannot look at him; I must get away from him. One should sympathize with the color, the beauty, the joy of life. The less said about life sores, the better.

—Rooms 614 and 615, please,—I said to the desk clerk.

—I'm sorry, Mr Wilde,—replied the perfunctory young man,—neither your nor Mr Holmes have paid your bill yet, and I have been instructed not to give you the key to your room until such payment is made.

—That is preposterous!—I shot back, raising my voice.— Mayor Kelly gave Holmes the Key to the City—how can you deny him the key to his room!?

—I'm sorry, sir, those are the rules of this hotel.

Who are these dictators of the desk who sway with such serene incapacity the office which they have so lately swept?

—I wish to speak to the manager!—I demanded, bristling with fury.

—He has gone to lunch and will return in an hour.

—An hour! People are put into prison for not paying their debts but they are never punished for the violation of oaths of love and friendship. Mr Sherlock Holmes is a sick man, and he needs rest and medical attention. Why just look at him!

I turned demonstratively toward Holmes, and discovered him to be gone. I dashed into the street and its roiling crowds, but a vast maddening parade of street life carried on, indifferent to my fate or Holmes!

What now? I suppose he'll turn up again.

---

* *He thinks too much about himself ... as much as is good for him.* Reprinted with the permission of The Free Press, a Division of Simon & Schuster Adult Publishing Group, from *LUDWIG WITTGENSTEIN: The Duty of Genius*, by Ray Monk. Copyright © 1990 by Ray Monk. All rights reserved. Published in the UK by Jonathan Cape. Reprinted with permission of The RandomHouse Group Ltd.

A hearse goes by. I sympathize with Holmes. Private investigators suffer so much on behalf of their clients. I, on the other hand, used to live entirely for pleasure. I shunned suffering and sorrow of every kind. I hated both. I resolved to ignore them as far as possible: to treat them, that is to say, as modes of imperfection. They were not part of my scheme of life. They had no place in my philosophy. My mother, who knew life as a whole, used often to quote me Goethe's lines—written by Carlyle in a book he had given her years ago, and translated by him, I fancy, also:—

Who never ate his bread in sorrow,
Who never spent the midnight hours

Weeping and waiting for the morrow,—
He knows you not, ye heavenly powers.

They were the lines which that noble Queen of Prussia, whom Napoleon treated with such coarse brutality, used to quote in her humiliation and exile; they were the lines my mother often quoted in the troubles of her later life. I absolutely declined to accept or admit the enormous truth hidden in them. I could not understand it. I remember quite well how I used to tell her that I did not want to eat my bread in sorrow, or to pass any night weeping and watching for a more bitter dawn.

I now see that sorrow, being the supreme emotion of which man is capable, is at once the type and test of all great art. What the artist is always looking for is the mode of existence in which soul and body are one and indivisible: in which the outward is expressive of the inward: in which form reveals.

Behind joy and laughter there may be a temperament, coarse, hard, and callous. But behind sorrow there is always sorrow. Pain, unlike pleasure, wears no mask. Truth in art is not any correspondence between the essential idea and the accidental existence; it is not the resemblance of shape to shadow, or of the form mirrored in the crystal to the form itself; it is no echo coming from a hollow hill, any more than it is a silver well of

water in the valley that shows the moon to the moon and Narcissus to Narcissus. Truth in art is the unity of a thing with itself: the outward rendered expressive of the inward: the soul made incarnate: the body distinct with spirit. For this reason there is no truth comparable to sorrow. There are times when sorrow seems to me to be the only truth. Other things may be illusions of the eye or the appetite, made to blind the one and cloy the other, but out of sorrow have worlds been built, and at the birth of a child or a star there is pain.

The fluid motion of the crowd takes me to the Bowery.

The wash hangs like flags in the tenements, billowing in the wind, collecting the ambient soot from factory smokestacks. The hubbub of the street features signboards that resembled English pub signs, and their language draws on a tradition stretching back to the Middle Ages: the druggists feature mortars and pestles; opticians, enormous eyeglasses; sporting-goods dealers, huge guns; tobacconists, meerschaums; wine merchants, demijohns. The hot-corn girls of idealized poverty and the unspeakable derelicts from the block and fall joints vie for the sidewalks with the *pullers-in* of local haberdashers, champions of assault merchandising who do not release their clients until they have made a purchase:—*It fits like der paper on der vall!*

Everything in the Bowery is loaded, fraudulent, or short-counted. Even the pushcart peddlers sell rotten fruit, cutlery made of scrap, ink bottles filled with water. Creative merchandising is everything.

Fex urbis, lex orbis.

I recall a young Harvard instructor once spoke to me about the early French explorers. America was the Dark Continent, and the French, *voyageurs* and adventurous aristocrats, with incomparable daring, moved up and down its uncharted rivers. La Salle, who was descending the Mississippi, to which no Anglo-Saxon had yet penetrated, left several men behind to build a boat. When he came back he found the boat only half-finished and his compatriots vanished. Upon the timbers were scrawled

these words: *Nous sommes tous sauvages*. All foreigners should bear this message in mind, scribbled upon a half-finished boat in the wilderness.[*]

---

[*] *I recall a young Harvard instructor ... upon a half-finished boat in the wilderness.* From AMERICA AND COSMIC MAN by Wyndham Lewis, copyright © 1949 by Wyndham Lewis. Used by permission of Doubleday, a division of Random House, Inc.

My dear Wilde, I write these few lines through the courtesy
of Professor Moriarty, who awaits my convenience for
the final discussion of those questions
which lie between us.
—Sherlock Holmes

Guns are pointed at me. Pearl grey and brown derbies tilted over one ear, suits in loud checks with a tight coat, worn over a pink striped shirt, wrapped in flaring box coats. Red Rocks Ferrel, Googy Corcoran, Slops Connolly and his brother, Baboon, hold me now at bay. They looked much as they did when I uncovered their look-out post behind the mirror in my room, except now the tables are turned: they are free on bail. This is the poetry of justice at work. Googy is particularly vengeful because of the gunshot wound he suffered at my hands. Dandy John Nolan restrains him from pistol-whipping me, then shoves me into a hearse they have acquired for the occasion. We proceed under cover of a mock funeral complete with black drapes in the vehicle and crepe bands for their hats, solemn festooning, and a coffin, presumably for my ultimate disposition. It is no secret. They are taking me to Moriarty. Evidently, my self-advertisement at *McGurk's* was indeed successful. I am blindfolded but make mental note of our orientation by tracking the hoof-count as well as the progression of left and right turns. I know we are at Houston and Crosby Streets when the blindfold is removed at our destination: a dive called *The House of Lords*, whose propinquity to Police Headquarters I can not ignore.

—That's police headquarters,—I remark.

—The nearer to church, the closer to God,—replies one of the Bowery B'hoys.

The House of Lords is a *shock house*, selling a concoction of whiskey, hot rum, camphor, benzene, and cocaine sweepings for six cents a glass, and caters to an enclave of crooks from the United Kingdom. The customers, the scum of the earth, surely

know the oblivion awaiting them. I am led through a long, dark corridor and emerge in the bar, tended by Ludovic the Vampire, a monster of a man who is afficted with hypertrichosis: they say he is a vampire, but I am disinclined to believe in the existence of such creatures. My analysis leads me to believe that he is a victim of porphyria, a metabolic disorder which evidences many symptoms commonly imputed to vampires.

I am led into the cellar, which is crammed with stolen merchandise from uptown mansions. All around are catacombs employed for the bagnio, consisting of dozens of featureless cubicles, one of which conceals the mouth of a tunnel that communicates with a large chamber, a capacious room with rough masonry walls and a vaulted ceiling that seem to conjure the devil's dominions. It appears to have been converted from a warehouse cellar into a fairly comfortable and secret office. There are no windows. Many charts of buildings are tacked up on the walls along with a marked map of New York. Books are visible on shelves—ledgers, railway guides, etc. The masonry has long ago been whitewashed but is now old, stained and grimy. There is a large, solid-looking door, fitted with mechanical devices for opening, closing, lowering. Such is Professor Moriarty's research laboratory for world-destruction.

Professor Moriarty himself is seated at a large circular desk where he pores over letters, telegrams, papers. A single light directly overhead illuminates his desk. His massive head of grey hair and beard evoke a Mephisthophelean figure. His face is full of character and intellectual force.

Moriarty picks up the telephone, deliberately ignoring me. There are less than three hundred telephones in New York City.

—Send Ryder in,—he orders.

Moriarty hangs up the telephone, thinking, poised to act, when a mincing gait heralds Ryder, a balding and bookish looking man with a nervous disposition.

—Any news from London?

—Nothing yet, sir.

—The others have reported?

—Yes, sir.

—I knew there was trouble ahead,—says Moriarty.—If we lose Myers—he's one of our top men! Send in Maxwell.

A fine-looking man of about forty signals his entrance with a cough.

—What happened in London?—demands Moriarty.

—The whole thing was a trap—set and baited by an expert.

—The letters and papers of instruction?—growls Moriarty with undisguised alarm.

—Ward disappeared and the documents are gone!

—Gone!—shouts Moriarty with sudden vehemence.

The men stand about in silent and disjunctive submission.

—Who could have done it?—asks Maxwell.

Moriarty's head vibrates from side to side, an angry vein throbbing in his forehead,—Say it yourself.

—Sherlock Holmes.

Moriarty nods slowly several times, then fixes his eyes histrionically upon me for the first time.

—Sherlock Holmes.

The room is filled with the sudden atmosphere of distress as all eyes follow the Professor's cue and turn upon me. This audience fears and pities me; I know this as sure as death. My mere presence aggrieves them one and all.

—He's got hold of between ten and fifteen papers and instructions on different jobs—and he's gradually completing chains of evidence that, if we let him go on, will reach to me as surely as the sun will rise. Reach to me! Ha!—sneers Moriarty.—You're playing a dangerous game, Holmes. Inspector Wilson tried it seven years ago in London, and we haven't heart from Wilson lately, have we?

—No, sir, we haven't,—answers Maxwell.

—Holmes,—says Moriarty with incisive mockery,—You're rather a talented man, but you didn't realize that there isn't a

street in New York that ever offered you safe haven once your
name was whispered into my ear.

I stand silent before my accusers.

The telephone interrupts him once again. Moriarty answers.

—Blaine is here? Send him in.—Moriarty returns his
attention to me, and continues unabated: —You are about to
meet the next President of the United States, James G. Blaine.

Blaine, a soft-looking man with a full grey beard and an elegant way of dressing, is shown into the room. He hands his top
hat and cane to Maxwell.

—My dear Moriarty,—Blaine says unctuously,—how are
you?

—Fair to middling, Blaine, but once you're elected, I will
be—*we* will be on top of the world!

—With the support of Tammany Hall, we shall be able to win
the election handily.

—We certainly can't monopolize the steel, rail and oil industries if we lose the election,—rejoins the Professor.

The moral standards of the young nation have touched a low
water mark. It is an epoch of rusty souls, war profiteers, con-
tractors in shoddy goods, manipulators of the stock market, vendors of quack medicines, brazen promoters of fake enterprises
... millionaires without taste, suavity or ordinary common
decency. Money is a raw force untempered by taste or elegance.

—Impossible. That blowhard Big John Kelly can steal more
votes from them than they can from us,—boasts Blaine.—You
and I are going to make money, a great deal of money.

—Yes, it is ripe for picking.

—And pick we shall,—chimes Blaine.—We'll do it just as
we built the Union Pacific Railroad through *Credit Mobilier.*
Just as when the country had to have a railroad to connect California to the East, a company was formed to build such a railroad; so with the steel and oil industries. And it cannot be done
without government involvement. Once I'm elected President,
Congress will give you aid with an open hand. Why, with *Union*

Pacific, I had Grant agree to lend the Company $27,000,000 in United States bonds. He trusted me. Congress then permitted the railroad to issue $27,000,000 of first mortgage bonds which took precedence over the government loan. That's when we got smart. Why turn all this wealth of land and money over to the Company? Why not keep it for ourselves by contracting to build the railroad and let the public be damned? Soon we made a contract with ourselves as the owners of *Credit Mobilier* to build the railroad at a price per mile more than three times the actual cost of the railroad. And even before that, we had mortgaged the nonexistent railroad and land grants for $37,000,000. Through some fancy financial hocus-pocus, most of these proceeds were turned over to *Credit Mobilier*. Everybody made money, except of course, Union Pacific, which kicked off its existence flat broke, with all of its actual assets in the hands of a no-name Pennsylvania corporation, and the government holding a worthless second mortgage. Whenever anybody in Congress wanted to know what was going on and where the government's money went, why, we just passed the sugar bowl around. And no one could point an accusing finger at us! That's the beauty of it! Let the public be damned!

The telephone sounds off again, whereupon Moriarty answers. Blaine pauses to light a dilatory cigar.

—Send him in,—orders Moriarty to the telephone,—Kelly is here.

—That blowhard!—says Blaine affectionately.

Kelly approaches the desk slowly, suspiciously as if he doesn't like the *genius loci*. He is the last and key agent of my putative destruction. Certainly he was responsible for the subtle espionage that confounded my efforts on behalf of the Governor. Hatred and a strong taste for revenge sear their ambitions into my brain. Evil machinations have sabotaged the law, compromised free elections, gelded free enterprise and pitched citizen against citizen in a war of greed. Evil is the oldest law on earth.

—Good evening, gentlemen,—says Kelly.

245

—Good evening.

—I understand that you have something to report on the subject of Sherlock Holmes,—is Kelly's opening gambit.

—Sherlock Holmes?!—cries Blaine with real fear.

—Gentlemen,—Kelly begins with suavity and confidence,— whenever Tammany is whipped at the polls, the people set to predictin that the organization is goin to smash. That was what was said after the throwdown in '80. But it didn't happen, did it? Not one big Tammany man deserted, and today the organization is as strong as ever.

—Brevity, Big John, is the soul of wit,—Blaine gently interposes.

—Truer words were never spoke,—says Kelly to Moriarty.— Me and the Republicans are enemies just one day out of the year—election day. Then we fight tooth and nail. But this election day, we're on the same side.

Kelly backslaps Blaine, causing that man of the people to choke on his cigar.

—Yes, Big John; I esteem your support,—answers Blaine, coughing his voice back to audibility.

—You see,—resumes Kelly,—we differ on tariffs and currencies and all them things, but we agree that when a man works in politics, he should get something out of it.

—Plato says man is a political animal,—quotes Moriarty.

—Precisely,—seconds Kelly, quick on the uptake,—and if Plato runs his organization like us, he knows we politicians have to stand together this way or there wouldn't be any political parties in a short time. The republic would fall and soon there would be a cry of *Vevey le roi!*

Big John Kelly decants a liberal glass of spirits for himself from a crystal gleaming on Moriarty's desk.

—The long and the short of it is after Sherlock Holmes bollixed up Uncle Jumbo's attempt to get the birth certificate of the little bitch-bastard he had by the sorrowful mother, a bleak mort

named Amber Halpin, Holmsey lost his mind. He's stark raving mad. A lunatic. A *bona fide* imbecile. No harm to anyone. —Oh really,—says the Professor in a suavely contradictory tone,—would you like to judge for yourself? A grim silence overcomes Blaine and Kelly. —He is here. Kelly, at last, becomes aware of my presence. A *true lightning change artist*, he blanches, and fear disfigures his face into a turpitudinous gargoyle. I steady my gaze on Honest John, my betrayer. —What are you going to do with him?—asks Kelly. —You have no choice. —No choice?—echoes Kelly. —If some law is about to be broken, Moriarty, it was unwise of you to invite me while a . . . a . . . a. . . .—stutters B-b-blaine. —No choice. No choice! No choice!!—shrieks Moriarty with casuistical force.—Then, calmly:—Have you got your full crew? —All here, sir. —No mistakes tonight?—he chides now with schoolmasterly joviality. —Extra careful tonight.

I am blindfolded and returned to the hearse. Moriarty is laughing. The Professor's laughter echoes, quartering from infinity to infinity the dimensionless unreality of this moment, where time and space have converged in a slowmoving hearse to conspire malevolent laughter, treachery, death.

The carriage comes to a halt. Brine. Gulls. The sea. The blindfold is removed. The Brooklyn Bridge, the seventh wonder of the modern world, looms ahead.

Night clips at the heels of this November sunset, the most terrible November in the history of the world. God's curse hangs heavily over a degenerate world: an awesome hush and vague expectancy pervade the cool, stagnant air. Sunset, one long, blood-red gash, is an open wound in the belly of the western sky.

247

Above, the stars are shining brightly and below, the lights of the shipping glimmer in the bay.

—Stop right there, Holmes,—orders the Professor.

I stop.

—Wait here, men,—the Professor instructs his accomplices.

—Holmes, just keep walking. We're going to settle our differences once and for all.

I toil up the stairs leading to the catwalk, Moriarty covering me with his revolver from a safe distance behind. I raise my eyes to the magnificent metal architecture that surrounds me in the splendorous cathedral of industrial progress. We gain the center of the bridge and Moriarty orders me again to *Stop*. A tide of weighted wagons and carriages speeds noisily along the roadways above us, and the rumble of the two iron paths upon which the trains move shears strident music from metal straining against metal. The busy river below carries schooners and steamboats in its strong, endless current, just as the fluid and indomitable fury of life propels itself over the edge of Time as I have heretofore known it to be.

A great synoptic panorama lies before me, a circuit completed by the villa-dotted Staten Island; the marshes, rivers, and cities of New Jersey; the Palisades walling the mighty Hudson; Long Island, fish-shaped Paumanok; the Narrows, with their frowning forts; the bay, where the colossal Liberty will rise; at last the ocean, with its bridging ships. Let the men and women of New York never lose sight of this bridge that will stand henceforth as a monument to the End of Time.

—This is an historic moment. I, Robert Moriarty, conclude the career of Sherlock Holmes. Have you any last request?

—May I write a note to Wilde? I would like to smoke a cigarette as well.

He does not object. I reach slowly for my cigarette case, unviolently removing a notebook and fountain pen as well. I strike a match and torch the cigarette.

248

Getting rid of *Sorge* is a religious experience, giving me the courage not to care what might happen, for nothing can happen to someone with faith. Now I have a chance to be a decent human being for I am standing eye to eye with death. Perhaps the nearness of death will bring light into life. God enlighten me! May I die a good death, wide awake. May I never lose myself.* I shall do my friends no wrong, for I have none to lament me; the world no injury, for in it I have nothing.

Moriarty watches me with keen pleasure.

> *My dear Wilde, I write these few lines through the courtesy of Professor Moriarty, who awaits my convenience for the final discussion of those questions which lie between us. I am pleased to think that I shall be able to free society from any further effects of his presence, though I fear that it is at a cost which will give pain to my friends, and especially, my dear Wilde, to you.*

I pause, balancing the pen in my hand. My finger taps the sagitate nib, and tells me that the pen is mightier than the sword. I smoke with relish, inhaling sharply, then conclude the letter. I append my signature.

—It is time,—says Moriarty

Now it seems that only two combatants are involved, Professor Moriarty and myself, but it is rather an open engagement between two detachments. Moriarty has the combined strength and intelligence of four men: Machiavelli, Napoleon, Blaine and

---

* *Getting rid of Sorge ... May I never lose myself.* Reprinted with the permission of The Free Press, a Division of Simon & Schuster Adult Publishing Group, from *LUDWIG WITTGENSTEIN: The Duty of Genius*, by Ray Monk. Copyright © 1990 by Ray Monk. All rights reserved. Published in the UK by Jonathan Cape. Reprinted with permission of The RandomHouse Group Ltd.

Kelly. My forces are comprised first of Time; second of Right; the third is vassal and servitor of Reason, loyal Sherlock Holmes; and the last is Willing Heart, which works wonders in extremities. Thus two detachments meet in open combat.

—Will you finally admit that you are beaten, Holmes? You never should have taken up an unjust cause. The wrongness of your case is now clearly established. If you wish to live, think upon how it may be done, while you still have the time. I will say this much, Holmes. It is indeed a burning shame to see so great an adversary as you brought low by a woman. In fact, it makes me laugh!

His scorching sarcasm eats my flesh and cuts a gully in my brain. He vomits forth the laughter composed of the undigested flesh and bones of men he has eaten to achieve his diabolical mission. Though the sting of open insult grieves me, I am enlightened, for it is his overbearing pride that leaves him vulnerable to attack, so proud and boastful as to laugh in my face, ignoring the moment of paralysis between spasms of laughter. That is my moment. I place the letter in the cigarette case, which I set on the catwalk.

—Yes,—I spit into his mocking face,—Now is the time of the assassins!

I fling the fountain pen, which spins three and one half times before the point strikes Moriarty's right eye, making a direct cyclopean hit. The gun, which he had aimed at my heart, misfires. The bullet rips through me like a thunderclap, piercing the flesh of my arm. Thanks to *li yuen*, I feel no pain. The wound is still only an idea—but it is real: a perforation, like the hole in my heart where love pours out. Moriarty loses grip of the gun as he attempts to pluck the fountain pen from his eye, and he falls to his knees, disoriented and raging. We struggle on the catwalk in an effort to reach the gun. This cursed limb of Satan strikes me so powerfully that his blows all but rob me of my senses. Some may now ask where are my comrades-in-arms, Time and Right and Willing Heart? Their battalion has taken a heavy beating. If

they do not come soon, it will be too late! When I finally sense their presence, my courage and mettle rise. Such a rain of blows do I deal him that I give him no chance to look up. I reach the weapon first but Moriarty wrestles with me, first inclining the gun to my chest, which I succeed in turning back. Driving the gun by main force into his chest, I pull the trigger and shoot Moriarty point-blank in the heart. His torso is blown back a full ten feet by the discharge, his arms and head whiplashing from the force of the blast. He falls back, supine. My hand relaxes, and the gun falls unintentionally from it, skips off the catwalk with a clang, and falls into the river below.

It is over now.

I stand myself up to breathe. Blood is soaking my shirt and trousers. My heart beats wildly in my shaking rib cage. I stand above the corpse of my enemy, humble yet victorious, as I vowed I would be. This alone spares me from being the last and the least among men.

By infallible decree, Time, Truth, Reason and Willing Heart have judged him wrong and restored justice to its own again, through me, their humble Instrument. May they long watch over me! This arrogance has been humbled!

But Moriarty's body twitches back to life, and much to my horror, he slowly rises from the dead, smiling sinisterly with insane and otherworldly rectitude, one eye filled with hate, the other with blood.

—I am not so easy to kill, am I?

He is not wounded at all.

—I am wearing a vest impervious to bullets, Holmes. Forty pounds of lead saved my life, in order to be able to take yours.

I stand my ground.

—I swear I will fight you to the death.

He rushes upon me. I bend him over the guardrail, trying to hurl him into the East River, when Moriarty turns. We rock back and forth in a death lock, for I am going to go over the railing with him. Back and forth, back and forth until with a single

overadrenolated surge, I heave myself along with Moriarty over the railing.

Stand still, ye ever moving spheres of heaven, that Time may cease. Let my life but flash before my eyes once again before I crash headlong into the gaping torrent of Oblivion.

I release Moriarty's throat because there remains no more than a heartbeat before our demise. In that short pocket of time I wish to devote myself to the tranquil contemplation of emotions I once felt. I can now succinctly state the theme of *The Book of Life*, which is dedicated to Lillie from her devoted servant in love, SH. It is written for her and a dozen other souls whom I will never see, but whom I love without having seen.

It is with humility really unassumed—it is with a sentiment even of awe—that I invoke the opening sentence of this thought; for of all conceivable subjects I approach the reader with the most solemn—the most comprehensive—the most difficult—the most august.

My general proposition, then, is this:—*In the Original Unity of the First Thing lies the Secondary Cause of All Things, with the Germ of their Inevitable Annihilation.* In the meantime bear in mind that all is Life—Life—Life within Life—less within the greater, and all within the *Spirit Divine.*

O God, doesn't anyone at all understand?

Pleasure for the beautiful body,
but pain for the beautiful soul.
                    —Oscar Wilde

Just as Greek sailors in the time of Tiberius once heard from
a lonesome island the soulshaking cry, *Great Pan is dead!* so the
modern world may be pierced by the grievous lamentation,
Theatre is dead! Art is dead! Sherlock Holmes is—
   The frou-frou of clothing shifts in the press of an embrace
until Frances leaves the room at last, blushing as she strides past
me in the outer office. Manning, who has been ignoring me, enters Cleveland's office.
   A sharp slap leaps off the Governor's desktop.
   —Blaine is a-whoring after votes,—declares Manning's
voice.
   I am straining to hear their every word from my position in
the outer office.
   —I know,—says Cleveland with resignation.
   —Perhaps you should consider campaigning actively for office.
   —Have you forgotten that I am the Governor of the great
State of New York? I will not shirk my gubernatorial duties in
order to make frantic appeals and degrading exposures.
   —The times are a-changing,—Manning insists, contradicting
the Governor in the most respectful manner.
   —Well, one thing hasn't changed. The President of the
United States is a statesman, not a partisan. It has heretofore
been the custom that candidates remain at home and mind their
own goddamn business—and it sounds like a good policy to
me—since we might as well admit that we've already lost the
election.—He pauses.—Is there any other bad news you wish to
convey?
   —Yes,—says Manning with uncertain tone.—Mr Oscar
Wilde is here to see you.

Disdainful mumbling and contrapuntal laughter swell and subside.

—*Has personal ridicule affected your judgment of the American people?*—It is Holmes' voice I hear. He speaks to me still. Answer: I rarely think of it, and when I do, I think nothing of it.

—*So, you do not fear ridicule?*

Indeed no. I want what I have to say to stand on its own merits. I shall ask no quarter. My mighty engine collided with the limitations of my partners, and my own immaturity. I shall come out of this affair bankrupt, ill, and liable to accusations of treachery and incompetence.

Manning motions to me informally from the inner office. I must exercise absolute self-command.

I see the man in his large bathrobe. His face is sullen, blanched from confinement and overwork. He regards me with great suspicion, holding his chin high with disdain. Discharge my obligation and depart. Holmes took half my life away with him. The devil will take the other half. For unless all the devils in hell pull the other way, my life is bound to become very sad if not impossible.*

—What can I do for you, Mr Wilde?

—Your Honor, I come to bring sad news. A great tragedy has befallen us. I regret to inform you that Sherlock Holmes is dead. The entanglements of your case must remain a mystery, for it has now drawn to an unexpected conclusion.

---

* *For unless all the devils ... very sad if not impossible.* Reprinted with the permission of The Free Press, a Division of Simon & Schuster Adult Publishing Group, from *LUDWIG WITTGENSTEIN: The Duty of Genius*, by Ray Monk. Copyright © 1990 by Ray Monk. All rights reserved. Published in the UK by Jonathan Cape. Reprinted with permission of The RandomHouse Group Ltd.

Cleveland throws his pen angrily at the table, then buries his face in his hands.

—Is there no justice at all?

* * *

Her home is not far away, but the night is dark and rainy, and as the hack splashes along the streets, the driver has trouble making out the number of the house. Moreover, he shows little compunction about jolting me over rough spots.

Finally I put my head out of the carriage window.

—I say, old fellow, what's wrong?

—Damme if I can find the dod-gasted house,—replies the loud-voiced driver.

—You ought to know it.

—Yes, but it's so tarnation dark.

Out pops my head again, with a second protest.

—Look here, you,—roars the driver in retort,—if you want me to fiddle around finding numbers, I'll stop and you can hold the horses. They won't stand tied.

—Bless me, I can't do that.

—Then back downtown we go!

He speaks with the force of an ultimatum, and my pride falls with my fortunes. I get out and stand in the wet minus even my ulster, and hold the horses' heads. Loyal beasts of burden. Can they comprehend death? Perhaps not, but they can smell it. I know that I shall never see Holmes again and I know that all palpable evidence of his being has disappeared, yet it is not a reality as of yet. I still hear Holmes' voice in the purple caverns of memory, and conduct imaginary conversations with him. But are they imaginary? They may be essential. Governor Cleveland must give audience to Holmes' voice, too, as he struggles through his disastrous campaign. I related to him all that I was told by Inspector Williams and his men, which they in turn inferred from evidence left at the scene where the encounter had taken place, and from fragmented testimony gathered from wit-

nesses found on a passing Brooklyn-Manhattan train. They know more, I suspect, than they are willing to reveal.

The driver returns. Good. I give him the wet reins. A funereal curtain of black rain parts as I enter her house.

I relate the news that has rent the fabric of my brain to one of the most beautiful personalities I have ever known: a woman, whose sympathy and noble kindness to me have been beyond power and description, one who has really assisted me, though she does not know it, to bear the burden of my troubles more than anyone else in the whole world has, and all through the mere fact of her existence, through her being what she is—partly an ideal and partly an influence: a suggestion of what my soul might become as well as a real help towards becoming it; a soul that renders the common air sweet, and makes what is spiritual seem as simple and natural as sunlight or the sea: one for whom beauty and sorrow walk hand in hand, and have the same message.

—There is enough suffering in one narrow London lane to show that God does not love man, and that whenever there is any sorrow, though but that of a child in some little garden weeping over a fault that it had not committed, the whole face of creation is completely marred.

—You are entirely wrong,—she tells me.

Only now can I fully understand it. Now it seems to me that love of some kind is the only possible explanation of the extraordinary amount of suffering that there is in the world. I cannot conceive of any other explanation. I am convinced that there is no other, and that if the world has indeed, as I have said, been built of sorrow, it has been built by the hands of love, because in no other way could the soul of man, for whom the world was made, reach the full stature of its perfection. Pleasure for the beautiful body, but pain for the beautiful soul.

Lillie is still crying. The letter is trembling in my hand.

—Go on, please,—she says, regaining her composure.

I have already explained to you, however, that my career had in any case reached its crisis, and that no possible conclusion to it could be more congenial to me than this. Tell Inspector Paterson that the papers which he needs to convict the gang are in pigeonhole M, done up in a blue envelope and inscribed Moriarty. I have made every disposition of my property before leaving England and handed it to my brother Mycroft. Pray send my greetings to Lillie, and believe me to be, my dear fellow, Very sincerely yours, Sherlock Holmes.

—A few words may suffice to tell the little that remains. An examination by experts leaves little doubt that a personal contest between the two men ended, as it could hardly fail to end in such a situation, in their reeling over the bridge into the East River. Any attempt to recover the bodies is absolutely hopeless (unless, I am told, their bodies wash up on Staten Island), and there, deep down in that dreadful cauldron of swirling water, will lie for all time and eternity the most dangerous criminal and the foremost champion of the law of their generation. As to the spies, there can be no doubt that they were among the numerous agents whom Moriarty kept in his employ. As to the gang, it will be within the memory of the public how completely the evidence which Holmes had accumulated exposed their organization, and how heavily the hand of the dead man weighs upon them.

—How he must have suffered,—Lillie sighs.

—It is rather remarkable that Holmes mentioned you in his last letter, especially after your recent contretemps.

She remains decorously silent.

—Blaine's spies obtained advance information on Holmes' plans and stole the birth certificate. If Holmes had gotten it, you can rest assured that it never would have become public.

—But that birth certificate belongs to me,—she protests.— She is my daughter, after all!

Nolo contendere. All I can do is change the topic.

257

—I had no inkling that you had changed your identity in order to bear Cleveland's child.

—That is another matter. Did I ever tell you that I knew Sherlock Holmes before he was Sherlock Holmes?

—Pray tell.

—I am certain that he was inspired to become a detective simply in order to discover my whereabouts.

—He said that you were the only woman he ever loved.

—He never quite understood. . . .—she says remotely.

—Were you angry with him?

—It's a personal matter, Oscar, I'm sure that you will understand: *de mortuis nil nisi bonum.* We're not all alone unhappy.

—Alas, that is true. Death *is* the doctor who cures all ills. But you still have Freddie and *As You Like It.*

—Yes, I do. Scandal never did keep paying customers away from the box office. But as for yourself?

—I don't know. This week I'll enjoy my freedom in New York, because next week I'll be brought to debtor's prison.

We lapse into silence. My roving eye finds delight and distraction from care in her lovely furnishings.

—I love your Japanese screen. Its style is *ukiyo-e, the floating world.* It expresses the transitoriness of life and its fugitive pleasures.

—Go on,—she says invitingly,—tell me more.

—Oh, I know very little. Jimmy introduced me as a correspondent to Ernest Fenellosa, who has devoted himself to the preservation of traditional arts in Japan. The Emperor has said to him, *You have taught my own people to know their own art, and I charge you to teach the Americans.* Since he cannot now carry out the Emperor's mandate personally, my correspondence with him has enabled me to carry on in some manner in his stead.

—What have you learned from Mr Fenellosa?

I place my teacup on the salver.

—It is a simple Japanese cup, roughly fashioned, asymmetrical, plainly colored. It is not unusual to find a crack in it. The

crack is the beautiful, aesthetic flaw that distinguishes the spirit of the moment in which this object was created from all other moments in eternity. The teacup possesses the quality of *wobi*. We are not aware of this feeling because we do not have a word or expression for it. Aesthetics is, therefore, something that can be learned, and more importantly, transmitted from generation to generation, from culture to culture. *A-ware* is another such concept. It is what we experience when a human being sighs because a rainstorm has washed the apricot blossoms from a tree. In other words, *a-ware* is our human quality and capability of recognizing these special aspects of the world. *Shiboui* is a sort of beauty that only the passage of time can reveal. It is the hidden nature of things that is revealed by time's passing. For example, you are beautiful now, but in twenty years, you shall possess another type of beauty as well, distinct from (though related to) the beauty you now possess.

—You know, Oscar, I know how you can make some money.

—How?

—A great deal of it! I'm sure of it.

—The suspense is unbearable.

—Oscar, my American agent is Sam Ward.

—Report speaks goldenly of his profit.

—He is working closely with D'Oyly Carte to bring Gilbert and Sullivan's *Patience* to New York. They want to open it soon because unauthorized productions of the show are already sprouting up.

—I don't think I can write an operetta.

—No, Oscar. I don't mean that. I mean no one in America . . . the only problem is Americans don't know anything about *Bunthorne* and don't know his type. Whitman in shirtsleeves isn't like him, and greybeard Longfellow isn't like him and neither is Emerson.

—*Bunthorne* is portrayed as James Whistler in the London production,—I added.—Jim and I are old friends.

259

—If you lecture on the subject of aestheticism, you will educate the American public to our renaissance, promote *Patience*, and *Patience* will promote you! The only traces of aestheticism that have reached America are women's gowns that hang from the shoulders in flowing folds, Queen Anne furniture, Morris wallpaper, Japanese screens—it's just beginning to be known. Oscar, you can gather the strands together and give them force in a program of lectures.

—Perhaps I can do readings in the manner of Dickens!

—Yes!

Objectivity seldom deserts her.

—Alas, he has a heart of stone who cannot laugh when he hears Dickens tell the story of the death of Little Nell!

She hustles me into her carriage and takes me to Sam's home before I can object.

* * *

Sam Ward is one of the most enchanting personalities that ever brightened this world. He is a ruddy, bald, Napoleanic Marshal of a man. His sixty-eight years have seasoned him with wit and good humor. I disagree with Sam Ward on almost every human topic, but when I have talked to him for five minutes I forget everything save that he is the most delightful company in the world. He is a *bon vivant* celebrated in New York, Boston, Newport, Washington, London, Paris and Berlin as a wit, a spendthrift and an epicure. He is an intimate friend of the Prince of Wales and Lord Roseberry. He knows the Pre-Raphaelite artists better than do I, and as an aesthete he could have made me feel very small indeed if it had not been for Uncle Sam's habit of making everyone feel very important.

—Oh, the British Invasion!—jests Sam upon greeting us.

We retire to the drawing room.

—Lillie, let's drop these shenanigans,—Sam says to Lilly.

—Yes, Sam.

—If you're going to open your own show, you better take the credit for it.

They soberly discuss the opening of the play with a view to box office. I keep out of the conversation until they conclude their discussion. It is agreed that Lillie is to open *As You Like It* under her own name. She then deftly turns the subject to that of *Patience* and my possible lecture series in connection with it.

—I am interested in making some money,—I say.

—Now yer talkin. I want to open Gilbert and Sullivan's *Patience* in New York. I'm certain we can do boffo box office here—even more profitable than the London production!

—Success for *Patience*, patience for success.

—Now yer talkin. I want to make *Bunthorne* an Oscar Wilde type of man in New York. You give the lectures about aestheticism to establish a context. *Patience* will fillip your lectures, and the lectures will fillip *Patience*. That's good business.

—We can make money!

—Now you're talkin American,—he replies with a gleam in his eye.—Being the originator of the aesthetic idea, you've made a profound sensation in English society. What do you propose to discuss in your lectures?

—I can easily prepare three lectures, the first being dedicated to the *Lyric Poem*.

—Nah, nah, America don't want to hear about no *Lyric Poem*.

—Another lecture, perhaps, illustrative of the poetical methods used by Shakespeare.

—Nah, nah, America don't want to hear about no Shakespeare.

—Well, perhaps a lecture devoted to the consideration of *The Beautiful* in everyday life.

—By jingo, that's it! *The Beautiful!* I can just see it now: Women's gowns that hang from the shoulders in flowing folds! Queen Anne Furniture! Morris wallpaper! Japanese screens! I can see it all now! We'll work up three/four lectures here in New York, and then we'll send you out to crisscross the American heartland.

Uncle Sam could even make the provinces alluring.
—May I bring up the subject of an advance?
—By all means.

I laughed, lit a cigarette, threw myself back on my chair, and replied precisely:
—Well, I'm a very ambitious young man. I want to do everything in the world. I cannot conceive of anything that I do not want to do. I want to write a great deal more poetry. I want to study painting more than I've been able to. I want to write a great many more plays, and I want to make this artistic movement the basis for a new civilization.*

At long last, the future belongs to me.

---

* *Well, I'm a very ambitious ... new civilization.* From OCSCAR WILDE by Richard Ellmann, copyright © 1987 by The Estate of Richard Ellmann. Used by permission of Alfred A. Knopf, a division of Random House, Inc.

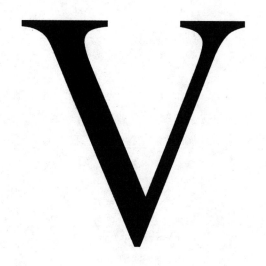

What transforms the day into night
and night into day?
Poetry.

—Sherlock Holmes

My ribs still hurt. I'm surprised that I didn't break them when I hit the water. I'm lucky that no one saw me swim to shore. But the fleshwound in my arm is going to take weeks to heal. So much remains to be done! It is better that I work alone now, and let one and all think me dead.

As the East River sweeps Moriarty's carcass into the ocean, I am swept again into the mighty river of time, the panther who claws me to shreds, but I too am a panther. Headlong I tumble into the labyrinth of Daedalus where so many philosophers have lost their way, where even a detective may be led astray. There are moments when the whole of creation becomes too complex and involuted for speech and thought; mythology, however, pervades life and gives it form.

I prepare by losing myself in the moment.

I have a well-worked-out psychological technique, enormous talent, and great physical and nervous resources. Wherever I may lack sufficient supplies of such resources, I must rely on inspiration. The organic bases of the laws of nature on which my craft is founded will shield me from taking the wrong path.

Clerical collar, vestments, eyeglasses. Can't dress without a mirror, but I must be very careful with its use. It has taught me to observe external manifestations rather than my soul, in spite of myself and my role. Act by looking behind the mirror.

—*Ye are the salt of the earth. This, then, is a corrupt world, and Christianity is the antiseptic that is to be rubbed into it in order to arrest the process of decay.*

There. Like a painter, I create the model in my imagination, then take every feature of it and transfer it, not to a canvas, but to myself. Who would ever suspect that I was not Rev. Samuel D. Burchard?

As a clergyman, I enjoy the freedom of the living and the freedom of the dead. I no longer have any regard for my corpse-like body, mutable, vulnerable to the wrath of enemies, disease and death. I have vomited forth my body to reoccupy it again. I am reborn with each passing moment, reanimating my body like a wandering spirit. Those who suppose me dead and gone are more vulnerable than ever.

What is the privilege of the dead? To die no more. What transforms night into day and day into night? Poetry. What is my faith? Allegiance to the immediate promptings of my consciousness.

On Broadway. Jangle and clatter of horsecar bells and hoofs. The avenues, roofed by the elevated roads where trains roar overhead. There. My destination.

The anteroom of Blaine's New York headquarters is somber. I am distracted by his official portrait and the hunting trophies. At the moment, externals are of great importance. They do not remind me of my room. At first, I find it difficult to retrieve my inspiration without this setting.

I gained admission to this elite group by offering to assemble a group of clergymen to speak on behalf of James G. Blaine. They must *believe* me, and if they do, they will tell me everything.

—Too bad about Moriarty. He was one smart guy.

The voice arising from Blaine's private office belongs to Mayor John Kelly.

Tammany Hall is literally an incarnation of the Devil. . . .

—It is a shame,—answers Blaine from the recesses of the office,—but there are others. The syndicate is vast, bigger than any one person, though Moriarty was a genius.

—I'll always remember him. He helped put us back on top,— says Kelly.

—Bah! The reason why we're on top, Big John, is because of Tammany and—

—And?

—My electrical effect upon voters,—says Blaine with no little vanity.

—Hey,—says Kelly,—wait just a tick, Jim. You were campaignin in the Midwest—that's Republican territory. If it weren't for our Tammany votes, you'd be smashed in New York, and you need New York cuz like you said, we gotta lotta lectrical votes.

—That's my point,—Blaine augustly replies.—I should travel up and down the great State of New York and communicate my great message directly to the people, thereby turning the tide of the election once and for all with my golden voice and Olympian powers of persuasion. I am the great communicator.

—Jimmy,—says Kelly,—the election's in the bag. Go home to Maine, rest, and wait it out. It's as easy as one, two, three.

—Big John, I cannot, because the American people find me irresistible. And it is my duty to give them what they want. I shall begin the final leg of my great campaign here in New York, and I will begin by addressing the clergy.

That is my cue. For a long time I cannot fit myself into my surroundings nor can I concentrate my attention on what is going on around me. Once I am summoned into the office, I am astonished that I continue to speak and to act mechanically.

—May I introduce His Honor the Mayor to Reverend Samuel D Burchard of Murray Hill.

The minute I meet the other characters in this drama, I feel myself possessed by a renewed power. At the same time some new unexpected sensations surge within me. The set hems in the actor.

—I propose,—I begin,—a gathering of ministers whom candidate Blaine may address on the subject of religion, politics, and morality. This would be an excellent manner of initiating his campaign effort in New York, for the event would be widely written up by the newspapers. . . .

I suddenly feel an obligation to interest my audience. This feeling of obligation interferes with my throwing myself into

what I am doing. I begin to feel hurried, both in speech and in action. My favorite places flash by like telegraph poles seen from a train. The slightest hesitation and catastrophe shall be inevitable.

—Furthermore, I suggest a dinner with New York's leading citizens at a suitable location, perhaps *Delmonico's*. . . .

—Splendid!—cries Blaine.—I *love* Delmonico's!

In spite of everything it seems as though I should get through to the end of the scene, yet when I come to the culminating moment in my role, the thought flashes into my mind: *Now I shall be stuck!* Whereupon I am seized by panic, and I stop speaking. I do not know what guides me back to an automatic rendering of my part, but once more it saves me. I have only one thought in my mind, to finish as quickly as possible and get out of the office.

> *The form of government that is most suitable*
> *to the artist is no government at all.*
>
> —Oscar Wilde

I spent the last three days in seclusion at the wonderful *Fifth Avenue Hotel* where I slept, ate, read and wrote. I spent my time reading Balzac's *Peau de Chagrin*, and Nerval:

> *Ou sont nos amoureuses?*
> *Elles sont au tombeau.*

The desk clerk will treasure for years his memory of me with a sunflower in my buttonhole, splashing my odd signature upon the register. Handsome, courteous bellboys showed me a charming two-room suite, 442 and 443, from whose windows I could see, on the south, Lester Wallack's new theatre. It is modern, all gas lights sheathed in tin. See the granite-pillared portico! Ironwork covered with old gold, the comfortable seats, the decorated proscenium. Wallack, who is over sixty now, is one of the oldest and finest actor-managers in New York. A big spender, too. He's to open his house with *School for Scandal*. Rose Coghlan is in the lead.

Daly's. Stars like John Drew and Ada Rehan play there. A clever young juvenile, Otis Skinner, is acting in *Kit, the Arkansas Traveller*. In dime museums, Miss Lizzie Sturgeon is playing the piano with her bare toes—and playing it very well, they say. So much to see and do in New York!

It is a vile night, bleak and bitter, however, I must brave even hurricanes to attend my dinner engagement with Uncle Sam and a few other privileged guests at *Delmonico's*. Long tentacles of lightning flash across the southern sky, followed by percussive thunderclaps. It is a testament to *The Fifth Avenue Hotel*'s high reputation for service that I have a cab waiting for me in this weather. I love civilization.

Upon my arrival at the restaurant, a man accosts me.

—'Scuse me, Sir!

269

He wears a short jacket which he opens. From neck to waist he is bare. He is one of many beggars who panhandle from the patrons of the expensive restaurant. The others lounge against the wall of a nearby building, sheltering themselves from the rain and cold. The society people routinely ignore them. I give this beggar two bits.

—That's all?—he says, rebuking me.

I simply take off my overcoat and put it about the man. Someone, to whom such simplicity must have appeared too Hugoesque, commented,—Why don't you ask him to dinner?

—Dinner is not a feast,—is my rebuttal to the well-dressed stranger,—it is a ceremony.

The stranger precedes me as we enter the restaurant. He looks familiar but I can't place him.

Delmonico's is even more crowded than usual. Moguls, captains of industry, pretty women wearing the smartest dresses. Mrs Schermerhorn stands at the end of the picture gallery, a heavy Tartar-looking lady, with tiny black eyes and wonderful emeralds, talking bad French at the top of her voice, and laughing immoderately at everything that was said to her. It is certainly a wonderful medley of people. Gorgeous peeresses chat affably to violent radicals, popular preachers brush coattails with eminent skeptics, a gaggle of reverends keep following a stout primadonna from room to room, and on the staircase stand several royal academicians, disguised as artists, and it was said that at one time the supper-room was absolutely crammed with geniuses. In fact, it is one of *Delmonico's* best nights.

Here is Edgar Saltus. I call his name.

—Oscar!

He looks well. Be generous. He is not a rival.

—I understand you just struck a deal with Uncle Sam.

I explain to Edgar the terms of Uncle Sam's contract as we wait to be escorted to the table.

—One thousand dollars. That's quite good!

—Mere starvation wages, my dear Edgar.

Sam Ward and Col Morse arrive and we are seated.

Haute cuisine, with the finest wines for every course, is the rule here, reflected in the handwritten menus standing upright in silver holders on the luminous tablecloth. The master chef and his assistants toiled all day to perfect the appearance as well as the taste of the food. All of our gourmet palates have been kept keen by visits to Paris, essential to our well-being. Not plain roast turkey but *dindon rôti aux truffes à l'Espagnole*; no barely warmed grouse but engraved silver platters bearing *faisan à la Flamande*. Hock, claret, burgundy and madeira flow as one dish succeeds another: turtle soup, two kinds of fish, game and roast meats, sherbets and deserts almost too magnificent to be divided.

Sam is a genuine epicure. He carries with him a set of specially designed silverware—a shallow spoon, a tiny fork and a blunt knife—to guard against his most lamentable weakness: a tendency to eat with *too great a rapidity*.

—It is a most unhappy failing,—he says,—to wolf down in *one* minute, what ought to have afforded a full *five* minutes of heavenly mastication. It is, indeed, a vice which deadens enjoyment, as well as abbreviates it.

Much to my surprise, I see we are seated adjacent to a lavish private fundraising party, which accounts for the many clergymen in attendance, and there is the stranger who made the Hugoesque comment to me. Wait—that's no stranger, that's James G. Blaine!

A gathering of clergymen. While Metaphysics has but little real interest for me, and Morality absolutely none, there is nothing that either Plato or Christ have said that could not be transferred immediately into the sphere of Art, and there find its complete fulfillment. It is a generalization as profound as it is novel. Perhaps I shall write a book, *Christianisme contre le Christ*. It shall be the Epic of the Cross, the *Iliad* of Christianity.

—What's all the commotion?

—James G. Blaine is going to address a convention of ministers. I should listen to his speech. Blaine has such skill in ly-

ing—it has so overwhelmed me that I don't seem to be able to lie with any heart lately.

I excuse myself to investigate the affair. Should try to meet him.

—There goes that damn fool, Oscar Wilde,—says a clergyman in passing.

It's extraordinary how soon one gets known in New York. The reverend is a medium-size, dark complexioned man with serious, myopic eyes, small, steel-rimmed spectacles, long curly hair, and sparse whiskers. Sober clerical clothes: a black waistcoat and a cleric's collar. Let me eavesdrop on a bit of his conversation. His lips are too straight, like Holmes' lips, declaring that everything on heaven and earth has already been settled in penny encyclopedias: *the lips of someone who has never lied.* I must teach him to lie, so his lips will be beautiful and curved like those of an ancient mask.

—Politically informed citizens understand that circumstances do not call for an imaginative leader, but for an executive who will purge government of rascals,—says the Presbyterian.

—We must, however, choose between the copulative habits of one, and the prevaricative habits of the other,—replies the Methodist.

—One Mugwump confided to me that we should therefore elect Mr Cleveland to the public office which he is so qualified to fill. . . .

—Of course,—interjects the other,—and remand Mr Blaine to the private station he is so admirably fitted to adorn.

—Your Reverences,—I interrupt,—Would you like me to tell you a secret?—They are astonished by my brilliant rudeness.—Do you know why Christ did not love his mother?—I pause.—It is because she was a virgin!

* * *

—Hey, Oscar!

It's Bury Dasent, the reporter from the *New York World* whom I met upon my arrival. He asked me the most intelligent questions and I took an immediate liking to him. We shake hands.

—I'm covering this for the Democrats, taking down the speeches in sound hand. Won't miss a word with this new method of transcribing living speech.

He displays his notebook proudly. I would love to have a secretary who took sound hand.

—Alas, I shall have to wait until my first theatrical success for such a secretary.

—Are you following the aesthetics of American politics, Oscar?

—Incidentally.

We take our seats just as Mayor Kelly introduces the Reverend Samuel D. Burchard, an elderly man, deformed by age, who takes the podium. It is he, the one who called me a fool!

—Thank you, fellow servants in Christ. I wish to extend a warm welcome to one and all.

He surveys the audience. His head vibrates slowly from side to side in reptilian fashion.

—In this city, every effort to make men respectable, honest, temperate, and sexually clean is a direct blow between the eyes of Governor Cleveland and his whole gang of drunken and lecherous subordinates, in this sense that while we fight iniquity, they shield or patronize it; while we try to convert criminals, they manufacture them; and they have three hundred dollars invested in manufacturing machinery to our one invested in converting machinery. Say all you please about the might of the Holy Ghost, every step in the history of an ameliorated civilization has cost just so much personal push. Therefore, the issue in this campaign is not between two great political parties, but between the brothel and the family, between decency and indecency, between lust and law. We are Republicans and, unlike the

273

Mugwumps, we don't propose to identify ourselves with the party of *Rum, Romanism and Rebellion.* There is an immediate and audible reaction to these explosive words from Mayor Kelly. Indeed, the remark unfairly discriminates against Democrats in broad lines, the Irish and the Catholic.

—*Rum, Romanism and Rebellion?*—echoes Bury in disbelief.

Blaine isn't even paying attention, letting the remark pass because he is lollygagging with a young actress seated at his table.

—Isn't that astonishing?—asks Bury.—He made no reference to the words, and this implies that he endorses them.

—This sentence must be in every daily newspaper in the country tomorrow, no matter what it costs!

—You're right,—he answers.—We may still have a chance to turn the tide of the election.

He earnestly seizes this dim opportunity. Enthusiasm. Only Americans behave in this antic fashion. It is one of their characterizing traits. They also leave without saying good-bye.

I circle round to Blaine's table.

—Looks like this fund-raiser will draw a pretty penny for you, Jim,—says Jay Gould.

I am supposed to meet Mrs Gould at a reception tomorrow night. Uncle Sam is wonderfully well connected.

—God manifests his divine love by making men wealthy,—replies Blaine confidently.

—Speaking of money, do you think you can exert some influence, casually, I mean, to keep the State Legislature from passing the Five-Cent Fare Bill? My contract with the State of New York allows me to charge ten cents at rush hour as opposed to the usual five-cent fare rate. This is government meddling with business.

—Speech, speech!

—Better give the people what they want, Jim,—says John Jacob Astor.

Blaine, the guest of honor, rises to speak:

—Ladies and gentleman, I wish to thank you for attending tonight's fund-raiser. It goes without saying that our war chest is full. The best way for me to show my appreciation to you is to deliver to you another four years of Republican prosperity. The guests applaud avidly. The millionaires are pleased. I must meet Blaine. It won't take but a minute. After the wild applause abates, I approach the table, but Gould leans over to Blaine and distracts him.

—Jim, what did he mean by that *Rum, Romanism and Rebellion* crack? The Democrats might make a big stink about it.

—Oh, hogwash and twaddle!—retorts Blaine.—I suppose all Rev Blowhard Burchard was trying to do was evoke my opponent's old saloon associates. But if they try to attribute that remark to me, I'm going to sue for libel.

—But it might be offensive to the Roman Catholic constituency,—adds John Jacob Astor.

—Well, it's not my fault, and I didn't say it,—says Blaine recoiling in defiance.

—And it furnishes an unpleasant reminder that the Democrats had been on the wrong side of the Civil War,—adds Russell Sage.

—It will blow over. The people love me. Besides, we're going to make a lot of money over the next four years, aren't we boys?

Blaine raises his glass in toast. Gould, Astor and Sage join their glasses to his.

—To us, and to the future!

This is not, I now see, the most opportune time to meet Mr Blaine. Better to return to my dinner companions lest I risk being inattentive.

* * *

—With the death of my father, I set up as a broker on Wall Street,—says Sam as I pick up the silver thread of his narrative,—and revenged myself upon the Puritan strictness of my youth, played the very devil with the checkbook, went

smash, and in 1848 struck off for Californ-eye-a and the gold mines. I was too gently bred to bend all day over a sieve in a creek, so I set up a mercantile house in San Francisco. By 1851 I made a fortune which I then lost in a fire. For the next nine years I roamed, living with the Piute Indians once to win a bet that I could learn their language in three weeks, then chased gold mines in Mexico, hunted concessions in South and Central America and once, in 1862, I represented the United States Government on a diplomatic mission to renew rights for the crossing of Nicaragua.

Romantic rumors about his travels drifted back to New York—women loved him, and one, in fact, is said to have adopted boy's clothing in order to be with him.

It was as a bachelor that Washington knew him on his return from Nicaragua, a bachelor and spendthrift with none of the re-former blood that his father, as founder of the New York City Temperance Society, had bequeathed to his sister, Julia. Mrs Howe was blowing the trumpets of abolition and woman's suffrage, while Sam settled down in Washington to practice and to perfect the newly discovered profession of lobbyist.

He was fond of telling Europeans how his sister Julia had come to write *The Battle Hymn of the Republic*. As a fellow poet, I am one to ask about it.

—Julia had gone to the army camps around Washington in 1861 with her husband, Dr Howe, who was doing relief work. One autumn day she rode in a carriage past soldiers who sang a new song, a great song, *John Brown's Body*. She sang it with them, and a preacher sitting beside her, James Greeman Clarke, said to her, *You ought to write some new words to that tune.* That night, the rhythm, the swinging, marching rhythm, beat in her veins. She couldn't sleep. One grandsire, far back, had rid-den and sung with Cromwell, and he rode again that night in the tent in Virginia. Suddenly, she found the wished-for lines ar-ranging themselves in her brain. She got out of bed, found a pencil and let *The Battle Hymn of the Republic* write itself on the

back of an envelope. It was quite a success. The *Atlantic Monthly* gave her five dollars for it, too.

I am enjoying myself far too much to wonder what all this means. The drinks go down my long throat endlessly. Whiskey and soda, soda and whiskey, all around, over again, and on and on. The night passes, and as the dawn is about to break, the guests begin to arise. They grip at phantom chairs and step elaborately over the shadows on the floor. Through a fog they see me, having arisen steady as a church, leading them firmly, steadily, calmly down the stairs. I move casually toward the door while they clutch at banisters, put on the wrong overcoats and fumble with each other's hats. On the street, Uncle Sam, standing amid the weaving group, says to me,

—Would you like to be escorted to your rooms?

—No, thank you. Really, it's a wonderful night for a stroll,— and stroll away I do as they help each other into cabs.

Sleep comes to me in silvery clouds in my hotel suite.

* * *

When I woke it was twelve o'clock, and the midday sun was streaming through the ivory-silk curtains of my room. I got up and looked out of the window. A dim haze of heat was hanging over the great city, and the roofs of the houses were like dull silver. In the flickering green of the square below, some children were flitting about like white butterflies. Never had life seemed lovelier to me, never had things of evil seemed more remote.

Then my valet brought me a cup of chocolate on a tray. After this leisurely recuperation, I anticipated the great ritual of my day: the long, portentous drama of my *toilette*. (Men once took great pains with themselves; they did not slouch and moon through life.) After I drank my chocolate, I drew aside a heavy *portière* of peach-colored plush, and passed into the bathroom. The light stole softly from above through thin slabs of transparent onyx, and the water in the marble tank glimmered like a moonstone. I plunged hastily in, till the cool ripples touched

277

throat and hair, and then dipped my head right under, as though I would have wiped away the stain of some shameful memory. When I stepped out, I felt almost at peace. The exquisite physical conditions of the moment dominated me, as indeed often happens in the case of very finely-wrought natures, for the senses, like fire, can purify as well as destroy.

I had all the newspapers brought up into my room. Ha HA! The shoe is on the other foot! The headlines read:

THE ROYAL FEAST OF BELSHAZZAR BLAINE
AND THE MONEY KINGS

At a merry banquet of millionaires held in Delmonico's Mr Blaine proceeded from Rum, Romanism and Rebellion to champagne and brandy, frothing and sparkling in glasses that glittered like jewels.

* * * * *

BLAINE HOBNOBBING WITH
THE MIGHTY MONEY KINGS

The clergymen were proud of Mr Blaine, no doubt holding their own in the midst of the mighty winebibbers.

* * * * *

MILLIONAIRES AND MONOPOLISTS
SEAL THEIR ALLEGIANCE

* * * * *

People sometimes enquire what form of government is the most suitable for an artist to live under. To this question there is only one answer. The form of government that is most suitable to the artist is no government at all.

Unde orta est culpa, ibi poena consistat.
—Sherlock Holmes

Children queue up for Sunday school. Innocent lambs of God. Clear eyes, fair skin, animated, high-pitched voices. I would like to be able to read Bible stories to them. Or fairy tales. It would please them and relieve the strain on me. It would be the one good thing in my life.

Ordinary men and women pass their entire lives, sweating, suffering, toiling and sacrificing to keep their families housed, fed and clothed. Others do not care and have children whom they neglect, mistreat, or abandon. If sexual love is the poem of the common man, then children are indeed its blossom and a new generation of men and women its full bloom. Love is the binding force. Poor children. They know not how bitter life tastes. Yes: God loves all his children, but I would prefer not to be loved by God, just as I wish I had not been loved by my parents or step-parents, just as I wish I had not loved anyone else myself. I wish that my heart were empty and had nothing to give to others, and that the hearts of others were empty and had nothing to give to me. The longer one lives, the longer one suffers. To make earthly existence bearable, men have created imaginary worlds vaster than this Cathedral on foundations of tobacco, strong drink, opium, cocaine and ether. I have sufficient hatred of life and everything connected with it to say that.

That is the reason why I shall never have children. Nevertheless, I can now see how children rejuvenate a person worn by *Sorge* and give the exhausted vacuum of existence replenishment with new spirit: makes life worth living.

What is my duty? Whatever each day requires. Submit to that requirement and I will have a tranquil heart.

I am so pleased with the bad publicity that the Delmonico's dinner created for Blaine. I can't help but laugh whenever I see one of the headlines. But that was yesterday's good deed. I am

more confident now in assuming the guise of a Roman Catholic priest. My investigations revealed that Big John Kelly takes confession in this Fifth Avenue Church every morning. Well, Father Sherlock has something in store for that bosthoon.

The strangeness of foreign life throws me back into myself but I find pleasure in the beautiful scenes contained within the Cathedral, which is almost completed. Only the Lady Chapel remains to be constructed. The architecture is styled in the manner of the cathedrals of Rheims and Cologne, and it occupies the entire block bounded by Fifth and Madison Avenues, and 50th and 51st Streets. Built of white marble, it is richly decorated, buttressed, pinnacled and spiring heavenwards.

Lead, kindly light, through the interior, which is scaled to awe-inspiring proportions. Massive, clustered marble columns support the lofty groined roof; and a magnificent rose window dominates the western end, refracting a God's palate of color, glazing the high altar in the sanctuary with warmth. I study the altar. It is made of Carrara marble, and its front is inlaid with alabaster and precious stones. The lower front is divided into niches and panels, the former containing statues of the four Evangelists, and the latter presenting in bas-reliefs the Last Supper, the Carrying of the Cross, the Agony, and the Betrayal. I finally enter the confessional magisterially, mindful of the billowing folds of my soutaine.

Here comes Big John, a great sinner looking to be shrieved. He shuts the doors of the confessional.

—Forgive me fadduh, for I have sinned,—says the man.

—Yes, my son?—as if I knew not what manner of man he was.

—I'm a big-time politician, fadduh,—he says chokily,—and I threw Tammany behind that fool Blaine, and now I'm mad at the insults he has heaped on Mother Church. See?

O God, if there be a God, save my soul, if a soul I have!

I am prepared to turn myself inside out, to give him everything I have; yet inside of me I feel so empty. The effort to

squeeze out emotion (of which I have none), the impotence in the face of an impossible task, fills me with a fear that petrifies my face and hands. My throat constricts and dries, my voice goes up a note. My hands, feet, gestures and speech rebel against my will. I am ashamed of every word, of every gesture. I blush, clench my hands, and press myself against the back of the chair. I am failing, and in my helplessness I am overcome with rage. I cut myself loose from everything about me.

—That is a grave sin indeed!—I say, graveling my voice with severity.

—There are only six days before the election, and I got to somehow undo my sinful deeds. What am I to do, Fadduh? How many Paternosters do I have to say?

—None.

—None, Fadduh?—he says, gulping with astonishment.

I hear him squirming in his seat, straining forward, listening.

The mysteries of the church are but the expressions in human language of truths to which the human mind is unequal. Rightly or wrongly, these mysteries shall be transmitted through me in order to influence his behavior.

—You must instruct your constituents to vote for Cleveland.

—That'll take a lot of doin, Fadduh!—he objects.

—*Unde orta est culpa, ibi poena consistat.* He that doth amiss, may do well.

—Fadduh, I thought that maybe some prayers would do the trick.

—Prayers won't save you if you choose to avoid facing the wicked deeds you have performed.

And here comes another feeling, of a personal nature, which has to do with severity in the case of any interference in his life. He thinks: *Why do you meddle? Why cannot you let me alone? You can do me no good; you know nothing about me; you may actually do me harm; I am in better hands than yours.* An impression of this kind is almost unavoidable in the circumstances of the case, when a man, who has acted strongly against a cause,

281

and has collected a party round him by virtue of such action, gradually falters in his opposition to it, unsaying his words, throwing his own friends into perplexity and their proceedings into confusion, and ends by passing over to the side of those whom he had so vigorously denounced.

—But Fadduh, everybody'll think I'm an idiot!

Answer a fool according to his folly.

—My son, there is a great difference between people *thinking* you're an idiot and people *knowing* you're an idiot.

My feeling is something like that of a man, who has said, and shall say, so many things that had been better left unsaid. Anyhow, no harm can come of bending a crooked stick the other way in the process of straightening it; it is impossible to break it.

—What will the Party say?

—The Party. There will ever be a number of persons professing the opinions of a movement, who talk loudly and strangely, do odd or fierce things, display themselves unnecessarily, and disgust other people: persons too young to be wise, too generous to be cautious, too warm to be sober, or too intellectual to be humble. Such persons will be very apt to attach themselves to particular persons, to use particular names, to say things merely because others do, and to act in a party-spirited way.

—But I owe my life to the Party!

—My son, you owe your life to God. We want, not party men, but sensible, temperate, sober, well-adjusted persons, to guide our civic life through the channel of no-meaning, between the Scylla and Charybdis of *Aye* and *Nay*. But when a man takes up politics, his *Via Media*, he is a mere doctrinaire; without ethics, he is like those who, in some matter of business, are ever measuring mountains with a pocket ruler or improving the planetary courses.

—Yes, Fadduh.

—Every breath of air and ray of light and heat, every beautiful prospect, is, as it were, the skirts of the Angels' garments.

The waving of the robes of those whose faces see God. And what would be the thoughts of a man who, when examining a flower or a herb or a pebble or a ray of light, which he treats as something so beneath him in the scale of existence, suddenly discovers that he is in the presence of some powerful being who was hidden all along behind the visible things he was inspecting—a being who, though concealing his wise hand, was giving them their beauty, grace, and perfection, as the instrument of God's purpose, the very being whose robe and ornaments those objects were, which he was so eager to analyze?

—I t'ink so, Fadduh.

—The Devil, torve and tetrick of countenance, is subtle, yet weaves a coarse web.

—The Devil?

The magic word: Devil. Kelly is silent for a long time. He will stuff his mouth during the holiday season with Christmas-pies of lawyer's tongues and clerk's fingers. Now drive the point home: he is begging for it.

—You must make an earnest attempt to undo your wrongs, or else your soul will go straight to hell!

—I unnerstand, Fadduh. I'll try my best.

—Pray whenever you feel that you must.

—Yes, Fadduh.

—*Domine vobiscum.*

His terrified figure shambles sadly away.

The scene is over. I may relax now. Get out of the character; return to myself.

One must preserve the purity of language by exposing to ridicule the confused thought that stems from its misuse. The nonsense that results from trying to say what can only be shown is not only logically untenable, but ethically undesirable.

My whole tendency and I believe the tendency of all men who ever tried to write or talk on Ethics or Religion, is to run against the boundaries of language. This running against the walls of our cage is perfectly, absolutely hopeless. Ethics so far

as it springs from the desire to say something about the meaning of life, the absolute good, can be no science. What it says does not add to our knowledge in any sense. But it documents a tendency in the human mind which I personally cannot help respecting deeply, and I would not for my life ridicule it.

I will describe this experience in order, if possible, to make you recall the same or similar experiences, so that we may have a common ground for our investigation. I believe the best way of describing it is to say that when I have it *I wonder at the existence of the world.* And I am then inclined to use such phrases as *how extraordinary that anything should exist* or *how extraordinary that the world should exist.* I will mention another experience straight away which I also know and which others of you might be acquainted with: it is what one might call the experience of feeling absolutely safe. I mean the state of mind in which one is inclined to say *I am safe, nothing can injure me whatever happens.*

Such things as one is inclined to say after such experiences are a misuse of language—they mean nothing. And yet the experiences themselves seem to those who have them, for instance to me, to have in some sense an intrinsic, absolute value. They cannot be captured by factual language because their value lies beyond the world of facts.

What is good is also divine. Queer as it sounds, that sums up my ethics.[*]

---

[*] *One must preserve the purity of language ... that sums up my ethics.* Reprinted with the permission of The Free Press, a Division of Simon & Schuster Adult Publishing Group, from *LUDWIG WITTGENSTEIN: The Duty of Genius,* by Ray Monk. Copyright © 1990 by Ray Monk. All rights reserved. Published in the UK by Jonathan Cape. Reprinted with permission of The RandomHouse Group Ltd.

Loving virtuous obscurity as much as I do, you can judge how much I dislike this lionizing, which is much worse than that given to Sarah Bernhardt I hear.
—Oscar Wilde

I can hardly fail. Chickering Hall has an audience larger and more wonderful than even Dickens had. Colonel Morse introduces me with a single sentence.

—Ladies and Gentlemen, Oscar Wilde.

A hush falls upon the audience when I make my entrance with a circular cavalier cloak over my shoulder. My audience appraises my attire, which is not at all what I was wearing to the receptions, and is far more daring than anything in the lecture. The costume of the nineteenth century is detestable. It is so somber, so depressing. My antidote is a dark purple sack coat, and knee-breeches which show off my well-turned legs and feet; black hose, low shoes with bright buckles; coat lined with lavender satin, a frill of rich lace at the wrist band and a low turndown collar; hair long, and parted in the middle. Some think this is the costume of court dress; I am certain, however, that no one will recognize it for what it is. My voice is clear, easy, and not forced. Change pose now and then, the head inclining toward the strong foot, and I keep a general appearance of repose.

I open my manuscript, which I keep in a costly morocco case. Now my words and tone stand in contrast to my costume. Having captivated the audience with ostentation, I held them with alarming solemnity of ritual. *By beautifying the outward aspects of life, we shall beautify the inner ones.* I evitate critics who are expecting me to define beauty by quoting Goethe in support of defining beauty by example, not by philosophical disputations. The English Renaissance is, I say, like the Italian Renaissance before it, a sort of new birth of the spirit of man. Under this rubric I discuss the desire for a more gracious and comely way of

285

life, the passion of physical beauty, the attention to form rather than content, the search for new subjects of poetry, for new forms of art, for new intellectual and imaginative enjoyments. The new Euphorion is, as Goethe had foreseen, the result of a union of Hellenism and romanticism, Helen of Troy and Faust.

I deal broad strokes to large matters. The French Revolution compelled art to respect the facts of physical life, but those facts have proved suffocating. The Pre-Raphaelites have gathered to make their protest against the dominion of facts. That the British public is unaware of these eminent artists has no bearing on the matter. *To know nothing about their great men is one of the necessary elements of English education.* Nor did the fact that these artists are frequently the objects of satire detract in any way from their worth. I amplified my comments on *Patience*: *Satire, always as sterile as it is shameful, and as impotent as it is insolent, paid me that usual homage which mediocrity pays to genius . . . In any case, to disagree with three-fourths of the British public on all points is one of the first elements of sanity.*

Some of the characteristics of the English Renaissance are difficult to document, I know. I assert (without much justification) that English artists celebrate form at the expense of content, being unconcerned with moral lessons or weighty ideas. (Pater had pointed out that for Plato form was everything, matter nothing.) They were right because it was not new ideas or old moral preoccupations but the discovery of Parian marble that had made Greek sculpture possible, as the discovery of oil pigments had made possible the Venetian school, and that of new instruments had made possible the development of modern music. The Pre-Raphaelites were in reaction against empty conventional workmanship. It is the capacity to render, not the capacity to feel, which brings true art into being. And once in being, art confers upon life a value it had not heretofore had. Its creations are more real than the living. As I heard Swinburne once remark at dinner (at Lord Houghton's), *Homer's Achilles is more real*

than England's Wellington. That is when I started piecing together my discovery.

Although at moments I imply, like Pater, that the renaissance is a recurrent phenomenon in history, at moments I insist that the present awakening of the spirit is more thoroughgoing than its predecessors. Although it lacks the divine natural prescience of beauty in Greece and Rome, it has a strained self-consciousness which I do not disparage. It is essentially a Western phenomenon, even if some of its decorative patterns come from the East. I hope that the Western spirit, so anxious and disquieted, might find some rest in comely surroundings that could foster a fuller existence. Hence the importance of decorative art.

—You have listened to *Patience* for a hundred nights and have listened to me for only one,—I say.—You have heard, I think, a few of you, of two flowers connected with the aesthetic movement in England, and are said (I assure you, erroneously) to be the food of some aesthetic young men. Well, let me tell you the reason we love the lily and the sunflower, in spite of what Mr Gilbert may tell you, is not for any vegetable fashion at all. It is because these two lovely flowers are in England the most perfect models of design, the most naturally adapted for decorative art.

On this note, I draw towards my ringing conclusion.

—*We spend our days looking for the secret of life. Well, the secret of life is art.*[*]

Recalled and applauded, I am now treated like the Royal Boy. I am torn to bits by Society. Immense receptions, wonderful dinners, crowds wait for my carriage. I wave a gloved hand and an ivory cane and they cheer. Girls very lovely, men simple and

---

[*] *We spend our days ... the secret of life is art.* From OCSCAR WILDE by Richard Ellmann, copyright © 1987 by The Estate of Richard Ellmann. Used by permission of Alfred A. Knopf, a division of Random House, Inc.

intellectual. I generally bahave as I have always behaved—
dreadfully.

The mob is so great I must leave by a private door. Loving
virtuous obscurity as much as I do, you can judge how much I
dislike this lionizing, which is worse than that given to Sarah
Bernhardt I hear.* Let me gather the golden fruits of America
that I may spend a winter in Italy and a summer in Greece amidst
beautiful things, and fleet the time carelessly, as they did in the
golden world.

* * *

The room is designed with a *motif japonnais*, reflecting the
aesthetic cognizance of my hosts, Mr and Mrs AA Hayes, Jr,
who are holding this reception for my benefit at their 112 East
29th Street residence.

I make my entrance wearing a tightly buttoned Prince Albert
coat, and holding in my hands a pair of light kid gloves. My hair
is long and alluring—it causes a subtle disturbance in the people
that I meet—they want to touch my hair but good manners forbid it. My appearance creates such a stir that I am posed in the
opening between two large parlors, a gigantic Japanese umbrella
behind me. Now I am treated as a *petit roi.*

I stand at the top of the reception rooms, and for two hours
they file past for introduction. I bow graciously and sometimes
honor them with a royal observation, which will appear the next
day in all the newspapers.

—Mr Wilde, who is now the leading painter in England?—
asks Mrs Hayes.

---

* *Loving virtuous obscurity ... given to Sara Bernhardt I hear.* From OCSCAR WILDE
by Richard Ellmann, copyright © 1987 by The Estate of Richard Ellmann. Used by
permission of Alfred A. Knopf, a division of Random House, Inc.

—Whistler is the first painter in England, only it will take England 300 years to find it out.

—Mr Wilde,—asks another,—what is the state of man's soul today?

—The Greeks had no clothes; the medievalists had no body; the moderns have no soul.

An atmosphere of jocosity pervades the soirée.

—Is it true, Mr Wilde,—asks yet another,—that David Belasco will produce *Vera* in New York if you make certain changes in the story?

—Who am I to tamper with a masterpiece?

I refresh my dry mouth at the bar. Wine and iced water. New York now appears to be an entirely different city from the one to which I arrived. I feel a sense of belonging and move in the society to which I am accustomed: young men and women *de la premiere volée*; the *haute grade* who enjoy the more *recherché* amusements—*The Elite*. And the canons of good society are the same as the canons of art. Form is absolutely essential to it. The gloom of recent days is paling. I am calm and self-centered, and complete, contemplating life, and no arrow drawn at a venture can pierce between the joints of my harness. Safe at last. I have discovered how to live, and now new life and discoveries lie before me.

Here's Sam's friend. My Mercury, Col Morse.

—Oscar!

He takes my arm and leads me to the window. Confidential matter. The trees obscuring Twenty-Ninth Street shield us in the privacy of their shadows.

—The box office receipts are in. You sold out Chickering Hall!

—Sold out?

—Even standing room!

—Splendid!

—The receipts amounted to $1,211!

—We're going to do well!

Col Morse breaks into a spontaneous jig, drawing me into it. We dance. Uncle Sam's words still ring in my ears. I stop. —Where will it all end? Half the world does not believe in God, and the other half does not believe in me.

While I pursued merrymaking more assiduously than speechwriting, I did not lose sight of the fact that a New York actress should play *Vera*. The two most likely prospects now are Mary Anderson and Clara Morris. I saw Miss Morris act for the first time as Mercy Merrick in *The New Magdalen* at the Union Square Theatre. She is a great artist, in my sense of the word, because all she does, all she says, in the manner of the doing and of the saying, constantly evoke the imagination to supplement it. That is what I mean by art. She is a veritable genius. I am however quite aware of how *difficile* she is.

I greet Miss Morris in the anteroom, where I take her hand in both of mine.

—I have heard much of you from Sarah Bernhardt,—I say,— Sarah told me, *Elle a du tempérament; c'est assez dire.*

She simply turns her back to me and walks away, whereupon I discover that I cannot be entirely spontaneous without misfiring on occasion. How could a halfhearted compliment from her eminent rival ever have won over Miss Morris?

—Excuse me, Mr Wilde,—says a pleasant young woman who timidly approached me.—Frances Folsom. Gov Cleveland, my fiancé, introduced us last week.

—Ah, yes.

And I thought she would never speak to me again!

—I wanted to ask you your advice on the arrangement of some decorative screens.

—Why arrange them at all? Why not let them occur?*
She is well pleased by my answer.
—Mr Wilde, would you be so kind as to join me and a friend this evening?
—Let me see. . . .
—It is election day, and I'm sure that even you would find the company distinguished.

* * *

Despite the fact I had put politics out of my mind, I could not refuse this invitation. Imagine my astonishment when, accompanying Frances to Mr Cleveland's hotel, we met *Honest* John Kelly at the door.

—I just got sumthin to say to the Governor,—he says sheepishly.

When Cleveland appears, he is surprised to see his erstwhile enemy.

—Yes, your Honor, what may I do for you?—asks Mr Cleveland icily.

—Mr Cleveland, I know we put the word out that Tammany is going to vote for Blaine. But this *Rum, Romanism and Rebellion* insult we wouldn't stand for. I tole my precinct captains to go to their people, to talk to them in their own language, and tell them we made a mistake—a big mistake. We still have a chance to get back on the beam. I tole 'em to nix Blaine and vote Cleveland. We're uniting our party behind you because you will give the nation a careful, honest, and conservative administration.

Cleveland is humbled by these words, and he shakes Kelly's hand when he offers it. Few moments in life are as dramatic as

---

* *Why arrange them ... let them occur.* From OCSCAR WILDE by Richard Ellmann, copyright © 1987 by The Estate of Richard Ellmann. Used by permission of Alfred A. Knopf, a division of Random House, Inc.

the conversion of an enemy to friendship. Mayor Kelly then quickly excuses himself and leaves.

—It takes all kinds to make a world,—mutters the astonished Governor.

We just took our seats in the parlor when Manning entered the room with a telegram.

—Hendricks can be counted on to carry Indiana, and despite the Republicans' claim that they carried New York, the ballots from the slum districts have not yet been counted.

Cleveland quickly dismisses Manning's aberrant optimism.

—Oh, let's forget about it. How about a stein of *Weissbier* for one and all!

The Governor is actually dressed in evening clothes instead of a bathrobe. In domestic matters, it appeared as though Miss Folsom had her say, and her fiancé actually listens. When it comes to food, dress, and deportment, she watches over him as though he were a child of hers. She succeeds in toning down his irascibility, polishing his manners, smoothing his relations with people, and getting him to relax and take vacations from time to time. She says once he bought an orange-tawny suit she disliked and she did everything she could to keep him from wearing it. Finally she told him he would lose the Irish vote if he appeared in public with it, and won her point.

—Wilde,—the Governor bids me as the steins of beer are served,—entertain us with a story. It would be a pleasant distraction.

I cast about for a story to tell, and in an instant I settle on this one.

—I was riding the elevated train the other day when a train boy punched me in the side and shouted, *Hoscar Wilde's poems for ten cents!* I started up to a sitting position and cried, *Great God, is it possible my poems have reached such a beastly figure as that?*

—*Three for two bits,*—said the boy, blindly heaping insult upon injury. He was offering some copies of the Seaside Library edition in paper covers.

—I grabbed the book and fixed my big eyes on the boy, as I asked him if he knew he was lending his countenance to a hellish infringement on the rights of an English author.

—The boy answered slowly, *Is that so? Do you suppose the feller that rit the book cares a damn? Why, he won't know it.*

—*I am the author of those poems,*—I said.

—*Ah, go away,*—snickered the boy.—*You're wringing in for a comish. 'Twon't work, Cully. Folks put jobs on me every day.*—He went on to say,—*If I thought such a loony looking chap as you rit them lines, d'ye suppose I'd peddle 'em? No, sir! They're cheap, d'ye see? Blarst my picture if I don't feel like a footpad every time I takes a short bit for the rubbish.*

—The crowded car resounded with laughter in which I heartily joined. A little later when the boy was assured that I was really Oscar Wilde, he came up manfully and, from his store, offered me a half dozen oranges by way of atonement.

—In America, there is no opening for a fool. You expect brains, even from a bootblack, and get them. There is no such thing as a stupid American. Many Americans are horrid, vulgar, intrusive, and impertinent, just as many English people are also; but stupidity is not one of your national vices.

Manning abbreviates our merriment when he re-enters the room, bearing yet another telegram.

—The ballots from the slum districts have been counted, your Honor, and you have taken the lead!

—I don't believe it,—objects Cleveland.

—After twenty-four years, the Democrats will once again have a president!—cries Manning jubilantly.

—Oh, Grover, you're going to win!—says Frances with genuine fear.—The newspapers will savage us!

—Newspapers,—ponders Cleveland unhappily,—I don't think there ever was a time when newspaper lying was so gen-

eral and mean as the present, and there never was a country under the sun where it flourished as it does in this. The people in our newspapers, while they are proof of the mental ingenuity of those engaged in newspaper work, are insults to the American love for decency and fair play, of which we boast. And I am in complete accord with President-Elect Cleveland. —Make it a law that no newspaper be allowed to write about art at all. The harm that they do is not to be overestimated—not to the artist, but to the public. To disagree on all points with the modern newspaper is one of the chief indications of sanity.

My writings and ideas are now easily assimilable into the very intellectual milieu they were largely a warning against.* I have ceased to care what they write about me—I have ceased to believe anything I say—*parce que le monde devient de plus en plus oscarisé*—my time being all given up to the Gods and the Greeks.

---

* *My writings and ideas ... largely a warning against.* Reprinted with the permission of The Free Press, a Division of Simon & Schuster Adult Publishing Group, from *LUDWIG WITTGENSTEIN: The Duty of Genius*, by Ray Monk. Copyright © 1990 by Ray Monk. All rights reserved. Published in the UK by Jonathan Cape. Reprinted with permission of The RandomHouse Group Ltd.

Midnight sounds. The icy fangs of the churlish
winter wind bite. A ghost may come.
—Sherlock Holmes

There is a humorous aspect to astrology. Attempts to incorporate the planets discovered since the Renaissance into the general scheme of astrology have failed. Some manner of statistical relation between planetary positions and human lives is also not demonstrable. No serious explanation seems to exist of the alleged spheres of influence of the planets, the alleged nature of their influences, or the manner in which they are received. In short, modern Western astrology, though of great interest and popular, is devoid of intellectual value.

I recall the story of the Duke of Lancaster who once asked an astrologer whether he would ever be king; and he told him no, but his son would be a king. When he had thus answered him, the Duke rewarded his wise man by hanging him from the neck till dead, so to prevent him from bruiting the news abroad or discussing it with others in England. This was a clever trick in popular opinion but I think it is the kiss of Judas to hang a man for telling the truth. Beware by this example powerful men and their fair words, and say little to them, lest they do the same to you.

For many, astrology provides dimensions for universal law, a code linking the eternal and incorruptible celestial spheres to the corruptible sublunar world by an all-pervading system of sympathies and antipathies. Judgments are based on the favorable or unfavorable positions of the planets in the zodiac, on their conjunctions, and on the harmonious or disharmonious character of their aspects in relation to each other. Thus, it is essential to know the place and time of birth with great accuracy, because even minor variations yield widely divergent results. Only in the last century, with the invention of timepieces, have precise astrological forecasts been possible.

James G Blaine, for instance, was born in the evening of January 31, 1830, in West Brownsville, Pennsylvania. Not knowing his exact time of birth, I cast horoscopes for the hours between sunset and midnight, but I could reach no final determination of the question.

The Ambassador of the U.K. kindly arranged this ruse for me. He explained to Blaine that Zora, the astrologer, had cast Queen Victoria's chart, so Blaine naturally wanted Zora to cast his own chart. There is no purpose to it at all except my own amusement. I can do no more for Cleveland. Now all I want is to savor the expression on Blaine's face when—oh, let's not be presumptuous.

I had taken great pains to wear the correct dress, so I chose a dark blue silk creation spangled by a star motif. I wore a crescent moon brooch. My handkerchief, stockings, fichu and laces are admirable, however, no wealthy Parisienne so readily follows the caprices of fashion. One can find a good, fast dressmaker in Paris who can run up a gown for half the New York price and with perfect fit and finish. I rather sympathize with Lillie Langtry's innovative disposal of stayed corsets for they are quite uncomfortable, and the whale-bone makes a tell-take creak with every movement, yet I must wear one to give my figure form.

Mr Blaine and his solemn company were quite inebriated by the time I had arrived. Despite his less-than-comprehensive state of mind, Mr Blaine insisted that I present the results of my researches upon the question he put forth, whether or no he would become President of the United States, and what would eventuate.

—What comes to light or is revealed by others may leave you stunned or surprised,—I said in preface.

—Ah hah!—Blaine guffawed, betraying his anxiety.

—However,—I continued,—since you may have suspected that was the case, you may already also have drawn up alternative plans.

—Alternative plans. You hear that, Jay?—Blaine cracked.

—Zora, will I be President or no?

—Mr Blaine,—I began diplomatically,—after consulting my ephemerides and almanacs, I find that a changeable Aquarian like yourself will remain a great statesman whatever the outcome of this election. Your particular position in relation to the planets and the twelve signs of the Zodiac indicate that—

An aide staggered into the room as if he had been stabbed, and mercifully interrupted me.

—It appears as though we lost New York by 1,149 votes out of a million ballots cast.

His words echoed in the dumbstruck silence long after he stopped speaking.

—We can charge vote fraud and demand a recount. You don't have to concede yet, Mr Blaine.

—All is lost,—Blaine finally muttered.—But for the intolerant and utterly improper remark of Rev Burchard, which was quoted everywhere to my prejudice and in many places attributed to myself, though it was in the highest degree distasteful and offensive to me, we would have won.

I savored the taste of victory secretly. Now things are as they should be. I have done something beautiful. Would this fall into Oscar's definition of beauty? Of course it would. I have authored *life* itself.

—You would have been wiser to have stayed at home, Jim— offered Gould with hindsight.

—I don't know,—Blaine whined,—I should have carried New York by 10,000 votes if the weather had been clear on election day and Rev Burchard had been doing missionary work in Asia Minor or Cochin China!

—Maybe Cleveland can be bought, and we can still assume control of the steel and oil industries,—said Gould with hope.— He vetoed the Five-Cent Fare Bill. I think he wants to get friendly with me.

—Don't kid yourself, Gould,—replied Blaine,—He acted on principle. If you can corrupt him, you are the devil himself. That man is . . . is . . . honest!

—Money talks,—Gould retorted.

—Yes, it does, and I have heard it say, *Good-bye! Good-bye!*
My services no longer being needed, I took leave of Mr Blaine's
company and walked slowly through the streets of Manhattan.
There was once a church on this block, and it had many a fair
monument within its peaceable confines. It is now defaced and
gone, destroyed by bad and greedy men of spoil. How it comforts
me to see decadence and moss grow over old buildings (not even a
lifetime old) and the destruction of the past.

Midnight sounds, and the great Christ Church bell and many
a lesser bell sound through the avenues. The icy fangs of the
churlish winter wind bite. A ghost may come.

In the multiple labyrinth of night, nests of brightness were
hewn by the large, colored lanterns in shop windows. I observed
the strangely ceremonial rites of autumn shopping.

A man whistles at me, and I blush.

I feel the wind gust under my skirt, where it is trapped like a
secret. This is how a woman traps the wild wet seed and fills her
belly with life. To dress within such a Goddess-shape is itself a
ritual act. We, the earth, its mounds, these streets, are the cosmic
womb of the pregnant Goddess.

Logic. Love. Illusion. Disillusion.

What is the connection between my thoughts on logic and my
reflections on the meaning of life? It is the distinction between
saying and *showing*. Logical form cannot be expressed *within*
language, for it is the form of language itself; it makes itself
manifest in language—it has to be *shown*.

It is true: Man *is* the microcosm: I am my world.[*]

---

[*] *What is the connection ... it has to be* shown. And *It is true: Man* is *the microcosm: I am
my world.* Reprinted with the permission of The Free Press, a Division of Simon &
Schuster Adult Publishing Group, from *LUDWIG WITTGENSTEIN: The Duty of Genius*,
by Ray Monk. Copyright © 1990 by Ray Monk. All rights reserved. Published in the UK
by Jonathan Cape. Reprinted with permission of The RandomHouse Group Ltd.

I luxuriated in the corn-colored sunlight that
flooded my window when a knock at the
door disturbed my reverie.
                    —Oscar Wilde

—What shall I do when I see him passing on the street? He
was once my friend. We used to laugh together.
I considered Theodor Tilton's remark about Henry Ward
Beecher, then replied:—Laughter is not at all a bad beginning
for a friendship, and it is by far the best ending for one.
I had just spent the morning with Theodor, a journalist and
writer who was at the center of the leading scandal of the last
decade when his wife was accused of a liaison with Henry Ward
Beecher of Brooklyn Heights, the most celebrated preacher in the
country. The eloquent pastor used his voice (the bell of his soul) to
persuade Mrs Tilton that he was not understood at home, and that
the beautiful love they had for each other was righteous and that,
eventually, it was to be expressed in ways more adequate than a
shake of the hand or a kiss of the lip. *Living on the ragged edge,*
paroxysmal kissing and *nest-hiding* were apposite expressions of
their love. I fancy Mrs Tilton is one of those very modern women
of our time who finds a new scandal as becoming as a new bonnet,
and airs them both in Central Park every afternoon at five-thirty.
The case went to trial but the jury failed to agree. All three lives
and reputations were ruined, so I'm encouraging Theodore to
move to Paris.
    —Deism and agnosticism have broken the grip Calvinism had
on American Religion,—remarked Theo.—Deism had been
clandestinely embraced by abolitionists and liberals, aided by
the quick spread of Darwinism. The raging orgy of political
corruption and industrial freebooting have shifted people's interest from hell-fire preachers to the new ethical preachers, like
Rev Talmage.

—Let me put it this way,—I said,—It is monstrous to compare Dr Talmage to Rev Beecher; it is like comparing Clown to Pantaloon.

Theo was kind enough to take me uptown this morning to visit the room where Poe, the marvelous lord of rhythmic expression, wrote *The Raven*. It is an old wooden house over the Hudson: low rooms, fine chimney piece, a very dull Corot day, a clergyman with reminiscences of Poe, about chickens. What can one say about America for putting to death a poet on the clearly proven charge of having written poems entirely composed of those three wonderful things: Romance, Music, and Sorrow.

The election to public office is a temporal station, and I am delighted to have been intimate with, and in my own useless way, instrumental to, Cleveland's campaign and election; Poe's station, however, is fixed, eternal and immortal. I take pride in having helped Cleveland give tongue to his personal conflicts, yet I am prouder still to have given tongue to the voiceless dead.

When I returned to lower Manhattan, I found ecstatic jubilation.

—Cleveland wins! Read all about it!—cried a quartet of newsboys. I hailed one lad who heaved a swelling bundle of papers onto the pavement. His apron jingled with coin. I saw the penumbra of my own youth in his eyes. Jostling crowds of jubilant Democrats spontaneously joined a demonstration, chanting:

> *Ma! Ma! Where's Pa?*
> *Gone to the White House, ha ha ha!*
>
> *Hurray for Amber! Hurray for the kid!*
> *We voted for Cleveland, and we're glad we did!*

I worked my way through the crowded streets, looking for a perch where I might read the story of Uncle Jumbo's victory (surely an inaccurate account and riddled with hearsay, malicious gossip, and lies) unmolested by the roiling crowd. So engrossed was I in my objective, heedless of where I was going, that I collided with an elderly man, knocking several books out

of his gnarled hands. His collar informed me that he was a reverend.

—Pardon me, Reverend! I am very sorry,—I said, avoiding his eyes.

I gathered the books, and noticed that one of the titles was *Poems* by Oscar Wilde. Favorably impressed, I handed the volumes back to the clergyman. The etiolated, severe face I know. Rum. Rev Samuel D Burchard of Murray Hill, himself!

—I'm very sorry, please forgive me.

Rev Burchard snarled with undisguised contempt and turned on his heels. His bent back and white side whiskers disappeared into the bustling street. There was something peculiar about the old fool, and now I know what it is. The copy of my *Poems* in his possession is the unauthorized Seaside edition. You know the Americans—they don't spend their money without a return, so why bother with incidental disbursements such as royalties? One would think that the poet would deserve a few dollars, but alas, no. Complain to the President-Elect but it does no good. Crucify the poet on a cross of gold.

—Oscar!—a pleasant feminine voice called out.

I turned to see Lillie and Freddie, waving from their carriage.

—Venus and Adonis!

—Come join us,—invited Lillie,—we just came back from dress rehearsal. *As You Like It* is opening tomorrow!

The enormous jewel that Freddie had given her adorned her finger. Lillie was firmly in command.

—Congratulations on your lecture,—added Freddie.

—May I invite you to my hotel room for a glass of champagne before you go off to the theatre?

—We have to visit Freddie's father first,—said Lillie,—we have to clear up some business. May we visit your rooms when we return from the theatre?

—Please do. I'll be waiting.

* * *

I was in the process of removing my gloves in my hotel room. I rested my cane neatly against the wall and luxuriated in the corn-colored sunlight that flooded my window when a knock at the door disturbed my reverie. I was astonished to find Rev Burchard at my door.

—You're surprised to see me, sir?—he said in a strange voice.

I welcomed him. Edgar Allen Poe had the civilized ability to entertain his enemies too.

—I merely wanted to tell you that if I was a bit gruff in my manners there was not any harm meant, and that I am much obliged to you for picking up my books.

—You make too much of a trifle, Rev Burchard. I couldn't help but notice that you were carrying an edition of my *Poems*. What good taste you possess!

—Indeed,—replied the reverend in his comical tone,—What turns night into day and day into night? It is poetry. I do not understand your poems, but their tone makes me happy. It is the tone of genius. And to express my thanks, here's *British Birds* and *The Poems of Catullus* and Nicetas Choniates' *O, City of Byzantium* in Greek.

He held up the books.

—A bargain,—he continued,—every one of them. These volumes might fill the gap in your shelf.

The gap-toothed shelf of books gaped at me. Of course there was room. I thanked him and shelved the charming volumes: *cormorant, odi et amo, the sack of Byzantium.* When I returned I discovered Sherlock Holmes smiling at me from across the table. Blood drained from my head quickly, darkness drooled over the panes of my vision, a buzz mutely roaring in my ears, circular motion round a motionless center, motionless center round circular motion. . . .

* * *

Brandy awoke my unconscious mouth. I had fainted. When my eyes opened I did indeed see Sherlock Holmes, my twin, my brother.

—My dear Wilde, I owe you a thousand apologies. I had no idea that you would be so affected.

—Is it really you, Holmes?—I asked.—Is it possible that you survived the Brooklyn Bridge?

—Are you indeed fit to talk, Wilde? I have given you a serious shock by my unnecessary reappearance.

I gripped his arm and he helped me to my feet.

—*On est bien changé, voilà tout!*

He brought the brandy bottle and cigarettes to the table.

—How did you survive?

Holmes lit a cigarette for me. He looked thinner and keener than before. There was a dead white tinge to his face.

—I never told you that I had learned to dive from three hundred foot cliffs off the coast of Brittany.

—Holmes, you rummy roaming rebel against death, you are absurd!

—My note to you was absolutely genuine,—began Holmes.—I had little doubt that I had come to the end of my career, so I allowed Moriarty to abduct me in order that I might confront him. He was wearing a bulletproof vest whose forty-pound bulk repelled my dead-on gunshots. During the ensuing struggle, we fell off the catwalk into the river. Due to the weight of Moriarty's armor, he sank to the bottom of the East River at once, while I simply swam to shore.

—Why didn't you inform me of your safety?

—I had only one confidante—my brother Mycroft. I owe you many apologies, my dear Wilde, but it was all important that it should be thought I was dead because I am still in danger from the survivors of Moriarty's gang. Mycroft supplied me with money and Scotland Yard is arranging for the arrest and refoulement of the remaining members of Moriarty's gang in New York. The exhausting labor has taken its toll on me. My intellect has never

quite recovered from the strain. I have been ever since definitely less capable of dealing with difficult abstractions than I was before.[*]

—So you were Rev Burchard! I heard you speak that night at Delmonico's. I *believed* you. I thought your gaffe was completely unintentional. Brilliant!

—*Rev Burchard* was merely one of several disguises I adopted. The character of Rev Burchard gave me an *entrée* to the highest circles of the Party. I deliberately planted the *faux pas* of *Rum, Romanism and Rebellion* into Blaine's welcoming speech to sabotage him, knowing that he would probably not disavow the statement and that it would be used against him. *Cardinal Newman*, my second incarnation, enabled me to shrieve Honest John Kelly of his heavy heart and motivate him to reverse the voting commitments of his Tammany constituents. My final incarnation was *Zora*, the Astrologer, who was invited to consult the stars for the agitated Mr Blaine on election night, whereupon I was able to savor the taste of victory at the expense of my enemy, a savor sweetened by the unconcealed bitterness of my rival.

If you take all these internal processes, and adapt them to the spiritual and physical life of the person you are representing, that is living a part. What Holmes did is a bold and provocative new direction for an actor. What stage but the world can confine the broad reach of his imaginative action? It is a pity that the stage lost such a genius as Holmes, who would have outshone Keene and Sir Henry Irving.

---

[*] *My intellect ... than I was before.* Reprinted with the permission of The Free Press, a Division of Simon & Schuster Adult Publishing Group, from *LUDWIG WITTGENSTEIN: The Duty of Genius*, by Ray Monk. Copyright © 1990 by Ray Monk. All rights reserved. Published in the UK by Jonathan Cape. Reprinted with permission of The RandomHouse Group Ltd.

My consternation, reappraisal of the recent events, wonderment, consideration, excogitation, unanswered questions, and sheer delight in the presence of my old friend was interrupted by yet another knock at the door. The likely assailants? Lillie and Freddie.

—Holmes, happy is your grace that can translate the stubbornness of Fortune into so quiet and sweet a style. Please resume your disguise. I shall need your assistance.

Holmes was back in character by the time I answered the door, where I found not Lillie and Freddie but President-Elect Grover Cleveland and a young girl. She must be *the* girl at the center of it all. We are the circular motion round the center and she is the motionless center round the circular motion, but we do not even know her name.

—I am indeed privileged to receive you, your Honor.

—Call me *Uncle Jumbo*,—he said winking,—just wanted to pay you a little visit. Mr Wilde, may I introduce to you my *niece*, Jeanne-Marie.

The young girl possessed a truly luminous presence, godlike, serene, at once capricious and eternal—an *Alice in Wonderland* blessing the occasion with her presence. We in Europe want to see what civilization you are making for yourselves and by yourselves in America, and she is the answer, for she herself is a work of art.

It is said that passion makes one think in a circle.

* * *

Love art for its own sake, and then all these things will be added to you. This devotion to beauty and to the creation of beautiful things is the test of all great civilizations. It is what makes the life of each citizen a sacrament and not a speculation, for beauty is the one thing that time cannot harm. Philosophies may fall away like the sand; creeds follow one another, but what is beautiful is a joy for all seasons, a possession for all eternity. National hatreds are always strongest where culture is lowest, but art is an empire which a nation's enemies cannot take away from her.

305

We in our Renaissance are seeking to create a sovereignty that shall still be England's when her yellow leopards are weary of wars, and the rose on her shield is crimsoned no more with the blood of battle. And you, too, absorbing into the heart of a great people this pervading artistic spirit, will create for yourselves such riches as you have never yet created, though your land be a network of railways, and your cities the harbors of the galleys of all seven seas. You call America a country. I call it a world.

All the world is full of inscape, and chance
left free to act falls into an order
as well as purpose.
—Sherlock Holmes

I sometimes have the feeling that my work might prove fruitless: when one has forged a path up a steep mountain that no one has climbed before, there must be a doubt as to whether anyone else will have the desire to follow one up it.* But folly will have its victims to the end of time—though few will be so heartless, so mean, so guiltless of its fascinating qualities. Oscar understands this. He is my friend.

I am nonetheless happy to be incognito in order to avoid any awkwardness that might arise. My self-command is in place when President-Elect Cleveland enters the room with the mysterious child so much in question during the campaign, the first cause of my case. I shall choose a propitious moment to reveal myself to Cleveland, reveal my findings to my client, and bring this case to its rightful conclusion.

I must confess that if anyone questioned me about my feelings with regard to my relations with Lillie Langtry, I would have assured them that nothing more had taken place than the incidents I recalled. But since the latent sensations of factual events that I call to mind are stimulated by my volitional memory, which conserves nothing of time past itself, I should never have pondered further over the ruins of my life with Lillie. To me it is in reality quite dead.

---

* *I sometimes have the feeling ... the desire to follow one up it.* Reprinted with the permission of The Free Press, a Division of Simon & Schuster Adult Publishing Group, from *LUDWIG WITTGENSTEIN: The Duty of Genius*, by Ray Monk. Copyright © 1990 by Ray Monk. All rights reserved. Published in the UK by Jonathan Cape. Reprinted with permission of The RandomHouse Group Ltd.

Forever dead? Possibly.

The mysteries of Time are often imprisoned within some substance, some material object (preserving the stimulus for the sensation which the said substance or object will provide to us) to which we have no clue. It remains to chance and circumstance whether or not we find the key to this ancient feast before we ourselves must die.

Am Anfang war die Tat.

The little stranger, however, commands my attention. She is quite lovely and possesses the angelic bearing and prescient beauty of her mother. Merely to behold her is to love her, the beautiful daughter of a still more beautiful mother. Strangely, she doesn't seem to bear a resemblance to Mr Cleveland, but takes all after her mother.

—This is the Rev Samuel D. Burchard,—says Wilde.—He is helping me prepare my lectures.

We exchange greetings tensely.

—The Rev Burchard of Murray Hill?—affirms Cleveland.

—The Reverend is a dear old friend,—says Wilde drolly in my defense,—and you may speak to him as freely as you do with me, for he is an extraordinary man. We wish to congratulate you on your,—he takes Jeanne-Marie into consideration at this point,—ahem—your new office and accompanying position of leadership in society.

Cleveland scrutinizes me closely.

—As you may recall,—continues Wilde with an air of farcical ritual,—the Reverend contributed to your campaign in his own inimitable fashion!

—A pleasure to meet you, Rev Burchard,—he says cautiously at last, preserving good form.—Jeanne-Marie is a great admirer of Sherlock Holmes, and I explained to her that I was once acquainted with him, and that you are the person in New York who knew him best. Jeanne-Marie begged me for an introduction. And I did not find it in my power to refuse!

308

—The Reverend knew Holmes, I dare say, better than I did,—says Wilde.

—I am delighted to meet you,—I say to the little girl. I notice the title of the little book she carries: *Elementary Chemistry*. My child, if I ever had one, would resemble her, and I rue the fact that she is not.

The girl turns her omniscient yet childlike eyes on me. Many years have elapsed since my *affair du coeur* with Lillie, and with the exception of the drama associated with my arrival in New York, none of it had any existence for me before coming face to face with my erstwhile paramour. But now, a much more subtle sensation sabotages my rational intellect. The warm and liquid smell of Jeanne-Marie's skin and hair affects me. No sooner had I recognized the lactose perfume of this girl than a shudder oscillated through me and I stopped, intent upon the astonishing moment that I am now experiencing. It is an exquisite pleasure that occupies my senses, something isolated and detached, with no suggestion of its origin. All of a sudden the variable fortunes of my life became trifling matters, disasters rendered harmless, the fabric of perception brief, mutable and illusory. It is as if I were a retort being filled with a rare substance, a new element perhaps, or rather this element is not in me, but *is* me. I cease feeling mediocre, contingent, mortal. Whence originates this all-powerful joy? The perfume of her hair communicates this unnamable sensation, but it transcends those savors, yet shares in some manner an identical nature. Whence did it come? What did it mean? How can I analyze this unknown something with which Reason collides when inspired by its paradoxical passion? Philosophy should be written as a poetic composition to rid us of the puzzlement of language. *

---

* *Philosophy ... to rid us of the puzzlement of language*. Reprinted with the permission of The Free Press, a Division of Simon & Schuster Adult Publishing Group, from *LUDWIG WITTGENSTEIN: The Duty of Genius*, by Ray Monk. Copyright © 1990 by Ray Monk. All rights reserved. Published in the UK by Jonathan Cape. Reprinted with permission of The RandomHouse Group Ltd.

—So, you are interested in chemistry? Sherlock Holmes was devoted to chemistry as well.

—Yes, Reverend, chemistry plays a part in every aspect of life. Even cooking is chemistry,—she avers, studying me closely.

—Indeed it is!—chimes Wilde.—I never thought of it that way before!

Jeanne-Marie allows me to peruse her chemistry book. I do remember in this precocious child some lively touches of myself.

—Chemistry. How very interesting. . . .

—Chemistry is a subject most congenial to me,—declares Jeanne-Marie.

The word rings a bell. It sounds like something I once said.

I draw closer to her to clandestinely smell her hair once again, but the result is rather a weaker voice in the swirling rondeau of sensation compared to the first magnificent impression. I withdraw and examine my own consciousness, which alone can unveil the truth. How? By what means? I am suspended over a chasm of uncertainty whenever I think of myself thinking, whereby the detective is simultaneously the means and object of his search through plutonian regions of not-knowing. It is, ultimately, an act of creation and imagination to body forth that which is inchoate, and transform it to reality.

Q: What is that unapprehended state or mode of being whose elusive memory banishes all other states of consciousness with its appearance as sunlight banishes shadows?

A: It is the unwobbling center around which my life circulates.

I frame in the center of my mind's eye the perfumery of Jeanne-Marie's unguentine hair. Something trembles within me, like manacles long ago nailed into a dungeon disengaging themselves from a stone wall; I cannot as yet define it but I can feel it loosen slowly, and I measure the slackening resistance.

No sooner do I detect a highlighting of thought than a whirlygig of sounds and colors washes the impression away, and I can-

not retain a form, and cannot ascribe either date or location or participants.

This present moment seeks out the memory of its long deceased ancestor, an identical moment so long lost, now *en route* to shake the foundation of my self. Now I feel the shape of a wayward life around a void. Will it return? I confess I shrink from the encounter, and the pangs of cowardice hinder me, urging me to rely on the here and now, masking my inner turmoil for the sake of good form.

And so I return to the source of that impression, Jeanne-Marie herself. It is a rare and isolated instance when we meet someone to whom we bear a strong psychic resemblance. Such was the startling first impression Jeanne-Marie made on me, with her clarity of vision, her articulation, her sensitivity.

The book she is reading is quite advanced for her age.

—I can't seem to find the definition of Avogadro's Constant,—I say as I flip through the pages, testing her pretensions to knowledge, hoping to demystify her.

—Oh,—she commences without hesitation,—it's a law of chemistry that states that under the same conditions of temperature and pressure, equal volumes of different gasses contain an equal number of molecules.

—What!?

—The specific number of molecules in one gram-mole of substance, which is defined as the molecular weight in grams, is 6.023×10^{23}, a quantity called *Avogadro's Constant*.

—Excellent! Bravo!

The tables have suddenly turned. Now Jeanne-Marie is studying me. I study her studying me.

—Is Mr Holmes really dead?—she asks after a brief deliberation.

Maybe there doesn't have to be a commonality of structure between world and language.

—Oh, you're a willful and inquisitive child!—interjects Cleveland, trying to save the situation.

311

WILDE ABOUT HOLMES

—Sherlock Holmes is not dead,—I reply, regaining my confidence.—He is in hiding because he's working on a big job for the President of the United States and Scotland Yard too.
—You see, Uncle Jumbo?—says Jeanne-Marie.—I told you he wasn't dead. You mustn't believe everything you read in the newspapers!
We resume our engaging conversation. I usually find children so dull, yet this little girl is utterly captivating. What is happening to me?
—You don't have to talk to me like a child, Mr Holmes, I can see right through your disguise.
I am astonished by the girl's perspicuity and veritable genius. If she weren't a child, I would be quite angry and upset!
—Even a ten-year-old can put on make-up better than that!
The struggle to be *anständig* for me means, above all, overcoming the temptations presented by my pride and vanity to be dishonest.* I have no choice but to remove my whiskers and reveal myself.
—Holmes!—Cleveland cries.—I thought you were dead!
Before I have any chance to explain, Jeanne-Marie seizes the initiative.
—See, Uncle Jumbo? I knew it was him. How come nobody ever believes anything I say?—she says, leaving him to his befuddlement.
Wilde is enjoying every moment, and explaining to President-Elect Cleveland how I orchestrated the sabotage of the ministerial gathering by injecting the *Rum, Romanism and Rebellion*

---

* *The struggle to be anständig ... vanity to be dishonest.* Reprinted with the permission of The Free Press, a Division of Simon & Schuster Adult Publishing Group, from *LUDWIG WITTGENSTEIN: The Duty of Genius*, by Ray Monk. Copyright © 1990 by Ray Monk. All rights reserved. Published in the UK by Jonathan Cape.Reprinted with permission of The RandomHouse Group Ltd.

remark. I am relieved to have Wilde explain it, for I want to speak with Jeanne-Marie. She converses with us all at once much like a child chess prodigy playing simultaneous games against old masters, and beating us one and all. What in heaven's name will she do next?

—You know what? My uncle has been elected President of the United States.—she says matter-of-factly.

—How did you know that?—asks Wilde.

—His picture's in the newspapers, for crying out loud! They can't lie about something like that.

—Shucks, Jeanne-Marie,—says Cleveland,—I just didn't want to brag about it, that's all.

—Mr Holmes, may I be one of your Baker Street Irregulars?—she asks so sweetly.

I can deny the irresistible little girl nothing.

—Why of course you may.

While Jeanne-Marie and I are quite engrossed in a conversation about chemical changes that take place during the cheese-making process, I hear Cleveland say: *I never would have guessed.* Then Wilde replies, *Nor would have I, but it appears to be so!*

What are they talking about? I want to know. Must remember to ask.

There is another knock at the door. *I love you from the bottom of my heart.* The force of what she had not said is more important that what she had. It is her: Wilde welcomes Lillie and Freddie. Lillie's eyes meet Cleveland's, then mine, then Freddie's. There is not a single ripple to her composure. Wilde usually speaks for Lillie, and her beauty speaks for itself—actual living beauty, that is, a woman *after* the first sin.

Now this was not what I expected, for I am now myself, Sherlock Holmes, undisguised, before Lillie, before the world. I fear that she will kick me in the shins once again, but instead, there is a tenderness to her features, and I feel that she may have forgiven my youthful ignorance and indiscretion.

—Lillie,—says Wilde,—I am delighted to see you.

—Amber—Lillie,—stutters Cleveland,—I am delighted to see you. Jeanne-Marie, this is your Aunt Amber. You used to live with her when you were young.

Jeanne-Marie studies Lillie with impish sagacity.

—I remember everything, and you're not my Auntie Amber—you're my mother!

Lillie kneels next to her daughter and tearfully embraces her, overcome by Jeanne-Marie's prescience.

—Clever girl! You seem to know everything,—flatters Oscar, heartily amused.

—You once said,—replies Jeanne-Marie,—that the old believe everything: the middle-aged suspect everything: the young know everything!

Lillie presses Jeanne-Marie to her bosom.

—*I love you from the very bottom of my heart,*—Lillie says to her daughter.

All bitterness has washed away from me. Things and actions are what they are, and the consequences of them will be what they will be: why then should we desire to be deceived?

Lillie looks fixedly upon me in pregnant silence.

—*You never listen to a word I say* . . . music—notes as facets in the *I love you from the very bottom of my heart* and the mind there, before them, moving *either you marry me or I shall go to America . . . I want to live where no one knows who I am* . . . so that the notes need not move.

Pregnant. With alarming immediacy, the memory of my dream announces itself. The bowl of tears, the beautiful flower, and the golden pond! The beautiful being who spoke to me: *whatifer piths you take hue may fund your way back to the golden pond.* . . .

All the world is full of inscape, and chance left free to act falls into an order as well as purpose.

I recall the perfumery of Lillie's hair and skin during the period in my life when I was attempting to create a synthetic *pa-*

paver somniferum. Nothing persists in time and space from the
remote past, after the people have died, after things are broken
and scattered; taste, smell, and words alone remain, more persistent, more faithful, and remain poised for a long time, like
souls, waiting, watching, hoping, remembering amid the ruins of
all the rest; and bear unflinchingly, in the tone and almost im-
palpable drop of their essence, the vast structure of recollection.
What is the difference between the mysteries of knowledge
and the mysteries of love? There is no mystery to love.

What a damn fool I am!

How often have I said that when you have eliminated the impossible, whatever remains, however improbable, must be the
truth? What other clue do I need to unmuzzle my wisdom? Now
there is no prison for me. I reach out to the stars, and through the
ages, and everywhere the radiance of her love lights up the world
for me. *Das erlösende Wort: Tochter!*

—Wilde,—I say through a catch in my throat,—do you
remember our wager?

—How could I forget?—he replies with wonderful hilarity,—
logic contends with love.

—I think love is winning,—I say, the catch getting stronger.

I kneel down before Jeanne-Marie, her mother is trembling
with emotion, holding her in her arms, looking me straight in the
eyes.

—Jeanne-Marie, do you know who your true father is?

Jeanne-Marie holds me in suspense as she casts a happy eye
round Wilde, Cleveland, Freddie and her mother before turning
to me.

—Yes I do,—says my daughter candidly, winking at Oscar.—
Can't you see that I'm just *Wilde about Holmes!*?

EPILOGUE

Speech is silver, but silence is golden.
—Lillie Langtry

14 October—Liverpool

My many friends and relations were within easy reach, and to leave them for unknown lands gave me a feeling of utter depression. That is why I begin this diary today instead of ten years ago when I first arrived in London, when I first saw the gulf that lies between the romantic and the sordid, when I was full of youthful enthusiasm and desired to see everything under the sun, when I still harbored illusions about genius, about love, about fame.

At sixteen, I knew that men and boys would do my bidding if I smiled at them. If I stared into a boy's eyes, he became flustered. I felt like a stream discovering that it could move a rock. Stories arose about me. *If you're as bold as you pretend to be,* Reggie dared, *prove it by chucking your clothes and running naked along Deanery Lane.* He supposed that all girls are uniformly silly, easily frightened, and full of qualms. I transformed my brother and his friends from mockers to supplicants well before I disengaged my feet from the fallen garments, emerging from a whorl of dress, skirts and lingerie as naked as a hand from a muff. I ran past the gray granite walls of the ancient deanery, streaking past the rouge, pink, and white damask roses that scaled the walls, and attacked the pantile roof;* I flew past the scattered and still-falling cherry blossoms that dappled the plum-colored twilight. The word quickly spread that I did not hesitate. . . . But it is not an easy

---

* *I ran past the gray granite walls ... the pantile roof.* From *The Prince and the Lilly*, by James Brough, Coward McCann & Geoghegan, Inc.: New York, 1974. By permission of Penguin Group (USA) Inc.

319

matter to change suddenly from the butterfly into the busy bee.*
Now I am twenty-nine, no more, no less, and the same passion
returns like a recurring dream, holding me in its heated grip.
Though my figure no longer retains its youthful slenderness, it is
full, elegant and well shaped. No one would imagine that I had
borne a child. My bust, my neck, my shoulders, and my arms are
extremely beautiful. Men still admire the smooth curves of my
body, seeing it as they do when the long flowing Grecian folds of
my simple gown stretch tightly across my mobile figure, revealing
and concealing it at once, receptive to even the faintest of
spontaneous impressions my body makes. My teeth are beautiful,
and I have all of them except one rear molar that I had extracted.
My legs are perfectly coltish, slender at the ankle, ending in small
feet, contrasting brilliantly with my tall, statuesque figure. My
hands, too, are slender, fine and white as Isolde's. Quite a portrait!
but as time unfolds, my moral portrait will emerge from these
pages as well.

15 October—The Sea

Alas, what danger it is for us to travel forth so far. Beauty
provokes thieves sooner than gold!

Henrietta had been corresponding with Henry E Abbey privately. She disclosed his terms. This was his offer: I was to pay
the salaries of my company, and in return I would receive fifty
percent of the gross box office receipts.

It was a good offer and Henrietta urged me to accept, but I
held out for sixty-five percent, with Abbey guaranteeing all traveling expenses, including those from England to America. I
asked for these terms because that's what Sarah got. *I' vaut mûs*

---

* *But it is not an easy ... busy bee.* From *The Prince and the Lilly*, by James Brough,
Coward McCann & Geoghegan, Inc.: New York, 1974. By permission of Penguin
Group (USA) Inc.

320

all ou ongri l'bras qué l'co. After several days of negotiations, I
brought the producer to his knees.

—Mrs Langtry, you're as tough a businesswoman as you are
lovely a lady,—he said.—You may smell of delicious perfume,
but nothing creases your hide except dollar bills.
Men are born to be slaves, and they know it.

16 October—The Sea

The Captain presented me with a king's ransom of precious
chocolates, wrapped in delicate golden foils: caramel almond,
roasted hazelnut and almond praline, almond mousse crême suspended in smooth chocolate cores enrobed in dark chocolate.

I hope it is no dishonest desire to desire to become a woman
of the world. I know that good things are happening to me.

17 October—The Sea

—You're no one's fool, Lillie,—Ellen T. once said to me. I
must ever strive to live up to those great expectations.

As I departed from the Captain's cabin this morning, a deck
hand had the insolence to whistle at me. I glared at him.

—You are rude!—I shouted.—And the Captain shall learn of
this.

He withered with dread anticipation of punishment and es-
trangement from the Captain's affection.

It is a peculiar world indeed. No one holds a gentleman in low
regard if he strays from home, conjugal bed, and hearth, provided,
however, that he is discrete and chivalrous, strictly observing the

---

* *I' vau mûs ... and they know it.* From *The Prince and the Lilly*, by James Brough,
Coward McCann & Geoghegan, Inc.: New York, 1974. By permission of Penguin
Group (USA) Inc.

** *I know that good things are happening to me.* From *The Prince and the Lilly*, by
James Brough, Coward McCann & Geoghegan, Inc.: New York, 1974. By
permission of Penguin Group (USA) Inc.

circumscribed bounds of propriety. Lord A, who may look down his nose at Lord B for keeping a mistress, himself entertains courtesans. People look the other way, and it proves Mr Darwin's theory, I think, because we are all descendants of not one but three monkeys: see-no-evil, hear-no-evil, and speak-no-evil.

18 October—The Sea

As You Like It will give me the opportunity to play Rosalind in buskin tights to show off my marvelous legs. You can do what you like in Shakespeare because people don't understand half of it anyway.

I am discovering that my real *forte* is in the character of heroines of genteel comedy.

I must not forget to wear my India rubber mouthguard for my recurring bruxism.

19 October—The Sea

Whatever else can be said about sex, it cannot be called a dignified performance.*

—Reginald! Reginald!—I cried out in my sleep, waking the Captain.

He supposed that Reginald was a lover. The dream vanished before my gathering wakefulness.

—Reginald was my brother. He is dead,—I told him.

> *Plaisir d'amour ne dure qu'un instant;*
> *Chagrin d'amour dure toute une vie.*

Bizarre accident. Old trouble at holmes.

---

* *Whatever else can be said ... dignified performance.* Reprinted with the permission of Abby Adams, from *AN UNCOMMON SCOLD*, by Abby Adams. Copyright © 1989 by Abby Adams. All rights reserved.

21 October—The Sea
I am straightforward in manner, even when the truth hurts.
—When was it we conquered Jersey?—said Gladstone when we first met.
—*Nous ne sommes pas Angleterre. Nous sommes les conquereurs d'Angleterre.* We conquered you, and England belongs to us! We became friends from that moment on. He said to me before I left:
—Mrs Langtry, you have become a truly public person, so you will be attacked, maligned, and slandered in your professional life and in your personal life as well. Never reply to your critics! Never explain, no matter what you've said or done! If you attempt to defend yourself, you'll keep alive a controversy.

23 October—New York Harbor
Sunrise. The *Arizona* crossed Sandy Hook bar to penetrate New York Harbor. Scheherazade is easy; the right dress is very difficult. What shall I wear? I have splendid gowns, made to order by an Irish seamstress on Dover Street, which run from grey satin fringed with beads, with matching hat and parasol, to white cream velvets and ecru lace. But the pride of my collection is my velvet mantles, one black and lined with white fox, the other brown, lined with Russian sable. I had not yet finished dressing in my cabin when I heard a brass band trumpeting *God Save the Queen*. Outside my porthole bobbed a tug that Henry Abbey had hired to meet the steamship in quarantine, bringing with him a large contingent of reporters. My nostalgia for London vanished that instant.*

---

* I have splendid gowns.... My nostalgia for London vanished that instant. *The Prince and the Lilly*, by James Brough, Coward McCann & Geoghegan, Inc.: New York, 1974. By permission of Penguin Group (USA) Inc.

Henrietta was in a sour mood because I had dodged rehearsals that she had stalwartly tried to arrange during the crossing. She concealed the true source of her displeasure. She is really jealous of all the attention I have received. She is further rankled by the sight of Oscar Wilde aboard the tug. As for myself, I fear nothing so much as a man who is witty all day long.

I waited for them all in one of the ship's public rooms.

I came out very demure, wearing no ornaments. Oscar had no chance to talk to me, nor to learn the details of how I had sat as a model for Burne-Jones's *Fortune at the Wheel*. Why should artists paint dead fish, onions and beer glasses? Girls are so much prettier.*

Oscar pressed forward with an anticipated bouquet of white lilies. On board the liner, passengers were asking each other who that was in the cowboy hat, long hair, and lilies. One immigrant who asked this question was answered, *That's an American unspoiled by civilization.*

No it's not. It's Oscar. Jellaby Postlethwaite the Great Poet, who, when first in London, laid determined siege to such notables as Ellen, Henry, and Sarah, writing them verses, sending them flowers, and making requests for photographs, inviting them to his rooms in Salisbury Street and having them write their names across the panels of his white walls.

Oscar's eyes, straining upward, suddenly settled upon my slender figure:

> *Lily of love, pure and inviolate*
> *Tower of ivory, red rose of fire!*

---

* *Why should artists paint dead fish ... Girls are so much prettier.* Reprinted with the permission of Abby Adams, from *AN UNCOMMON SCOLD*, by Abby Adams. Copyright © 1989 by Abby Adams. All rights reserved.

I am one of those unhappy people who inspires bores to great flights of art.

I had never faced a throng of utterly shameless newspapermen before, but nobody had to teach me how to handle men. I was brought up in a clergyman's household, so I am a first class liar.*

I advanced. I am made of ivory and gold. The curves of my lips rewrite history.

—What do you think of America, Mrs Langtry?

—I have spent nine days aboard an American ship,—I said,— so I already know your kindness and your hospitality. I am enchanted.

—What is your opinion of American women?

—I have often been told they are the most beautiful in all the world, and I am sure the reports are accurate.

—Have you seen the Prince of Wales lately, Mrs Langtry?

I ignored that question and awaited the next. I kept my composure and just stared the little weasel down. He had not the courage to repeat the question.

The reporters crushed closer.

—What do you think of New York?

I laughed.

—When the fog lifts, perhaps I will tell you.

—What did you think of the voyage?

—It had disappointed me. There had been wind, but not enough. I wanted to see the ocean run mountains high. It ran only hills high.

I praised Mrs Labouchère, who was at my side.

—What are your emotions regarding your approaching debut?

—Oh, I'm not over my stage fright yet.

I was patient during their endless, idiotic, impertinent and irrelevant questions and managed to charm them by good-natured answers.

* * *

What I saw of the city as I went ashore delighted me. A forest of sailing ships' masts broke the townhouse skyline over the piers of lower Manhattan. The iron-shod hooves of drayhorses and wagon wheels rang on the cobbled streets. The few withered trees that endured the chimneys' smoke were tinged by autumn's fiery red and gold.

Abbey provided an ancient carriage to carry me from the pierhead, a contractual obligation he fulfilled to encarriage me in the style to which I was accustomed.

* * *

Telephone for a monthly fee of ten dollars a head. The elevated railroad on Second Avenue. Brooklyn Bridge is almost complete. Bicycling is a rage, with a new rink available for devotees. Lawn tennis can be played indoors at the Armory. Old English, Flemish, and French masterpieces in the Metropolitan Museum in Central Park just three miles away.

More reporters rushed upon me at the hotel, where I spent two more hours answering their questions. At 2 p.m. finally went out with Henrietta to see New York. Much to my astonishment, I was recognized immediately. It has become risky for me to indulge in a walk on account of the crushing that would follow my appearance.[*] My coach was surrounded by a large

---

[*] *It has become risky ... follow my appearance. ....People rushed ... and I was mobbed.* From *The Prince and the Lilly*, by James Brough, Coward McCann & Geoghegan, Inc.: New York, 1974. By permission of Penguin Group (USA)Inc.

crowd that snarled traffic on Fifth Avenue, and the police had to unblock traffic and rescue me from my admirers. I attempted to visit the Taylor & Lord dry-goods store on Broadway, where a riot almost broke out when someone raised the cry that it was *I*. People rushed toward me and before the police could interfere, I was mobbed. I was unable to do any shopping at all. I was finally escorted to the manager's office and a squad of policemen took me back to the *Albermarle*.

New York has gone mad. I feel that I should apologize to the mayor for all the fuss I am creating. I shall have to disguise myself as a boy continually to walk the streets safely.

24 October

I am startled by the lusty vigor of New York living but I am disturbed by the fact that Americans are relatively indifferent to European cultures. Charles Dickens described the United States as barbarian. Oscar told me that America is a land of unmatched vitality and vulgarity, a people who care not at all about values other than their own, and who, when they make up their minds, love you and hate you with a frightening, passionate zeal.

We went to *Delmonico's* and saw several members from London society and greeted them. Lord X and Lady Y snubbed me, reminding me that I was barred from many of London's best homes, intimating that I would not be admitted to New York's aristocratic circles.

I will make them pay.

25 October

I telephoned Abbey today. Marvelous invention. A good way to talk to someone without offering them a drink.

Such a great demand for tickets for my opening inspired Abbey to conceive of an unprecedented stunt. He is auctioning all opening night seats except those to be used by the drama critics, at *The Turf Club Theatre* on Twenty-Sixth Street. The normal price for orchestra seats is two dollars, for the balcony one dol-

lar and for the gallery fifty cents. Front box seats are being sold for $325. The cheapest orchestra seats for ten. Headlines.

26 October

Generous Americans! A wine merchant delivered a case of French champagne, and all he wants in return is for me to order a bottle at a restaurant. Two competing piano manufacturers, Baldwin and Kimball, insisted that I accept their products, and asked nothing in return. Dressmakers somehow managed to learn my precise measurements, and inundated me with gifts of gowns which they begged me to wear. Milliners, shoemakers, glovers and corsetmakers followed. New York's finest restauranteurs invited me to dine in their establishments as their guest. The owner of a fleet of hansom cabs placed a carriage at my disposal for the duration of my stay in New York. What a horn of plenty America is!

27 October

We rehearse at the *Park Theatre* in Madison Square from 8:00 a.m. to 8:00 p.m. Then Henrietta and I rehearse privately from 9:00 p.m. to midnight. I am utterly committed to the plan, and through the long hours devoted to *As You like It*, I am discovering the majesty of Shakespearean drama. Once the reading and interpretation are in place, we work on the blocking, stage effects, and timing and expression until the play becomes a single event.

Where will love take me next?

> *It was a lover and his lass,*
> *With a hey, and a ho, and hey nonino,*
> *That o'er the green corn-field did pass.* . . .

28 October

The *New York Herald* assigned a reporter, Bury I. Dasent, to accompany me on my rounds whenever possible and cover every minute of my day, because they recognize the value of the con-

tinuing stream of stories that flow through me. Bury, of course, is falling in love with me and is writing the most ecstatic stories. He will do anything I say. He would kiss my feet if I requested him to do so.

29 October

My allure rested in exciting rumors that preceded me, imparting an advance impression of delicious wickedness. Women, rich and poor, reproduce something of my appearance in their own. The Jersey Lilly hair style—a single, heavy plait reaching halfway down the neck with bangs covering the forehead—is showing up everywhere.

* * *

I dressed seductively. I was ready to discuss business with Sarony. In return for a commission, he would have exclusive rights to make new portraits of me, and woe betide him if proofs he submitted did not come up to my expectations.

30 October

Bury came up with the wonderful advertising stunt. He suggested that I go down to Wall Street. Huge throngs gathered in the narrow streets. The police had to rescue me again. When we were finally admitted to the Stock Exchange, Bury guided me to the observer's balcony amid the hellish pandemonium of grown men screaming orders to buy and sell stocks like savage lunatics. When word came around that I was there, the traders dropped their business presently. They fell silent with awe. They broke precedent when they suspended transactions on the Exchange long enough to greet me formally.

31 October

The true subject of any conversation is myself and my career in drama. Oscar, having heard that I was to play Rosalind in *As You Like It*, persuaded me to dispense with the long-legged boots that Rose Coghlan introduced to the role. We conversed

profoundly upon the relative merits of curling irons and the proper arrangement of curled locks.

1 November

We rehearsed with the company until 2:00 A.M. We left the carpenters to toil over the lavish settings. Mrs Labouchère gave me her final notes.

Afternoon. David Belasco, the young manager of the *Madison Square Theater*, saw me when I was at the Park to see the workings of the double stage, designed by Steele McKaye. Belasco showed me how it worked, then about five o'clock went with me, Abbey, and Mrs Labouchère back to the Albermarle, where we were talking when Pierre Lorillard came running into the room crying:

—I'm afraid the *Park Theatre* is on fire!

We all rushed to the windows and saw the roof of the theatre ablaze, billows of smoke writhing in the orange flames, which lit up the early winter darkness. Fire had broken out in the carpenter's workshop backstage and raced through the auditorium. I watched from my window as smoke darkened the red sky over Madison Square.*

Fire-bells were clanging. Belasco saw me wipe a tear from my eyes. I stood watching the flames leap around the signboard on the roof—the signboard with my name upon it. Superstition and willpower clashed. If it stands, I'll succeed. If it burns, I'll succeed without it.

When the fire faded to embers, two men were dead, the building was destroyed, but my sign survived. Hot tears of rage

---

* *Fire had broken out … to hire clothes for the company.* From *The Prince and the Lilly*, by James Brough, Coward McCann & Geoghegan, Inc.: New York, 1974. By permission of Penguin Group (USA) Inc.

and sorrow filled my eyes, and my hands were clenched into a fist.

—Well, we'll try again some other day,—I said to Belasco.

Our scenery, properties, and costumes were all gone except for my dresses, which I had the foresight to keep safely in my hotel.

Abbey took the fire in stride. He rented another, larger house while Henrietta bustled around to the *costumier* to hire clothes for the company.

2 November

Leonard Jerome introduced him to me. He fell in love with me but I felt nothing. It irritated me that he began to pursue me. He invites me to go riding and ice-skating. He takes me driving and we take long walks. We dine alone together, sometimes in tony restaurants, at other times in German beer gardens where we would escape public recognition.

Freddie has led a completely undisciplined life. It is rumored that he has never heard the word *no* spoken to him. He will inherit $5,000,000 from his father—provided, however, that he marries. He lives off the interest, which at 5% I reckon to be $250,000 per annum. He is a rebel who never worked a day in his life, never learned how to read and write well, and who consorts with jockeys, prize fighters, and prostitutes.

His attitude to life is very concise: *I have an income of $250,000 per annum. The Public be damned!*

He brought me a costly necklace, which he flung at me.

I played with his tie.

—Oh, Freddie, off with these!

* * * * *

Oscar visited me not long after Freddie left. My complexion was still flushed and redolent of lovemaking. I hurled the necklace at Oscar and giggled. I startled him.

—When I saw Freddie just now,—I explained,—he took that out of his pocket and flung it at me across the table, saying, like

331

the surly bear he is, *If you want that you can keep it.* So I felt that I must positively fling it at someone else.*

Oscar was not amused, nor was he to be outdone.

—I think I shall keep it!—he said with comeback, admiring the necklace.

He finally returned it to me before he left.

The day was quick in coming, for Lester Wallack telegraphed Abbey a message, which the latter interpreted as an offer to use Wallack's Theater for my opening. Abbey fell to work as the front pages of American newspapers told the story of the fire. Curiosity in me doubled, and in the week that I awaited the building of new scenery, reporters telegraphed distant editors about what I thought of the national elections (which were to come the day before my debut), what I thought of American dress, whether I had or had not a headache. In the craze for items about me, some reporters grew weary, if not bitter, one of them writing:

> *On her voyage to America, Mrs Langtry won the steamer pool, thirty pounds. It is customary to give this to the ship's charities, but Lillie Shylock Langtry quietly pocketed all but one pound.*

It's not true!

3 November

Oscar is trying to write a play. How pretentious! He creates his silly characters spouting exquisite nonsense, characters who are by his own admission extensions of his *personality*. I, on the other hand, author the very beliefs men hold, and as my daughter will attest, I am the inventor of life itself.

---

* *When I saw Freddy just now ... someone else.* From OCSCAR WILDE by Richard Ellmann, copyright © 1987 by The Estate of Richard Ellmann. Used by permission of Alfred A. Knopf, a division of Random House, Inc.

If you have a room which you do not want certain people to get into, put a lock on it for which they do not have the key. But there is no point in talking to them about it, unless of course you want them to admire the room from the outside! The honorable thing to do is to put a lock on the door that will be noticed only by those who can open it, not by the rest.[*]

Speech is silver, but silence is golden.

* * * * *

—You have made me pretty,—I scolded Sarony,—I am beautiful.

I know the value of the commodity which I exemplify. If I had lived in the days of the Stuarts, I would have been a duchess in my own right.[**] I am a continuing stream of stories, all of which flow through me in a grand confluence. Edward sees one aspect of my life that does not include Jeanne-Marie, and supposes me to be one type of person; Sherlock is much the same; and Freddie sees Lillie Future but not Lillie Past. To theatre audiences, I am *Rosalind, Kate Hardcastle, Hester Grazebrook*, mother and hot whore all at once. I am the grand mistress of majesty and elegant illusion. A photograph is a secret about a secret. The more it tells you, the less you know.[***]

---

[*] *If you have a room ... not by the rest.* Reprinted with the permission of The Free Press, a Division of Simon & Schuster Adult Publishing Group, from *LUDWIG WITTGENSTEIN: The Duty of Genius*, by Ray Monk. Copyright © 1990 by Ray Monk. All rights reserved. Published in the UK by Jonathan Cape. Reprinted with permission of The RandomHouse Group Ltd.

[**] *You have made me pretty ... a dutchess in my own right.* From *The Prince and the Lilly*, by James Brough, Coward McCann & Geoghegan, Inc.: New York, 1974. By permission of Penguin Group (USA) Inc.

[***] *A photograph ... the less you know.* Reprinted with the permission of Abby Adams, from *AN UNCOMMON SCOLD*, by Abby Adams. Copyright © 1989 by Abby Adams. All rights reserved.

4 November

First night attendees included my old friend Grover Cleveland and members of New York's most prominent families: the Vanderbilts, Goulds, Belmonts, Lorillards, and Cuttings, who jostled together in a crowd that filed into Wallack's Theatre, the men splendidly starched, pressed, and pomaded as London clubmen, the women ablaze in diamond tiaras, necklaces, and stomachers. Two wagonloads of flowers stood waiting by the stage door before the curtain rose. Two hundred and fifty reviewers and reporters filled rows of stalls, with Oscar in his glory as guest critic for the *World*.

A cablegram arrived from Bertie, wishing me success on my opening night. This was no surprise to me. I had written it out myself before I left London, leaving him to perform the act of friendship for me.

Le plus beau jour de ma vie. It is all a dream, a delight, a wild excitement. I slid down the stairs of the theater on a silver salver and crashed into Freddie's arms.[*]

5 November

The opening night receipts were almost seven thousand dollars, a record in the American theatre. Long lines at the box office assure me of success regardless of the critics' verdict.

Oscar began his review: *It is only in the best Greek gems, on the silver coins of Syracuse, or among the marble fringes of the Parthenon frieze that one can find the ideal representation of the marvelous beauty of that face that laughed through the leaves last night as Rosalind. . . .*

---

[*] *Le plus beau jour ... into Freddie's arms.* From *The Prince and the Lilly*, by James Brough, Coward McCann & Geoghegan, Inc.: New York, 1974. By permission of Penguin Group (USA) Inc.

My idea was to meet Winter by accident and charm him. I don't care what is written about me so long as it isn't true.[*] Henry Abbey arranged to meet Winter for dinner at *Pfaff's*. I shall happen to be dining alone a few tables away.

Henrietta's husband writes me:

—I marvel at your ability to remain on good terms with that termagant, who is not happy unless she is creating misery for someone else.[**]

6 November

It is a good idea to write down one's thoughts. It saves one having to bother anyone with them.

I always found Oscar a terrible bore. He and I are using each other for our separate purposes.

I thought he got what he wanted with the lecture in aesthetics. But no, he is so high minded and ambitious. Ward is selling his notoriety, his aesthetic clothes, his mannerisms, his resemblance to a comic character in a light opera, and his appeal to public curiosity of the lowest sort, as if he were an anomaly or a curiosity of medicine.

—Yes, it's a good offer,—he said, utterly blind to what people really thought of him.

> *HE IS COMING!!!*
> *WHO IS COMING???*
> *OSCAR WILDE!!!*
> *THE GREAT AESTHETE!!!*

---

[*] *I don't care ... as long as it isn'*. Reprinted with the permission of Abby Adams, from *AN UNCOMMON SCOLD*, by Abby Adams. Copyright © 1989 by Abby Adams. All rights reserved.

[**] *I marvel ... creating misery for someone else.* From *The Prince and the Lilly*, by James Brough, Coward McCann & Geoghegan, Inc.: New York, 1974. By permission of Penguin Group (USA) Inc.

People notice Oscar when he moves in my shadow. A *New York Herald* man saw him sitting in the *Albermarle*, on the Sunday after my arrival, waiting for me to return with Abbey, Mrs Labouchère, and other admirers from a steam yacht trip up the Hudson. When I came to my room, Oscar sat silently listening at one side while the reporter plied me with questions. Nothing spoils a good party like a genius.

—How did you like the Hudson?

I never know how much of what I say is true.*

—I think it is simply lovely, grand, magnificent, or rather, let me use that expressive, American, somewhat paradoxical phrase, and say I was agreeably disappointed. I don't wonder that you call it *The Rhine of America* ... But do you know, there is one thing that would prevent me from settling down somewhere upon the banks of the Hudson and becoming Americanized.

—And what is that?—the reporter demanded.

—Why, that horrid railroad that runs all the way along the bank. It destroys very much of the beauty. Why do you allow it there? I suppose now I must see Niagara Falls, that great American attraction.

At this, Oscar came out of silence, as if on cue.

—Oh, don't go to Niagara falls,—he said.

—Why not?—I asked, then before he could speak, I rippled on laughingly.—Oh, I remember now your experience in pulling up the car window curtain and asking disappointedly, *Is that Niagara Falls?* pulling down the curtain again and going to sleep.

—They told me that so many millions of gallons of water tumbled over the fall in a minute,—said Oscar, taking the

---

floor.—I could see no beauty in that. There was bulk there, but no beauty, except the beauty inherent in bulk itself. Niagara Falls seemed to me to be simply a vast unnecessary amount of water going the wrong way and then falling over unnecessary rocks. People are beginning to ask why he hangs around any longer. The real reason appears to be that he has nothing special on his mind and that there are enough silly people afflicted with the English craze to flatter and amuse the fellow.

* * * * *

11:00 P.M.

Must inquire about my negligees that I had lined with ermine. Freddie will delight in them for brevity is the soul of lingerie. And that ball gown I want trimmed with silver fox. . . .*

The enterprising Dasent discovered that Freddie purchased a necklace and bracelet of matching diamonds for me at *Tiffany's*, and enlightened the *Herald's* readers with the details. He sent me the gems in a huge bouquet of flowers, and I did not return the gift. Much to his annoyance, Freddie was catapulted over-night into international prominence.

7 November

Freddie does not get along well with Henrietta, who disapproves of him. She is no prude but she thinks it is disadvantageous for me to consort openly with a young millionaire. She wants me to spend more time rehearsing *An Unequal Match*, which we must take on tour. She didn't like the idea of me accepting the costly necklace and bracelet or the publicity it

---

* *Must inquire ... trimmed with silver fox.* From *The Prince and the Lilly*, by James Brough, Coward McCann & Geoghegan, Inc.: New York, 1974. By permission of Penguin Group (USA) Inc.

caused. Of course not, no one ever gave her such a present. Then she unearthed a story about Freddie: He was a brawler, an iconoclast, a gaudy dresser, a drunk and a hedonist who thumbed his nose at the world. He drank, and when drunk, became pugnacious. Gladys Leslie, an actress whose sole distinction was being a blonde, pressed charges against Freddie when he began treating her like a punching bag during a night on the town. Henrietta is surely trying to poison me against him.

I'm telling her to mind her own business.

8 November

A kiss can be a comma, a question mark or an exclamation point. That's the basic spelling that every woman ought to know.[*]

I took Freddie into the bedroom, which I furnished with Parisian elegance and simplicity, with soft velvet carpets, and clouds of pink and white draperies.

His appearance and physique suggested the glories of Noirmont, conjuring the image of the most valiant of my forebearers, Raul Le Breton, a man after my own heart. King John is honored by the Le Bretons not so much for signing the *Magna Carta* as for entrusting Raul with the mission of cutting a path up along the Seine with a few hundred retainers to capture Paris from his liege's rival for the throne, Arthur of Brittany.[**]

Freddie requested that I remove my bonnet, cloak and dress, those abused inventions of modern barbarism. I hesitated,

---

[*] *A kiss can be a comma ... every woman ought to know.* Reprinted with the permission of Abby Adams, from *AN UNCOMMON SCOLD*, by Abby Adams. Copyright © 1989 by Abby Adams. All rights reserved.

[**] *His appearance ... Arthur of Brittany.* From *The Prince and the Lilly*, by James Brough, Coward McCann & Geoghegan, Inc.: New York, 1974. By permission of Penguin Group (USA) Inc.

merely to prolong his sweet agony. He whispered words of love
into my ear, and with no unpracticed hand unfastened the various hooks and eyes, and buttons, ribbons, and lacings with
which modistes are wont to incase me. I stepped out of my fallen
clothing, arranged about me like fallen petals. He is a young
Adonis, made out of ivory and rose leaves—a brainless and
beautiful creature.

He pressed me to him, disengaged the fallen garments, and
laying me upon my side he slowly passed his hand up and down
my spine, over my bosom, and down my arms, till my whole
frame trembled beneath his touch, and I could not tell whether it
was pain or pleasure that I felt. He whispered into the ear-
between-my-legs.

I had no power to move but I moved; a dreamy intoxication
came over me; my breath came quick and panting through my
parted lips; I was in a trance—dead I seemed to the outward world
with no thought of past or future; indeed no distinct speculation of
the present, yet I was in a state of most unspeakable, most
profound and ecstatic enjoyment, and satisfied by the holy rites of
love the passions he had excited to the highest pitch.

Then I fell half-asleep happy but inexplicably sad. I dreamed
about that boy again. I skipped out of the house to meet him as
we had arranged that evening. We were sauntering together
down *Patier Lane*, not far from the deanery, when my father saw
us. A single glance sufficed to inform him the mutual warmth of
feeling we possessed, but he seemed needlessly disturbed. My
father summarily ordered me home.*

At home, he closed the study doors behind me, then spoke
with unaccustomed sternness. *I forbid you ever to go out again*

---

* *Then I fell half-asleep ... before breakfast the next day.* From *The Prince and the Lilly*, by James Brough, Coward McCann & Geoghegan, Inc.: New York, 1974. By permission of Penguin Group (USA) Inc.

with that young man, he said. I asked boldly why he objected with such violence to a boy who so resembled him. My father at first only repeated his edict. I continued to press him for an explanation, until it was given with no little reluctance.

—Because he is your own half-brother. You must endeavor to understand. He is another son of mine.

My composure did not desert me. I was adept by now at controlling my feelings. My brothers' training had taught me to think more like a man than a weeping girl. I still ponder the implications of his honest answer. I wonder how many others like my forbidden admirer were on the island. Perhaps only *Le Tcheziot* could guess at the dirty dean's full score. I know thee, *Le Tcheziot,* consorting with witches who conjure storms at sea and dance naked in covens at Rocqueberg Point where you, the devil's deputy, left a print of his cloven hoof in the stone.

Henrietta stumbled upon us. She occupied the bedroom on the far side of the sitting room in my suite, saw lights burning there, and investigated. She was astonished and horrified to discover me and Freddie drinking champagne in a paradisiacal state of nudity.

—Make yourself at home. We ain't bashful!—Freddie chimed in, inviting her good-naturedly (!) to join us.

Henrietta found no humor in the remark and left before breakfast the next day. She is naive, like Edward, like Sherlock. She left me a scathing letter.

Mrs Labouchère wanted me to have more *dignity* in New York, and I forced her into a back seat; it hurt her. When she said, *You much choose between us,* my response was, *My choice is already made.*

10 November

THE LANGTRY SCANDAL

Mrs Labouchère officially announced that she disap-
proved of Mrs Langtry's proceedings in this country,

340

*had no further connection with her, personally, or
with her theatrical engagements, and intends to return to England after visiting friends in Washington.**

That is not true! I offered Henrietta her share of the profits
but my mentor refused remuneration. The highly moral newspapers are enjoying a bonanza portraying Henrietta as a champion
of virtue, myself as a fallen angel, and Freddie as a conniving
seducer. Late at night I ponder these developments. Moonlight
gleams through the windows. Suddenly, I hear a weird rustling
like the whirring of huge wings. I wonder if I may command the
mysterious forces of the universe** and keep box office receipts
high in the face of such a hostile reception by the press.

11 November

I am convinced that the Muses and the Graces never thought
of having their breakfast anywhere but in bed.

Freddie is so precious! He considered the *New York Sun* to be
our chief journalistic malefactor, and took it upon himself to answer them.

*Times must be pretty bad, I sez, if a gentleman can't
make a present a lady, who every man in America
admires, with flowers as a token of admirashun.*

*Mrs Langtry could do no wrong, even if she wonted
to, because she is watched by Mrs LaBooshare, by a
yunger sister of that woman is a better actres than*

---

* *Mrs Labouchère officially announced ... friends in Washington.* From *The Prince
and the Lilly*, by James Brough, Coward McCann & Geoghegan, Inc.: New York,
1974. By permission of Penguin Group (USA) Inc.

** *Suddenly, I hear ... forces of the universe.* From *The Prince and the Lilly*, by James
Brough, Coward McCann & Geoghegan, Inc.: New York, 1974. By permission of
Penguin Group (USA) Inc.

> *she is a watchdog, which ain't saying much, by a*
> *Miss Pattison of Mrs LaBooshare's staff who never*
> *stops spying on Mrs Langtree, and in my opinion she*
> *is jelus, by the manger of the hotell, by the hotell*
> *servints, and even by the peeple on the staff of the*
> *Wallax Theeyater. I am wiling to wagger that these*
> *spies are also on the payroll of the snooping Mrs La-*
> *Booshare. I challenger to produce her own marage*
> *certtificat, as proof that she has a right to cridisize a*
> *lady who has done no wrong.*

Quel mignon! His grammar and spelling errors colored his anger so boyishly. But after all, a man who has an annual income of $250,000 does not need to know grammar and orthography. His secretary should do that for him. In fact, it's the secretary's fault. Freddie should dismiss him at once!

12 November

Pus nou-s'etiboque la saltai, pus on pu.

The English actors in the company are badly shaken by Henrietta's defection, but Kate Hodson, Henrietta's sister, saved the day. She announced that she had no intention of quitting. Kate said in print that her sister was a lifelong troublemaker who couldn't get along with anyone. The company is regaining its composure. I have taken the role of actor-manager.

Reporters visited me in my rooms. I gave them tea, smiled pleasantly, and talked about the raw weather and the early winter. No one really listens to anyone else, and if you try it for a while you will see why.[*]

---

* *No one really listens... you will see why.* Reprinted with the permission of Abby Adams, from *AN UNCOMMON SCOLD*, by Abby Adams. Copyright© 1989 by Abby Adams. All rights reserved.

13 November

Everybody forgot about the reviews of *As You Like It*. We were sold out four weeks in advance and had done more than sixty thousand dollars of box office. Moral controversy is good for business.

Freddie berated Wilde when I sat on his lap this afternoon: *You can't sit on his lap. It's not at all compromising!*

15 November

They call me *Miss Lillie*. I am unapproachable by any common actor or actress in the company. I had learned from both Holmes and the Prince the techniques for maintaining distance between myself and lesser beings. During working hours, I am a businesswoman, exacting obedience from those who serve me. I refuse to be hurried or flustered by any calamity, and I seldom speak an unnecessary word. I merely have to say softly, *Let us not fuss, please,* and it has the impact of a command.

I am more regal offstage than on, if that is possible.*

20 November

These men in show business are impressed by neither charm nor money. I'm always tough with them.

—Freddie is accompanying me to Chicago as my bodyguard,—I said.

Abbey's hairs stood on end.

—Such things are not done,—he said,—a married woman traveling with a handsome young bachelor who does not conceal his affection for her. That is simply not done in America. The moral public will reject you.

Lillie doesn't care!

---

* *The call me Miss Lillie ... it has the impact of a command.* From *The Prince and the Lilly*, by James Brough, Coward McCann & Geoghegan, Inc.: New York, 1974. By permission of Penguin Group (USA) Inc.

26 November

O, how full of briars is this working-day world!

Arthur Elwood is my leading man. He is a fine actor but lacks the *je ne sais quoi* that would make him a theatrical luminary. He has made a serious mistake by falling in love with me, his employer and co-worker. I have been able to hold Elwood's off-stage attention in check, even though I typically enjoy seeing men make fools of themselves over me. But business is business.

Elwood eventually began to discharge his contained emotions in the form of jealousy directed against Freddie. I am quite familiar with the effects of adverse publicity, so I have developed new techniques. I arrive in a city and am accorded a grand reception with much fanfare, then Freddy arrives quietly the next day. I outmaneuver the press, so we suffer no repercussions.

Elwood's acting, however, began to deteriorate whenever Freddie arrived. On stage he stuttered, blew lines, missed cues, all in all enormously complicating the entire production and annoying cast and crew alike. But worst of all, Elwood forced his way into my dressing room and created a scene. He demanded an immediate audience with me after a performance.

So I was speaking to Elwood in my dressing room about his shortcomings. I told him quite frankly that I would have to let him go unless he stopped this calf-loving immediately. We are professionals.

That is when Freddie burst into the dressing room. It is a familiar dilemma: telling someone something he does not understand is pointless, even if you add that he will not understand it. That so often happens with someone you love.[*]

---

[*] *telling someone something ... with someone you love.* Reprinted with the permission of The Free Press, a Division of Simon & Schuster Adult Publishing Group, from *LUDWIG WITTGENSTEIN: The Duty of Genius,* by Ray Monk. Copyright © 1990 by Ray Monk. All rights reserved. Published in the UK by Jonathan Cape. Reprinted with permission of The RandomHouse Group Ltd.

Freddie had been drinking and lost all self-command when he saw me with Elwood. First he accused me of cheating, and when Elwood tried to intervene, Freddie knocked him down repeatedly and threw him bodily out of the dressingroom.

Haro! Haro! À l'aide mon Prince! On me fait tort!*

His rage unabated, Freddie made a shambles of my dressingroom. He ripped paintings and tapestries from the walls, overturned and smashed furniture. He ripped to shreds several new gowns I had just ordered from Worth, and he scattered the contents of my dresser drawers.

He then assaulted me and blackened my eye.

My hands were full, but I swore the cast and the crew to secrecy. I love the lie that saves my pride, but never the unflattering truth.

Freddie is guilt-ridden as he ought to be. I detest him, but he is giving me a small house on Twenty-Third Street to make amends.

2 December

When my turn came with the reporters, I smiled my Mona Lisa smile and said, *Who is Mr Gebhardt? A mere boy, only twenty-three. Is he so important that my recognition of him must set all tongues wagging?*

I permit Freddie to visit me now only if he is sober.

* * *

I behave more haughtily than a duchess and teach my daughter to do the same. I strive to create an atmosphere of impassive frostiness of demeanor, as does Jeanne-Marie, in the company of strangers. I do not want people to be agreeable as it saves me the

---

* *Haro! Haro! À l'aide mon Prince! On me fait tort!* From *The Prince and the Lilly*, by James Brough, Coward McCann & Geoghegan, Inc.: New York, 1974. By permission of Penguin Group (USA) Inc.

trouble of liking them.* I will sit in an armchair with the splendor of the queen-empress, extending her hand to be kissed, acknowledging a greeting with a stately nod. When the crowd is gone, I dismount my high horse. Then I hitch up my skirt, jump up from the chair, and cry, *Thank God, that's over for a while. Now let's play!* One of the survivors knuckles down on the piano's keyboard, the lively and intimate conversation and laughter begins, and champagne glasses clink.**

I would be hurt, if people thought me cruel, for I have far more heart than I am given credit for, but I will not endure stupidity or incompetence, and any lack of straightforwardness is with me unforgivable.

8 December

The easiest kind of relationship for me is with ten thousand people. The hardest is with one.***

20 December

We board *The City of Worcester*, which boasts a living room, three bedrooms and a private bath. Diamond Jim Brady is lending it to me just for the privilege of being seen in my company at *Delmonico's*. Freddie threatened to punch a reporter who made the mistake of trying to interview him.

* * * * *

---

*   *I do not want people ... liking them.* Reprinted with the permission of Abby Adams, from *AN UNCOMMON SCOLD*, by Abby Adams. Copyright © 1989 by Abby Adams. All rights reserved.

**   *I behave more haughtily ... champagne glasses clink.* From *The Prince and the Lilly*, by James Brough, Coward McCann & Geoghegan, Inc.: New York, 1974. By permission of Penguin Group (USA) Inc.

*** *The easiest kind of relationship ... hardest is with one.* Reprinted with the permission of Abby Adams, from *AN UNCOMMON SCOLD*, by Abby Adams. Copyright © 1989 by Abby Adams. All rights reserved.

I am an attraction no matter what the critics think of me.

* * * * *

Richelieu Robinson of the House of Representatives attacked me in a speech he delivered on the floor of the House. He accuses me of demoralizing the American stage and corrupting American society, and suggested that I be deported. The time has come for me to behave with great discretion at all times. Who is he? What is he? Is he anything at all? A Congressman, an illiterate hack whose fancy vest is spotted with gravy and whose speeches, hypocritical, unctuous, and slovenly, are spotted with the sauce of political patronage.

We women are a slave society in the grip of men who are priests and politicians. They accuse us of everything and act punitively toward us, by making us women out to be evil, flawing the world by the act of procreation. They conjure up the bogeyman of *original sin* to keep us guilty. For such an unjust system to work for any prolonged period of time, it is necessary for the people to think they deserve the injustice.

Where is Freddie when I need him? I would rather have a fool to make me merry than experience to make me sad; and to travel for it too!

9 January—Chicago

An eighteen-hour journey, and then came to the rambunctious, fast-growing, somewhat ramshackle metropolis of the Central West.

We reached it after dark. Twinkling lights in Indiana farmhouses and glimpses of sullen way-stations are replaced by hints of the great city. Shadows of factories and grain elevators stand black against a cold grey sky. The traveler can feel the presence, close by the train, of an immense inland ocean; for we are passing the southernmost curve of Lake Michigan. In the night, and in its winter mood, it is a spectral sea, shrouded in light fog and breathing mystery.

In a short time, the molten hearths of the South Chicago steel works cast scarlet and purple flares through the train windows from their huge forges.

My train begins to rattle over switch-points and run warily across streets as dismal as those of East London, if not worse. Then it enters areas a little better lighted and more cheerful. And at length it draws in slowly at the terminal bordered by slums, its shed roaring with escaping steam, its exterior surrounded by hacks, by barkers for hotels, by rat-faced men seeking to trap immigrants, by shrieking newsboys and whining beggars.

* * * * *

Reporters met me in my suite in the *Grand Pacific Hotel*: I shall never get used to not being the most beautiful woman in the room. It is intoxicating to sweep in and know every man has turned his head. It keeps me in form.[*]

They press the inevitable question: How did I like America after living here four months?

—It improves upon acquaintance,—I answered grandly.

—Do you like the people?

—They have been pretty kind to me.

Was there any prospect of my husband joining me?

—I am sorry to say no,—I said without the slightest hesitation.—Poor man, he can't spare the time to come over just now. He is in trouble and has to stay in England.[**]

Lying increases the creative faculties, expands the ego, lessens the friction of social contacts . . . It is only in lies,

---

wholeheartedly and bravely told, that human nature attains through words and speech the forebearance, the nobility, the romance, the idealism, that—being what it is—it falls so short of in fact and deed.[*]

23 January—Chicago

From the beginning of our life together, my husband seemed to accept the inevitability of my having a train of admirers. I could not help it. There they were. It was all a great game, but he could not cope with it.[**]

Edward is making a nuisance of himself again. He is woeful and miserable, still begging to be taken back. *Quel sentiment de ferveur!* He threatens to come to America and pay me visits at the theatre. He is dissipated, gone to seed, and incapable of even menial labor. Now he says his father has cut off his allowance. I didn't believe him and I wouldn't give him any more money. Then he threatened to make trouble for me by revealing more than is proper regarding our personal relations. . . . I'm agreeing to support him with a monthly allowance on the condition that he never come to see me again. Should he break the agreement, I will have the right to cut him off. George Lewis will disburse his monthly allotment.

* * *

America, I decided, grows on me. I was terrified at first. Curiosity is expressed here with a roughness of manner to which I have not yet become accustomed. I found a lack of cultured and

---

[*] *Lying increases the creative faculties ... it falls so short of in fact and deed.* Reprinted with the permission of Abby Adams, from *AN UNCOMMON SCOLD*, by Abby Adams. Copyright© 1989 by Abby Adams. All rights reserved.

[**] *From the beginning ... could not cope with it.* From *The Prince and the Lilly*, by James Brough, Coward McCann & Geoghegan, Inc.: New York, 1974. By permission of Penguin Group (USA) Inc.

349

intelligent gentlemen. But since I can make a fresh fortune every season by exposing myself to vulgar curiosity, I shall have to learn to live with it.[*]

1 February—Chicago

I discovered that the fastest-growing city in the United States is tough and rude, pugnacious and incredibly energetic. It stands on ceremony with no one. Men fight for the sheer love of combat and shout at attractive women in the streets. A dozen languages are spoken, fortunes are made overnight, and the race goes to the swift, the strong, and the bold.

Chicago is not even a hundred years old and has less history than New York, and none of that real, solemn history that is Europe, which I cannot be interested in: The quarrels of Popes and kings, with wars and pestilences on every page; the men are all so good for nothing, and hardly any women at all. *How wonderful it must have been for the ancient Britons,* my mother once said, *when the Romans arrived and they could have a hot bath.* That is genuine history.

14 February—Chicago

I wrote to George Lewis to learn if there was a chance that Edward would agree to a divorce, and discovered there was no chance he would consent. I am deeply in love with Freddie and want to marry him. Abe Hummel suggested a way out of my difficulties.

—You could always become an American citizen,—he said.

---

[*] *America, I decided, ... learn to live with it.* From *The Prince and the Lilly,* by James Brough, Coward McCann & Geoghegan, Inc.: New York, 1974. By permission of Penguin Group (USA) Inc.

20 February—Chicago

I am at last permanently reunited with Jeanne-Marie. Nothing shall separate us ever again.

30 March—San Francisco

In addition to the real estate purchase I made in Chicago, I bought a house in San Francisco and applied for United States citizenship as a resident of California. I am beginning the clandestine course of ridding myself of Edward. At a private hearing in a judge's chambers in Lakeport, California, I stated my claim for my marriage to be dissolved on the grounds that Edward had long since deserted me.

O, that woman that cannot make her fault her husband's occasion, let her never nurse her child herself, for she will breed it like a fool!

—I have always treated Mr Langtry with affection,—I declared,—never giving him cause to disregard his duty to me as a husband.

Humility is not my *forte*, and whenever I dwell at any length of time on my own shortcomings, they gradually begin to seem mild, harmless, rather engaging little things, not at all like the striking defects in other people's characters.

Adultery is meanness and stealing from someone what is rightfully theirs, a great selfishness, and surrounded by lies lest it should be found out. And out of the meanness and selfishness and lying flow love and joy and peace beyond anything that can be imagined.*

Edward was unaware of the proceedings; and I had no difficulty in gaining my freedom. . . . Thank God! We are now rid of such a damned blackguard!

No man may occupy the role of father to Jeanne-Marie, even though Freddie is living openly with me, and the girl is the focus of his attention. She goes riding with him. He takes her to the circus and the New York Zoo, but I am not ready to marry him, in spite of his apparent fondness for my child.[*] A man is so much in the way in the house, and besides, I have yet to hear a man ask for advice on how to combine marriage and a career.[**]

The monthly allowance to Edward continues.

17 March—San Francisco

Oh, these ghastly women reporters! They are so deadly in earnest, and are so naive, and know so little about anything! I accepted an invitation from one of them to go to a function where I should meet a lot of interesting people. But when we left together, the creature wanted to interview me on the proceedings and asked me if I was not very much impressed. That was really *too* quaint. *My good woman,* I said, *you forget that I'm in the impressing business myself.*

28 May—Kansas City

We played in decrepit wood frame buildings that dated back to the days of Junius Brutus Booth, father of the notorious John Wilkes. We performed in halls where the company jack-of-all-trades had to pipe in a gas supply to feed the footlights. We

---

[*] *No man may occupy ... for my child!* From *The Prince and the Lilly,* by James Brough, Coward McCann & Geoghegan, Inc.: New York, 1974. By permission of Penguin Group (USA) Inc.

[**] *I have yet to hear a man ... combine a marriage and a career.* Reprinted with the permission of Abby Adams, from *AN UNCOMMON SCOLD,* by Abby Adams. Copyright © 1989 by Abby Adams. All rights reserved.

came to know the fantastic theatrical palaces of Western boom towns that rose in marble splendor out of the plains, surrounded by shacks that a landed English gentleman would refuse to keep pigs in.[*]

27 July—New York

Wilde paid an afternoon call on me with a manuscript under his arm. Placing it on the table, he made a sweep with his right hand: *There is a play that I have written for you.*

I was not sure that he was in earnest. His chatter sometimes amused me, but the thought that he might have pretensions as a playwright—well, he tried so hard to get money from Freddie that I stopped taking him seriously.

—What is my part?—I asked cautiously.

—A woman,—he said,—with an illegitimate daughter.

If he were trying to rattle me, I would not let him.

—My dear Oscar, am I such a person?

I refused to touch the manuscript or allow him to read a line of it to me.

—Put it away for twenty years,—was my parting advice. Twenty years.

The middle age of buggers is not to be contemplated without horror.

Why he ever supposed that it would have been a suitable play for me, I cannot imagine. *Lady Windermere's Fan* is the title of the blasphemous manuscript. It is in such bad taste![**]

---

[*] *Oh, these ghastly women reporters ... to keep pigs in.* From *The Prince and the Lilly*, by James Brough, Coward McCann & Geoghegan, Inc.: New York, 1974. ` By permission of Penguin Group (USA) Inc.

[**] *Wilde paid an afternoon call ... in such bad taste!* From *The Prince and the Lilly*, by James Brough, Coward McCann & Geoghegan, Inc.: New York, 1974. By permission of Penguin Group (USA) Inc.

14 August—Washington, D.C.

I visited Uncle Jumbo to settle some unfinished business that still existed between us, which consisted of my repayment (with interest) for the money he disbursed for Jeanne's upbringing in Philadelphia. I came on a day when his wife was gone. Needless to say, I was not invited to their wedding. I noticed a lovely piece of colonial furniture and paused to admire it.

—Like that stuff?—he asked.—Know anything about it, or just like the looks of it?

I told him I was quite fond of antique furnishings.

—Well,—said Cleveland.—I suppose if you like it, you like it.

Then he told me how the piece found its way into his home.

The preceding summer, according to Uncle Jumbo's tale, his wife, Frank had paid a visit to an island off the coast of Maine.

—Not long after her return,—narrated Cleveland,—a great, damn vanload of junk came rolling down the avenue toward the house. *What the hell have you got there?* I asked the pantechnicon driver. *Old Furniture for Mrs Cleveland,* said the mover. *It came from some place up in Maine.* Blaine's Maine, that goddamn State of Maine! I cast a scornful eye on the old chairs, bureaus, beds and desks with contempt and cried, *You turn around and take that damn kindling pile back downtown!* I forgot about it as soon as the van left. Well, a couple of weeks later I took a trip to Manhattan and when I returned, I saw a new old piece of furniture that Frank was adorning. *Frank,* I said to my wife, *where'd you get that? Where'd it come from?* She looked preoccupied. *That?* she said airily. *Why, we've always had that. We've had that for years.* I grunted and banished all thought of it. Now the next time I spent the day in New York, an enormous chair manifested itself in the parlor. *Where'd that come from, Frank?* Quite nonchalantly she said, *Oh, that old chair, we got it out of the attic; we've had that for a long time.* Then one day I went into our spare bedroom and there was a new bed, shiny and polished, so I felt I ought to say something about it. And in six or seven months, what do you think? Frank had slipped every damn sliver of that furniture into

the house, one piece at a time, and she thought I didn't know it. And one day I told her, and we had a good laugh. I suppose it is all right, if that's the sort of thing you like, why you like it!*

27 September—New York

A San Francisco newspaperman excavated the hitherto unknown story of my divorce. It made headlines all over the world. Almost immediately, my worst fears were realized. Soon a Hearst reporter obtained an interview with Edward. *However cruel it may be*, he said, *I affirm that I never heard that my wife gave birth to a child of which I am reputed to be the father, until I learned of our divorce. That should dispose of the question of desertion.*

10 October—New York

Several workmen found Edward wandering the railroad tracks near Chester. He was rather worse for wear, his clothes were rags, he was filthy and he spoke incoherently. He was emaciated, and he reeked of whiskey. They took him to the Chester jail where he sobered up but still spoke nonsense. I paid for three prominent physicians to examine my former husband, and they declared him to be *non compos mentis*.

The press heaped a torrent of abuse upon me. In any event, it is against my principles to comment on personal matters.

* * *

Gladstone sent me a copy of his new book, *Homeric Synchronism*, a learned thesis arguing that Homer was no mytho-

---

*   *a gread damn vanload of junk ... if that's the sort of thing you like, why you like it!*
From *Autobiography of William Allan White*. The Macmillan Company: New York, 1946, p. 362-363. By permission of the Estate of William Allan White.

logical creator but the true author of the *Iliad* and the *Odyssey.* [*]
Butler thinks Homer is a woman. It was he who wisely pointed out in *The Way of All Flesh* that the four Gospels do not agree in their account of the life of Christ. Both of them are enthusiastic about Schliemann.

18 October, New York

I have decided to go to Paris to enroll in the *Conservatoire* of François Joseph Regnier. No one of my standing has ever reduced herself to the role of a student, but I am determined to win recognition for more than my beauty.

Dion has written to Regnier from New York, and the instructor agreed to devote the entire winter to working exclusively with me. For three months he will handle no other pupils himself; he respects my desire for self-improvement, and he writes that he will do everything in his power to help me. How simple are the great!

22 November, Paris

Coquelin is extraordinary. He says more in a pause than most actors can say in hundreds of words. He drops a hand, he raises an eyebrow, and one feels the controlled power of his gestures. Under his tutelage I have brought new color and depth to Rosalind's closing lines.

> *I would kiss as many of you as had beards that*
> *pleased me, complexions that liked me, and breaths*
> *that I defied not; and am sure, as many as have good*

---

[*] *Homeric Synchronism ... Iliad and the Odyssey.* From *The Prince and the Lilly*, by James Brough, Coward McCann & Geoghegan, Inc.: New York, 1974. By permission of Penguin Group (USA) Inc.

beards, or good faces, or sweet breaths, will, for my
kind offer, when I make curtsy, bid me farewell.

As for Bernhardt, she is magnificent! I despair of becoming a real actress when I work on the stage with her, and I would gladly exchange my beauty, such as it is, for a soupçon of her great talent. I know I will never be a Bernhardt or a Coquelin, but must emphasize as best I can my own assets. I can make you one pledge, my dear friend. When I return to America I will not disgrace myself... and even the assassins of the press will applaud me.[*]

The Wheel of Fortune. Bourne-Jones saw me as I really am when I posed for him:

> *Scholars named me Fortune long ago, whom you,*
> *Holmes, once accused of murder. You are a man with*
> *no name at all compared to mine. I've broken better*
> *men than you by poverty, chaingangs, and hard*
> *labor. Do tears run down your cheeks merely*
> *because you live in disgrace? You are not alone, so*
> *don't complain. Look and see what I've done in days*
> *of old. I've clashed with kings and many a brave man*
> *has dropped dead because of me, and you are a*
> *runner, a scullion, a factotum compared to them.*
>
> *I poisoned Alexander, blinded Oedipus, and hanged*
> *the Absalom by the neck till dead. This is my way and*
> *I give no reason, so hear me well: Were I not bridled*
> *by the powers of heaven, there would not even be a*

---

[*] *As for Bernhardt, ... the press will applaud me.* From *The Prince and the Lilly,* by James Brough, Coward McCann & Geoghegan, Inc.: New York, 1974. By permission of Penguin Group (USA) Inc.

shadow left behind by you or anyone else, and for each back I've broken, I'd have broken ten!

You had better take things as they come, Holmes!

THE END

AFTERWORD

As soon as the authenticity of *Wilde About Holmes* appeared to have been proven beyond cavil and doubt, the editor's Olympian triumph was extinguished upon the altar of sobering truth: someone, somewhere, had perpetrated a hoax! No sooner had this edition been printed than the original manuscript was discovered to be a forgery. The editorial team had been so preoccupied with the reconstitution of the text from a photocopy of the shorthand original that signal clues to the work's true nature were overlooked. First, the manuscript paper and ink were determined to date from the 1990s. Then more scholarly heads than mine cited learned borrowings from twentieth century authors. It was discovered that passages from the published works of Oscar Wilde and Sir Arthur Conan Doyle had been incorporated into the text verbatim or with slight adaptation, and linked by an anonymous author/editor. *Wilde About Holmes* is nothing short of a fake. It was therefore right and just to append this afterword to disabuse our readers, lest erroneous reports of the book's purported authenticity supersede its true nature.

Despite the historical accuracy of many of the incidents described in the novel, and the many real events it contains, these have been subtly distorted by alterations of the sequence and context, their emphasis shifted, uniformly it seems, for dramatic effect. The most evident of these achronological incorporations is Wilde's lecture tour in America, which took place in 1882–1883. Grover Cleveland, however, was elected to the presidency nearly two years later. Only time and reflection on the internal evidence in the story could reveal insights such as these.

As Oscar Wilde pointed out, the mere effort to convert anyone to a theory involves some form of renunciation of the power of credence. This editor attests to the truth of this remark. And on the subject of forgery, Wilde states that:

> . . . *to censure an artist for a forgery is to confuse an ethical with an aesthetic problem.*

It was the content of the story that suggested attribution to the works of Conan Doyle and Wilde, just as the *Homeric Hymns* were once attributed to Homer, though we now know they were certainly not authored by him. The perplexing question of the nature of authorship tempts one to recall the Homeric Problem instigated by the great German scholar F.A. Wolf in 1795 with the publication of his pivotal work, *Prolegomena ad Homerum*, a controversy that continues into the present day with devoted adherents on either side. Wolf's severely critical analysis of the form and the contents of the *Iliad* and *Odyssey* posed the following questions: by whom, when, where, and from what materials were the *Iliad* and the *Odyssey*, as we have them, composed? The traditional view that the poems were composed by a poet named Homer at Chios or Smyrna around the ninth century B.C. was generally rejected. Many concluded that the poems were not by the same author; that even separately they were not unities in themselves, but collections of shorter epic poems, probably by different authors, although put together rather inefficiently by seventh- or sixth-century editors. The controversy did not end there. Millman Perry's classic studies of oral transmission and the spontaneous composition of oral poets, as exemplified by Yugoslav epic poets (upon which Alfred Lord's classic study, *The Singer of Tales*, is based) have once again turned the traditional notion of authorship on its head.

Moreover, the implications of the research conducted by Dr. Roberto Salinas-Price in his revolutionary work *Homeric Whispers* has received a limited response in the West. His research places Troy on the Dalmatian coast in Gabela instead of Hissarlik, which was excavated by Heinrich Schliemann in Asia Minor in the 1880s and presented as "Troy." The publisher's description of *Homeric Whispers* states: "Furthermore, he [Salinas-Price] argues, internal linguistic evidence suggests that these works were originally created in a Slavic dialect but later became translated by a bicultural society into "Homeric Greek." However, he adds, somewhere along this process of translation

AFTERWORD

the tutorial guidance necessary for an adequate understanding of these texts became lost, to the detriment of subsequent generations which never understood that the *Iliad* and the *Odyssey* were sister compositions never intended to be separated from each other." Salinas-Price describes the effect of his meeting with Dr. Olga Luković-Pjanović, author of Срби ... народ најстарији (The Serbs ... The Oldest of Peoples) in 1985 when she first introduced him to this hypothesis: "I went into a state of cultural shock, so to speak, but, with time, I learned to think differently. Those who dismiss this hypothesis as unlikely, if not altogether ridiculous, cannot even begin to give rational explanations on the etymologies of names like *"Iliad"*, *"Troy"*, *"Hellespont"*, *"Pygmies"* ... or several hundreds of them, in fact, and have no recourse but to offer meanings (where these are possible) derived from a language-base—Greek—that did not come into existence until some three, or perhaps four, centuries after the fact."*

In closing, there is no conclusion that can be drawn about the nature of *Wilde about Holmes*, except for, perhaps, Wilde's most striking insight on the subject:

All art is at once surface and symbol.
Those who go beneath the surface do so at their own peril.
Those who read the symbol do so at their own peril.
It is the spectator, and not life, that art really mirrors.
Diversity of opinion about a work of art shows that the work is
new, complex, and vital.
When critics disagree the artist is in accord with himself.

—The Editor

---

* *Homeric Whispers*, by Roberto Salinas-Price, Scylax Press, San Jerónimo Lídice (Mexico): 2006.

AFTERWORD